W9-BRV-303

THE DEL REY BOOK

OF SCIENCE FICTION

AND FANTASY

DEL
REY

BALLANTINE BOOKS NEW YORK

THE DEL REY BOOK
OF SCIENCE FICTION
AND FANTASY

Sixteen Original Works by
Speculative Fiction's Finest Voices

Edited by Ellen Datlow

A Del Rey Trade Paperback Original

Compilation and preface copyright © 2008 by Ellen Datlow
"The Elephant Ironclads" copyright © 2008 by Jason Stoddard
"Ardent Clouds" copyright © 2008 by Lucy Sussex
"Gather" copyright © 2008 by Christopher Rowe
"Sonny Liston Takes the Fall" copyright © 2008 by Elizabeth Bear
"North American Lake Monsters" copyright © 2008 by Nathan Ballingrud
"All Washed Up While Looking for a Better World" copyright © 2008 by Carol Emshwiller
"Special Economics" copyright © 2008 by Maureen McHugh
"Aka Saint Mark's Place" copyright © 2008 by Richard Bowes
"The Goosle" copyright © 2008 by Margo Lanagan
"Shira" copyright © 2008 by Lavie Tidhar
"The Passion of Azazel" copyright © 2008 by Barry N. Malzberg
"The Lagerstätte" copyright © 2008 by Laird Barron
"Gladiolus Exposed" copyright © 2008 by Anna Tambour
"Daltharee" copyright © 2008 by Jeffrey Ford
"Jimmy" copyright © 2008 by Pat Cadigan
"Prisoners of the Action" copyright © 2008 by Paul McAuley and Kim Newman

All rights reserved.

Published in the United States by Del Rey Books, an imprint of The Random House Publishing Group, a division of Random House, Inc., New York.

DEL REY is a registered trademark and the Del Rey colophon is a trademark of Random House, Inc.

Library of Congress Cataloging-in-Publication Data

The Del Rey book of science fiction and fantasy : sixteen original works by speculative fiction's finest voices / edited by Ellen Datlow.
    p. cm.
  ISBN 978-0-345-49632-4 (pbk)
  1. Science fiction, American.   2. Short stories, American.   I. Datlow, Ellen.
  II. Title: Book of science fiction and fantasy.
  PS648.S3D45 2008
  813'.0876208—dc22

                                                        2008004948

Printed in the United States of America

www.delreybooks.com

2 4 6 8 9 7 5 3

Text design by Karin Batten

short story (including novelettes and novellas). My initial brief at *OMNI* was to publish science fiction, but over the years I was able to showcase some of the best fantasy and horror being written during that period as well—and once in a while published fantasy by writers better known outside the field, such as Patricia Highsmith, Daniel Pinkwater, William Kotzwinkle, T. Coraghessan Boyle, Joyce Carol Oates, William Burroughs, and Julio Cortázar.

This volume reflects the kinds of fiction I published while at SCI FICTION: fantasy, science fiction, a touch of horror—and even a possibly unclassifiable or two. I did not go out and try to pick a story to represent every type of SF, every type of fantasy or dark fantasy. You won't find off-planet stories or hard science fiction, but you will find two very different alternate histories, some aliens, and some powerful, very timely political science fiction. There's no sword and sorcery or elves but there are cities in bottles, a twisted fairy tale, and a woman who loves filming volcanoes.

I'm often asked about the future of the short story. I can't answer to the market question, but I can certainly respond to the quality of what is being written. That's a happy constant, with some of my favorite established writers and talented new voices creating new worlds and re-imagining existing ones. I hope you enjoy your excursion into some of those following.

Ellen Datlow

SEPTEMBER 2007
NEW YORK

Preface

As a child I was encouraged to read anything I chose, and that included books lying around the house like *Bulfinch's Mythology*, Modern Library collections of Nathaniel Hawthorne and Guy de Maupassant, fairy tales from all over the world. A little later I read collections by Ray Bradbury, Harlan Ellison, and Richard Matheson, plus anthologies like *Dangerous Visions* and *Again, Dangerous Visions*, *The Playboy Book of Horror and the Supernatural*, the Carnell original anthologies from England, and many best-of-the-year anthologies. Still later, I was an avid reader of Angela Carter's *Fireworks* and *The Bloody Chamber* and T. Coraghessan Boyle's *Descent of Man* and *Greasy Lake*, and I continue to revel in short-story writers in and outside the field. As you can see, I was seduced early by short fiction. I didn't differentiate among science fiction, fantasy, and horror—I loved imaginative fiction any way it clothed itself. To me short stories are the heart and soul of fantastical fiction—especially science fiction. They are the medium in which writers can experiment in voice, in style, in structure. A writer can try out a theme that may later be expanded into a novel. A short story can introduce a reader to an unfamiliar writer's work without the investment of time that reading a novel requires.

As fiction editor of *OMNI* magazine and OMNI online for seventeen years, and editor of *Event Horizon: Science Fiction, Fantasy, and Horror* and SCI FICTION, the fiction area of the SCIFI.com website, I've been lucky enough to be able to indulge my preoccupation with the

Contents

THE DEL REY BOOK
OF SCIENCE FICTION
AND FANTASY

The Elephant Ironclads

Jason Stoddard

Jason Stoddard lives in Newhall, California, with his wife, Lisa (who writes under the name Rina Slayter), and a motley assortment of tortoises and cars. He has gone from the discipline of engineering to the halls of advertising, then on to the wild world of interactive marketing.

His short fiction has appeared in SCI FICTION, Interzone, Strange Horizons, Fortean Bureau, Futurismic, and GUD, and he was a finalist for both the Theodore Sturgeon Memorial Award and the Sidewise Award for Alternate History. Jason is currently working on novels based on his short fiction. His website is www.xcentric.com.

"The Elephant Ironclads" is another alternate history—based (as most of the best of the subgenre) on some unbelievable but actual historical events.

N ow, those are healthy elephants," Niyol Chavez said.

Wallace Chee ground his teeth. Ahead of them, a caravan loaded with Mexican sugar was coming down the dusty road from the Albuquerque airfield. On top of the lead elephant, a fat merchant in a gaudy Hopi outfit bounced, wearing the satisfied grin of a man who has made an excellent deal.

"See how they almost prance," Niyol said, pointing. "Healthy."

"Stop it," Wallace said.

"Look at how they shake their heads."

"Stop it!"

"They even sound like—"

Wallace turned and pushed Niyol, hard. Wallace caught a glimpse of his friend's broad, playful smile, then Niyol's legs tangled and he fell sideways into the scrub.

"I was joking!" Niyol said, his dark eyes flashing anger.

I didn't know the elephant was sick, Wallace wanted to say. Images of the dead elephant, lying in the dust outside the skeleton of his father's burned-out workshop, came unbidden. The slack stares of Niyol and Patrick and Jose, who had given all their Diné pesos for Wallace's tales of an elephant of their own, a trade route that would bring them riches before they were fourteen. The flaming anger of his mother when she'd discovered he'd taken her precious tourist dollars to fund his dream. Her tears when she saw the carcass. The way she looked from the elephant to the workshop and back again. And, finally, the few pesos he'd been able to get from the butcher as he began the grim job of rendering the elephant down to dog food and bonemeal.

"I told you I'd pay you back."

"No. You won't." Niyol picked himself up and brushed dust from his jeans.

"No?"

"We'll both pay your mother back." Niyol eyed the Diné airships that dotted the faraway field. "If there's any work left, that is."

"What do you mean?"

"The caravans are already coming south, so they've probably already unloaded."

Wallace grimaced. Niyol was as sharp of mind as he was of tongue. He would probably go back to school next year, to The-Years-That-Finish-You. And after his years at the Americanized school, he'd be able to get a job in California or Mexico, rather than Dinétah.

"There'll be other airships," Wallace said.

Niyol scanned the empty blue sky and shrugged.

As the caravan passed, the elephants' trumpeting sounded like laughter.

At the Albuquerque airfield, a half dozen airships hung motionless in the clear blue winter sky. On one of the ships, Diné airmen were making repairs to the skyshields, their bright orange-and-red-tunics in sharp contrast with the blue fabric that shielded the airships from the ever-watchful eyes of the Diyin Diné. None of the ships wore gray stormshields, so they must be expecting the clear weather to continue. The sun was bright, but the early-March chill still bit with every breeze.

On the ground, nothing moved. Stacks of crates and bags of sugar in the cargo shacks showed that the airships had already been unloaded. Big men lounged on the rough wood porches of the shacks, smoking cheap American cigarettes and telling poor jokes that poked fun at one another's clans. Several of them gathered around a radio, which was chattering in English about a new war the Americans were starting in a place called Korea.

Wallace remembered the days when the Americans always seemed to be at war. His own war games with Niyol. Japs and Americans. Like Cowboys and Indians, or Elephant Ironclads and Cavalry. He was only nine when he'd heard about the end of the Second World War, coming in softly in Navajo over the Dinétah station. It was hard to believe the war had been over for five years.

Niyol hung back, so Wallace introduced himself to one of the men and said they were looking for work.

The man, cigarette dangling loosely from his lips, looked them up and down and laughed. In that moment, Wallace saw himself and Niyol through those men's eyes, two scrawny kids looking to do heavy labor. Something seemed to crumple and collapse in his heart.

I'll have to go back to Isleta, he thought. I'll have to be a shepherd.

"You see?" Niyol said, after they'd walked out of earshot.

"Maybe I'll become an airman," Wallace said.

Niyol opened his mouth as if to say something, then seemed to think better of it. He grinned. "You, in Mexico? In America?"

Wallace frowned. He remembered black-and-white newsreels showing impossibly smooth streets and sleek, glossy cars. He remembered making fun of them, loudly, so the theater attendants came and made him and his friends leave.

"I could do it."

Niyol looked doubtful.

"I could become an elephant tender."

"Not elephants again!"

"I could earn it this time!"

Niyol shook his head. "Elephants are for rich men."

"Elephants are the gift of the Diyin Diné!"

"To try our resolve," Niyol said. Completing the common wisdom.

Wallace grimaced. He'd heard it from his mother. *Elephants aren't efficient pack animals. Their role in Diné independence was more luck than divine will.*

They ate too much. They tied us to the land. But he didn't care. Just once, he wished the Diyin Diné would send a vision of the Elephant Ironclads, standing watch at the edges of the Four Corners. But that was just a story, too, if you believed the common wisdom.

Even if it was only a story, it should be true, Wallace thought.

"Let's find some work," Wallace said, and walked away, not caring if Niyol followed.

At the airstrip office, gaudy color posters of Benjamin Hatathlie hung outside. Block capitals declared, CHIEFTAIN-AHNAGHAI. Wallace frowned. He knew from the newscasts that Hatathlie was running for president, but he frowned at the bald Americanization of the Diné word. They could have used the Diné alphabet, or tried to render the proper pronunciation.

"Brother," Niyol said, smiling ironically.

"You share clan with him?"

"Yeah. We're both Chiricahua Apache."

"So if he wins, my friend is the president's brother."

Niyol grinned. "The president'll have many brothers, all asking favors."

Wallace laughed. That was a good joke.

Wallace went to talk to the white-shirted office keeper, but the story was the same. No work here, especially for youngsters. Try when you're older. There's a guide who might employ you in a couple of years.

Wallace saw himself a shepherd, old and bent, watching dirty and indifferent sheep. He felt tears gather at the corners of his eyes.

Outside the office, Niyol put his hand on Wallace's arm. "I'm sorry."

"It's all right," Wallace said.

But it wasn't. It really wasn't. Wallace looked down at the earth and asked the Diyin Diné, *What have I done to offend you?*

A distant buzzing came from the sky to the north. Wallace looked up and saw a white speck in the distance. As it drew closer, he could make out wings, sticking out stiffly from a bright white fuselage.

An airplane. Like the Americans used. Wallace grimaced. Loud, dirty, noisy . . . a terrible mockery of the powerful Thunderbird.

The little plane drew closer and dropped toward the airfield. The laborers came out from under the shed awnings to look up at it. The Diné airmen paused in the middle of their work to turn sun-brown faces to the apparition.

The airplane flashed across the sky, impossibly fast, impossibly loud, shattering the stillness of the day. Diné on the outskirts of Albuquerque came out of their hogans to squint up at the sky.

The plane lunged at a long dirt road that paralleled the airships, sunlight glinting off its windshield. It touched down and bounced along the dirt runway, sending a long streamer of dust toward the dun-colored hills.

"Come on," Wallace said.

"Why?" Niyol said.

"Maybe they need to be unloaded."

"I don't think they have much to unload."

"They're rich men from America. They'll need something."

Niyol shook his head. "I don't know."

Wallace sighed. "I'm going to make some money," he said, and walked off toward the plane. After a few moments, he heard Niyol's footsteps behind him.

By the time they reached the runway, two men had emerged from the plane. They stretched in that big, lazy American way and looked out across the plains, as if the distances were too far for them to grasp. One wore a dark brown suit and a thin black tie. The other wore a gray suit of some coarse fabric, with a royal blue tie knotted over an off-white shirt. Dark-tinted sunglasses covered their eyes. Their shoes, polished black, were already coated with the rich orangish dust of the Dinétah desert.

Not even dressed for the trip, Wallace thought. In men this stupid there had to be opportunity.

Brown-suit noticed them first. He tapped his companion on the shoulder. Two heads swiveled to look at him. Their eyes were completely hidden behind dark glasses, their faces motionless and expressionless. It was like being looked at by insects.

"What do you want, kids?" Brown-suit said.

"I'm Wallace Chee of Big Water Clan," Wallace said.

"So?" Brown-suit said.

"Can I carry your bags for you? To your hogan?"

"No hotel. We have a car waiting."

A car? In Dinétah? Wallace didn't know what to say. When he found his voice, he croaked, "Guides. Do you have guides?"

Brown-suit snorted. "We have maps."

"Maps won't help you when the car breaks," Wallace said.

"Who says it'll break?"

Wallace grinned. "No highways. No service stations."

"We're loaded with gas."

"And water?"

"Yes."

"And a spare axle, for when you get caught in a rut?"

The two men looked at each other.

"And a guidebook to all the friendly Diné, who will help someone as strange as yourself?"

Another look.

"And maybe some padding in those clothes to keep you from picking up some buckshot?"

"Buckshot?"

"From the people who think you're a skinwalker?"

"Skinwalker?"

"Dead returned to walk," Gray-suit said. His English was thick with a strange accent.

Wallace started. An American who knew something about Diné? He didn't know men like that existed.

"Okay, okay," Brown-suit said. "How much? Will twenty do it?"

"Twenty dollars?" That was almost a thousand Diné pesos. More by half than he spent for the dying elephant.

"Twenty-five, then."

Wallace struggled to keep his face expressionless. "We're worth thirty," he said.

Brown-suit frowned, rummaged in his pocket, and pulled out a thick leather wallet. He extracted a twenty-dollar bill and handed it to Wallace. "Do a good job, and maybe there'll be another when we're done."

Wallace folded the bill out of sight quickly, resisting the urge to look around. He could feel the eyes of the laborers on them. Hopefully they weren't watching close enough to see the bill.

"I am Wallace Chee, of Big Water Clan," Wallace said. "Pleased to do business with you."

Niyol stood stunned. Wallace elbowed him. "Niyol Chavez, of Chiricahua Apache Clan."

"What's with the clans?" Brown-suit said.

Gray-suit smiled. "They say that to honor you in formal greeting." He held out a hand. "I am Frans Van der Berg, of no particular clan."

Wallace took his hand, briefly, remembering that this was what white men did. It was cool and greasy.

The other didn't offer his hand. "Herbert Noble. No clan."

As the men started unloading their heavy, olive-colored canvas bags, Niyol leaned close to Wallace. "What are you doing?" he whispered, in slow Spanish.

"Making us a lot of money," Wallace said.

"We don't know where they're going."

"We'll find out."

"We don't know what they want."

"Does it matter?"

"You're being male again."

"I know," Wallace said. But, as the drunks say, spend enough stupid and sometimes there's a return.

The two men led them to a low shack that fronted stables, grinning as the boys struggled with the heavy bags. Wallace worked happily, the slick paper of the twenty-dollar bill sticking to his leg inside his jeans.

Outside, a small sign read: ALBUQUERQUE HORSE STABLE AND RENT—NONLOCAL WELCOME. A smaller sign hung below, newly painted: AUTOMOBILE.

In front of the shack was an even more ramshackle stand that advertised FRIENDLY INDIAN GUIDES in faded sky-blue paint and shouted SAFE PASSAGE—UNIQUE SIGHTS—LOCAL HOSTESSES in weathered white below. Smaller, it said, GERALD MANYCOWS, HOOGHAN ANI, PROPRIETOR. A chubby Diné sat cross-legged in front of the low wood counter.

"Can I offer you gentlemen guide services?" the chubby Diné asked.

"Already have them," Herbert said, nodding at Wallace and Niyol.

The chubby Diné—presumably Gerald Manycows—frowned. His eyes followed Wallace and Niyol as they passed, as if asking, *Who are you to steal my custom?* Wallace was glad that the rental shack was out of sight of the runway. There was no chance Gerald could have seen the money that changed hands. Still, his heart pounded.

The rental shack was little more than a front to the stables. Inside the front door was a tiny room and a low counter. A grimy window looked out onto a dirt area in front of the stables. Three horses grazed in the shade of the gray, warped wood roofs.

In the middle of the dirt area, a sleek Ford sedan sat. It was the color of new cream. Chrome sparkled in the sunlight. Around the Ford, traditionally dressed Diné chanted and whirled through a Blessingway ceremony.

Herbert and Frans pushed through the back door to the dirt area and watched the Diné, hands on hips. Eventually, a stable boy came forward to the office.

"Nice of them to do this all for us," Herbert said, nodding at the ceremony.

Wallace hid a smile. He didn't know what the Blessingway was for, but he knew it was more likely to protect the land from damage by the car than to assure the safety of a couple of foreigners. But of course they wouldn't understand.

The stable boy pretended not to hear. After the Blessingway, money changed hands.

Wallace and Niyol loaded the bags into the car. The rental-office men watched them out of the corners of their eyes. None of them could be younger than fifty. Wallace felt he was being measured against some Diné standard he couldn't hope to understand.

What was the bigger insult? Wallace wondered. Helping the men find their way around Dinétah, or renting them a car?

The sun was setting as they drove off into the eternal west. Herbert drove. Wallace sat beside him, watching the great chrome gauges swing and chatter. The car even had a radio, but it produced only static. Niyol and Frans made the backseat a country of silence.

Wallace tried to imagine the car was a great Elephant Ironclad, like the ones of legend that won Dinétah its freedom. But it didn't work. It was just another loud, ugly mechanical thing, alien and wrong.

The big Ford roared and bounced into the setting sun. Behind them, the airships were beginning their long trip north.

They didn't go far before nightfall. The lights of Albuquerque's airfield were still visible in the valley below when Herbert Noble gave up and pulled the car off the road. He looked back toward Albuquerque with a look like he'd just bitten into a sour peach.

"You weren't kidding about the roads being bad," Herbert said. "If you could even call that a road."

"Not many cars here," Wallace said.

"Should have gotten an elephant," Niyol said.

"Really?" Herbert said.

"No," Wallace said. Niyol was making fun of him.

"Why not?"

Elephants are for Diné, Wallace thought. "They're not good pack animals. They eat too much." In the gathering dusk, Wallace could imagine Niyol's grin, hearing the blasphemous words come out of his mouth.

"I believed Lincoln's elephants were the reason for Dinétah independence," Frans said. His accent was thick, guttural, almost familiar.

"Not Lincoln's," Niyol said.

Frans raised his eyebrows, politely surprised.

"Some escaped on their way over the Rockies. Most came from the Confederate States, after the American Civil War."

That was what they taught in school, Wallace thought. He preferred the old story, the one that said the elephants emerged from the ground like the Dinétah themselves, a gift of the Diyin Diné. Still, he remembered old filmstrips showing photos of grizzled southerners working in smithies, riveting iron plate in curves suggestive of an elephant's flanks. But they'd never shown a completed Elephant Ironclad.

We did it, Wallace thought. The Elephant Ironclads are ours.

Frans nodded. "Nevertheless, they are impressive beasts."

"Are you German?" Niyol said.

Bang. That was the accent. Wallace had heard it in a dozen bad American war movies.

But Frans just smiled. "I am Dutch. It's said Dutch sounds Deutsch, if you speak with enough force."

"Dutch?"

"A small country in Europe, with beautiful windmills," Frans said.

"I've heard of it," Niyol said. He opened his mouth to say something else, but Herbert interrupted.

"Give me five dollars, and I'd keep going." Herbert peered out along the road.

"You would break something," Frans said.

Herbert sighed. "Probably."

"There will be time tomorrow."

For what? Wallace wondered. He glanced at Niyol, but his friend refused to meet his gaze.

The two men insisted on setting up camp by themselves. They pitched two camouflage-patterned tents with US ARMY SURPLUS stenciled on the side in dripping black, and sparked Coleman gas lanterns, throwing pale light on the green of the early-spring grass and scrub. They hauled two small, heavy bags into one of the tents and zipped it shut.

Wallace sat with Niyol on a big boulder, watching the last color bleed from the twilight sky.

"What did you get us into?" Niyol said.

"A lot of money," Wallace said, pulling out the twenty-dollar bill. He'd seen American money before, mainly coins. His mother pulled in dollar bills from time to time for her pretty skystone and silver jewelry. But he'd never seen such a big number printed on a bill. "I'll have money left over, even after I pay everyone back."

"We'll have money left over."

Wallace felt his face go hot and red. "Yeah. We."

"They'll ask us where we got it, back in town."

"So?"

Niyol rolled his eyes. "Just don't buy any more elephants."

Herbert and Frans lit a small camp stove and called them to come over. The stove hissed gas into blue flame. They boiled water for coffee and heated pork and beans from cans.

"How long are you staying?" Niyol said.

Herbert and Frans looked at each other before Herbert answered. "A week, we think. Could be longer."

"Thirty dollars gets you a week," Wallace said.

"You'll get more if we stay longer."

"What are you doing here?" Niyol said.

Another shared glance. "We're rock hounds," Herbert said.

"Rock hounds?"

"People who collect rocks."

"I know."

"You flew into Dinétah for rocks?" Niyol asked.

"Niyol," Wallace said.

"It's okay," Herbert said. "If I was you, I'd ask, too. Probably a lot earlier. Wouldn't want any furriners poking around, taking things we shouldn't."

"Is that what you're going to do?"

Herbert laughed. He looked at Frans.

"We are looking for unusual stones. We will take some photographs. If you do not want us to remove the stones, we will leave them where they are."

"Why?"

"We're rock hounds!" Herbert said, as if that explained all.

Niyol nodded and looked down, frowning.

Herbert sighed. "We're allies. Remember the codetalkers."

"They won World War Two," Wallace said.

"They helped," Herbert admitted.

"Without them, you wouldn't have a way to whisper secrets. You might've lost the Pacific. We read about it in school." Just like the prophecy said. *Diné will save the white man.* But you didn't talk about that to foreigners.

"Maybe." Herbert drew the word out.

"The atomic bomb won the war," Frans said.

For a long time, there was no sound except the low sigh of the wind. Wallace remembered photos from the atomic tests in Nevada, and the famous photos of the blast over Hiroshima.

Eventually, Herbert and Frans started clearing the plates and scraping the pans. Wallace and Niyol helped in silence.

The two men shared one of the tents, and the boys shared the other. Night breezes made the dark fabric snap and mutter. It was what Wallace imagined a skinwalker might sound like as it stalked past outside. Their sleeping bags were musty and rough, and the darkness was absolute.

"What if we're gone for weeks?" Niyol said softly in Spanish.

"What if?" Wallace shrugged inside his bag.

"Your mother will kill you."

"Not when she sees her money back."

Niyol said nothing.

Wallace sighed and turned over to face the invisible wall of the tent. Eventually he slept.

The Diyin Diné sent Wallace a dream. He dreamed of elephants with shining steel armor, marching beneath a sky full of iron-plated airships. But the elephants carried no Diné. And Wallace knew that armored airships were impossible. They would never fly. The riderless elephants advanced into the setting sun, unstopping, like machines. Wallace smelled acrid smoke and turned. Behind him was the Canyon De Chelly and the peach orchards, burning.

Wallace awoke with a start into pitch darkness. The wind had died to a whisper on the tent's fabric. Niyol breathed softly beside him.

Wallace squeezed his eyes tight and waited for sleep.

He waited a long time.

After a bland breakfast of powdered eggs, they set off into the west again, through the old Valencia land grant toward el Rito and Paguate. The foothills of the San Mateo Mountains rose in the distance, still wrapped in early-morning mist. The scrub shimmered with dew, silver-green in Dinétah's brief spring.

The road wasn't much more than a donkey track, narrow and heavily rutted from the recent rains. The Ford bounced and groaned over the ruts. The tires spun and the engine roared. Herbert cursed and fought the wheel.

In the backseat, Frans Van der Berg looked up from a map that was marked in smeared blue fountain-pen ink. "Beautiful," he said, pointing at an airship that floated in the west. They could see the tan-colored gasbag above the groundscreen. A blue-painted passenger cabin poked through the screen, pierced by many small round windows that reflected glints of the sun. Perhaps tourists heading for the Grand Canyon.

Or people like Niyol, heading for the opportunities in California, Wallace thought, frowning.

"Creepy," Herbert said.

"What is creepy?" Frans said.

"That camouflage."

Frans sighed. "From what I understand, the fabric barrier is not for camouflage."

"The skyshields keep us from marring the sky," Wallace said. "In case the Diyin Diné are looking up from their homes in the earth."

"Diyin Diné?"

"Gods," Niyol said.

"Gods in the earth, looking up," Herbert said, shaking his head. "Now I've heard everything."

"Do not insult our guides," Frans said.

"What did I say?" Herbert asked.

Frans just shook his head. "It is a beautiful way to travel. Silent and slow, like a bird soaring."

"It keeps us from marking the land with our presence," Wallace said. Not that it mattered, this far out of Four Corners. But he supposed all of Dinétah should be respected, even if they had overreached their ancestral lands.

Herbert snorted but said nothing.

They didn't go far before Frans called a halt. The two men got one of the heavy bags out of the trunk and extracted rock hammers and a hinged aluminum box.

Wallace followed the men, but hung back. They knelt at the ground and picked at rocks, turning them over in their hands like raccoons given a blob of dough. The chill of early morning still bit deep through Wallace's thin chambray shirt.

"I need the money," Wallace said.

Niyol just looked at him.

"Not just to pay you back. I need to make something for myself."

"We all do."

"You're going to go to The-Years-That-Finish-You. Then you'll be gone."

"Who said that?"

"Everyone can see it," Wallace said. "You're smart."

Niyol shook his head. "Nothing's certain."

Silence for a time. The men moved to a shallow stream channel, already dry from the last rains. Wallace and Niyol followed. Niyol walked closer and watched them carefully.

"What do you think they're doing?" Wallace asked.

"I don't know."

"You seem worried."

"I'm worried they'll find something they want."

"So? They said they won't take anything we won't want them to."

"What if they come back with more men?"

"Then we bring more men, too."

"And if they bring the army? Will your beloved Elephant Ironclads appear out of the earth, to save the Diné once again?"

Wallace looked away. Compared with the powers that strutted on the newsreels, even armored elephants and airships seemed small, easily swept away. He remembered his dream from last night and shivered, wondering what it meant.

"What do we do?" Wallace asked, finally.

"Just watch. For now."

The two men knelt in the streambed and picked at rocks in its side and bottom. They opened the aluminum box, did something with it, shook their heads. After a while, they moved to another location and did the same thing.

When they finally headed back toward the car, Herbert wore a fake smile and Frans a convincing frown. Wallace suppressed a grin. Whatever they were looking for, they hadn't found it. Maybe there was nothing to worry about.

The rest of the day was the same routine, endlessly repeated. Drive west, stop, pick at rocks. The San Mateo Mountains seemed as remote as ever. Wallace scuffed his foot on the thin brown dust, wishing something would happen. The men came back with the same expression, a little grimmer every time.

At their last stop, a Diné shepherd watched them. He stood silent and motionless as his sheep milled and cropped the new grass. His black, unblinking eyes were like a weight on Wallace. Like an accusation.

Is this a sign? Wallace thought. Is this a man, or one of the Diyin Diné, clothed in the form of a man?

Wallace walked closer to the two men, who were using the aluminum box again. Frans took a slender metal wand out of the metal box and held it near some of their rocks.

Niyol jumped, as if he had been goosed.

"What?" Wallace said.

Niyol shook his head and walked closer. Wallace followed. The metal wand was connected to the aluminum box with a coiled black cord. Inside the aluminum box was a big dial and a cluster of black Bakelite switches. It made a slow clicking noise.

Frans looked up as Niyol approached. He saw him looking at the box and put on a big fake smile.

"What's that?" Niyol said.

"It's an instrument."

"What does it do?"

"It tells us what the rocks are made of."

Wallace felt his stomach lurch and slide. Something seemed wrong, very wrong. Would rock hounds have something that was so obviously sophisticated and expensive? Was America that rich? For once, he wished he knew more about America than the newsreels and whispers from the radio stations in Kansas and Colorado.

Wallace expected Niyol to ask more questions, but the other boy nodded, as if satisfied. They walked back toward the car. The shepherd still watched from amid his sheep.

Niyol's eyes flickered from the shepherd to Wallace and back again. He rubbed his hands together, as if trying to scrub the dirt off them.

"What's wrong?" Wallace said.

"We have to get out of here," Niyol said.

"Why?"

"Shh." The men were coming back from their little dig, looking more disappointed than ever. Wallace noticed that their ties had disappeared during the course of the day, and their suits were smudged with orange and brown earth. Herbert had a handprint in the center of his forehead, dark against his pale skin.

Before they got in the car, Wallace drew Niyol aside and said, in Spanish, "What's happening?"

"Not now," Niyol said.

Wallace ducked into the car. The sound of the door slamming was leaden and final.

*   *   *

Wallace didn't get to talk to Niyol until they were done with dinner. Herbert and Frans hung close, as if sensing that something had changed. Niyol chattered, complaining about the blandness of the American food, saying that the food they were used to was more Mexican than traditional Diné, and that all you had to do was look around at the place-names to see they were more Spanish than anything else. Wallace frowned at him. Niyol was acting like a scared old man, talking to keep the silence away.

The two men eventually drifted off to the car and came back with a bottle of whiskey, which they shared in little tin cups. Wallace watched them, feeling a slow burn of anger. That's why I don't have a father, he thought. White man's booze.

Niyol saw his gaze and pulled him away into the darkness, claiming he needed to take a piss. Wallace didn't know whether to be angry or relieved.

"That was a Geiger counter," Niyol said, pissing.

"A what?"

Niyol sighed. "You should stop making fun of the newsreels and watch them once in a while. A Geiger counter measures radiation."

Wallace started, remembering similar clicking wands from the footage of Hiroshima. Except those didn't click. They buzzed. "So they're going to bomb here?"

"No," Niyol said. "I think they're looking for uranium."

"Uranium?"

Niyol rolled his eyes. "The stuff they make atomic bombs out of. Didn't you pay any attention to that American film, *The Promise of the Atom*, in Science Track?"

Wallace shook his head. He might have slept through it. Or skipped class.

"Why do they want more uranium?"

Niyol frowned. "To make more bombs, probably."

"Why would they want to do that?"

Niyol laughed, long and hard. Wallace saw the two men swivel to look their way, then go back to their bottle. "Why would a boy want to buy an elephant?" he asked.

Wallace looked down. Because it was my destiny, he thought. He remembered his excitement. Coming home from Pepe's Bar, his head ringing with the thought that here was an elephant, almost affordable. He'd even started to rebuild his father's burned-out workshop. He'd even started to imagine beating steel into shapes that would cover his elephant.

"We need to get out of here," Niyol said. "We have to tell someone."

"Who?"

Niyol shrugged. "Chief of Albuquerque. Or Benjamin Hatathlie, if he's campaigning. Someone who can take it to the president."

"What will they do?"

"If these guys are American army, it might not matter what they do. But they don't seem like army."

He remembered meeting one of the codetalkers who was out recruiting. There was a certain distance to him, a faraway look in his eye, a comfort in silence. Like Diné, but more. These men seemed just . . . men.

"Wait until they're asleep, then head back?" Wallace said.

Niyol looked at Wallace, his eyes reflecting sparks of stars. "Exactly."

"I'm not a sellout."

"I know that," Niyol said softly. Wallace saw the curve of his smile and grinned back.

Wallace looked back down the road, east toward Albuquerque. The glow had long since disappeared behind them. Wallace had never been so far from home. But they hadn't gone that far. Not with all their stops. If they walked fast, they could be in Albuquerque by morning. They could wait outside the town adobe and wait for the chief to come in.

They'd be heroes.

Wallace wondered if there might be a reward.

*   *   *

In the perfect darkness, Wallace felt a hand on his arm. He jumped and almost cried out.

"It's time," Niyol said.

Wallace felt his face go hot. *He'd fallen asleep!* If it was up to him, they'd have slept until morning, and been trapped with the men for another day. *Some hero.*

"I . . . I . . . ," Wallace began.

"Shh," Niyol said.

Niyol pushed the flap of the tent open, and starlight slashed into the tent. The moon was only a tiny sliver, but to Wallace's dark-adjusted eyes it seemed almost as bright as day.

Wallace followed Niyol back to the road. It stretched in front of them, a stark relief of charcoal and black in the low-slanting moonlight. They walked softly until the camp had disappeared behind a low rise, then picked up the pace.

"I'm sorry," Wallace whispered.

"For what?"

"For getting us into this."

"No harm done," Niyol said. "In fact, if Dinétah can do something about it, you may have done us all a great service."

Pride swelled in Wallace, and he walked a little faster. Maybe he would be a hero. Maybe there would be a reward.

They crested a low rise. Ahead of them was a small campfire, casting long flickering shadows from four men. Two horses stood alongside, heads down, enjoying the new grass. The sound of laughter, low and rough, carried on the night breeze.

Wallace had a sudden sinking feeling in his stomach. "Go back," he hissed, grabbing Niyol's arm. Niyol nodded and turned around.

Wallace glanced back at the four men. One now stood. He shielded his eyes and looked toward them. The sliver of moon sat low on the horizon ahead.

They can see us, Wallace thought.

From behind them came rough cries.

Wallace ran off the road, toward thicker scrub that might have some chance of hiding them. He heard the crash of Niyol's feet behind them. Then, moments later, hoofbeats.

The horses galloped past them, throwing up white moonlit dust. The riders brought them around to a quick stop in front of Wallace. He skidded to a stop, and Niyol stumbled to the ground beside him.

Both horses carried two riders. One hopped down and approached. In the dim moonlight, his face looked familiar. The chubby Diné from the guide shack. Gerald Manycows. Many cows, many hogans, Wallace thought desperately.

"Where were you two going?" Gerald said. "Did you already steal all their money?"

"We got homesick," Wallace said, squeezing his eyes shut and willing tears. He snuffled and let the tears cut channels down his cheeks.

Gerald laughed. "Sure," he said. "We believe that, don't we?"

Titters from his companions.

"What do you want?" Niyol said.

"The money."

"What money?" Wallace said.

Gerald stepped closer. His breath smelled like sour beer. "Everyone at the airfield saw money change hands. Don't make me hurt you." He pulled a long knife from his belt.

Wallace dug in his pockets and handed Gerald the sweat-slick bill. Gerald held it up in the moonlight. "Twenty dollars? Twenty dollars!"

The others drew closer, as if pulled by invisible threads.

"Why did they give you twenty dollars, kid?"

"They set the price, not us," Niyol said.

Gerald shook his head and turned away, muttering something that Wallace couldn't hear.

"How much more money do they have?" Gerald asked.

"I don't know," Wallace said.

"Maybe a lot, if they're dumb enough to give you this." The calculation of greed spread an ugly grin on Gerald's face. Wallace's stomach flipped over. He imagined that was what he'd looked like, when he'd told Herbert and Frans they were worth thirty dollars.

"Search the boys," Gerald said. "See if they're holding back."

Wallace and Niyol were disrobed and thoroughly groped. The night air froze Wallace's skin, and his teeth clacked and chattered. The flunkies noticed this and laughed. After an age, they were allowed to get back into their clothes.

"What now?" Niyol said.

Gerald laughed. "You're going to help us get the rest of the money."

"How?"

"We're all friends here. You can introduce us to your other friends."

"They're asleep," Wallace said.

"That's even better. Maybe nobody gets hurt."

Wallace saw the men, their throats slashed, their bodies buried in shallow graves. Like the stories you sometimes heard, Diné gone bad, imagining all the old conflicts. "You don't need us."

Gerald laughed. "I don't need you telling the police, either."

"We wouldn't do that!"

"Not after helping us."

"They're looking for uranium," Niyol said. "We left so we could turn them in."

Gerald frowned. "They're looking for what?"

"Uranium. What they make atomic bombs out of."

For a few moments, there was silence. Then Gerald shrugged and said, "I don't care if they're looking for Changing Woman herself."

"But—" Niyol said.

"Shut up," Gerald said, and punched Niyol in the face. Niyol fell to his knees, grabbing his nose. Blood seeped through his fingers, black in the moonlight.

"Any more questions?" Gerald said.

Wallace shook his head.

Gerald remounted his horse. One of the other riders stayed dismounted, to prod them along with a knife. They made their way back to the Americans' camp, silent except for the snuffle of the horses and the crunch of their feet on the dirt.

The two tents stood silently under the moonlight. The big Ford sedan was painted white like a ghost. The fire, long dead, still tele-graphed the scent of smoke into the night.

Gerald had them all dismount when they spotted the camp. Ger-ald's knife prodded Wallace forward. Wallace thought of yelling to try to warn the men, but he couldn't make his mouth open. He couldn't bring himself to look at Niyol. He knew his friend's accusing eyes would be dark and sad.

Diyin Diné, I ask your help, Wallace thought. *If we escape this, I will learn to be content.*

Gerald had them stop by the Ford, positioning it between them and the tents. The front flaps of the tents faced the car, making it easy to see if anyone emerged. Gerald told them all to stop moving. Silence descended. No sound came from the tents.

"Look at all the stuff," one of the flunkies said, pointing inside the car. Tools glittered, spilling from an open bag on the backseat.

"Neat," Gerald said. One of the others opened the trunk. It popped open with a metallic *bonk* that was incredibly loud in the still night.

"Even better," Gerald said, looking at the bags. "We do the car first, then the face-to-face."

"Maybe the car's enough, Gerald," one of the flunkies said.

Gerald shook his head. "I'll say what's enough."

"But they might have guns."

Gerald turned to Wallace. "Do they have guns?"

"I didn't see any," Wallace said.

"You sure?"

"Yes."

"Good. Because you'll be first in line if bullets come our way," Ger-ald said, watching Wallace.

Wallace just looked at him.

They cleaned out the car first, gingerly easing the heavy bags out of the trunk and carrying them over to the horses. Wallace kept hoping for them to drop one of the bags and raise the alarm, but they made lit-tle noise other than a few muffled thuds and a quiet whinny from one of the horses.

"After this, you introduce us to your friends," Gerald said. "Just re-member, you'll be standing in front."

Gerald popped the car door open and handed the tool bag out. He left Wallace and Niyol in the care of one of his companions and disap-peared into the car, running his hands under the seats, looking for more loot.

The flunky in charge of Wallace and Niyol took no chances. He held them close, pressing twin blades against their necks. He breathed heavily, and Wallace could see his eyes darting back and forth.

There was a sharp crack and the flunky's head exploded in a foun-tain of gore. Wallace felt warm blood spatter his cheeks. The flunky made a single surprised sound, something like a sigh, and the pres-sure of the knife at Wallace's throat fell away. The flunky crumpled to the ground.

Wallace moved without thinking, snatching the knife out of the flunky's hand. Niyol watched, wide-eyed, then bent and did the same.

The flunky who had been watching the tents moved fast to get behind the car, but he wasn't fast enough. Another crack split the night, he went down, clutching his stomach and screaming. Another crack and muzzle-flash from the tent, and the screaming stopped.

Gerald wriggled back out of the car, like a fish on land seeking water. He saw the boys huddled in the lee of the car. He saw their knives. He grabbed his own knife out of his belt and held it at the ready. Wallace tried to copy him, crouching below the roofline of the car. He knew nothing about knife fighting.

Out of the corner of his eye, Wallace saw movement. The tent flap opened, and Herbert Noble emerged. He pointed a long rifle out at the car.

"Come on out," he said. "This is a thirty-ought-six. I'll shoot right through the car if I need to."

Gerald just ducked below the level of the windows. Wallace and Niyol copied him. Three knife points faced one another in the Ford's shadow.

"I'm not kidding," Herbert said. "I'll shoot you right through the car." His voice was dead calm, as if it was something he said every day.

"First we dance," Gerald said, lunging at Wallace with his knife. His face was an insane mask of anger.

This is the last thing I'll ever see, Wallace thought.

"Stop," Frans said from the scrub behind Gerald. There was the click of a pistol cocking.

Gerald snarled and turned away from Wallace. Wallace saw Frans lying in the scrub, holding a small pistol. Somehow, he'd gotten out of the tent and circled the back of the car and they hadn't noticed.

There was another crack from the direction of the tent, followed by a thud. Wallace risked a glance in the direction of the horses, and saw Gerald's third flunky crumpled there.

"Drop the knives and stand up," Frans said, getting to his feet.

Wallace and Niyol dropped their knives. Gerald grabbed his tighter and rushed at Frans. Frans frowned and squeezed the trigger once, twice, three times. Gerald rocked back and fell dead at Frans's feet.

Frans prodded Gerald once with his shoe, then turned his gun on Wallace and Niyol. Herbert came around the other side of the car, his rifle held at the ready.

He raised his rifle and pointed it at Wallace. Wallace felt the world go swimmy and gray. He clutched at the door handle, his legs suddenly weak. *Diyin Diné, I am sorry if I offended you, I should never have helped the outsiders who can never understand.*

"What were you doing?" Herbert said. "Trying to leave us?"

"No . . . we were . . . we . . ."

"Bullshit! We saw you leaving!" Herbert screamed.

"We were scared!" Wallace said, closing his eyes against tears. "We wanted to go home!"

The barrel inched closer. "How true is that guide crap you fed us? Do we really need you?"

"Yes! Yes!"

"Why?"

"Some Diné shoot without asking. Some only help Diné."

Frans put a hand on Herbert's rifle barrel, forcing it down. "They are only children," he said.

"We're sorry!" Wallace said, letting the words pour out of him. "We won't try to leave! We'll be good guides!"

"We were just homesick," Niyol whispered.

That was enough. Herbert's rifle barrel dropped the rest of the way.

"Time to clean up the mess," Herbert said.

The two men made Wallace and Niyol help them dig a long, shallow grave. Wallace dug steadily, trying not to think about what kind of men could be so unaffected by the killing. Army? He didn't think even the army could be so cold.

But that's what Americans do, his father had always told him, in the days before he drank his mind away and disappeared. *They're always fighting. That's just how they are.*

Wallace let his body settle into the pattern of digging. He cursed the tiny folding shovel as blisters formed and began to run. He didn't dare look at Niyol. He could only imagine the black disgust on his face.

When they were done, Herbert transferred the bags from the horses to the car. "What do we do with the horses?" he asked.

"Take their saddles and let them go," Niyol said. "Someone will be happy for the gift."

"We shouldn't shoot them?"

"I don't think we can dig a grave that deep."

Herbert frowned and unbuckled the saddles. Wallace noticed that he was wearing Manycows's knife in his belt, as if it were some great prize.

They buried the saddles with the bodies. Gerald Manycows's blank eyes looked up at them, his mouth open in a silent scream. Wallace winced as the first shovelful of dry earth struck the chubby man's face.

Light painted the eastern sky when they were done covering the bodies. Wallace wanted nothing more than to crawl into the tent and sleep, but they had to pack up the camp and move on.

As they bounced along the dirt path south of the San Mateos, Wallace realized he'd never pulled the twenty-dollar bill out of Gerald Manycows's pocket. It was now under a couple of feet of dirt, miles behind them.

He felt laughter welling up inside of him. He clamped it down. If he started, he was afraid he wouldn't be able to stop.

Instead, he remembered Frans Van der Berg's words.

They are only children.

Later that morning, they had to swing the car off the road for a small caravan of three elephants, weighted down with heavy bags and crates. A merchant sat on a thick padded platform atop the lead elephant. He wore a bright white shirt and new blue jeans. Two children rode the other elephants, frowning as they bumped along the road.

Wallace looked at Niyol, daring him to say anything. Niyol just shook his head.

The merchant waved at the car as he passed, offering a puzzled grin. Probably wondering why Diné and white men were sharing a car in the middle of Dinétah. Wallace waved back, trying to smile. He wanted to get out of the car and tell them, *It's all a mistake, I only did it for the money, but I don't even have the money now, can I take it all back, can I go with you.*

"They may be impractical, but they are impressive," Frans said, watching the elephants recede into the distance in his rearview mirror.

They stopped at a long channel that had been cut by runoff coming out of the San Mateos. The land at the base of the hills was rugged and rutted, carved into fissures where raw rock and earth showed. Nothing like the unearthly beauty of northern Dinétah, but better than flatland and scrub.

The men had Wallace and Niyol stay close. Herbert wore a pistol in his belt, and Frans used the Geiger counter openly. They dug deep into the riverbed and appeared excited when they found some yellow rock. But the Geiger counter clicked only slightly faster when they placed the wand near it. Frans wiped off the yellow dust and frowned.

Maybe they won't find anything, Wallace thought. Maybe we'll get out of this yet.

After seeing the guides die, though, he doubted it. Wallace rubbed at his face, remembering the dried blood he'd washed off that morning. He still felt unclean.

No. They will keep you around as long as you're useful, and then they will dig two more graves.

Unless they could find a chance to escape. Wallace tried to catch Niyol's eye, but his friend wouldn't look at him. When he tried whispering in Spanish, Herbert frowned and told them to speak in English.

They took the car farther into the mountains. Another stop. Another slow clicking from the Geiger counter. Lunch came and went. They passed a Diné man leading a group of donkeys, heavily laden with bags. He stopped and watched the car pass, his head swiveling to track them. His expression didn't change, and he didn't try to wave.

Another stop. They were well into the foothills. A ravine rose nearby. Wallace kept looking at it, wondering if it was a possible escape route.

Niyol saw the direction of Wallace's gaze and shook his head slowly. Wallace looked away. Niyol was right. Even if he made it to the ravine before he was shot, he didn't know how deep it would go. He imagined Herbert following him until the ravine narrowed, his own Canyon De Chelly.

The Geiger counter clucked a little faster this time, but the men still looked disappointed. Wallace suppressed a grin as they walked back to the car.

Another airship passed over them as they reached the car, almost invisible against the blue sky. This one's skyshield was taut and seamless. A cargo ship, perhaps heading for California. Wallace remembered his jest about becoming an airman. *You could be on that ship now, heading for California,* he thought.

But this was his path. He created it. He would have to walk it to the end.

They drove past the little town of Paguate, where shepherds watched over dirty brown sheep that cropped the new grass. It wasn't yet birthing time, so there were no new fluffy white babies among them. The shepherds watched, but they didn't wave, as the car chugged past the little adobe village.

Another stop. This one at the base of Mount Taylor. Herbert and Frans paused at an outcropping of loose rock that bore a darker stain running through it. They chipped away at the rock with their hammers. Wallace noticed that Herbert's suit was torn at the shoulder, and a huge orange-brown ring of dust and sweat had worked its way into his open collar. Frans had removed his suit jacket and rolled up his sleeves, exposing arms lightly frosted with pale hair. The backs of his hands bore strange ridged scars, as if his flesh had melted and been made whole again.

They struck more yellow rock and wanded it with the Geiger counter. The counter buzzed loudly, and the two men exclaimed, juggling the yellow rock in their hands. They dug deeper with their rock hammers, beads of sweat flying in excitement.

"This is bad," Niyol whispered.

"We could run. Now." While they're distracted.

"Boys, stop talking!" Herbert said. He pulled his gun out of his belt and held it at the ready as Frans continued digging.

"Looks like a whole vein, running right into the mountain," Frans said.

"Is that good?" Herbert said.

"It is amazing!"

They collected some of the yellowish stone and brought it back to the car.

"I thought you said we could decide what you took back," Niyol said.

Herbert smirked but said nothing.

They followed a thin trail up to the north, now to the west of

Mount Taylor. At the next stop, the Geiger counter buzzed excitedly again, and the men collected more stones. These were dark and looked like nothing more than ordinary rock.

They want the magic of the sacred land, Wallace thought, remembering tales of Mount Taylor. "Pulling out the heart of the Diyin Diné."

"What was that?" Herbert said.

Wallace shook his head. He wasn't aware that he had spoken his thoughts. He felt numb from lack of sleep and constant fear.

"You said something. What was it?"

"You're pulling out the heart of the Diyin Diné," Wallace said. "The gods."

Herbert chuckled. "Stupid superstitions!"

"Do not insult them," Frans said. "Navajo mythology is very specific about where their gods reside."

Herbert shook his head and muttered.

Their last stop was far into the foothills. Barren land that grew no scrub and little grass. Not even suitable for grazing. And yet Wallace saw that someone had set up a tiny shack at the base of the hills. It had fallen in on itself, its contours gone swaybacked.

The first rocks they uncovered made the Geiger counter click with only moderate speed. They followed a streambed up toward the mountain, toward the shack, pulling more rocks. The buzzing got steadily faster. Wallace thought of a wasps' nest, buzzing anger into the summer heat.

"This is a rich land," Frans said when the counter finally buzzed frantically. "There's ore virtually everyplace we look."

Herbert just smiled. It was a terrible expression, like that of a naked skull.

They were close to the shack. Close enough that Wallace could see how strange it was. It appeared to have been covered with metal scales at one time. Rust coated the lumpy remains heavily, bleeding down into the pale earth. From within, smooth pale timbers poked through the sides.

No. *Not timbers.*

Wallace walked toward the shack, his heart beating frantically. He heard his breath coming in short gasps. He heard a shout behind him. He ignored it and walked faster.

Another shout.

He could see it now. *Bone.*

He ran. Expecting the shot. Not caring.

He stopped just short of the remains. His feet scuffed through the blood-red rust into pale soil. He saw the tusks thrusting out of one side of the rusted armor. Bright white ribs showed where metal links had broken and the armor's plates had separated. A large leg bone was half buried in rust-red dirt.

Wallace shivered. *They were real. The Elephant Ironclads. They were real.*

Herbert skidded to a stop and took Wallace's arm. Wallace shook him off and stepped forward to touch the rusted metal plates. Oxidized iron flaked off on his fingers. He rubbed them together in front of his face.

Real. They were real.

Their remains had been here all along. No reason for passersby to go look at the old collapsed shack. Here was the proof that everyone wished for, but nobody really believed. The elephants had been more than just beasts to scare the settlers. Chee Dodge's friends had come to Dinétah after the fall of the South. They had made Elephant Ironclads. It wasn't just a story. It was like all the old men whispered about.

It was true.

"What is it?" Frans said, bringing Niyol. Niyol's eyes widened, looking past them to the pile of bones and rusted iron plates.

"It's an Elephant Ironclad," Wallace said.

"A what?" Herbert said.

Wallace just shook his head.

Frans stared down at the remains of the Elephant Ironclad. Something that could have been understanding flickered in his eyes. Wallace imagined Frans telling Herbert it was okay, they should let the boys go.

"This is an amazing sight," Frans said. "But we have larger concerns."

Herbert nodded, glancing down at the remains one more time. They could have been dust and rock.

They exist, Wallace thought. He wondered if, like the shepherd, it was a sign. And if it was a sign, what did it mean? Did it mean their fate was to slowly dissolve into the sand? Or was this supposed to fire his heart and make him into a great warrior?

Wallace realized just how little he knew. If he had taken the time to visit Grandfather's hogan and really learn the ancient ways, he might understand more of the signs.

Diyin Diné, if I live through this, I will learn.

Herbert Noble flogged the poor Ford north as the sun painted the western sky. He hummed a happy tune. The flat-topped Zuni Mountains tracked their passage, purple-gray in the sunset. Wallace stared straight ahead, wondering if he would die that night.

"This is good," Frans said when the path had become little more than a trail. Ahead of them was nothing but scrub and dirt. Farther north was Chaco Canyon, where men who had attracted the attention of the Dinétah authorities were said to hide.

They stopped and made camp. The two men made Wallace and Niyol work as they drank whiskey from the bottle and watched. Wallace caught shards of conversation:

"Need to run a full radiographic survey . . ."

"What kind of skills do we need . . ."

"We need to let the fearless leader know . . ."

When the tents were up, Herbert unpacked one of the larger bags. Inside was a gray metal box with a big round knob on the front, a wet-cell battery, and many feet of wire. Wallace recognized it instantly from class: a shortwave radio. Frans strung the antenna as Herbert connected the battery. Vacuum tubes bled orange light from the louvers in the radio's case. Herbert twisted knobs and mumbled into the mike. The radio blatted unintelligible answers. Frans watched the boys, never looking away for a moment.

Who are they calling? Wallace wondered. The scofflaws in Chaco Canyon? Or Colorado, where the Americans were supposed to have an army base? Which would be worse?

"I'm sorry," Wallace said.

"You already said that," Niyol said.

"I needed to say it again."

Niyol looked down. "I'm sorry, too."

Wallace frowned. "Why are you sorry?"

Silence.

"Niyol!"

"Remember when you built the airship?" Niyol said.

Wallace smiled, remembering. They were eleven. One chill winter's end, like this one. Niyol had brought a paper bag and had shown Wallace how it could be made into a little airship by holding it over a hot fire. Something he learned on the Science Track.

Seeing the floating paper bag, Wallace had a vision. He would build his own airship. He would fly over Isleta, and people would look up in wonder. He would float north to Albuquerque, where the airmen would swarm around, their eyes bright with wonder at the boy who had built his own airship. He might even be able to carry goods, like a merchant. He saw himself rich and happy, beaming down at the shepherds and their flocks.

Over the next weeks, he spent his savings on the lightest linen he could find. He borrowed his mother's sewing machine and frantically worked the treadle, sewing together a patchwork gasbag. Eventually, he had a thing that was twenty feet long and almost as wide. Wallace tied a small harness to the bottom and made padded loops for his arms.

Niyol watched and helped, telling him stories about Thomas Baldwin, the southerner who had brought his balloon act to Dinétah in the 1880s, then worked with them to build airships in the new century. Wallace tried to ignore him, wanting to keep his airship to himself, to the Diné.

Wallace cut a hole in the tin roof of his father's old work shed and pulled the fabric bag up on top of it. It hung like a hand-me-down dress. He filled the work shed with kindling and firewood while Niyol told him that he'd kill himself.

Don't, Niyol said, when he lit the match.

Wallace lit the kindling carefully and went outside to grasp the harness, imagining his ascent into the sky.

The big fabric bag rippled and began to billow upward from the shed. It began to take on the roundness of an airship, but in a crazy patchwork way. He'd used remnants of every color. Pink, blue, orange, sand, ocher. Fabrics with stripes and zigzags and flowers.

The top of his airship rose higher. Soon it would rise over the small hillock that separated their hogan from the town proper, and the people of Isleta would come out to see.

But the groundshield. It had no groundshield.

Wallace gritted his teeth. Hopefully the gods wouldn't be looking that day. Or maybe they would laugh at the young-man-that-would-fly.

Wallace felt the harness tug his hands. He grinned at Niyol, whose eyes had gone big and unbelieving. He was going to fly!

The bag burst into flame.

Not slowly. Instantly. One moment it was a smoothly swelling patchwork, the next it was a collapsing wall of burning linen. Wallace fell to the ground and saw flames falling toward him. He scrambled away frantically, kicking his legs to escape the burning fabric. He shrugged out of the harness and ran. Flames struck just behind him. Hot wind pushed him.

Wallace turned to see flames engulf the work shed. Niyol ran to the pump to bring buckets of water. Wallace followed. It was futile. The flames grew, and the shed folded inward on itself, as if it were made of paper.

Wallace shook his head, coming back to the present. "I'm an idiot," he said softly.

"But you dream," Niyol said.

"You should have stopped me."

Niyol shook his head. "Sometimes you have to dream."

* * *

After dinner, Niyol tried to get himself killed.

"So you're going to make a bomb?" Niyol said.

Herbert paused with the second bottle of whiskey halfway to his mouth. Frans turned to look at Niyol, giving him an ironic grin.

"If only it were that easy," Frans said.

"You're not Dutch. You're probably some German scientist. What's your real name? Viktor?"

"Niyol!" Wallace hissed.

"It seems you know all our secrets," Frans said. "My name is still Frans, however."

"You can take our land, but you can't take our souls," Niyol said, looking at Wallace.

The two men snorted and went back to drinking.

"We won't help you," Niyol said.

"Niyol, stop!" Wallace said.

"You might as well kill us now."

Herbert Noble returned the grin. "Nope. Radiographic surveys are a hell of a lot of work. You'll be helping, plenty."

"We won't help," Niyol said.

"Yes, you will."

"No, we won't," Wallace said.

Herbert opened his mouth as if to say something, but the low drone of a plane from the west cut him off. He looked out over the moonlit valley, where red and white lights blinked slowly in the sky, falling steadily lower. Herbert went to the car, got a flare, lit it. The little plane circled once, falling lower.

This is the end of the path, Wallace thought. He imagined a dozen big army men piling out of the plane, ready to finish the job the white men had started, so many years ago.

The plane aligned itself with the rough road and fell out of the sky. It bumped down the road and coasted to a stop in a cloud of dust. A single man got out and walked toward them.

When the light of their fire touched his face, Wallace started. He looked at Niyol, but his friend only nodded, as if he wasn't surprised.

It was Benjamin Hatathlie, the vice president of Dinétah.

Hatathlie's expression didn't change as his eyes paused for an instant on Wallace and Niyol. In the flickering firelight, they were dark and impenetrable, like chips of obsidian.

"Who are the boys, Mr. Noble?" Hatathlie said.

"Guides," Herbert said, his jaw set stubbornly.

"Should we walk and talk?"

"No. They know what we're doing."

"They know?"

"Some other assholes came after us. Had to kill them. They saw it."

Hatathlie turned to Wallace. "Who did they kill?"

"Gerald Manycows, of Many Hogans Clan. And three of his friends. We didn't know them."

Hatathlie blinked, once, slowly.

"It was them or us!" Herbert said.

"What did you do with them?"

"We buried them," Wallace said.

Hatathlie nodded.

"This is the smart one," Frans said, nodding at Niyol. "He saw the Geiger counter and knew what we were doing."

"Is that true?" Hatathlie asked. "How does a boy know this?"

"Movies," Niyol said.

Hatathlie grinned. "Of course. Education from the screen. I should have known the American fables would have effects."

"And now you've sold us out to them!" Wallace said.

Hatathlie chuckled. "To the Americans? No. They have their weapons. It's now time that we develop our own."

Oh my Diyin Diné, living in the earth, Wallace thought. This couldn't be happening. A Diné who rode willingly in a plane. A Diné willing to tear out the heart of the earth. It wasn't possible!

"Should we be telling them this?" Herbert said.

Hatathlie nodded. "Of course. This is our new path. There's no turning away from it."

"I don't know," Herbert said. "They seem pretty stubborn."

Hatathlie knelt down in front of the fire and turned to face Wallace and Niyol. He let a big grin spread across his face. It transformed him from a scary, powerful man to someone who would look at home telling stories in front of a fireplace.

"Would you like to hear how Dinétah can become great again?" Hatathlie spoke softly.

Herbert shifted uncomfortably. "And Texas."

Hatathlie ignored him.

"Tell us," Niyol said.

Wallace almost protested. He almost said, *No, not for any reason. If you are to rip out the heart of the earth and kill the gods, I don't want to know how great it will make us.* But he looked at his friend and saw the intense and desperate look in his eye, and said nothing. Maybe it would be better to know. Maybe, for once, it would be good to follow Niyol's wisdom.

"Once, the Diné were great," Hatathlie said. "We owned this land and the land beyond. Where we walked, others fell by the wayside. The Apache and Hopi respected us. We were the most powerful tribe on the continent."

And we still are, Wallace thought.

"But we were fooled. I no longer believe the elephants were a gift of the First Ones. I think they were a gift of Coyote, to fool us into following a path and losing our soul."

"We won Dinétah!" Wallace said.

"Yes!" Hatathlie nodded. "And now we're surrounded by America. Rich, strong America. Infecting our brightest with their own ideas." He looked at Niyol, and Niyol looked away.

"To the south, Mexico. Still richer than us. At all points of the compass we're surrounded by more powerful countries. We're trapped in a cage of our own making. We could be so much richer if we embraced the present and changed with the world.

"And the world is changing. You've seen it. The atomic weapon ended World War Two with a single stroke. It is the greatest power the world has seen. And in a few short years, many nations will have their own. Including ours."

"And Texas," Herbert said.

"Yes," Hatathlie said. "Dinétah, joined with a newly independent Texas, will be a great force in the world. Where we lead the change, rather than turn away from it."

"Who are you, then?" Niyol asked Herbert. "The Texas governor?"

Herbert laughed. "No! He's just a lapdog of the Americans. I'm an independent businessman. With connections."

"A mobster, in other words."

Herbert frowned. "Kid, your movies make you too smart for your own good—"

"Shh," Hatathlie said. "We're having a friendly conversation. Let's keep it that way."

Herbert grumbled and fell silent.

"If Dinétah is rich in uranium," Hatathlie said, throwing a glance at Frans, who nodded enthusiastically, "we have three choices. One, we can wait for the Americans to discover it, and decide that letting us keep Dinétah was a bad idea. Two, we can try to sell it to them, which will make some of us very, very rich. But in the end, they will have the uranium and the bombs, and they will decide what we do. If they decide they want Arizona and the New Mexico territories back, if they want to make Colorado and Nevada slightly larger, they'll do it. And there's nothing we can do to stop them. Three, we can mine it ourselves, develop our own weapons, and establish ourselves as a nation with the foresight to be a true world power. Which would you choose?"

Wallace sighed. It all sounded so reasonable. So proper. So right. But why couldn't they just leave the uranium where it was? Why couldn't they just hide it, forget it ever existed? Why did Hatathlie bring these men out here? Why did he have to start this whole thing?

Wallace shook his head. He wished for words, old words, powerful words that could change the world. Words that would make Hatathlie change his mind in an instant. He opened his mouth, but nothing came out.

Hatathlie shook his head. "No choice? None?"

Wallace shook his head and looked at Niyol. Niyol looked away.

"I understand," Hatathlie said. "It's a difficult thing to think about. We've been small and poor for so long that we can't think of ourselves as rich and powerful. But it's time to end the tyranny of that idea."

"I never thought we were poor," Wallace said.

Hatathlie laughed. "You've seen the American movies, their sprawling modern homes, the families with two cars and a television, and you think we're not poor?"

"Those are only *things*," Wallace said.

"Things matter."

Wallace shook his head. "I am Wallace Chee of the Big Water Clan. That matters."

"And I'm Niyol Chavez, Chiricahua Apache Clan. Hello, brother."

Hatathlie frowned and put his hands on his hips, as if confronting a stubborn mule.

"You look Diné, but you are white," Wallace said.

Hatathlie's frown deepened. "If President Lincoln hadn't accepted King Mongkut's gift of the elephants, this might be a very different world today. It is time for us to accept our own elephants."

"No," Wallace said.

"No," Niyol said.

Hatathlie sighed. "Maybe you'll listen to reason in the morning."

Not if it's your reason, Wallace thought.

He turned away from the boys and addressed Herbert and Frans. "I understand we're in business."

"There's an entire vein of high-grade ore running into Mount Taylor," Herbert said, pointing at a map. "And more, scattered here and here."

"This appears to be an area extremely rich in uranium ores," Frans said.

The three men shared a new bottle of whiskey around and huddled over the map, laughing and gesturing excitedly. The boys could have been statues. More than once, Wallace thought about running, but he couldn't imagine outrunning the men.

The men eventually finished their discussion and agreed to take turns watching the boys as they slept. Wallace sighed and lay down on the ground as far from the fire as he could. Niyol lay beside him.

Wallace looked up at the stars, bright and cold and uncaring. Even though he was exhausted, sleep wouldn't come.

"I'm going to leave," Wallace whispered. Herbert had been watching them. Now he sat by the fire, head down, apparently sleeping.

"Where?" Niyol hissed, eyeing Herbert.

"Away from here."

"Who are you going to tell?"

"Everybody."

"What can they do?"

Wallace frowned. "I have to try."

Silence for a time. Wallace wished that an airship would pass over them, low enough that he could shout for help. He wondered if they would stop.

"I'm going," Wallace said.

"I'll stay here," Niyol said. "In case he's not asleep."

"What will you do if he isn't?"

A crescent of white teeth showed in the moonlight. "I don't know."

Wallace smiled back. He turned over on his belly, as if rolling in his sleep. He waited, then edged forward, pulling himself away from the camp. Slowly, over a period of several minutes, he crawled away from the camp.

No noise from Herbert. He snuck a look back. The man's head still hung at an uncomfortable angle.

When Wallace was about twenty feet away, he moved to hands and knees, crawling fast. Still nothing from Herbert.

Wallace stood and jogged as quickly as he dared, his feet making soft shushing sounds on the loose sand and dust. His shoulder blades itched, as if an invisible sight were trained between them. He remembered the flunky's head exploding, drops of gore spattering his face.

He resisted the urge to look back. Soon he would be far enough away, over a series of low hills and behind some of the taller scrub. Then he'd have a real chance.

Wallace sprinted up the first hill, rising like a bread-loaf mound in the desert. He held his breath as he crested it and dropped out of the camp's line of fire. At the bottom, he grinned and looked back, happy to see that he could no longer see the embers of the fire, the car, or the plane.

"Stop right there," said a voice, behind him. In Navajo.

Wallace froze.

"Turn around."

Wallace turned, slowly, to face the voice.

A man stood in front of him, clothed in traditional Diné garb. The bright colors were gray and pastel in the moonlight. His skin glistened as if oiled. Smooth black hair piled above deep eye sockets. He looked like a picture out of a history book.

"I am Ahiga, of Shining Elephant Clan," the man said, in Navajo. Wallace frowned, the words running ahead of his ability to translate. When they'd all registered, he said, clumsily, "I am Wallace Chee, of Big Water Clan."

Ahiga bowed. "Greetings, Wallace Chee. Why are you here? Why are you leaving your companions?"

"I, uh . . ." Wallace searched for words. "Men come . . . to steal land."

"Speak English, if it's easier." In English.

"Yes. Thanks," Wallace said. He started a quick account of who the men were and why they were there, but his voice died when he saw the elephants.

Two of them, standing quietly in the shade of one of the low hills. Covered with some kind of blankets. If they hadn't moved, he never would have seen them. One still carried a rider.

Ahiga's gaze flickered to the elephants and back to Wallace. He cocked his head to the side and told Wallace to go on.

Wallace had to explain that the men had found a precious metal and were plotting to take over Dinétah. He told Ahiga about Benjamin

Hatathlie. He told him about Niyol, still in the camp. He asked for Ahiga's help.

Ahiga said nothing. He made a gesture with the fingers of his right hand, and the elephants walked over to stand at his side. They moved almost silently.

Up close, Wallace could see that the rider of the other elephant was an older man, also dressed in traditional garb. Wallace couldn't see his eyes, but he got the feeling the old man was looking at him.

"I am Yiska Laguna, of Shining Elephant Clan," the old man said, his voice thin and reedy.

Wallace told him his name and clan. Yiska nodded once, as if satisfied.

Shining Elephant Clan. Like the Elephant Ironclads, shining in the orange light of sunset in a thousand old paintings. But the elephants they rode weren't armored. They were covered with heavy blankets, layered like scales.

Blankets with frayed edges that exposed tiny lines of shining metal. Blankets that clapped against one another with a faint metallic song.

They'd padded the armor. Of course. That made sense.

Wallace felt suddenly light-headed. The Elephant Ironclads still exist, he thought. They're real, and they're still here!

Wallace knew he had to be dreaming. He slapped himself in the face, willing wakefulness.

Nothing changed. The elephants still stood before him. Ahiga gave him a strange grin. Yiska sat imperturbably on top of the other elephant.

"Are you . . . are they the Elephant Ironclads?" Wallace asked.

"They have been called that," Ahiga said.

"They're beautiful," Wallace said.

And they were. They were everything he imagined. They stood towering over him, topped by the multicolored warriors of legend. Wallace imagined the scene set against a backdrop of sunrise, with airships rising from the east. It was Diné, it was Dinétah, it was everything that Benjamin Hatathlie wasn't.

"Where have you been?" Wallace asked.

Ahiga smiled and looked around, as if indicating all the land. "Everywhere."

"But . . . nobody believes you really exist."

"People who need to know, know."

"You don't know how important you are!"

Ahiga just looked at him.

"Will you help me?" Wallace asked.

"With what?"

Wallace realized he hadn't finished his story about Herbert and Frans and Benjamin Hatathlie. The mention of uranium produced only blank looks. Wallace tried to explain about nuclear weapons. More blank looks. Finally, he settled for telling them uranium was something like gold, and the men wanted to mine it.

Finally, Yiska stirred. "These bilaganna want to tear out the heart of Mount Taylor?" Yiska said.

"That's where they said the vein was," Wallace said.

Yiska's ancient face puckered into a deep frown. "This Hatathlie . . . he agrees?"

"He's helping them," Wallace said.

The frown deepened. Yiska motioned Ahiga over to his side, and they had a short conversation in Navajo.

"We will help you," Ahiga said.

Ahiga mounted his ride and reached down to help Wallace up. Wallace sat behind Ahiga. The warmth of the elephant, even through the plates and fabric, was almost overwhelming. Wallace realized he could feel the beat of its heart, a low thudding beneath his legs. He laid his head on the elephant's back and heard the rush of breath in its lungs, the faint creak of bones and muscles, the singing of tendons.

Ahiga made a small noise, and the elephant started moving. It was like his first time riding a horse when he was very, very small and the horse seemed very, very large. It was like nothing he'd ever experienced before.

Wallace looked up at the stars. They were no different from the stars earlier. But they no longer seemed cruel.

The elephants approached the camp almost soundlessly. Wallace saw the last embers of the fire, tiny red sparks in the charcoal-drawn landscape. Herbert was slumped to one side, snoring. The other two men lay on the ground, unmoving. Niyol was still wrapped in his sleeping bag.

"Which is your friend?" Ahiga whispered.

Wallace pointed at Niyol.

Ahiga caught Yiska's eye and pointed at Niyol. Ahiga nodded.

Yiska made a low, harsh bark.

The elephants charged. Wallace grabbed at the fabric to keep from being thrown off. He felt wind in his face. He didn't know elephants could move that fast.

The elephant's footfalls merged into continuous thunder. They raised their trunks and trumpeted.

In camp, Herbert was first to jump up. He grabbed at the .30-06 and started bringing it up, squinting into the night. Then he stopped and stood openmouthed, the .30-06 dropping butt-down in the dirt.

Ahiga's elephant charged straight at Herbert. And for a moment, it was as if Wallace were watching the elephants through Herbert's eyes. Monsters from hell, huge trumpeting demons with scaly gray skin and great shining white fangs that shrieked in anger and towered over them. Painted in nothing but moonlight and darkness, they were impossible, heart-stopping.

Wallace smiled. *This is the weapon of the Diné.*

Benjamin Hatathlie and Frans Van der Berg threw off their covers and scrambled for weapons. When they looked up, they also stopped, eyes wide in terror.

Ahiga's elephant struck Herbert with its head. Herbert's .30-06 flew into the night and Herbert tumbled to the ground. He scrambled to get back up, but Ahiga's elephant had already stopped. It put a foot on Herbert to hold him in place. Herbert scrabbled at Many-cows's knife, still at his side. The blade glinted with reflected fire-light. The elephant bore down on him. Herbert groaned and dropped the knife.

Three shots rang out in quick succession. Wallace saw Benjamin Hatathlie calmly firing at Yiska's elephant as it charged toward him. The elephant bellowed and shook its head. Hatathlie's eyes went wide as the beast bore down on him. He squeezed off another shot and turned to flee.

Yiska's elephant picked up Hatathlie with its trunk and shook him like a rattle. Hatathlie tried to point the gun at the elephant's skull. The elephant shook him harder and Hatathlie dropped the gun.

Ahiga leaped off his elephant to chase Frans, who was running toward the car. Ahiga caught him when he was opening the door, slamming the bigger man into the car with a sharp metallic *bonk*. Frans's head cracked against the window frame and he slumped to the ground.

"Wallace?" Niyol's voice came from below him.

Wallace looked down at his friend and grinned. "Who else?"

"I thought I was dreaming." Niyol stepped forward to touch the ele-phant's fabric-wrapped armor. The beast turned its head to look at him, but did nothing more.

Ahiga dragged Frans back to camp. Soon, all three men were se-curely tied, facing a new fire that cast their shadows into the night. The elephants grazed calmly in the background, their fabric-covered armor making soft rustling noises.

"Fellow people, why do you bind us?" Hatathlie asked, speaking Navajo.

"We bind for truth," Yiska said. He sat facing the three men, back-lit by the fire. "Strong accusations have been made."

"What has the boy said?"

"He said that you will tear out the heart of our land for some metal that shines like gold. He said you will give our land to our enemies."

Hatathlie sighed. "May I speak my vision?"

"Yes," Yiska said.

"You are a proud group," Hatathlie said. "Descendants of the men who won our land from the Americans. I did not know you existed. I salute your bravery and what you have done. I hope your resolve will help you understand what I see for Dinétah, and for the Diné."

Yiska nodded, his expression blank.

"I see the Diné rising again. It has been said that we will one day save the world. Some people say this is what our codetalkers did. I do not think they did. I think the prophecy is literal truth, and we will save the world.

"You may know that the United States has an atomic bomb, as does the Soviet Union. Two powerful nations, now both with the power to destroy the world. Dinétah is a small nation, rich in culture. Now we find we are gifted with the resources to make our own atomic bombs, to become a nuclear power. Two legs do not make the stool. We can be the third leg. We can be the counterbalance. We can stand aside and say no, this land is sacred, it shall not be destroyed."

"After you've mined all the uranium," Wallace said.

Yiska looked at Wallace and shook his head. Wallace felt his face grow red.

"With this atomic bomb, we would be as powerful as the Americans?" Yiska asked.

"Yes!" Hatathlie said. "We would never have to worry about losing our land again. We could go to Washington and speak as equals. Maybe even more."

Yiska nodded again. "Diné could sleep secure in their hogans, knowing this."

"Yes!"

"And we could keep the land as we once did."

"Yes."

"After we remove the heart of a sacred mountain."

Hatathlie's mouth clicked shut.

"You did not introduce yourself or your clan when we met," Yiska said.

"I . . . I was scared. I'm Benjamin Hatathlie of Chiricahua Apache Clan . . ."

Yiska sighed, stood up, and turned his back on Hatathlie.

"What . . . what does that mean . . . ," Hatathlie said.

Ahiga stepped out of the shadows from behind Hatathlie. He held a long blade that glowed orange in the reflected firelight.

The blade fell, swiftly, slashing Hatathlie's neck. He gurgled and screamed and fell over on his side, tugging at the ropes that bound his hands and feet. His eyes, wide and dark, seemed to settle on Wallace. Wallace tried to keep his face expressionless, but he wanted to smile.

You were not Diné, he thought.

Hatathlie's struggles became weaker. Eventually, he lay motionless. A great sigh passed out of him, and he was still.

Wallace heard a sob. Beside him, Niyol was crying.

"Why are you crying?" Wallace asked.

Niyol just shook his head and turned away.

Was it possible that his friend believed what Hatathlie said? Did he stay with them because he wanted to be part of the great new nation?

A low noise from Frans broke his thoughts. The man was mumbling something, his eyes heavenward. Praying.

Herbert looked Ahiga directly in the eye. There was no fear in his expression.

"Go ahead," Herbert said. "Kill me. It doesn't matter. There are lots of others like me. And it's either us or the United States. And you know what the United States did to you. You could have worse partners than the mob."

Yiska shook his head. "We will not kill you."

"What?" Herbert said.

Frans stopped praying and looked up.

"This is for Diné. You are not Diné."

"They killed Diné!" Wallace said. "They killed four of us!"

"Is this true?" Yiska said.

"They attacked us first!" Herbert said.

"Is this true?" Yiska asked Wallace.

"They . . . these men shot first."

Herbert frowned. "If we hadn't, they would have taken the money. And maybe killed these kids."

"Is that true?" To Wallace.

Wallace looked away. It was true. He doubted if Gerald Manycows would have left any witnesses.

But they had to kill them! What Herbert said was true! It was them or America. Eventually, one of them would come in and take everything away. Wallace envisioned US Army tanks rolling across the orange-red desert, to face a line of Elephant Ironclads ridden by brightly clothed Diné warriors. It would be an incredible sight. In its own way, it would be beautiful.

It would be a massacre.

"It's true," Niyol said.

Wallace turned to look at his friend. Anger clenched his hands into fists. He wanted to strike him to the ground, and keep hitting until black blood flowed.

"Is this true?" Yiska asked.

Wallace looked at Yiska. What would he do if I said no? Would I sit facing the firelight like Hatathlie?

"It is," Wallace said.

Yiska stood up. "Then we do nothing."

Herbert tugged at the ropes that bound his arms. "Let us go!"

Yiska nodded. "We will."

"Now!"

Yiska ignored him and went to talk with Ahiga.

"Hey!" Herbert said.

Ahiga and Yiska pulled down the tents and piled the fabric and aluminum rods next to the car, ignoring Herbert's protests. Frans remained silent, perhaps satisfied enough in keeping his life.

"Why'd you cry?" Wallace asked Niyol.

"He was my brother."

"He'd kill us all."

Niyol shook his head.

"Do you want us to be like America?"

"No," Niyol said. "I don't know. I just want to go home."

Home. Back to Mother and her little skystone jewelry stand, back to the sheep and the shepherds. Wallace just shook his head.

When Ahiga and Yiska began to push dry brush under the car, both Frans and Herbert yelled in protest. Wallace laughed and went to help.

Soon, the night was lit by two new fires: the car and the plane. Both burned uncertainly for a time, then fountained upward in pillars of fire as the gas tanks caught. It was bright enough to illuminate the far hills.

When the fires guttered and went out, Ahiga and Yiska untied Herbert and Frans. Herbert rubbed his wrists and gave the two elephant men a calculating look.

"You may go," Yiska said.

"Where? You've killed us," Herbert said.

"I do not believe that is true."

"We'll be back."

Yiska smiled. "And we will still remain."

"Let's go," Frans said, pulling at Herbert's arm.

"You think you'll stop us, but you won't!"

Frans tugged harder.

"We'll be back!"

One more tug. Herbert tore his arm away from Frans, but walked away with him. The two men shrank into the distance, following the road back toward Paguate.

Yiska and Ahiga mounted their elephants. In the wan moonlight, they looked like ghosts drawn in shadow. Wallace looked up at them. They were what Diné should be.

Wallace heard Niyol's footsteps crunching away into the night. He turned to see his friend walking down the road, following the two men.

"Niyol!" Wallace cried.

Niyol kept walking.

"Niyol!"

Niyol didn't look back.

He has something to go back to, Wallace thought. I have nothing.

Wallace looked up at Yiska. "Can I stay with you?"

"That is one path," Yiska said.

Wallace imagined himself atop a great shining elephant, leading the Diné against whatever might come. Maybe even helping them understand this strange new world they lived in. He could be the avatar of change. He could be the one who saved them all!

"And there is your friend, and what he follows," Ahiga said.

Wallace turned to look at Niyol's shrinking figure. Yes, there was his friend. And the men who had promised to come back.

"That is another path," Yiska said.

The elephants were beautiful. Wallace looked at them for a long time, burning the image into his mind. Tears welled, but he willed them away. He was not their savior. He might not ever find any great path.

"Good-bye," Wallace said.

Yiska's expression never changed. He nodded once and turned his elephant around. Ahiga followed. They were almost completely silent.

Wallace waited until they were nothing more than shadows against the stars. Then he went back to camp where Herbert had fallen. He picked up Manycows's blade.

He stuck it in his belt and started walking, back toward the men, back toward Paguate.

Ardent Clouds

Lucy Sussex

Lucy Sussex was born in the South Island of New Zealand and lives in Australia, where she works as a researcher and writer. She has published widely, with a particular interest in crime and Victoriana.

Her fiction has won Ditmar and Aurealis awards and been shortlisted for environmental awards and the International Horror Guild Award. Her short stories have been collected in My Lady Tongue, A Tour Guide in Utopia, *and* Absolute Uncertainty. *She has also written three books for younger readers, two for teenagers, and one adult novel,* The Scarlet Rider. *Of the four anthologies she has compiled,* She's Fantastical *was shortlisted for the World Fantasy Award.*

She also writes the "Covernotes" column for The Age *and* The West Australian *newspapers and is completing a nonfiction book,* Cherchez les Femmes, *on early women crime authors and detectives.*

Sussex is an expert at creating vivid, believable characters, flaws and all. She does so in "Ardent Clouds," a story about an extremely dangerous profession and those who embrace it.

C all me suicidal (many do). Call me a paparazzo, specializing in subjects blowing their top. Call me a groupie for danger. I just love the smell of sulphur in the morning . . . or any other time. Someone from film school said it best: "You, Bet, are a powdermonkey."

Yeah, powdermonkey, those boys employed by the British navy to feed gunpowder to the cannons, darting through the noise and smoke of battle. I can just see myself in navy breeches and pea jacket, my A-size breasts concealed beneath a bandage, wrapped tight. Way back then, if a girl wanted a career that didn't involve babies, wanted adventure, she disguised herself and went to sea. I'd have loved it!

But in terms of fire, noise, and explosion, a cannon just doesn't cut it for me. Give me a volcano anytime. That's how I make my living, travelling from eruption to eruption, filming the biggest, most explosive, most uncontrollable things on earth.

It started with an SMS from Spider, as I call him. To others, he's Herr Professor Dr. Sigurrson, theorist of volcanology. Spider makes his lair at a university in a cold and geologically stable part of Europe. There he sits, at the centre of a web of information stretching all over the planet, like lines of longitude and latitude, provided by seismological sensors. If there's a twitch from a volcano anywhere, Spider knows about it.

But he can't go and investigate, because he's in a wheelchair, some
sort of fragile bone syndrome. He doesn't travel, and we met only
once, at a conference on his home turf. When we met, he couldn't even
risk shaking my hand, in case I squeezed *his* too tight and broke a finger. That's how some tell if others are okay, by the handshake. Spider
does it at one remove, visually. The clear blue Viking eyes behind
those bottle glasses, they looked me up and down.

It wasn't with desire, either: I tend to the stocky and have no-
nonsense hair. I also dress super-sensibly—that's not a gun in my
bulging pocket, but a spare lens. Volcanologists do fall in love and get
married, even Spider, who has Magga, a devoted nurse-wife, always
one pace away from his wheelchair. But their real passions are elsewhere. You could see lust in the eyes watching my film, of an undersea
volcano hitting the ocean surface in a maelstrom of steam, stink gas,
and lava.

In my accompanying presentation, I threw in a few specialist volcanological terms, to show I was smarter than the average nature documentary maker. And, to show I meant business, told how I'd bribed
the coast guards to take me into the danger zone. The boat had been
bucking underneath me, I had to keep wiping pulverized pumice off
the lens, I was drenched in sulphur-tinged spume—and none of that
mattered, because I got great footage.

I also gained something else: a boss. Every grouping has its moi-
eties, opposing parties. I privately grouped volcanologists into Spiders
and Powdermonkeys. My family, who are old air force stock, distin-
guished between Shiny Ass fliers and Aces. The former flew desks, the
latter Spitfires. If I'd had the math to be a volcanologist in actuality, instead of just a hanger-on paparazzo, I'd have been an Ace, yes siree! If
Spider hadn't been doomed by nature to a life lived apart from his pre-
cipitous, dangerous objects of research, he might have been the same.
Instead, he was king of the (computer) desk fliers, and as such needed
a proxy.

Spider and I have a deal: He tells me where the volcanological action is, I go there and film it. I also report back: I've been his ears and
eyes all over the world. In the process, though I've never seen him

again, we've developed a rapport. He gets oddly solicitous: If I'm going to Alaska, he tells me to wrap up warm; or in the Philippines, he'll recommend insect repellent. All this for someone at a far remove, going places he can never physically visit.

"Do you envy me?" I e-mailed him late one night.

The reply came at the end of a long list of technical data, stuff I really had to know for the latest hot spot in volcanology. Then he got, briefly, personal.

"No. Sometimes when I see your footage, almost. Then I remember that I'm better in my office, away from the explosions. Magga says she doesn't know why anyone would marry a volcanologist otherwise. Someone like you gets up close, but I get the big picture. I don't envy Bet the ant, walking on a ticking bomb."

Which was to me, and to many of the people I met in the field, or at conferences, precisely the fun of it. The Powdermonkeys, we got dirty and dangerous, taking photos or collecting gas from steaming fumaroles; the Spiders kept their distance, analyzing the figures, building mathematical models.

I guessed that more likely Spider-proxies, grad students or colleagues, were ruled out for reasons of possible professional jealousy. And in choosing me, I don't flatter myself falsely that he'd been very astute. Not even top volcanologists can go where I've gone. Money is tight in universities these days; business schools are more important than science. What with teaching, grant applications, and admin, few volcanologists can drop everything and dash off to an incipient eruption. But I have connections to TV networks, specialist heat- and chemical-resistant cameras, and an ever-increasing reputation for spectacular images.

"I don't know how you do it," said Cody Veitch from CNN. "Always the money shot."

I bit my lower lip. Network execs tend to the crass, but it was true—although my money shot was large-scale, rather than in the intimate, bedroom realm.

"It's like you go there, the volcano blows. I remember being an anchorman way back with Mount St. Helens, waiting God knows how long for the fucker to shoot its load. And thinking: Hurry up, it's a real slow news day! With you, it's like you're in and out of the hot spot within twenty-four hours, with your footage. So what's the secret?"

"Connections. The best."

Silken ones, I thought, leading to my master, sitting in his wheel-chair in front of a computer screen.

But latterly I had begun to wonder: How come Spider gets it so right? Sometimes a volcano can get active, but just sits and grumbles, letting off gas or steam without doing anything newsworthy, let alone cataclysmic. The locals would get evacuated, a costly exercise, and nothing would happen. Spider might have the best information, but clearly he had something else. Scientists don't sacrifice goats and consult their entrails, even for something as unpredictable, even godlike, as a volcano. Spider was a theoretician, and I figured he was perfecting a theory, perhaps a formula: If $x = y$ to the power of z, then the volcano will blow. Being able to predict eruptions would have huge prestige—it would pay to get it absolutely right.

Someday, I thought, I'll be at the Nobels, filming Spider as he wheels himself up for his glittering prize. In the meantime, though, I was having the greatest of times. I went everywhere from Iceland to Antarctica, following volcanic action. I've even been undersea in the Mir submersible, filming the weird and wonderful fauna that hang around hydrothermal vents, and their warm, mineral-rich emissions. After that anything seemed possible, like a trip to Jupiter and its volcanic moon Io. A girl can dream . . .

When the mobile peeped, five AM in my Miami hotel room at a documentary film fest, I knew we were in European time, and that Spider was calling.

It was an SMS message, one word: CHILLIPEPPER.

That was the nickname of a volcano in South America. The real name signified some unpronounceable pre-Columbian fire god; *Chilli-pepper* was the easy alternative. Obvious, since it was dead centre of an area famous for its chilli production. The soil around volcanoes is typically fertile—it's one reason why people don't keep the hell away from them. Chillipepper's pickles had a cult following, almost an *appellation contrôlée*, as the hottest and tastiest peppers around. The jar labels even featured an erupting volcano, a bit of a fiction, as Chillipepper had rumbled into life a few times last century, causing a stir, but nothing really dramatic.

The name rang a recent bell, but I couldn't recall anything more. Early in the morning is not a good time for my synapses. I ordered coffee, double strength, from the dozy room service and got onto the Net, Googling for more information. A name instantly familiar hit the screen: JOE BOY BARRETT. I groaned. Spider might rule the desk fliers, but Joe Boy, Emeritus Professor Barrett, was King Ace and thus eternally at war with Spider & Co. He proclaimed that no theorist could predict an eruption; you had to get up there, smell the sulphur. Like some of the flying aces I'd met as a kid (okay, the family were ground crew), Joe Boy had elephantiasis of the ego. He was big, boomed a lot, and shook hands like it was a strength contest. He had a cowboy image, too: boots, Texas buckle on his jeans, and once he'd hosted a formal conference dinner in a genuine Nudie suit, complete with sequinned volcanoes.

When I started out, I might have idolized him like the postgrads he trailed in his wake, as the man who would stick sensors into smoking fumaroles while the mountain shook beneath him and lightning danced in the air. After working for Spider, I saw things differently; in his quiet, abstracted way my master was getting things right, while others strode around, trailing sulphuric glory and yelling: Look at me, Look at me!

Now I avoided Joe Boy, especially since he'd started putting the hard word on me, not sexually (he had another of these devoted faculty wives) but to make a documentary about him. He even had a title for it, *The Danger Man*.

I shuddered, sipped more coffee, intent on my laptop screen. This long weekend Joe Boy would be keynote speaker at a Chillipepper conference, to be held in a city literally underneath the volcano. I scanned the list of speakers: mostly Joe Boy's pals or, if not, considered to be no threat, or easily put-down-able. Not like Spider, the ultimate physical weakling, but who on an intellectual level fought like Shelob. Relations were so poisonous between the two they wouldn't even e-mail.

I sent an SMS back to Spider:

JOEBOY! MUST I?

(Spider's response to *The Danger Man* had been in Icelandic and, he assured me, obscene.)

A few moments later, he replied.

YOU HAFTA

ITS WORTH IT

GETTAMOVEON

I glanced at my multi-time-zone watch: Networks would not welcome a call now, nor would my travel agent. And I was feeling a little unwelcoming myself. Over the past year there had been—for lack of a better term—a husbandly tone to Spider's missives, as if he'd got used to having me at his beck and call. I was starting to bridle at it. Okay, so he thought Chillipepper was worth it. But *I* needed something else.

I got onto Volcano-Lovers. In Internet-land, there's discussion groups for everything, from morris dancing to (coded) incest, and several on volcanology, varying from the highly technical to the fannish. Deep down, those who love volcanoes are simply groupies for the baddest, deadliest, most temperamental things on the planet. They just talk in different languages. I could understand scientific papers, though Spider's recent publications were eye watering. But for simple gossip, easy info, and, yes, like souls, I turned to Volcano-Lovers.

Alluringly, there was a thread for Chillipepper. I read through it, stopping at a message sent from a Russian server:

LARISSA: MY ALLOWANCE CAME THROUGH! SO CHILLIPEPPER HERE I COME!

That settled it. Chillipepper here I come, too!

*   *   *

I first met Larissa on a grubby little ferry crossing the Bay of Naples. She walked up to where I leaned on the railing, gazing at the waves.

"This should be Roman galley," she said.

I looked up, registering the small figure, the raven-wing of hair, and her arctic eyes. Identifying the accent took slightly longer. Unlike some Russians I'd met, including a volcanologist I termed Ivan the Incomprehensible, she spoke clear, if slightly MTV English. But I blinked: How could she know what I was thinking?

As if registering that thought, too, she said: "If Bet Murray, famous volcano photographer, is crossing Bay of Naples from Cape Miseno to Vesuvius, then she's being pilgrim, on trail of first volcano-lover."

Russian has no articles, so those learning English as their second language have problems with *a* or *the*.

"You're right, I am following the sea trail of Pliny the Elder," I said.

Pliny, commander of the Roman navy, had on a fine August day in AD 79 seen what would later be called a Plinian eruption column arising from Vesuvius. And set off across twenty sea miles for a closer look.

She had a book under her arm, and though I couldn't read the Cyrillic on its cover, I could guess it was a translation from the Latin of Pliny the Younger, the commander's nephew. He provided the eyewitness account, since Uncle Pliny did not survive his Powdermonkey curiosity.

"You know who I am, but you are . . ."

"Larissa."

"You're from Volcano-Lovers."

"Also PhD student. My diss is on Bezymianny."

Larissa might look childlike, but she had picked a volcano that even the most macho of volcanologists found scary. In 1956 Bezymianny blew its top off, creating a crater over a mile wide, with a Plinian eruption column reaching twenty-one miles skywards. It would have been lethal but for Bezymianny being in relatively uninhabited Kamchatka.

"Bezymianny? *Bozhe moy!* My god!" I said, in my minimal Russian.

She smiled, a faux-pas smile, but not unkind.

"My pronunciation?"

"No. But Russians say *Bozhe moy* for ordinary things like cabbages and people. Not volcano."

"I'm sorry."

"*Nichevo.* That means, no matter."

We fell silent, watching the expanse of water, the cone of sleeping, silent Vesuvius, as if seeing two thousand years ago. I thought of how Pliny the Younger had stayed behind but nearly got killed anyway. He saw a terrifying black cloud, torn as if by giant lightning, with massing flames at its centre. It sank down from the volcano, onto the sea, and rolled the twenty miles across the bay. Darkness came with it, like a light going out in a closed room. Ash began to fall on young Pliny, a teenager, and his mother. They thought the world was ending.

Yet Pliny had survived to provide the first existing account of pyroclastic flows—from the Greek "cracked fire," the lethal, fast-moving clouds of gas and ash that are the real volcanic killers. You can outrun a lava flow, but not something moving at three hundred miles an hour, at its worst hot enough to BBQ you or suffocate you with hot ash.

"Larissa, what do Russians call pyroclastic flows?"

She looked wry. "Loan word. *Piroklastichesky potok.* Why not borrow *nuées ardentes?*"

It was French, glowing clouds—ardent clouds, too, if we were punning.

"It sounds better, yes."

"I want to see one!" From her face, an ardent wish.

"I might have wanted to be the first to film them, but Maurice and Katia Krafft"— alias the volcanic Cousteaus—"got there first."

"And died for it."

"At eight hundred forty degrees Fahrenheit, their clothes and hair alight, instant human carbon."

Even for a pair of Powdermonkeys, it was sobering. I looked over the sea at modern Naples, the sprawling houses, and thought of teenage Pliny, watching the *nuée ardente* rushing towards him like a hellish bat, fire on its wings. He was lucky: In the twenty miles across the bay much of its force, heat, and hydrogen sulphide were dissipated. Otherwise he would not have survived to tell his tale.

Still in Vesuvius mode, we visited Pompeii the next day. I'd been before, but Larissa never had, and she was duly professional when regarding the famous casts of the volcano's victims, the father and son holding hands, or the leashed dog, twisted in agony. We heartlessly speculated about temperature, velocity, and ash distribution. Only the sight of a doll's head, found with the bones of an eight-year-old girl, clutched for comfort in a horrific death, gave Larissa teary pause. "So sad!"

Then we separated. I had a meeting with an Italian production company keen to use my footage in a projected remake of *The Last Days of Pompeii*. They were paying, so I wasn't going to tell them what the *Lord of the Rings* special-effects guys had done to simulate a lava flow from Mount Doom: CGI graphics on top of K-Y jelly.

Larissa had to go to a wedding: "My cousin. They hired Versailles for reception. Why didn't they hire somewhere with volcano!"

In the new Russia, nobody asks where people get their money. At the least, Larissa's family were oligarchs; at the worst, mafia. I got the impression they were so relieved at an heiress not behaving like Paris Hilton, they would subsidize an expensive volcanological habit. It was probably cheaper than cocaine, anyway.

I continued to the next port of call, some serious talks with *National Geographic*. Life continued as usual: dangerous, solitary, and rather too weird for friends, unless they happened to be fellow obsessives. Now Larissa was a frequent guest in my in-tray: a photo here (the Versailles wedding looked like Fellini gone Slavic), a comment or professional query there. I figured at first she was networking, then that life had so blessed her that she simply gambolled through it like a friendly puppy.

Finally I realised that I liked her, and that unless she was a really good actress, it was reciprocated.

I could put up with Joe Boy Barrett for Larissa's sake.

What was it about Chillipepper? Spider and his department had compiled a huge form guide to the world's and even some extraterrestrial volcanoes. I would be sent an extract, everything I needed to know this time. But on my preliminary e-research, it wouldn't seem that Chillipepper rated significantly in the volcano stakes. It wasn't snow-peaked, nor did it have glaciers draping from its slopes like bridal trains (and—if melted by eruptions—causing torrential, lethal floods). It didn't have the stately cone of Fuji, nor fountains of picturesque, fiery lava. Sure, it was an active stratovolcano, which means explosive, but not very, on the available evidence. It didn't have a body count, not like Vesuvius nor Krakatau (thirty-six thousand in 1883).

That was off-putting, as was the fact that the Chillipepper region was currently in a state of—if not active—then grumbling civil war. For twenty years government forces and rebels had been at odds: holdups, murders, even massacres. The US State Department did not recommend the area for tourists, to put it mildly. There were only two entry points, a minor airport with an indifferent safety record, and a highway frequented by both guerrillas and the local bandidos. My travel agent would freak, and I didn't know how I was going to pitch such a relatively boring volcano at the powers-that-pay. I could always write the conference off as a business expense . . .

But, but, I thought, I'm the Powdermonkey who brings home the footage. I could simply trade on my reputation. I reached for my address book. Then my in-tray beeped as it received a huge infodump from Spider. The accompanying message read: WHAT ARE YOU WAITING FOR?

What indeed? What do you know, my master?

* * *

It took some time to get down to Chillipepper. I only got the fare together after promising Cody Veitch some footage of the chillis for use in a lifestyle gourmet program. As it was, I missed most of the first day of the conference after further delays caused by fog in transit. It was dark by the time the elderly prop plane passed the volcano, and I perceived Chillipepper only as blackness between the lights of the city and the stars. And when I got to the site of the conference, I found a major traffic headache.

"Festival time," said the taxi driver. His day job was teaching English, he said, which spared him my dog-Spanish.

Outside, a gaggle of girls, wearing scanty frills in various shades of red, yellow, and orange and a lot of glitter, banged on the rear window.

"It's okay," said the driver. "They don't mean robbery, they just want to give the gringa a present."

I wound down the window and received a necklace of fresh chillis, pointed as shark teeth. Dependent from it was a doll made of one large chilli, wearing a peasant scarf, shawl, and frilly skirts roughly fashioned from corn husks.

"Chilli harvest festival?"

"And Don Nestor's day. Our Saint Nestor, if he makes it past the gringos in the Vatican."

He sounded doubtful.

I was intrigued. "Isn't sainthood automatic since the pope abolished the devil's advocate? All you need is a miracle."

Outside, a conga line of costumed animals—pumas, parrots, jaguars—passed gyrating wildly to the amplified beat of drums, electric guitar, and some screeching local variant on the fife.

"We've had our miracle: No eruptions since eighteen seventy-two."

I'd read Spider's form guide to Chillipepper, so I knew the driver was slightly exaggerating. There'd been no major eruptions, but plenty of tremors, rockfalls, and clouds of ash.

"And how did Don Nestor achieve that?" Volcanology wasn't a science in the 1870s; otherwise some rival researcher would probably have killed Don Nestor for getting there first.

"He sprinkled holy water on the volcano."

Remind me to suggest that to the Shinto priests near Unzen, I thought, the Japanese volcano where the Kraffts and forty others died. But the driver continued:

"That's what they say in the church. But *outside* the church, they say different. You see, Don Nestor wasn't *just* a Catholic priest. That's Rome's problem."

A gap in the traffic appeared, and as the driver accelerated to fill it before someone else did I glimpsed a procession, priests in robes, banners, huge crosses. The Catholic Church might be the religious supremo in South America, but underneath the veneer of Christianity are all sorts of wild and woolly variants, with pre-Columbian elements, or incorporating deities brought from Africa, given a quick scrub and a name change, just like their worshippers, the slaves. Santeria, Candomblé, Vodoun; it was interfaith in practical, colourful action.

"What's the story they tell outside the church?"

"Don Nestor, he hiked up his skirts and climbed the volcano. And when he got to the top and looked into the crater he saw fire: a god, woken from a long sleep, hundreds of years, and mad as hell to find that in the meantime all his temples had been razed. Now, Don Nestor, he grew up here, he knew how things worked. He sat on the crater rim, his feet dangling, and explained. Like how people might go to church on Sunday, but they'd hedge their bets, show respect to what was here first. When they planted crops, they'd turn towards the mountain, and say please silently, and when they harvested, they'd show thanks. But to the gringo priests they'd pretend that the dollies made outta chillis and corn husks were kid stuff. Nobody would say why the dolls get thrown into the harvest bonfire."

"Displaced sacrifice," I said.

"Whatever you call it. Don Nestor, he cut a deal. You're feeling a bit neglected, hey? How about we throw a volcano party each year when the chillis get harvested? I'll host it, to keep the monsignor happy, but everyone will know who's really being honoured."

Outside firecrackers popped, the partygoers broke into raucous song.

"And in return you lay off the fire from above, for your people, who show you the proper respect."

"And what about other people?"

He grunted, gunned the motor, which backfired in response.

"You'll have to cut your own deals."

I hedge my bets, too. Once I'd dumped my baggage at the hotel, I took an everyday, nonvolcanological camera and went out to the street party again. If nothing happened with the volcano, I had just the footage to chilli-spice up Veitch's cooking program, or even a travel show. It was two AM by the time I hit my pillow, totally wrecked. I made a very late entry to breakfast, when most of the conference attendees were heading to the day's papers. Still, I managed a few greetings and had pressed into my hand the latest issue of a volcanological journal. I flicked through it, while breakfasting, then became riveted by the lead article.

"It's Professor Barrett's keynote address from yesterday, mostly," said a lugubrious voice.

I looked up to behold Zapata, to a T, complete with drooping mustaches. The name tag said: GONZALES. He was director of the Observatorio Volcanológico, a local boy who had been studying the volcano most of his life. The conference had been his idea—he headed the organising committee. Then Joe Boy had decided to take it over. Which meant Joe Boy got the glory, Gonzales got a heap of extra work.

We swapped pleasantries, how nice the conference could accommodate me at such short notice, even without space on the program to show my films, yes, such a pity, some other time, maybe. But his mind was not on chat, from the way his gaze kept returning to the article, which was practically burning a hole in the tablecloth beside my orange juice.

"It's fighting words," I said. The usual stuff, but positively incendiary, this time.

He frowned. "He and Professor Sigurrson, pistols at dawn . . ."

"On top of some volcano."

An almost-smile, interrupted by several flunkies dashing in with a computer printout. Whatever it was, they didn't want me to know, for they hurriedly withdrew. I finished my breakfast, studied the conference program. Tomorrow was excursion day, including a field trip to the volcano; today was speakers and the conference dinner. Currently Ivan the Incomprehensible was speaking on the chemistry of cooling magma. About as interesting as watching . . . magma cool, I decided. I went back to my room, checked Spider's Chillipepper file against last night's information. Yes, there had been an eruption in 1872, smallish in volcanological terms, but which had nonetheless sent a *nuée ardente* shooting down the mountainside for several kilometres. No casualties, but clearly enough for Don Nestor to gird his loins and ascend the volcano.

My SMS chimed, again Spider:

LPE.

Oh! I thought, suddenly realising what the huddle had been over the printout. Had I looked over Gonzales's shoulder, I would have seen an image like a fringed caterpillar, a seismic signal. They were called Long Period Events, and measured the vibrations caused by superheated steam within an otherwise peaceful volcano. Spider had published about them lately, articles studded with ornate equations. If he was right, then Chillipepper was suddenly going to get much more interesting.

I eyed the doll, now hanging from my mirror, then threw the window curtains open. Revealed was my quarry, a brooding bulk, dominating the landscape as volcanoes inimitably do. I sat back on the bed, gazing at it. A familiar adrenaline surge began to build in me, which—if I intellectualize it—is the closest I get to sex.

Chillipepper here I come!

Downstairs, it was morning teatime. I went looking for Larissa but found her conversing with Joe Boy.

"Bet! Goodtaseeya!" He was a man who went in for bear hugs, unfortunately. As I disengaged, I noticed that his beard had whitened and his big mitts were liver-spotted. "Bet, loved your work on Redoubt"—an Alaskan volcano overlooking a major oil field, which had meant lots of lovely oil money. "Any more on *Danger Man?*"

Larissa was standing to one side, just looking at me and smiling. Somehow I had to get Joe Boy to piss off. So I opened my mouth and said the very thing to piss him completely.

"Well, no, I got an approach from a European network for a documentary on Professor Sigurrson. The Stephen Hawking factor, you know."

For a moment I thought he was going to explode.

"Sigurrson! When he's trying his best to ruin this conference!"

He stormed off towards a group of what, to judge from the concerned, adoring glances, were his grad students.

"Ruin?" I said to Larissa.

"Professor Sigurrson sent out—what do Americans call it on police shows? An APB. Watch out for perp, one stratovolcano, ten thousand feet tall, armed with explosives and dangerous."

I glanced around, looking for Gonzales, who was bailed up in a corner, pulling at his mustaches and talking glumly into his mobile.

"I was behind him in coffee queue, US Geological Survey rang. Next city council."

An LPE, if I'd followed Spider's math correctly, was no joke. Neither was the possibility of having to evacuate a city. In the process a major volcanological conference would be disrupted, in which, I would bet, knowing how Joe Boy operated, substantial US funds had been sunk, with the lure of more in the future. If Gonzales wanted up-to-date instruments for his Observatorio Volcanológico, something no Third World government could easily afford, he couldn't annoy Joe Boy. And Joe Boy, I thought, recalling the article, had no time for LPEs, preferring magmatic quakes—vibrations you could feel underneath your boots, goddammit, a real man's seismic shock.

"Field trip's off?" she queried.

"Over Joe Boy's dead body." What, miss an opportunity to show off?

"But Gonzales has say, surely?"

"Not a very loud say. He'll mumble something like: On your own head be it."

She shrugged. "We had paper on Chillipepper yesterday, it's not Bezymianny. I'm going on field trip."

"And I am, too, Larissa."

In the morning, at six AM, packing for the mountain, I sent an SMS to Spider to tell him what I was doing. It was a message that brooked no opposition, he'd know that.

A reply came: REMEMBER WHEN I ASKED YOU WHAT YOU WANTED?

I remembered, from last year, in that curious remote intimacy we'd reached, when I'd asked him if he envied me. What I wanted . . . I'd thought of the Kraffts, then of volcanologists David Johnston and Harry Glicken riding a helicopter to Mount St. Helens the day before it erupted. They were all dead now, from *nuée ardentes*: Johnston the day afterwards, at St. Helens, Glicken at Unzen with the Kraffts.

I had told Spider then: I want to take the ultimate volcano photographs, no matter what. I repeated that now, signed off. Dawn was rising over Chillipepper; the mountain—and the field trip—awaited me.

Downstairs, in the lobby, I found a milling crowd of scientists, and Gonzales, shouting to be heard:

"I said, we have a new field-trip option, courtesy of the Provincial Agricultural Co-operative: tasting tour of chilli farms and wineries."

Clever, I thought. If there was one thing to compete in the macho stakes with volcanoes, it was chillis. I wandered out of the hotel, to find a waiting line of jeeps, and warmed up with a brief recap of my nicotine habit. As I blew smoke rings—top that, volcanoes!—I watched Joe Boy commandeer the newest and biggest jeep. A group formed around him: the co- and junior authors of his incendiary paper, his grad students, Ivan the Incomprehensible and Boris, his twin and much more understandable brother, me and Larissa.

"Don't we get a guide?" I said.

"I've been up the mountain before," Joe Boy almost snarled, plainly not forgiving me from yesterday.

Russians sit down quietly just before a journey, I knew that from Mir. I check my backpack.

"What's that?" Larissa asked. We'd been drinking chilli-flavoured vodka last night, which had left her apparently untouched, now she was lurid in magenta and green Gore-Tex.

"The corn dolly? Local colour, for my film."

She shook her head, pointed at the air canisters. "You're not diving."

"If I'm caught in a *nuée ardente*, then I don't want to die with a lungful of scalding ash. That is, if I'm not totally crisped first."

She stared at me, the steel-capped boots, the photographer's multi-pocketed vest and my backpack over thermo-safety overalls, with a hard hat dangling on its string from my neck, like an old-fashioned bonnet. Nobody else on the field trip was dressed so protectively.

From the other side of the jeep, Joe Boy distinctly said: "Old woman."

Without looking at him, I replied: "The networks won't insure me otherwise."

Our driver arrived. We piled in and set out through the sprawling city, passing through slums, then outlying farms, and, as we ascended the foothills, thick fog.

Chillipepper consists of two parts, like a layered pudding. One, the bulk of the volcano, is an ancient caldera, broken in parts like battlements; the second is within it, a much smaller and recent cone. We drove up pitted and winding roads, stopping at a small building just below the rim of the caldera, no more than a hut for mobile phone transmitters and geological instruments.

The driver got out a comic and a packed lunch, settling in for a long stay. There was no way to go but down, into the crater via a guideline of posts, connected with rope. Nothing could be seen except mist.

I gazed into it, trying to locate the cone and its own personal fog. The caldera looked like San Francisco on a bad day, hardly something to get the adrenaline flowing. While I brooded, Larissa bummed a cigarette from me. And as I watched her head in its beanie bend over the flame, something really strange happened: I felt the chemical surge I should have got from Chillipepper. When I stared into the volcano again, it dissipated. Shit! What was wrong?

Barely able to see beyond an arm's length, we formed a descending crocodile down into the crater. At the bottom, the combination of the rising sun and a stiff breeze wrought a miracle: The fog cleared, blown through the battlements, and we could see. The caldera looked, as usual this close to a volcano, like the surface of the moon, but smelly. The cone rose in the centre, the colour of an ash heap, and to my jaded eyes not much bigger. An unimpressive dribble of steam rose from it.

That mattered not; we had work to do. I got out my best camera, now I had something to film. All around the scientists scattered, the equipment of their various arcane specialities in hand: geochemistry, seismology, petrology. But for the babble in various languages, the soft phonemes of Russian, Joe Boy's Texan drawl, it was completely silent. My boots crunched new-laid-down rock, kicked up soft ash. I still hadn't got the expected surge—well, not from the volcano—and that bothered me. It was messing with my head, as were the remnants of the vodka, and I knew my personal edge was missing. I was like a lens that couldn't focus: nothing seemed clear, or right.

Shots of the caldera soon palled, and that left only the cone. It got bigger as I neared and started to climb, not as steep as the ancient walls around us, but still not for the unfit. Halfway up I passed a grad student, examining rocks through a lens, and a little later the co-authors, collecting gas from a steaming fissure. One yelled as I passed: "A hundred ninety-five degrees C!" At the top I paused, not at the sight from the summit, of the surrounding landscape, Chillipepper's domain, but into the crater. It was slightly domed in the centre, a clot of cooled, sealed lava, with who knew what beneath. Nonetheless Joe Boy and Larissa were racing across its surface, like a pair of science-crazed kids.

My mobile beeped. "Oh shut up, Spider!" I muttered. On the other side of the crater, the twins glared at me. I reached into the pack, switched the mobile off, and as I did touched vegetable matter: the doll. Without thinking consciously, I pulled it out and tossed it into the crater. The doll came to rest against a rock, bizarrely upright in its skirts, as if stopped for a rest. Larissa looked up, laughed, then went back to what she was doing. *Now* I felt the surge, and I filmed the doll, filmed her and Joe Boy's antics.

What happened next? There are gaps in my mental records, where the film is my only witness. The earth shook, I knew that, and I froze as beneath me, with a deafening roar, the floor of the crater split up and open in a cascade of fire. The view skews up, catching a glimpse of the twins, now cowering. Then a handheld blur, of rocks beneath my running feet, some grey, some eggs new-laid, red-hot, and shot from the volcano. The angle careers as I dodge more rocks, boulder-size and spat out with incredible force. I must be off the cone now, and running across the caldera floor, the most dangerous place to meet a *nuée ardente*. Then I fall, and the camera view tilts upwards wildly, recording Chilli-pepper's latest Plinian column as it reaches for the skies. The film goes blank.

I woke up in an air ambulance chartered by CNN that was flying me to the best medical treatment network money could buy. I had a broken ankle, burns from sulphuric acid and red-hot rock, also a compound fracture of the skull, from a projectile that would have mashed me without the hard hat. As I lay looking up at the nurse, a seasoned emergency evacuations professional, she cooed: "Your camera's okay, you were protecting it beneath your body."

And thus the footage was saved, much more valuable than any photographer.

I opened my mouth, found it dry and cracked. "And everybody else?"
"They're all fine."
"Liar," I said, a good line on which to pass out. I knew nobody could

have escaped from the crater, and the rock barrage would have felled an army. Later I learned the rescue workers found most of the others in pieces, burned and bloodied traces. Joe Boy's Texas belt buckle somehow got spat out recognizable, if twisted and half melted. Of Larissa there was no sign, as if she had been vapourized.

When I next woke, I wept: survivor guilt, the worst loneliness.

I spent a long time in hospital, which I largely remember in short film clips. Cody Veitch, walking in with a big grin and a humongous basket of hothouse orchids. Cut to a trayful of blackened objects in front of me, all of which I had carried up the mountain. The backpack and vest had smouldered; only the thermal overalls stayed largely intact. I picked up my mobile, its case singed, but miraculously still working. Then I turned it so that the network team, the bland interviewer and her cameras, could read an SMS on the screen, from Spider: BET! GET OFF CHILLIPEPPER! NOW! The date was two minutes before the eruption, when nobody standing on the cone had any indication, from gas emissions or perceptible tremors, of the fiery force about to surface. But Spider knew, the formula or whatever it was deadly accurate. His Nobel was assured.

Cut again, to an Orthodox priest, bearded, yet with a strong resemblance to Larissa. I asked him for a prayer, in Russian, for his sake as much as mine. He obliged, the unknown words flowing over me like an aural balm.

Cut, to more family, this time my parents, prepared to take me home and nurse me. As they said: "We've been expecting far worse . . ."

Cut one last time, to the network team again, filming me as I watched my Chillipepper footage on a wide-screen console. This was their climax, a pound of flesh or vicarious emotion. The only way I could view it was at a technical remove, ignoring the hype: "The ultimate volcano footage, from someone totally on the spot!" Thus detached, I watched, thinking I'd filmed bigger and better volcanic explosions, though at a greater distance. The eruption of Chillipepper wouldn't have killed anyone, if people hadn't been fool enough to be actually standing on the damn thing as it blew.

I dabbed my eyes discreetly for the team, the expected network emoticon. When they were safely gone, I cried rivulets, for the deaths I had just seen, even Joe Boy's. I'd wished him harm, but not that much—he was simply an aging insecure man, protecting his scientific glory. At least he went the way he wanted to, pure Powdermonkey. I guessed all of them had. But *I* didn't want to, not anymore. My Powdermonkey days were gone, the surge, the thrill lost with Larissa on the volcano. So was my career, I guessed. Could I ever look through a lens again, after filming the fiery death of someone I had only just begun to realise I loved?

The only thing to do was . . . . do things. First was an e-mail to Spider. I sent him two words, terse as our relationship had always been: I RESIGN. No reply was needed, but I got it anyway: I UNDERSTAND.

Next I summoned Cody Veitch and resigned in person.

"Call me when you need a book agent," he said.

Cody might be a network asshole, but he reads people well. Words weren't entirely a new tool for me: I'd always written to the family, even if it was all about volcanoes. I'd also loved posting to Volcano-Lovers. Could I make something of a new medium, get it to say what I wanted?

One day, months later, I was sitting in the family backyard, the new spring filling the trees with blossom. I had the laptop on my knee, playing Scrabble, that's how boring and invalid I'd become. Suddenly I closed the game and started typing frantically.

There are ways to tell a story. Something had happened on Chilli-pepper to make me the only survivor, but there was no easy way to express it.

A dream? Too pat.

Magical realism? Don Nestor and the volcano god arguing my fate? Too arty.

Crime? There was more to it than that. Horror? Beyond the wildest imaginings. A ghost story? Maybe.

What was the best form for my truth?

I let my fingers do the typing or talking, and left it at that. If my film and my writing are at variance, then consider Don Nestor and the volcano, the tales told inside and outside the church. Both have equal validity.

I'm back at the volcano, amid the roar and the fury, running down the slope for my life, and I hear someone coming behind me, a girl's voice, swearing in Russian, of which I understand two vital words:

"Piroklastichesky potok!"

I know the recommended procedure, find a hollow, don gas mask, and cover myself. A hideous wait would follow as the *nuée ardente* passed over me on its fiery journey down the mountain. Should I be really lucky, it *might* not be hot enough to char the flesh off my bones. I eyeball the craterscape frantically, seeking sanctuary. Next moment I trip, go sprawling into . . . just the ticket. I place the camera underneath me, heap ash over my steel-capped but possibly not fireproof boots, lie down with the backpack over my head.

"Larissa! I've only got the one gas mask, you'd better have it."

"Nichevo. I'll lie on top, protect you."

And although she is so small, she stretches my body length and more over me, her skirts and shawl like a thick, rustling blanket. She wraps both arms around me, clasping them beneath my chest. The lappets of her long headscarf trail down into the ash, sealing me off from what is coming.

"Here it is!" she says. Hot darkness flows over us, and all I can hear is the crackle of the corn husks all around, as they burst into flame.

Gather

Christopher Rowe

Christopher Rowe lives in Lexington, Kentucky. He attended both the Clarion West and the Sycamore Hill writing workshops. With his wife, writer Gwenda Bond, he runs a small press, The Fortress of Words, which produces the critically acclaimed magazine Say . . .

His story "The Voluntary State" was a Hugo, Nebula, and Theodore Sturgeon award finalist. The best of his early short fiction was collected in a chapbook, Bittersweet Creek.

Rowe has been writing a series of stories that portray a very weird, reconfigured Kentucky. "Gather" is one of them.

At the very end of autumn, Gather had thirty-four coins to spend. Commerce—that's the kind of buying things that used coins instead of goods—was not an opportunity that arose in the north town very often. He planned to spend all thirty-four.

There was a lot to regret about that. All of Gather's coins were beautiful. They had curling, unknowable writing on one side and little pictures of God on the other. Gather loved to study the coins. He was intimately aware of all their differences and similarities, and aware, too, that with winter coming he'd have few chances to get more.

Besides his work assignments, his sisters would usually each give him a coin for good-bye and remembrance when it was their turn to go down the river to wife for the bad batch men. He'd found one copper coin in a wagon track, where the ground had split from thawing and refreezing in the inconstant autumn temperatures. It showed God's eyes, all steaming. He'd won a rough gray coin at a fair, when he'd rowed a skiff faster than a sweepsman off a southern barge.

Another obstacle to transactions was the way the act of spending could complicate itself so hypnotically. Offer the merchant a coin for those pepper seeds spilling out of twists of dead, unflickering paper, then put the coin to heart, to lips. Do it again and rock forward and backward and then forward and then backward and put the coin to forehead, to heart, to lips, and on like that, and on until the merchant loses patience and raps one hand against the table and shakes the seeds with the other, *arrhythmic*. All wrong.

"Liveborn fool," the merchant said. "A grown man, getting lost in counting games! Buy if you're buying, we're closing this fair down."

Gather snapped to, because these barges were the last before winter, and it would be long years to huddle with just the cold comfort of money before spring.

The merchant spoke again. "Ice chokes the river, boy, and if it freezes over it'll be you pushing our barges, skate-like, you and all these holy men down from their chapterhouse." The southerners were bad batch men, mostly, with useless legs bundled up under them if they were merchants or captains, legs self-amputated if they were hard men who needed speed, like the sweeps handlers.

Gather had liked rowing the skiff so quickly, and would have asked about a job on the barge, but he had to stay up the river with the preachers and his sisters. *Only bad batch men can be southerners.* That was from a bible. So he worked on the docks or on the fishing boats for now, and would work chopping holes in the ice when the river was frozen. Gather was stout and steady.

He considered whether to buy the twists, which would yield long red wreaths of hothouse peppers, if he was careful. He considered his thirty-four coins.

"You can plant a coin," one of his sisters had said when he'd accumulated two dozen of the coins. "You can *plant* them, but they won't grow into anything useful out here."

But that wasn't quite true, it wasn't *exactly* the truth, and Gather required things to be very exact indeed. Precision was his watchword and his sacrament.

In the end, he bought four twists of seeds from the southern merchant. He bought an old blanket that the seller claimed had been woven by a machine. He bought forty candles, forty pounds of sugar, and forty minutes' worth of a storyteller's time.

Forty minutes was long enough for the national anthem, the long night in the garden at Gethsemane, and the history of the first people to come down onto Virginia, who were called Pilgrims and who had starved to death before they were born again for God.

Counting coins again.

The twists and the blanket and the candles and the sugar and the time and that's down to eleven left for imperishable food. Eleven coins on smoked fish like muskie, or eleven coins on ground grains like spelt, or eleven coins on dried pulses like beans.

Peas and lentils all winter, then.

Weeks later, when the river was frozen hard enough for foot traffic, some of the children came to Gather and asked him to pull their sledge across to the far side. This was forbidden, but their leader, a little girl with green eyes, was PK—a preacher's kid—which warranted a lot of deference. But more than that she said, "One, two, three, *four*, Gather walks across the *floor* . . ." and on like that—a very clever little girl, very good at rhymes *and* rhythms. So Gather bundled up in his heaviest coat and his machine blanket and trudged out onto the ice with a towrope slung over his shoulder.

The PK girl had him skirt north of the island where the watchtower stood. ("Thirteen, fourteen, fifteen, *sixteen*, further up so we are *not* seen.") There were no preachers manning the tower top that Gather could see, which was a curiosity. Then he heard hammering and work-chanting farther down the river and remembered that today was the first day the preachers would be pushing the big wagons across to the far side to cut up big blocks of frozen soil—the good kind of soil that things would grow in. Many work points, but only for preachers, who had special dispensation from God and specific instructions on where to gather the soil from their bibles.

The PK snapped her fingers in time with her counting to get Gather moving again, and he pulled them on up and across. Her voice faltered with her courage, a dozen yards shy of the eastern shore. The bank was choked with evergreens right down to the ice, towering pines that cut off any view of what lay farther back. Which was just as well, because God lived on the far bank and to go to the house of God was forbidden. That was from a bible, too.

"S'ko back, y'all." One of the other children finally spoke. Earlier, the PK had hushed the girls whenever they started to speak, which Gather had appreciated because it was rare for a pair and nearly impossible for a group to keep the rhythm.

Gather was pretty sure the speaker was a niece of his, or possibly a very young aunt, some kin anyhow from the tangled net of cousins and sisters who stayed up the river for the preachers. She said, "S'kome."

The option of returning to town lay out there on the ice, but the PK was clearly not convinced. She stood, considering, and nobody moved to turn the sledge around.

A thick shelf of snow slid off the lowest hanging branch of a nearby tree. It made a noise like *shhhh-choom*. None of the children jumped or screamed or carried on, but Gather said, "Oh, Lord," because he thought that maybe God was coming down the bank.

The PK girl said, "Home home home home."

For Gather, home was his apartment in the carriage house behind the post office. Once he and the children were back on the side of the river where people lived, Gather walked down Dock Street with the river to his left.

He turned in to the alley between the post office and the courthouse—he'd shoveled the brickway clear the day before—and crossed the courtyard to his door.

Gather's apartment was on the ground floor of the carriage house, so he didn't have to worry about navigating the treacherous wooden staircase tacked to the fieldstones of the exterior wall. The stairs were thick with ice and snow, because Miss Charlie, who lived upstairs, didn't use them. Instead, she clambered up and down along the rope contrivances she engineered for bad batch men wealthy enough to afford her work. One was always hung through the trapdoor in the ceiling of Gather's kitchen.

Before he opened his front door, Gather pulled a canvas tarp back from where it covered his rick. He took an armful of split yellow wood, well seasoned, for the kitchen stove. Yellow was native Virginia wood, not like the Pilgrim pines on the bank. Not good for making useful soil, but good enough for burning.

Inside, Gather found Miss Charlie working at his kitchen table. She was tipping the pepper seeds out of one of his twists and into a clay jar. Gather saw that she'd already emptied the other three—the dead papers were spread across the tabletop.

"You told me, Gather, I remember your very words, you said, 'I don't like those hot old things.'" Miss Charlie was suspended amongst pulleys and weights, testing a new configuration. She was wrapped up in one of the soft hides people made from deerskins sometimes. Getting them soft was hard—Gather'd had a job doing that for a while but he hadn't been good enough at it.

"I can grow 'em in the house, though, Miss Charlie," he said, then dumped the wood into the metal box beside the stove. "And if you share your dried apricots, I can make the spicy jelly the preachers like."

"*Strong* thinking, Gather," said Miss Charlie. "Stronger than you were doing this morning when you let that pack of children lead you off into trouble." Gather started to say that they hadn't gotten into trouble but he remembered a lesson: Not getting into trouble isn't the same as not getting caught.

Miss Charlie untwisted the paper she held and smoothed it flat next to the others with her skinny, clever fingers. Miss Charlie was a scientist. Everything about her was skinny and clever.

She arranged the four papers into a pretty, even line. They were rectangular, but not the same rectangular as the oiled wood top of Gather's kitchen table. The ratios of the different rectangles were plenty enough different, which was a good thing. If they'd been close-but-not-quite, it would have been upsetting.

Miss Charlie leaned over each of the papers in turn and examined them through her glass. Gather could see that there were letters on the papers.

"Is that writing the same as on the"—Gather thought of the word—"*exempla* you've got upstairs in your kitchen?" Gather glanced up at the open trapdoor. Miss Charlie looked up at him but forgot to take the glass away from her face, so her eyes were huge—one green, one brown.

"My la*bor*atory," she reminded him. "I'm a scientist, we don't have kitchens. The ones I have upstairs have a little life in them. This writing here is stuck on dead paper."

Gather was afraid that she might lecture him for a while then, which she sometimes did, but she was too distracted by her work. Her work, Gather remembered, was always *the question at hand*. The question at hand meant something Gather didn't know about.

"And anyway," said Miss Charlie, "I don't think these letters written here are like the letters on my papers upstairs, or on coins. They're more like the letters on the mayor's stick, or in a bible. Not quite, but that's closer." Gather had seen the mayor's stick before—he'd *felt* it be-fore, the bad way, across his backside—but he'd never seen the inside of a bible, as only preachers were allowed to uncover their tops. Once one of his sisters had pointed out that if the preacher reading from it wore a glass, you could see the writing in the green glow reflecting off his face.

"The paper—the *medium*"—and she looked at him and raised her eyebrows the way she did when she used a word she wanted him to learn—"the paper is about the same as what I've seen before, though."

Miss Charlie chewed on her thumbnail for a second, then said, "Let's do an experiment."

"Oh, Lord," said Gather. "Oh, Lord."

"Hush," said Miss Charlie. "It'll be fine. I'll go upstairs and get our aprons and goggles. You'd better go get a bucket of water."

Miss Charlie swung up onto a rung threaded through the web of ropes hung from Gather's ceiling, then hand-over-handed up to the la*bor*atory above. Gather had never seen the la*bor*atory except from this oblique angle. *Oblique.*

He felt a little bit concerned about what was likely to happen next, but Miss Charlie did outrank him, so he went back out into the court-yard to sweep snow into a saucepan, then popped it onto the stove for melting. Gather breathed the metal smell of the new water and hoped it wasn't meant for an experiment that would leave him with less furni-ture, as so many of them had in the past.

The heavy leather aprons slapped onto the tile floor, then Miss Charlie dropped down onto the table, free of her harnesses and crouching on her skinny legs. Two pairs of leaded glass goggles hung from her cord belt.

"Suit up!" she said. "I'll let them know at the hall that you worked for me today, get you some credit."

Which was better than chopping holes in the river ice, so long as he finished the assignment intact.

Miss Charlie took four of Gather's baking pans from the cupboard and laid them on the table. Gather liked to make cookies, when he could get eggs, and so had lots of pans. She laid each of the papers in its own tray and that made three different rectangles, three different ratios, with one table and four trays and four papers for the quantities. "Oh, Lord," said Gather. "Oh, Lord."

Miss Charlie made comforting noises and slung the heavy apron over Gather's head. "Put on your goggles, young man. How often do you get to play with fire?"

Not often. It was true that Gather did not often get to play with fire. But this wasn't comforting.

The first part of the experiment was designed to determine if the paper could burn. Gather had never seen paper that would burn, but Miss Charlie claimed to have heard of it, to have heard of paper that would *immolate*. So Gather tonged a coal out of the stove and placed it squarely on each of the papers, one by one. That was called the scien-tific method.

None of the papers even curled up brown like burning things do when they start to burn, so Miss Charlie had Gather fetch down a rag from the cupboard while she pulled a tiny clay bottle from a pouch at her belt. She poured a scant two or three drops from the bottle into the water from Gather's saucepan, then took the rag from Gather and swabbed it around and around. The water went from smelling of metal to smelling of lemons. Miss Charlie then squeezed the rag over the papers. Each of them flickered on and off once, then shriveled up, twisting back almost to how they'd looked when they still held pepper seeds.

"That's a *datum!*" said Miss Charlie.

Which was very exciting, but it was well into the afternoon by then, and the children had coaxed Gather onto the river without his breakfast. Between those labors and now all this science, he was very nearly starved.

Since the pans were laid out, and since he had plenty of sugar and even a few eggs, the thing to do seemed to be to bake cookies. Miss Charlie, long resident above Gather's kitchen, knew his baking and was very excited by this plan.

"I'll do more on this tomorrow," she said, and swept the papers together onto a single pan. While she cast around looking for a receptacle she might deem appropriate to carry the papers upstairs, Gather pulled a mixing bowl out from beneath the dry sink.

He went to set it on the table and saw the soaked, twisted papers gathered all together. He raised his hands above his shoulders and keened. He began to breathe in and out and in and out *fast*.

Miss Charlie took his hands and hummed. She breathed slower, slower, slower, slower . . . slow.

Then she saw the papers, too. She saw how'd they flickered back on and smoothly scuttled together into a new, single sheet. She saw that the words had crawled to the edges and she saw the finely detailed, heretic drawing that took up the center of the page.

"Why—" Miss Charlie was not a churchgoer, but she saw it. "Why, it's God."

How Miss Charlie convinced Gather not to go to the mayor or to the preachers with news of the picture was to: sing to him for one hour; tell him the names of all of his sisters that she'd ever known; give him the dried apricots she had tucked away in a burlap bag beneath the eaves in her apartment; promise him that the two of them knew as much about what God needed as anybody on the side of the river where people lived.

The whole time she was singing and listing and fetching and talking, Gather kept watching the paper on the table. It kept being God. God *with people*.

There was God, *all* of God, not just a little bit like on a coin, not just told about like in a sermon. All of God was on the papers on Gather's table, and more. Because, unheard of! Untellable! There was a man with his hand on God's flank and a woman kneeling next to God's ferocious mouth. God, *with people*.

People lived on this side of the river. God lived on the other. Even should God want to cross, the river was too swift in the summer. The ice would not bear God's weight in the winter.

It was impossible to know what to do, so Gather decided to let Miss Charlie decide. He was frightened, too frightened even to bake the cookies.

"I think there are three things we can do," said Miss Charlie. "We have to choose one of these *three* things." Miss Charlie held up three of her fingers and waved them around in a scientific way. Gather didn't like threes. They made people mad. They were *odd*.

"Take it to a preacher," she said, "but we've struck that already." Gather saw then that she'd only started with three so that she could get to two right away, which was easier and soothing.

"We can hide it and never speak of it." Miss Charlie looked at Gather very carefully when she offered that up. "Gather, could you do that? Could you never speak of it?"

Gather scrunched up his face and thought. "I think I would do a pretty good job for a pretty long time, Miss Charlie," he said. "But I think that then I'd forget and tell."

"That's what I think would happen, too," Miss Charlie said. "And I think you are very wise to be able to predict things like that. Don't tell *me* you can't be a scientist!"

"But what is number two?" Gather asked. He remembered that there were really only two.

"God . . ." Miss Charlie was thinking very hard. "God must be lost. God must need to get back across the river."

Gather attended every Sunday service. Most times, it was the same preacher—the little green-eyed girl's father—up there. Sometimes, though, if that preacher was away, then it was the mayor up there because he was the lay leader. There were even times when it was a different preacher altogether. And all of them did different homilies—a little bit different, anyway—and all of them always led three songs, an *odd* number of songs. But the thing that was always the same, no matter who was up there, was the way it ended, when they would say, "This is *my* God, and this is his body, and this is his blood." And then everybody would eat the bread.

"Does God need to go across . . ." Gather paused. "Does God need to go back across, because otherwise, everybody will eat God all up?"

Miss Charlie could pitch her eyebrows up as steep as rooftops. "Yes, Gather," she said. "Yes, I think that's it exactly."

Miss Charlie said that Gather should stop taking the work assignments he was given at the hall every morning. "You can work for me full-time," she said. She tucked her bottom lip under her teeth, which meant she was performing a sum. "I have enough points for that to work for a time. For as long as we'll need anyway."

Gather had never had a permanent assignment. It was a comfortable distraction, even when Miss Charlie made him practice being quiet for the whole next morning before they went to arrange it with the mayor.

The mayor was outside the hall, watching preachers push wagons full of soil up the road to the chapterhouse. He spotted them as they approached and fled inside, but forgot to bar the door.

Miss Charlie marched straight past the glaring preachers and on through the door. Gather didn't know whether his *proscribed* silence had started while they were still outside, but to be safe he didn't answer their calls for him to lend his shoulder to their wagon wheel.

The big chimney in the hall had a poor draw, and the air was thick with smoke. The mayor had taken refuge behind his desk and was pushing beads back and forth on a calendar rod when Miss Charlie cornered him.

"Charlie," said the mayor. "Charlie with the questions."

"I want—" Miss Charlie began, but the mayor said, "No!"

He stood up suddenly and reached for his stick. Words ran around it in a loop, blinking on and off when he tamped it against the ground in time with his words to Miss Charlie.

"No, you cannot go to the chapterhouse. No, you cannot have an . . . *exemplum* of the soil before the preachers bless it. You cannot take a skiff south unless you pair with a bad batch man, and you will *never* have a bible!"

At that last, he struck the stone floor so hard that his stick made a buzzing noise and went dark. The three of them all stared at it together for a moment until it flashed back on.

"I want to hire Gather for the rest of the week," said Miss Charlie.

Even in the dark, Gather was able to follow his sledge tracks from the PK morning back across the river. At first, Gather wanted to find a sledge and pull Miss Charlie on it, but she said that they were equal partners. She said that it was an equal *endeavor*.

At night, the fires in the watchtower seemed to burn as bright as a pinewood fire, but Gather knew they weren't, not really. He had a job once hauling yellow logs out of the water and stacking them to dry by the watchtower fire, but only while the regular man was sick.

They were close enough to the fire for them to cast flickery shadows on the ice, but in the afternoon, Miss Charlie had gone to see the night watchman with some cookies she had made herself—

unprecedented—and said that he would be sick tonight. He would not raise the hue and cry.

When they got to where the tracks ended, Gather said, "*Shhhhh-choom*," as quietly as he could.

"Is that how God talks?" asked Miss Charlie, and Gather remembered that she could never have been so close to the other bank before.

"The only time I ever heard God was that morning, Miss Charlie," said Gather. "And that is what God said."

"Did you know that makes you a prophet, Gather? If you hear God, I mean?" she asked him.

"All those little girls heard it, too. Little prophets," said Gather. "Little prophet*esses*."

"Maybe I'm wrong, then," she said. "Like on an initial hypothesis. Maybe you have to hear and listen both."

Gather didn't understand, but his feet were very cold from the nighttime ice. He shuffled the last few yards to the shoreline and noticed that he wasn't afraid anymore. He reached his mittened hand up to a branch to steady himself, then gestured back to Miss Charlie. "Give me God," he said. "I'll put God up in this tree."

Miss Charlie had wrapped God up in white clothes from the laboratory. *Neutral. Sterile.* She pulled the bundle out from the bottom of her leather pack. Mysteriously, she had filled the pack with food and blankets and tinder. She handed the bundle to Gather.

"When God is back on the bank, there, Gather, what about those people? What about the man and the woman with God?"

Gather lowered his hands to his sides. The bundle hung in the loose grip of his left mitten. He waited to see if Miss Charlie would keep talking, but she didn't.

"Is this another experiment?" Gather asked her. He felt himself getting agitated and didn't know whether to push it down.

"I don't think so," said Miss Charlie. "I think this is an *exploration*."

That was another word to learn, so Gather said, "What does it mean?"

Miss Charlie put her mitten around the bundle and pressed it against Gather's palm, so they were holding God there, holding God up and between them.

"I think it means we keep going," she said.

Then there was no agitation in him, and no hesitation. Then there was some *clarity* in him. "I think so, too," he said.

Sonny Liston Takes the Fall

Elizabeth Bear

Elizabeth Bear was born on the same day as Frodo and Bilbo Baggins, and very nearly named after Peregrine Took. She is a recipient of the John W. Campbell Award for Best New Writer as well as the Locus Award, and she currently lives in southern New England, where she claims that she is engaged in murdering inoffensive potted plants and writing science fiction and fantasy.

Her most recent books are a science-fiction novel, Carnival, *from Bantam Spectra; an urban fantasy,* Whiskey and Water, *forthcoming from Roc; and—with Sarah Monette—a Norse heroic fantasy called* A Companion to Wolves, *forthcoming from Tor.*

I know that Bear is best known for her fantasy novels, and I'm familiar with her dark Lovecraftian stories because I've published some of them. But "Sonny Liston Takes the Fall" is something very different from either.

gotta tell you, Jackie," Sonny Liston said, "I lied to my wife about that. I gotta tell you, I took that fall."

It was Christmas Eve, 1970, and Sonny Liston was about the farthest thing you could imagine from a handsome man. He had a furrowed brow and downcast hound-dog prisoner eyes that wouldn't meet mine, and the matching furrows on either side of his broad, flat nose ran down to a broad, flat mouth under a pencil-thin mustache that was already out of fashion six years ago, when he was still King of the World.

"We all lie sometimes, Sonny," I said, pouring him another scotch. We don't mind if you drink too much in Vegas. We don't mind much of anything at all. "It doesn't signify."

He had what you call a tremendous physical presence, Sonny Liston. He filled up a room so you couldn't take your eyes off him—didn't *want* to take your eyes off him, and if he was smiling you were smiling, and if he was scowling you were shivering—even when he was sitting quietly, the way he was now, turned away from his kitchen table and his elbows on his knees, one hand big enough for a man twice his size wrapped around the glass I handed him and the other hanging between his legs, limp across the back of the wrist as if the tendons'd been cut. His suit wasn't long enough for the length of his arms. The coat sleeves and the shirtsleeves with their French cuffs and discreet cuff links were riding halfway up his forearms, showing wrists I couldn't have wrapped my fingers around. Tall as he was, he wasn't tall enough for that frame—as if he didn't get enough to eat as a kid—but he was that wide.

Sonny Liston, he was from Arkansas. And you would hear it in his voice, even now. He drank that J&B scotch like knocking back a blenderful of raw eggs and held the squat glass out for more. "I could of beat Cassius Clay if it weren't for the fucking Mob," he said, while I filled it up again. "I could of beat that goddamned flashy pansy."

"I know you could, Sonny," I told him, and it wasn't a lie. "I know you could."

His hands were like mallets, like mauls, like the paws of the bear they styled him. It didn't matter.

He was a broken man, Sonny Liston. He wouldn't meet your eyes, not that he ever would have. You learn that in prison. You learn that from a father who beats you. You learn that when you're black in America.

You keep your eyes down, and maybe there won't be trouble this time.

2.

It's the same thing with fighters as with horses. Racehorses, I mean, thoroughbreds, which I know a lot about. I'm the genius of Las Vegas, you see. The One-Eyed Jack, the guardian and the warden of Sin City.

It's a bit like being a magician who works with tigers—the city is my life, and I take care of it. But that means it's my job to make damned sure it doesn't get out and eat anybody.

And because of that, I also know a little about magic and sport and sacrifice, and the real, old blood truth of the laurel crown and what it means to be King for a Day.

The thing about racehorses is that the trick with the good ones isn't getting them to run. It's getting them to *stop*.

They'll kill themselves running, the good ones. They'll run on broken hearts, broken legs, broken wind. Legend says Black Gold finished his last race with nothing but a shipping bandage holding his flopping hoof to his leg. They shot him on the track, Black Gold, the way they did in those days. And it was mercy when they did it.

He was King, and he was claimed. He went to pay the tithe that only greatness pays.

Ruffian, perhaps the best filly that ever ran, shattered herself in a match race that was meant to prove she could have won the Kentucky Derby if she'd raced in it. The great colt Swale ran with a hole in his heart, and no one ever knew until it killed him in the paddock one fine summer day in the third year of his life.

And then there's Charismatic.

Charismatic was a Triple Crown contender until he finished his Belmont third, running on a collapsed leg, with his jockey Chris Antley all but kneeling on the reins, doing anything to drag him down.

Antley left the saddle as soon as his mount saw the wire and could be slowed. He dove over Charismatic's shoulder and got underneath him before the horse had stopped moving; he held the broken Charismatic up with his shoulders and his own two hands until the veterinarians arrived. Between Antley and the surgeons, they saved the colt. Because Antley took that fall.

Nobody could save Antley, who was dead himself within two years from a drug overdose. He died so hard that investigators first called it a homicide.

When you run with all God gave you, you run out of track goddamned fast.

3.

Sonny was just like that. Just like a racehorse. Just like every other goddamned fighter. A little bit crazy, a little bit fierce, a little bit desperate, and ignorant of the concept of defeat under any circumstances.

Until he met Cassius Clay in the ring.

They fought twice. First time was in 1964, and I watched that fight live in a movie theater. We didn't have pay-per-view then, and the fight happened in Florida, not here at home in Vegas.

I remember it real well, though.

Liston was a monster, you have to understand. He wasn't real big for a fighter, only six foot one, but he *bulked*. He *loomed*. His opponents would flinch away before he ever pulled back a punch.

I've met Mike Tyson, too, who gets compared to Liston. And I don't think it's just because they're both hard men, or that Liston also was accused of sexual assault. It's because Tyson has that same thing, the power of personal gravity that bends the available light and every eye down to him, even when he's walking quietly through a crowded room, wearing a warm-up jacket and a smile.

So that was Liston. He was a stone golem, a thing out of legend, the fucking bogeyman. He was going to walk through Clay like the Kool-Aid pitcher walking through a paper wall.

And we were all in our seats, waiting to see this insolent prince beat down by the barbarian king.

And there was a moment when Clay stepped up to Liston, and they touched gloves, and the whole theater went still.

Because Clay was just as big as Liston. And Clay wasn't looking down.

Liston retired in the seventh round. Maybe he had a dislocated shoulder, and maybe he didn't, and maybe the Mob told him to throw the fight so they could bet on the underdog Clay and Liston just couldn't quite make himself fall over and play dead.

And Cassius Clay, you see, he grew up to be Muhammad Ali.

4.

Sonny didn't tell me about *that* fight. He told me about the other one.

Phil Ochs wrote a song about it, and so did Mark Knopfler: that legendary fight in 1965, the one where, in the very first minute of the very first round, Sonny Liston took a fall.

Popular poets, Ochs and Knopfler, and what do you think the bards were? That kind of magic, the old dark magic that soaks down the roots of the world and keeps it rich, it's a transformative magic. It never goes away.

However you spill it, it's blood that makes the cactus grow.

Ochs, just to interject a little more irony here, paid for his power in *his* own blood as well.

5.

Twenty-fifth child of twenty-six, Sonny Liston. A tenant farmer's son, whose father beat him bloody. He never would meet my eye, even there in his room, *this* close to Christmas, near the cold bent stub end of 1970.

He never would meet a white man's eyes. Even the eye of the One-Eyed Jack, patron saint of Las Vegas, when Jackie was pouring him J&B. Not a grown man's eye, anyway, though he loved kids—and kids loved him. The bear was a teddy bear when you got him around children.

But he told me all about that fight. How the Mob told him to throw it or they'd kill him and his momma and a selection of his brothers and sisters, too. How he did what they told him in the most defiant manner possible. So the whole fucking world would know he took that fall.

The thing is, I didn't believe him.

I sat there and nodded and listened, and I thought, Sonny Liston didn't throw that fight. That famous "Phantom Punch"? Muhammad Ali got lucky. Hit a nerve cluster or something. Sonny Liston, the unstoppable Sonny Liston, the man with a heart of piston steel and a hand like John Henry's hammer—Sonny Liston, he went down. It was a fluke, a freak thing, some kind of an accident.

I thought going down like that shamed him, so he told his wife he gave up because he knew Ali was better and he didn't feel like fighting just to get beat. But he told *me* that other story, about the Mob, and he drank another scotch and he toasted Muhammad Ali, though Sonny'd kind of hated him. Ali had been barred from fighting from 1967 until just that last year; he was facing a jail term because he wouldn't go and die in Vietnam.

Sensible man, if you happen to ask me.

But I knew Sonny didn't throw that fight for the Mob. I knew because I also knew this other thing about that fight, because I am the soul of Las Vegas, and in 1965 the Mob *was* Las Vegas.

And I knew they'd had a few words with Sonny before he went into the ring.

Sonny Liston was supposed to win. And Muhammad Ali was supposed to die.

6.

The one thing in his life that Sonny Liston could never hit back against was his daddy. Sonny, whose given name was Charles, but who called himself Sonny all his adult life.

Sonny had learned the hard way that you never look a white man in the eye. That you never look *any* man in the eye unless you mean to beat him down. That you never look *the Man* in the eye, because if you do *he's* gonna beat *you* down.

He did his time in jail, Sonny Liston. He went in a boy and he came out a prizefighter, and when he came out he was owned by the Mob.

You can see it in the photos and you could see it in his face, when you met him, when you reached out to touch his hand; he almost never smiled, and his eyes always held this kind of deep, sonorous seriousness over his black, flat, damaged nose.

Sonny Liston was a jailbird. Sonny Liston belonged to the Mob the same way his daddy belonged to the land.

Cassius Clay, God bless him, changed his slave name two days after that first bout with Sonny, as if winning it freed up something in him. Muhammad Ali, God bless him, never learned that lesson about looking down.

7.

Boxing is called the sweet science. And horse racing is the sport of kings.

When Clay beat Liston, he bounced up on his stool and shouted that he was King of the World. Corn king, summer king, America's most beautiful young man. An angel in the boxing ring. A new and powerful image of black manhood.

He stepped up on that stool in 1964 and he put a noose around his neck.

The thing about magic is that it happens in spite of everything you can do to stop it.

And the wild old Gods will have their sacrifice.

No excuses.

If they can't have Charismatic, they'll take the man that saved him.

So it goes.

8.

Sometimes it's easier to tell yourself you quit than to admit that they beat you. Sometimes it's easier to look down.

The civil rights movement in the early 1960s found Liston a thug and an embarrassment. He was a jailbird, an illiterate, a dark unstoppable monster. The rumor was that he had a second career as a standover man—a Mob enforcer. The NAACP protested when Floyd Patterson agreed to fight him in 1962.

9.

Sonny didn't know his own birthday or maybe he lied about his age. Forty's old for a fighter, and Sonny said he was born in '32 when he might have been born as early as '27. There's a big damned difference between thirty-two and thirty-seven in the boxing ring.

And there's another thing, something about prizefighters you might not know. In Liston's day, they shot the fighters' hands full of anesthetic before they wrapped them for the fight. So a guy who was a hitter—a *puncher* rather than a *boxer,* in the parlance—he could pound away on his opponent and never notice he'd broken all the goddamned bones in his goddamned hands.

Sonny Liston was a puncher. Muhammad Ali was a boxer.

Neither one of them, as it happens, could abide the needles. So when they went swinging into the ring, they earned every punch they threw.

Smack a Sheetrock wall a couple of dozen times with your shoulder behind it if you want to build up a concept of what that means, in terms of endurance and of pain. Me? I would have taken the needle over *feeling* the bones I was breaking. Taken it in a heartbeat.

But Charismatic finished his race on a shattered leg, and so did Black Gold.

What the hell were a few broken bones to Sonny Liston?

10.

You know when I said Sonny was not a handsome man? Well, I also said Muhammad Ali was an angel. He was a black man's angel, an avenging angel, a messenger from a better future. He was the *way* and the *path,* man, and they marked him for sacrifice, because he was a warrior god, a Black Muslim Moses come to lead his people out of Egypt land.

And the people in power like to stay that way, and they have their ways of making it happen. Of making sure the sacrifice gets chosen.

Go ahead and curl your lip. White man born in the nineteenth century, reborn in 1905 as the Genius of the Mississippi of the West. What do I know about the black experience?

I am my city, and I contain multitudes. I'm the African American airmen at Nellis Air Force Base, and I'm the black neighborhoods near D Street that can't keep a supermarket, and I'm Cartier Street and I'm Northtown and I'm Las Vegas, baby, and it doesn't matter a bit what you see when you look at my face.

Because Sonny Liston died here, and he's buried here in the palm of my hand. And I'm Sonny Liston, too, wronged and wronging; he's in here, boiling and bubbling away.

11.

I filled his glass one more time and splashed what was left into my own, and that was the end of the bottle. I twisted it to make the last drop fall. Sonny watched my hands instead of my eyes, and folded his own enormous fists around his glass so it vanished. "You're here on business, Jackie," he said, and dropped his eyes to his knuckles. "Nobody wants to listen to me talk."

"I want to listen, Sonny." The scotch didn't taste so good, but I rolled it over my tongue anyway. I'd drunk enough that the roof of my mouth was getting dry, and the liquor helped a little. "I'm here to listen as long as you want to talk."

His shoulders always had a hunch. He didn't stand up tall. They hunched a bit more as he turned the glass in his hands. "I guess I run out of things to say. So you might as well tell me what you came for."

At Christmastime in 1970, Muhammad Ali—recently allowed back in the ring, pending his appeal of a draft evasion conviction—was preparing for a title bout against Joe Frazier in March. He was also preparing for a more wide-reaching conflict; in April of that year, his appeal, his demand to be granted status as a conscientious objector was to go before the United States Supreme Court.

He faced a five-year prison sentence.

In jail, he'd come up against everything Sonny Liston had. And maybe Ali was the stronger man. And maybe the young king wouldn't break where the old one fell. Or maybe he wouldn't make it out of prison alive, or free.

"Ali needs your help," I said.

"Fuck Cassius Clay," he said.

Sonny finished his drink and spent awhile staring at the bottom of his glass. I waited until he turned his head, skimming his eyes along the floor, and tried to sip again from the empty glass. Then I cleared my throat and said, "It isn't just for him."

Sonny flinched. See, the thing about Sonny—that he never learned to read, that doesn't mean he was *dumb*. "The NAACP don't want me. The Nation of Islam don't want me. They didn't even want Clay to box me. I'm *an embarrassment to the black man*."

He dropped his glass on the table and held his breath for a moment before he shrugged and said, "Well, they got their nigger now."

Some of them know up front; they listen to the whispers, and they know the price they might have to pay if it's their number that comes up. Some just kind of know in the back of their heads. About the corn king, and the laurel wreath, and the price that sometimes has to be paid.

Sonny Liston, like I said, he wasn't dumb.

"Ali can do something you can't, Sonny." *Ali can be a symbol.*

"I can't have it," he drawled. "But I can buy it? Is that what you're telling me, Jack?"

I finished my glass, too, already drunk enough that it didn't make my sinuses sting. "Sonny," I said, with that last bit of Dutch courage in me, "you're gonna have to take another fall."

12.

When his wife—returning from a holiday visit to her relatives—found his body on January 5, eleven days after I poured him that drink, maybe a week or so after he died, Sonny had needle marks in the crook of his arm, though the coroner's report said *heart failure*.

Can you think of a worse way to kill the man?

13.

On March 8, 1971, a publicly reviled Muhammad Ali was defeated by Joe Frazier at Madison Square Garden in New York City in a boxing match billed as the "Fight of the Century." Ali had been vilified in the press as a Black Muslim, a religious and political radical, a black man who wouldn't look down.

Three months later, the United States Supreme Court overturned the conviction, allowing Muhammad Ali's conscientious objector status to stand.

He was a free man.

Ali fought Frazier twice more. He won both times, and went on to become the most respected fighter in the history of the sport. A beautiful avenging outspoken angel.

Almost thirty-five years after Sonny Liston died, in November 2005, President George W. Bush awarded America's highest civilian honor, the Presidential Medal of Freedom, to the draft-dodging, politically activist lay preacher Muhammad Ali.

14.

Sonny Liston never looked a man in the eye unless he meant to beat him down. Until he looked upon Cassius Clay and hated him. And looked past that hate and saw a dawning angel, and he saw the future, and he wanted it that bad.

Wanted it bad, Sonny Liston, illiterate jailbird and fighter and standover man. Sonny Liston the drunk, the sex offender. Broken, brutal Sonny Liston with the scars on his face from St. Louis cops beating a confession from him, with the scars on his back from his daddy beating him down on the farm.

Sonny Liston, who loved children. He wanted that thing, and he knew it could never be his.

Wanted it and saw a way to make it happen for somebody else.

15.

And so he takes that fall, Sonny Liston. Again and again and again, like John Henry driving steel until his heart burst, like a jockey rolling over the shoulder of a running, broken horse. He takes the fall, and he saves the King.

And Muhammad Ali? He never once looks down.

North American Lake Monsters

Nathan Ballingrud

Nathan Ballingrud lives with his daughter outside Asheville, North Carolina. His fiction has appeared in SCI FICTION, The Magazine of Fantasy & Science Fiction, The Third Alternative, *and* The Year's Best Fantasy and Horror, *among other places. He can be found online at* http://nballingrud.livejournal.com.

Nothing is poetical if plain daylight is not poetical; and no
monster should amaze us if normal man does not amaze.
—G. K. CHESTERTON

G rady and Sarah shuffled out of the cabin, bundled in heavy jackets and clutching mugs of coffee that threw heat like dark little suns. Across the wide expanse of Tipton's Lake the Blue Ridge Mountains breached the morning fog banks, their tree-lined backs resembling the foresty spines of some great kraken trawling the seas. Together they descended the steps from the front porch onto the unkempt grass and made their way down to the lake's edge, and the small path that would lead them a couple of hundred feet along until they came to the body of the strange creature that had washed ashore and died there.

They did not speak much as they walked. Out of jail for only three days after six years inside, Grady was struggling to recognize his thirteen-year-old daughter in the sullen-eyed, cynical presence striding along beside him. She had undergone some bizarre transformation since he'd last seen her. She'd dyed her hair black; strange silver adornments pocked her face: she had a ring in her left eyebrow, and a series of rings along the curve of one bejeweled conch of an ear. Worst of all, she'd put a stud through her tongue.

"Man, I can really smell that thing," he said. Sarah had discovered it last night, and was eager to show it off. The early cold snap had held off the smell to some degree, but it was beginning to creep toward the cabin.

"Wait till you see it, Dad, it's amazing."

Sarah had not come to see him during his last three years in prison. At first that had been at his own insistence, and she'd taken it badly: He told her of his decision while she and her mother were visiting, and she threw a tantrum of such violence that the guards were obliged to cut their session short. His reasons, he thought, were both predictable and justified: He didn't want his little girl to see him in that environment, slowly eroding into a smaller, meaner, beaten man. But the truth was simply that he was ashamed, and by keeping his daughter away he spared himself the humiliation he felt in her company. After less than a year of that, though, his resolve failed, and he asked his wife to start bringing her again. But Sarah never came back.

They rounded a thick copse of pines, cutting off their view of the cabin. From this vantage point it was easy to imagine themselves far from civilization and all its attendant rules. Cold air blew in off the lake. Grady lowered his chin into his jacket and closed his eyes, smelling the pine, the soft wet stink of the mud, the aroma of real coffee. He'd smelled nothing but sweat, urine, and disinfectant for so long, it seemed to him now that he was walking through the foothills of Heaven.

"I don't know what you think you're gonna do with it," Sarah said, ranging ahead. She cradled the mug of coffee he'd made for her like a kitten against her chest. "It's way too big to move."

"Won't know till I see it," he said.

"I was just telling you," she said, sounding hurt.

Grady was immediately irritated. "I didn't mean it like that." Christ, managing her moods was like handling nitroglycerin. Wasn't she supposed to be tough, with all that shit on her face? The old anger—irrational and narcotic in its sweetness—stirred in him. "So who's this boy your mother told me about? What's his name . . . Tracy?"

"Travis," she said, her voice muted.

"Oh. *Travis.*"

She said nothing, picking up her pace a little bit. She was on the defensive, which only provoked him. He wanted her to fight.

"What grade is he in?"

Again, nothing.

"Does he even go to school?"

"Yes," she said, but he could barely hear her.

"He better not be in fucking high school."

She turned on him; he noticed, with some dismay, that she had tears in her eyes. "I know Mom already told you all about him! Why are you doing this?"

"Jesus, what are you crying about? Never mind what your mom told me, I want to hear this from you."

"He's in ninth grade, all right? You should be glad I'm dating an older boy, he's not an immature shithead like the boys in *my* school!"

Grady just stood there, trying to decide how to feel. He felt a calmness descend over him, in an inverse proportion to Sarah's distress. He studied her. Did she really believe what she was saying? Had she grown so stupid?

"Well. I guess I ought to be grateful. Do I get to meet this Travis when we get back to Winston-Salem?"

She turned and continued down the path.

After a few more moments of trudging in strained silence, they rounded a small bend and came upon the monster. It was as big as a small van, still partly submerged in the lake, as though it had lunged onto the ground and expired from the effort. Grady drifted to a halt without realizing it, and Sarah went ahead without him, walking up to the huge carcass as casually as if she were approaching a boulder or a wrecked ship.

"Jesus, Sarah, don't touch it."

She ignored him and pressed her fingertips against its hide. "What are you afraid of? It's dead."

He was having trouble apprehending its shape. It looked like a huge, suppurated heart. It seemed a confusion of forms, as though the weight of the atmosphere crushed it out of true: He had the strong impression that underwater it would unfurl into something sensible, though perhaps no less strange. Its skin, glistening with dew and sickly excretions, was dark green, almost black. Enfolded in the flesh near the mud was an eye: saucer-size, clouded, eclipsed by a nictitating membrane that covered it like a bone-white crescent moon. A two-foot-long gash was partially buried in the mud; it could have been a mouth, or the wound that killed it. An odor seeped from it like a gas, candy-sweet.

Grady felt his stomach buckle. "What . . . what is it?"

"I don't know," Sarah said. "It's a dinosaur or something."

"Don't be stupid."

She went silent, pacing calmly around it.

"We need to uh . . . we need to get rid of it. Push it in or something." The thought of this smell rolling into the cabin windows at night fueled an irrational rage inside him. It wasn't right that this atrocity should ruin his homecoming.

"You can't. I already tried."

"Yeah well. Maybe I'll try again."

He placed his hands on it with great reluctance and gave it a cursory push to get a sense of its weight. The flesh gave a bit, and he felt his hands sink. He wrenched them away, making a high-pitched sound he didn't recognize as his own. His hands were covered in a sticky film, as though he'd gripped a sappy tree. Nausea swelled in his body; the ground swung up to meet him and he vomited into the mud.

"Oh my God. Dad?"

He continued to dry-heave until it felt like his guts were crawling up his throat. He smelled coffee on the ground in front of him, and he crawled away from it. "Oh Jesus, oh Jesus."

Sarah pulled at his shoulders. "Dad? Are you okay?"

He managed to lean back into a sitting position, rubbing his hands hard against his pants, trying to wipe off the sticky residue. He thought that if he moved it would trigger another spasm, so he sat still for a few moments and gathered himself. He could hear his daughter's voice. It seemed to come from an immeasurable distance. He crawled over to the water and thrust his hands into it, trying to scrape the residue from them without success.

The thing would have to be destroyed. Maybe if he hacked it up he could push it back into the lake. They were staying at his father-in-law's cabin; surely the man kept a chain saw or an ax around for chopping wood.

Eventually, he grabbed her arm, hauling himself to his feet. His mug lay near the monster, splashed in mud. He decided to leave it there.

"Let's go," he said. He started back along the path without waiting to see if she'd follow. He continued to scrape his hands on his thighs, but he was beginning to doubt the stuff would come off.

Tina was awake by the time they returned. She was leaning against the porch railing, one hand clutching her robe closed at her neck and the other holding a cigarette. Her eyes were heavy-lidded, her hair sleep-crushed, her hangover as heavy as a mantle of chains. She stood up there like a promise of life, and something stirred in Grady at the sight of her, grateful and tender. He summoned a smile from some resolute part of himself and raised a hand in greeting.

"You look like shit," she said amiably.

He looked down at himself. "I fell."

"So did you see it?"

"Oh yeah, I saw it."

"Mom, he got sick!"

He closed his eyes. "Sarah . . ."

"You got sick, baby?"

"Just, I—yeah, okay, I got sick. It's fucking disgusting."

They climbed the stairs and joined her on the porch. Tina brushed at his pants with one hand, her cigarette clenched in her teeth. "Sarah, go get a towel from the bathroom. You can't walk into the cabin like this."

"It's all over my hands," Grady said.

"What is?"

"I don't know, some weird sticky shit on the, on the thing. I think it gave me a reaction or something."

"We should get you to a doctor, Dad," said Sarah.

"Don't be stupid. I just got a little dizzy."

"Dad, you–"

"Goddammit, Sarah!" She stepped back from him as though she'd been struck.

Tina gestured at her without looking, still brushing her husband's pants. "Sarah—honey—a towel. Please."

Sarah's mouth moved silently for a moment; then she said, "Fine," and went inside. Grady watched her go, fighting down a spike of anger.

"What's *your* problem?" said Tina, giving up on his pants.

"*My* problem? Is that a joke?"

"You been gone six years, Grady. Give her a chance."

"Well, it was her choice not to see me for the last three of them. I didn't ask her to stay away. Not at the end. And anyway, is that what *you're* doing? Giving her a chance? Is that what the rings in her face and that shit in her tongue is all about?"

He watched a door close somewhere inside her. "Grady . . ."

"What? 'Grady,' what?"

"Just . . . don't, okay?"

"No, I want to hear it. 'Grady,' what? 'Grady, I fucked up'? 'Grady, our daughter is a walking car wreck and it's because I spent so much time drunk I didn't even care'?"

She wouldn't look at him. She smoked her cigarette and focused her gaze beyond him: on the lake, or on the mountains, or on some distant place he couldn't see.

"How about, 'Grady, I spent so much time banging Mitch while you were in jail that I forgot how to be a wife *and* a mother'?"

She shook her head; it was barely perceptible. "You're so goddamned mean," she said. "I was kinda hoping you'd of changed."

He leaned in close and spoke right into her ear. "No, fuck that. I'm more me than ever."

* * *

Grady showered—discovering that the substance on his hands was apparently impervious to soap—and the girls retreated to their rooms, nurturing their hurts, stranding him in the living room. He drank more coffee and flipped through the channels on TV. It was not unlike how he spent rec hour in jail, and he felt a profound self-pity at the realization. Goddamned evil bitches, he thought. I'm back a few days and they're already giving me the cold shoulder. It's disrespectful. He knew how to handle disrespect in prison; out here he felt emasculated by it.

He knew he should use this time to go out to the monster and start breaking it down. He'd only regret it if he allowed it to stay longer. But it would be gruesome, grueling work, and the very thought of it made his body sag into the couch. And anyway, it wasn't fair. These two weeks at the cabin were supposed to be for him, a celebration. He shouldn't have to climb up to his waist in fucking monster gore.

So instead he watched TV. He turned on VH1 and was pleased to see that the countdown of the hundred best 1980s songs he'd started watching in prison was still going on. It chewed through his day. From time to time Tina emerged from their bedroom and drifted silently past him into the kitchen, still wearing her robe; he heard the tinkle of ice in her glass and the hum of the freezer when she retrieved her vodka from it. Whenever she came back through he refused to look at her and he supposed she returned the favor—certainly she said nothing to him. That was fine, though; he'd already proven he could live with hostile motherfuckers. She brought nothing new to the table.

Left to itself, though, his self-righteousness dissipated, and he fell into examining his own behavior. These women had been his beacons while he was in prison and within days of his return he had driven them into hiding. He remembered it being like this sometimes, but it seemed worse now.

What's the matter with me? he thought. Why do I always fuck it up?

Eventually Sarah came out of her room. She was dressed to go outside, and she held a large pad of paper under her arm. She strode through the living room with a purpose and without a word. Just like her mother, Grady thought.

"Where are you going?"

She stopped, almost at the door, her back to him. She raised her face to the ceiling, as though imploring God. "Outside," she said.

"I can see that. Where to?"

She half turned, looking at him finally. "What does it matter?"

His teeth clenched. He stood up quickly, in a fluid motion: It was an abrupt and aggressive action, meant to convey threat, a holdover from the vocabulary of violence he'd spent years cultivating. "Because I'm your father," he said. "Don't you forget that."

She took a startled step backward; Grady felt a flare of satisfaction, and was immediately appalled at himself. He sat back down, scowling.

"I want to draw the monster," Sarah said, her voice markedly subdued.

"You—why would you want to do that?" All the anger had drained from him. He tried speaking to her now in a reasonable voice, the kind he thought a regular father might use.

She shrugged. She looked at the floor in front of her, looking for all the world like a punished child.

"Sarah, look at me."

Nothing.

He put some steel into it, not wanting her to make him angry again. "I said look at me."

She looked at him.

"You don't need to be going out there," he said.

She nodded. She tried to say something, failed, and tried again. "Okay."

But as she turned and headed back to her room, her face a cramped scrawl of defeat, his resolve washed away completely. He hadn't expected her to acquiesce so quickly, and he experienced a sudden need to show her that he could be giving, and kind. "You know what? Go ahead."

Sarah stopped again. "What?"

"Just go on. Go ahead."

She seemed to consider it for a moment, then said, "Okay," and turned back to the door. She walked out, shutting it quietly behind her.

She's so weak, he thought. Goddammit.

Despite the fact that she'd only been staying there three days, Sarah's room was a wreck. Her suitcase was open and clothes were stacked precariously on the bed, the ones she'd already worn strewn across the floor. He went into the little bathroom and looked in the medicine cabinet, which was empty, and into the trash can, where he found spent cigarettes. They were only half consumed, which he supposed was a small blessing. He figured she was training herself to like them. Maybe there was still time to put a stop to it. He spent a futile moment at the sink, trying once more to clean his hands.

Back in the bedroom he opened the bureau drawers, thinking that he might find her diary. He was encouraged when he saw a spiral-bound notebook in one of them, until he opened it to find lists of chores and a draft of a letter to someone named Tamara about an impending trip—his mother-in-law's notebook, which made it eight years old at least. He looked under her mattress; he looked beneath her clothes in the suitcase. In a large zippered pouch on the lid of the suitcase he found large sheets of paper covered in pencil sketches.

They were drawings of a nude teenage boy. Her boyfriend, he guessed. The infamous Travis. He sat carefully on her bed and looked at them, breathing carefully, concentrating on holding his hands steady. He tried to reason with himself: The drawings were not lewd; he supposed they were classical poses. He even recognized, dimly, that the drawings were good. There was talent at work here. But mostly he felt a rising heat, a bloody flush of anger. A bead of sweat fell from his forehead and splashed onto the sketch, obliterating the boy's shoulder like a gunshot.

Well. No hiding it now.

He tore the drawings down the middle, turned them sideways, and tore them again. He returned the quartered papers to the pouch in the suitcase and determined that she would never, ever see that predatory little fuck again. He would see to it. He left her room and stationed himself in front of the TV again. He couldn't decide what he should do. He would wait for her and reason with her. He would scream at her and put the fear of God into her. He would go into the other bedroom and beat Tina until she bled from her ears. He would let it all go, and not say a word. He would go outside and get the goddamned ax or chain saw or whatever he could find and go down to the lake and lay into the moldering pile of garbage until his arms hurt too much to move, until he filled the air with blood, filled his lungs and his heart and his mouth with blood.

What he did was watch more TV. After about forty minutes he even began to pay attention. He forced himself to focus on whatever non-sense was on display, forced himself to listen to the commercials and consider the shiny plastic options they presented to him. It was a trick he'd cultivated in prison, a sort of meditation, to prevent himself from acting rashly, to keep himself out of trouble with the guards. Most of the time it worked.

He would not go down to the lake. He would not go into Tina's room, where she was steering herself into oblivion. He would sit down and be calm. It was easy.

He went into the kitchen and grabbed a bottle of vodka from the pantry. He left the one in the freezer for Tina; unlike her, he liked to feel the burn.

A couple of hours passed. Sarah stayed gone. He killed half the bottle. The TV show became something else, then something else again, and his thoughts blundered about until they found Mitch. Tina had told him about Mitch while he was in jail. She started seeing him after he'd been in about four years, well after Sarah stopped coming to see him. He'd received the news stoically—he was proud of himself for that, even to this day. He inflicted operatic violence on some guy later that day, sure, but no one who wasn't going to get it anyway. On the whole he thought he handled it all exceptionally well. And good news: Mitch got dumped after about six months.

Grady told himself he could live with it, and he did.

But it ate at him. Just a little bit.

Now seemed as good a time as any to explore his feelings on this matter with his wife. To have an intimate discussion with her. It would bring them closer together.

Grady lifted himself off the couch and plotted a course to the bedroom. He placed his hand on the wall to steady himself; the floor was trying to buck him. He would show it. He took a few lurching steps and halted, one arm held aloft for balance. When it seemed that doom had been skirted, he took a few more steps and reached the far wall. There was a window there, and he cracked it for some fresh air. The sun was failing, little pools of nighttime gathering beneath the trees. He smelled something faintly sweet riding the air, and he breathed deeply and gratefully before he realized it must be the moldering corpse of the monster. Shaken, he pulled away from the window and went into the bedroom.

Tina was awake, lying flat on the bed and staring at the ceiling. A photo album was open at her feet; some of the pictures had been removed and spread atop the covers. When he came in she rolled her head to look at him, and flopped an arm in his direction. "Hey babe," she said.

"Hey."

He sat heavily on the bed. The room was mostly dark, with only a faint yellow light leaking through the curtains. He picked up one of the loose photos: It was a picture of her father standing by the lake, holding up a big fish. "What the hell are you looking at?"

She plucked the picture from his hand and tossed it to the floor, laughing at him. " 'What the hell are you looking at?' " she said, rolling her body onto his legs.

"Don't do that."

" 'Don't do that.' "

He laughed despite himself, grabbing a handful of her hair and giving it a gentle tug.

"Ain't you mad no more?" she asked, her fingers working at the button of his pants.

"Shut up, bitch," he said, but affectionately, and she responded as though he'd just recited a line of verse, shedding her robe and lifting herself over and onto him, so that he felt as though he were sliding into a warm sea. He closed his eyes and exhaled, feeling it down to his fingertips.

They moved roughly, urgently, breathing in the musk of each other, breathing in too the smell of the pines and the lake and the dead monster, this last growing in power until it occluded the others, until it filled his sinuses, his head, his body, until it seemed nothing existed except that smell and the awful thing that made it, until it seemed he was its source, the wellspring of all the foulness of the earth, and when he spent himself into her he thought for a wretched moment that he had somehow injected it with the possibility of new life.

She rolled off of him, saying something he couldn't hear. Grady put his hand over his face, breathed through his nose. Tina rested her head on his chest, and he put his nose to her hair, filling it with something recognizable and good. They lay together for long moments, their limbs a motionless tangle, glowing like marble in the fading light.

"Why couldn't you wait for me?" he said quietly.

She tensed. For a while he could hear nothing but her breath, and the creaking of the trees outside as the wind moved through them. She rubbed her fingers through the hair on his chest.

"Please don't ask me that," she said.

He was quiet, waiting for her.

"I don't know why I did it. I don't know a whole lot about that time. But I just don't ever want to talk about it. I wish it never happened."

"Okay," he said. It wasn't good enough. But he was just drunk enough to realize that nothing would be. He would have to figure out whether or not he could live with it. It was impossible to say, just now.

So he lay there with her and felt the weight of her body against his. When he closed his eyes he imagined himself beneath deep water, part of some ruined structure of broken gray stone, like some devastated row of teeth.

"I should make dinner," Tina said. "Sarah's probably hungry."

Her name went off inside him like a depth charge. He lurched upright, ignoring the swimming sensation in his brain. "Sarah," he said. "She went out."

"What?"

"To that thing. She went out to that thing."

Tina seemed confused. "When?"

"Hours ago." He swung his legs out of bed. "Goddammit. I've been drunk!"

"Grady, calm down. I'm sure she's fine."

He hurried through the living room, his heart crashing through his chest, a fear he had not believed possible crowing raucously in his head. He pushed her door open.

She was there, illuminated by a slice of light from the living room, lying on her belly, her feet by the headboard. Her arms were tucked under her body for warmth. Her suitcase was open, and the pictures he had destroyed were on the floor beside it.

"Sarah?" he whispered, and stepped inside. He placed his hand on her back, felt the heat unfurling from her body, felt the rise and fall of her breath. He crept around the bed and looked at her face. Her eyes were closed and gummed by tears, her mouth was slightly parted. A little damp pool of saliva darkened the blanket underneath. The rings in her ears caught the light from the living room.

He stroked her hair, moving it off of her forehead and hooking it behind her ear. Anything could have happened to her, he thought. While I was drinking myself stupid in the other room, anything could have happened to her.

Tina's voice came in from the other room. "Grady? Is she all right?"

Christ. I'm just like her. I'm just as fucking bad. He went to the door and poked his head out. "Yeah. She's sleeping."

Tina smiled at him and shook her head. "I *told* you," she said.

"Yeah." He went back into the room. He pulled off Sarah's shoes and socks, slid her jacket off her shoulders. After a lot of careful maneuvering he managed to get her turned around and underneath the covers without waking her. He leaned over to kiss her on the forehead, and smelled the vodka on his own breath. Self-loathing hit him like a wrecking ball. He scrambled into her bathroom and barely made it before puking into the toilet, clutching the bowl with both hands, one leg looking weakly for purchase behind him. He'd had nothing but vodka and coffee all day, so there wasn't much to throw up.

When he felt able, he flushed the toilet and headed back to the bedroom. He leaned over and picked up the torn pictures, so he could throw them away. Beneath them he found the new ones, the ones she'd spent all day working on.

He didn't recognize them at first. She'd used colored pencils, and he initially thought he was looking at a house made of rainbows. Upon closer inspection, though, he realized that she'd drawn the dead monster: as a kaleidoscope, as a grounded sun. His mind reeled. He dropped it to the ground and here was the monster again, rendered larger than it was in real life, its mouth the gaping Gothic arches of a cathedral, its eyes stained glass, ignited by sunlight. There was another, and another, each depicting it as something beautiful, warm, and bright.

Why couldn't she get it? Why was she forever romanticizing vileness? His breath was getting short. He rubbed his temples, his body physically rocking as waves of anger rolled through him. She was just stupid, apparently. It was too late. Maybe he'd fucked her up, maybe Tina did, but the damage was done. She'd have to be protected her whole goddamned life.

Might as well start now, he thought.

Tina was in the living room as he walked through it, shrugging into his jacket.

"Where are you going?"

"Is the shed locked?"

"What?"

"Is the shed fucking locked?"

"I, no, I—"

"Good. Stay here."

When he opened the front door the cold slammed into him like a truck. The temperature had dropped precipitously with the sun. He paused to catch his breath, then jumped down the stairs and headed around back to the shed. He slid the door open and flipped on the light. Inside was a dark, cobwebby tomb of stacked wood and garden appliances with the untroubled appearance of dead Egyptian kings. No chain saw was evident, but he did find an ax leaning against the wall behind a rusting lawn mower. He reached gingerly through a shroud of webs, wary of spiders, and grasped the handle. He pulled it out, trailing dust and ghostly banners.

It had changed since this morning. It actually was shedding light, for one thing, though it was a dim phosphorescence, the result of some strange fungus or bacterium running amok through its innards. The creature looked like some ghastly oversized night-light. The gash that was either a mouth or a wound had borne fruit: A weird and vibrant flora spilled from it like fruit from a cornucopia, pale protuberances with growths like outstretched arms listing this way and that, a dozen vegetable christs. Life abounded here: Small chitinous animals hurried busily to and fro, conducting their miserable business in tunnels and passageways in the body, provided for them by nature or their own savage industry; a cloud of insects, drunk on the very perfume that had driven him into fits, alternately settling on its carcass and lifting away again in graceful curtains, like wind blowing through a wheat field.

Grady raised his ax and took a few tentative steps toward it.

Something moved near him: a raccoon startled from its feast and gone crashing into the underbrush. The flesh around where it had been eating sloughed away and more light spilled into the forest: Hundreds of small insects, their backs coated with the glowing fluids of this dead thing, moved about the wound like boiling suns.

The ax was heavy, so he let it drop. He couldn't process what he was seeing. He had to figure it out. He sat down in the mud several feet away from all that moving light and stared at it for a while. Maybe there was beauty in there somewhere. Maybe you just had to look at it the right way.

He looked at the palms of his hands. They cast light.

All Washed Up While Looking for a Better World

Carol Emshwiller

Carol Emshwiller grew up in Michigan and in France and currently divides her
time between New York and California. She is the winner of two Nebula Awards
for her stories "Creature" and "I Live with You." She has also won the Life
Achievement award from the World Fantasy Convention.

She's been the recipient of a National Endowment for the Arts grant and two
New York State grants. Her short fiction has been published in many literary and
science-fiction magazines; her most recent books are the novels Mister Boots and
The Secret City, and the collection I Live with You.

Emshwiller's whimsical tone sometimes disguises the seriousness of her themes.
Here, a woman's search for an exotic escape from her mundane existence takes her
to an island with some unpleasant surprises.

I wanted to be washed up on a foreign shore, but this can't be it. I wanted, first, a long, long beach, so I could lie there and recover for a while. After all, I'd be tired. I'd have fought the waves for, maybe, days. Or it certainly would have seemed like days. I *am* tired. I must have rowed for hours but one can't judge time at a time like this.

I didn't want to fight a surf and then sharp rocks. I wanted beauty, palm trees, coconuts, a freshwater stream flowing down not far from where I would have collapsed. And natives of course. They would find me and bring me to their huts or caves. Nurse me back to health.

But there doesn't seem to be anybody here.

As far as I can see this is all beach. More like a desert. It *is*. I may have to walk for miles before I can get help. If there is any help.

I won't start yet. I have to rest first. I'll just lie here, my cheek on wet sand and sharp little shells. Periwinkles. I know you can eat them, but it's a lot of work. It takes half a dozen to make one decent bite.

Actually, I liked it well enough back where I was. I liked my boss and my fellow workers, but I'd been there ten years. I'd turned forty. I thought it was time for something different, but not this different.

I should say my job was in a huge windowless library, pillars all across the front. Greek Revival pediment and all. Wide steps up to the colonnade. Inside, the offices were small, the stacks huge. There were no windows except little high ones in the basement. In the spring we could look out at the forsythia in bloom. At other times it was just a little bit of green.

I must have slept or passed out, my nose down with the crabs. And then I hear someone say, "What sort of creature is it?"

First I think they must be talking about some odd shell. I'm curious, too. I roll over to see what they're looking at and it's me.

"Never saw anything like it before."

"Look, it's wearing clothes."

"What's it worth?"

"A pitcher or two."

I say, "No," and, "No, no, no."

"Hear that? It thinks it's talking."

"Sounds almost human."

Far as I can see they look just like me, or more or less. But it's foggy. They might not be here at all. I'm thinking it would be nice if they weren't.

This isn't the kind of thing I wanted. Where are the palm trees and the kind brown natives with their little grass huts and soft springy beds of reeds? These people are as pale as city folk. Even their eyes and hair are pale. How can you be so pale on a desert island? If that's what this is. Or maybe it's always foggy.

I try to sit up. I'm dizzy and my leg hurts. I reach to touch it. What if it's broken?

"Look, it can sit."

"It's a her."

"Yup."

I look at myself and see that I'm still wet and my blouse is clingy.

"Maybe it'll get up and walk."

"Won't that be funny? If it does, it'll be almost just like us."

"We could take it home and show Ma."

"Wonder what it eats."

"How about sheeshoosh?"

That makes them laugh.

I'm thirsty, but I don't think I'll get anything from these . . . people. Even so I make a gesture to my mouth. I say, "Drink. Please."

"Listen to that. If you didn't know better, you'd think it was speech."

I say, "It *is* speech."

"Did it say it's speaking speech?"

"Couldn't have."

"Do you think it has a name?"

"We could name it."

"How about Jo or Bo. Those are easy ones. It could even call itself to come to itself if it wanted to."

At that, they all flop down on the sand laughing.

It's still foggy out though the sun is well up—a murky gray ball. You'd think it would have burned off the fog by now.

They're not paying any attention to me. I feel at my leg again. I can't tell if it's broken or sprained or what. I'm beginning to wonder if I shouldn't have stayed home even though I was so tired of never being out in nature. We didn't even have windows. What little bit of nature I saw was when I walked home . . . bits of flowers or weeds around the bottoms of the trees. Pigeons. Not that I don't like pigeons.

Well, trust nature to give you a broken leg and make you so thirsty you can hardly stand it.

I pick up a periwinkle and pull out the sliver of sandy meat and eat it. I do it again. I look at the creatures. There are five. Still laughing. They look leggy—long arms, too. Adolescents? Preadolescents?

One says, "Let's name it Rex."

"Does it look like a Rex?"

The creatures roll onto their stomachs and stare up at me.

"So that's what it eats."

"A lot of bother for nothing much. Must take all day. You'd think it wouldn't be so fat."

I'm not fat, just fat compared to them.

"Let's get it going."

They prop me up and I try to take a step or two, but then I go down on all fours.

I say, "I can't walk unless you help me."

"Come on Jo, Bo . . ."

"Rex."

" . . . we have to get on home."

"Give it a couple more shell things."

One comes close and peers into my face and I peer into its. Its hair is pale and long and lank. I can't tell if it's a boy or girl. Its eyes look sleepy because of their droopy lids.

It says, "Ugh," and hands me two tiny shells.

I say, "Thank you."

"Listen to it try to talk. Ma will like it."

"Maybe, but you never know with Ma."

They pull me up again and I take a couple of steps, but I just can't. Three of them have already started off and are way ahead. I drop down on all fours and start to crawl.

"Look how it's going."

"It's too slow."

They yell for the others to "Wait up!" and off they go.

I follow. Not hard. I mean it's hard crawling, but not hard to see where they're headed. They've left a trail in the sand much wider than need be.

After a few minutes, I raise up as high as I can but I can't make out whether there are any cliffs or palm trees or grass houses in the distance.

Of course not very likely they'd help me even when I get someplace. But I'm so thirsty and there's no fresh water around here that I can see. They've got to have some.

I crawl for what seems a long time. Then I hear, "Hey, look how far it got."

"Not bad."

"Let's help it."

And so they grab me again, one on each side. (There are only two of them this time.) They try to hold me up, but they're not very strong. Still, they keep me on my feet, which I wish they wouldn't. I say, "Slow down. Please."

They don't and I didn't expect them to.

They bring me to a steep-sided pit in the sand. They throw me . . . or rather let me fall, slipping and sliding, down into it. And there is . . . I suppose it is . . . Ma.

"What in the world have you dragged in now?"

"It chatters. It's wearing clothes. It can do lots of things. Maybe it can help."

"It's useless. Its leg is all swollen up."

"That's the way it's supposed to be."

"I doubt it."

"We can sell it."

"Poosh."

"Can we have it?"

"I don't see why not."

"Yay."

They all begin to dance and kick up sand.

I say, "Now, listen for once. I'm no different from you. I'm talking your language. Can't you see that?"

"Maybe we can tame it."

"I'll do anything you want if you just give me a drink. I'll give you my silky blouse and my silver bird pin. I'll give you my turquoise ring." (I wore these especially to give to the natives who might rescue me.) "I've lost my shoes but I'll give my socks, though I'd like to keep my underwear."

"It's trying to give a speech."

"Wonder what it thinks it's saying."

"Let's listen."

But they don't.

"I wish there were two of it. Then we could both have one. Where can we get another one?"

"Hang out on the beach is where. Things get washed up all the time. Maybe we could even get a better one."

They tie a piece of frayed twine around my neck and I have to scrabble out of the sandpit—as much sliding down as climbing up. One pulls me along while another pushes. I'm not worried about getting choked. I think the twine will break any minute.

But how to get a drink? I wanted broth and a caring hand lifting my head to help me drink it.

We've been going slightly up for a while, me crawling and them pulling on the string. I turn around and see the view of the shore beyond. It's a spectacular view now that the fog has burned off, but right now I don't care. If I could drink a view . . .

Later, here come the other three. One asks, "Can it dance?"

"We don't know yet."

"Well?"

"We don't know how to make it do it."

"Drink," I say. "I'll dance if you give me a drink."

I keep pointing at my mouth.

They start slapping their hands on their thighs and making clicking sounds. One finds two stones to pound against each other.

They sing, "Diggity thump, diggity thump."

I wave my arms to show them I'm willing.

We do that for a while until one says, "Whoa. Ma'll be mad."

"Is it getting dark already?"

Suddenly they all run off. I'm not sorry. A little peace and quiet. Maybe I can find a drink by myself. I pull myself along, but to the side where I think I see a bush. Maybe I can find a hiding place.

Natives! At least not cannibals. So far, anyway. Why didn't I think twice about leaky boats instead of just once. I was taking a bigger risk than I thought—heading off toward nowhere. Nowhere is exactly what I wanted, but I didn't want this kind of nowhere.

I always thought, especially recently, that I was born to be washed up someplace odd and lost and unknown. A place unlike anyplace I was used to. Or perhaps born to crash in an airplane in a jungle, or on the top of a mountain. Someplace with rushing streams and gnarled thousand-year-old trees. Surely a spectacular setting of some sort.

And I was born to start over, to have a whole new life, a second chance, new friends, new surroundings, even new ideas. *Especially* new ideas. Born to not, anymore, think my same old thoughts that I've been thinking over and over. Even born to speak another language. One I never heard of before, full of glottal stops and hisses.

The more I saw the recommended movies, read the bestsellers and the book reviews, went to plays I couldn't afford, saw the latest art shows, the more I knew that I was only marking time. That something more important awaited me.

But now I suppose you could say the moral of my adventure would be "There's no place like home." Even so, no matter what happens, I won't believe that. No matter how this ends up—it'll probably end up with me dying for lack of water and food—anyway, no matter how, I'll not believe it. Home is never best. Home is everything as usual. Who wants that?

It is a bush. Just one. It's not as big as it looked to be from down the beach. I hunker down next to it. It's a wonder I sleep at all, thirsty and hungry as I am, but I do. In the morning my leg feels some better. I guess it isn't broken. I'm going to try and stay off it and I'm going to try to avoid those . . . whatever they are. I crawl yet farther, sideways along the beach. I hope away from them. There's another bush. I head for it when . . .

"Hey, here it is."

"Yay, I thought it was lost."

"Don't worry. Even if it was, we could look for another one. If one gets washed up, other ones must get washed up, too."

"Well, then how come this is the first one we ever saw?"

They prop me up again, one on each side. By now I know it's useless to say anything.

It looks like they're chewing gum. Is this a sign of contact with the outside world? Or has this always been the outside world, so that I've not really moved that far from my usual surroundings—as if I'd gone to Coney Island on a cold day when hardly anybody else was there?

They bring me back to that sandpit, me crawling and hopping, and at last give me a drink and food—in a dog's bowl. In fact it says DOG right on it. And the food looks like kibbles. I'm grateful anyway. I say, "Thank you."

The ma says she doesn't want me in the house, but where *is* the house?

"Can't we have it inside? Please. Just this once."

"We don't even know what it is. Besides, it's too sandy."

Actually, there seems to be nothing but sand all over everything anyway.

I feel so much better after having eaten and drunk, I curl up around the water bowl to fall asleep, but they don't want me to.

We spend the day at all sorts of games. Hide-and-seek. They hide me under sand. Not my head, thank goodness. And: Can they crawl as fast as I can? (They can.) How many periwinkles can they eat?

Then one says, "If we can find a male, we could have babies."

"And we could watch them do it."

"Yay."

They all (and I also, pulled and pushed along) go back to the beach to look for a male. They walk up and down, but not very far.

I'd have a fellow feeling for anyone washed up. I hope they find somebody, though I wouldn't wish this on anybody.

They find shells they like. They make a little sort of harness with a plastic bag on each side of me. (Is this another sign I haven't gone far or have plastic bags blown all over the whole world?) I carry them, crawling.

Back at the pit, the ma asks, "Did you feed it?"

"We forgot."

"Well, *I'm* certainly not going to do it."

They bring fresh water and food. I say, "Thank you. You're very kind." I'll be polite. Maybe something will get through to them.

I want to stay awake to see if they go anywhere outside of this sandpit, but I'm too tired.

In the morning they forget to feed and water me. Talking hasn't helped so I bark and meow. I even say a couple of big "baaaaas." It feels good to do it.

I don't know if they hear me or not, but they do feed me.

Then it's back to the beach to look for more like me.

They forget why they're there. They get to playing a sand-in-the-face game. I crawl away and they don't notice.

I stay down on the harder wet sand. It's easier going. Maybe I can get out of sight.

I think I see, way, way down the beach, that there's a rowboat pulled up on the shore.

I crawl even faster.

I hope the oars are still there. I'll be off to some other, better desert island. I'll sing as I row.

"Hey, don't let it get away."

Here they come.

I get up and hobble but they catch me before I can get to the boat. And even if I'd made it, I'd have had to push off. I never would have gotten away.

They see the boat, too, and forget all about me.

I follow, but slowly. They're all jumping around in it. I sit down beside it.

"Not bad."

"And look, the oars are still here."

"Too bad nobody's here. I thought maybe we'd find another one and then you others could have one, too."

"There's got to be another one or even two around here someplace. Maybe three. Maybe we could all have one."

I look around for tracks leading from the boat, but they look around for tracks, too, and kick up so much sand there's no way to tell anymore.

Escape was so close it gives me hope. A boat is all I need. Or maybe even just a log to float away on.

I search the sea and the beach for signs of driftwood. There's only small stuff, but I collect a pile, anyway. Maybe I can build a fire and a ship will come, though there'll be the problem of matches. I wonder if these creatures have any.

My pile is getting bigger. It takes me a long time crawling to gather stuff, but at least they're not bothering me.

Then they notice my pile. They love it. They crawl in and out of the branches and old planks and mess it all up.

I say, "You could make a nice bonfire," and one of them says, "Hey, we could make a nice bonfire."

Do I actually have some influence? Except it *is*, clearly, the makings of a bonfire.

I say, "What about matches?" and they say, "Let's get some matches," and off they go.

I crawl over to the rowboat. I try really hard, but I don't have the strength to push it back into the surf. I wonder if I can get them to do it. I climb in. Fall onto the bottom. Could I hide here? Of course then I wouldn't have any chance of getting water and food.

The sound of the water lapping nearby is restful. I wake when I hear them coming back—good grief, they're noisy—but I don't move.

"Oh no, where has it got to?"

Meaning me, of course.

And then I see their heads all along the gunwale. Five of them. They smile and wave when they see me.

I say, "Push the boat off. We can all go for a ride," but they turn away to the pile of driftwood.

I look over the side and watch them. It lights instantly.

Playing with fire. Not a good idea. I hope they don't all get burned up. They're my only hope for water and food.

But someone is striding down the beach toward us. At first I think he's naked, and I feel good because, for sure, he's one of those native brown people I was hoping for, but then I see he's wearing shorts and a T-shirt, everything tan, and he's just a regular person. I hope he can hear what I say.

The creatures all run and hide behind the boat while I climb out and crawl to greet him. He's a long way off so I manage to get well away from them before we meet.

When we get close, I sit up. I straighten my blouse and brush some of the sand off. I try to do something with my hair though I know it's a lost cause.

He's good looking and about my age, though, unfortunately, not my type.

He sits down beside me, and right away he says, "I've been all the way around it, and there's nothing here," as if he's not surprised to see me. Not even surprised to see me crawling first and then sitting here with my swollen leg stretched out in front of me.

I don't tell him about the others. I just say, "Oh."

He had come on shore early in the morning and it had taken him all day to get back around to his boat.

"This isn't much of an island."

The good news is, he, also, had wanted to be washed up on a foreign shore.

I say, "I presume you're looking for a whole new way of life, with adventures and interesting natives, in an exciting setting. I suppose you wanted naked ladies, but this isn't the place."

"You've made a bonfire. You want to be rescued."

"This isn't where I meant to come. I'm starving and thirsty and I'd like to leave with you."

"You're not what I'm looking for."

"No, no, nothing like that, though, considering, we must have a lot in common. I just want to get away. Actually if I had a comb and could wash my hair I'd look a lot better. But I just want out of here."

They're still hiding behind his boat. I hear them giggling. The man hears, too.

"Are there other people here?"

"Sort of."

They jump out and run to us yelling, "Yay, yay, yay, another one."

"Who are they?"

"I've no idea."

Before he can stop them they feel at his crotch.

"Yay, it's a male."

They dance around us and kick up sand until he's as sandy as I am.

He wants to get out into the surf to wash off, but they keep getting in the way.

I say, "It's useless."

He starts hitting out at them but misses every time. How can that be? He's using up all his energy and it looks to be as useless as trying to tell them something.

"Stop. Wait," I say. "We need them. There's no water or food except if they give it to us back at their pit. I have to crawl there, but at least you can walk."

He stops.

And then the creatures do it again. Yell, "Oh no. Ma will be mad." And off they go.

What if they get so distracted with him that I can leave him here instead of me? Maybe they'll forget about me even though they want to have babies. Maybe if I had enough time, I could push the boat off by myself. Maybe I could even take days to do it. They might not notice that it was inching out little by little. Then I could be starting off on my *real* adventure.

"Go on," I say. "Follow them. It's your only chance for food."

He trots off, but I head back to his boat. I wonder if he left any food or water in it.

First I push at it. And push and push. I do move it a little. About a half inch every push. If I didn't have a bad leg, I'd do a lot better. I keep pushing until I'm exhausted and it's dark. I've gone about three or four feet. Then the moon comes up—not a full moon, but I can see fairly well except in the shadows. I get into the boat and look around for supplies.

There's a dirty backpack tucked under the backseat. It's wet. I find wet crackers in it. I think they're cheese crackers and might have been good once. I eat them all. There's an inch of stale-tasting water left in a plastic bottle. I drink that.

The bonfire smolders outside. I wonder if anybody will see it and come. Maybe I should be working at keeping it burning, but I don't.

I sleep in the boat, though it's not as comfortable as the sand. At least with sand you can make yourself a hip hole.

In the morning they all come rushing back. I hear them a long ways off. The man gets here first and they trail after. First thing he looks over the side and sees the empty water bottle and cracker wrappers.

But even so he's relieved. "I thought you might have taken off in my boat."

I say, "Their water tastes a lot better than yours."

I hope he doesn't notice that his boat was moved a few feet.

Maybe he is my type after all. He looks less like a boy and more like a man than I thought. Or is it just that he spent a sleepless frustrated night? The circles under his eyes make him more attractive, and there's something pleasantly worried about his face.

He hops into the boat and sits beside me—says, "At least *you* can hear me."

He's found out what it's like not to be able to say anything.

All five of the creatures follow him into the boat. There's hardly room for all of us. The way they're crowding around and pushing at us, they obviously want us to sit closer to each other. He moves to the front of the boat to be farther away.

"Hey," they say, "how about it?" and make lewd gestures.

"Sorry I didn't save any crackers for you. I couldn't help myself."

I wonder if I look better to him this morning, just as he looks better to me. Can we already have gotten to the point where anybody of the opposite sex starts looking good?

They crowd us and push us so much we leave the boat and sit down, one on each side of the ashes of the bonfire.

He says, "My name is Brad."

I wonder who I should be. I say, "My name is Melody," which of course it isn't—any more than he's Brad. (I don't know why that name popped out. I don't even like it. And I don't even look as if my name is Melody.) I'm sure he doesn't believe me, either.

This night they don't let me stay in the boat by myself. I try hard against their pulling. The boat only needs another three or four feet. But then there's the dog food and more or less clean water. I go. Three stay with me as I crawl back, and two go on ahead with him.

Ma is really mad when she sees two of us. "Out! Out! Both of them! I never even wanted one. What will you be dragging in next?"

She makes them push us out of the sandpit.

There's another little bush nearby. (There don't seem to be any trees, just these bushes. Probably some sort of saltbush, considering.) They tie us up to this bush with frayed twine. Then they feed us and water us. As I figured, just one bowl. We take turns.

"You know, we could put some of this dry food in our pockets and take it down to the boat and save it until we have enough to leave."

"What can we do about water?"

"Bring up that plastic bottle and fill it from the dog bowl?"

"Where does their water come from?"

"That's the question."

Later, by moonlight, we untie each other and climb back into the pit. There they are, in a bundle in the middle, sleeping. We make a survey. He does, I do the best I can crawling. As far as we can tell, it's just an empty pit, debris strewn around. We find plastic bags, clothespins, rubber bands, old Coke bottles with water in them closed with wine corks, a collection of string and wire, insoles but no shoes . . . We take several plastic bags for dog food, and five of the Coke bottles with water. Then we climb back to the bush, hide our loot under sand, and tie ourselves up again.

We're feeling quite happy with each other. I can see it on his face and I'm sure he can see it on mine.

We talk. He tells me a long story about three women lovers who left him. He says they were bitches, all three of them. I don't think that can be true and say so. I say maybe he's been choosing the same kind of women every single time. "Psychologists say that happens a lot."

He says, "They really were bitches."

I say, "I don't think so, not all three."

He says, "What do you know?"

I say I've had a lover or two, but he isn't paying attention. I say, "I know I'm a mess now. It's been days since I had a shower or a good night's sleep."

He's not listening. You'd think, after being with these creatures for a couple of days, he'd know enough to listen to somebody—even me.

He says he wanted, just as I suspected, naked native women. Naïve and unsophisticated. He says I'm not to his taste.

I say, "All I was looking for was a new life, not a mate." I go on and on, but then I notice he's asleep.

Back at the beach the next morning we put our water and kibbles in the boat. Not enough of either yet for the two of us, but might be enough for one. Depending, of course, on how far away the next foreign shore is.

I wonder if he'll try to take off without me. It wouldn't be hard, what with my bad leg making me so slow.

The creatures don't seem to notice our packages, but then they open one of the water bottles and drink it themselves. They taste the kibbles, make faces, and spit them out.

Then we work on the bonfire. All of us do. They seem to enjoy it.

This time, when we head back to the pit, me crawling, as usual, I turn back. Brad and the other three are far ahead. I stand up. My leg is much better. I limp, but I go much faster this way. Of course I've got two of them with me.

I push and push at the boat. The two help. I wonder if they realize what they're doing.

And then the sun is on the horizon again.

"Hey, look." And off they run.

The surf is up. The tide is in. I do it. I give the boat one last push. I get in and row away as fast as I can.

How beautiful it is in the moonlight. Wouldn't you think whatever it is I'm looking for would be found on a beach just like this? But now I'm thinking maybe prison or a nunnery would be better. I'd like a regimented life with bells to tell me what to do and when. Why didn't I think of that before I took off that first time? I can't wait to get into a cell of some sort.

I'm going to land somewhere with mountains. Or if I should happen to land on Coney Island, or some such place back in civilization, I'm going to commit a crime and go to jail.

When he finds me gone off with his boat, Brad will have more tales to tell about how bad all women are and I guess they are if I'm an example. But I wouldn't have gone without him if he hadn't been so mad at women in general, or if he'd listened to me just once.

Brad! How ridiculous can you get? But Melody . . . It's ridiculous, too, and I don't really like it much, but I'll keep it. Names can change your life just as much as places can. Maybe a new name is all I needed in the first place. Nobody named Melody would be working in a library.

Special Economics

Maureen F. McHugh

Maureen McHugh recently moved to Austin, Texas, with her husband and two dogs.

She has written four novels and a collection of short stories and does freelance work in the video game industry. Although probably best known for her first novel, the Tiptree Award winner China Mountain Zhang, her short fiction is collected in Mothers & Other Monsters, which was a finalist for a major nongenre award, the Story Prize.

McHugh returns to China with a novelette about a young woman who dreams of a better life.

J ieling set up her boom box in a plague-trash market in the part where people sold parts for cars. She had been in the city of Shenzhen for a little over two hours but she figured she would worry about a job tomorrow. Everybody knew you could get a job in no time in Shenzhen. Jobs everywhere.

"What are you doing?" a guy asked her.

"I am divorced," she said. She had always thought of herself as a person who would one day be divorced so it didn't seem like a big stretch to claim it. Staying married to one person was boring. She figured she was too complicated for that. Interesting people had complicated lives. "I'm looking for a job. But I do hip-hop, too," she explained.

"Hip-hop?" He was a middle-aged man with stubble on his chin who looked as if he wasn't looking for a job but should be.

"Not like Shanghai," she said, "not like Hi-Bomb. They do gangsta stuff, which I don't like. Old-fashioned. Like M.I.A.," she said. "Except not political, of course." She gave a big smile. This was all way beyond the guy. Jieling started the boom box. M.I.A. was Maya Arulpragasam, a Sri Lankan hip-hop artist who had started all on her own years ago. She had sung, she had danced, she had done her own videos. Of course M.I.A. lived in London, which made it easier to do hip-hop and become famous.

Jieling had no illusions about being a hip-hop singer, but it had been a good way to make some cash up north in Baoding where she came from. Set up in a plague-trash market and dance for yuan.

Jieling did her opening, her own hip-hop moves, a little like Maya and a little like some things she had seen on MTV, but not too sexy because Chinese people did not throw you money if you were too sexy. Only April and it was already hot and humid.

> Ge down, ge down,
> lang-a-lang-a-lang-a.
> Ge down, ge down
> lang-a-lang-a-lang-a

She had borrowed the English. It sounded very fresh. Very criminal.

The guy said, "How old are you?"

"Twenty-two," she said, adding three years to her age, still dancing and singing.

Maybe she should have told him she was a widow? Or an orphan? But there were too many orphans and widows after so many people died in the bird flu plague. There was no margin in that. Better to be divorced. He didn't throw any money at her, just flicked open his cell phone to check listings from the market for plague trash. This plague-trash market was so big it was easier to check online, even if you were standing right in the middle of it. She needed a new cell phone. Hers had finally fallen apart right before she headed south.

Shenzhen people were apparently too jaded for hip-hop. She made fifty-two yuan, which would pay for one night in a bad hotel where country people washed cabbage in the communal sink.

The market was full of secondhand stuff. When over a quarter of a billion people died in four years, there was a lot of secondhand stuff. But there was still a part of the market for new stuff and street food, and that's where Jieling found the cell phone seller. He had a cart with stacks of flat plastic cell phone kits printed with circuits and scored. She flipped through: tiger-striped, peonies (old-lady phones), metallics (old-man phones), animé characters, moon phones, expensive lantern phones. "Where is your printer?" she asked.

"At home," he said. "I print them up at home, bring them here. No electricity here." Up north in Baoding she'd always bought them in a store where they let you pick your pattern online and then printed them there. More to pick from.

On the other hand, he had a whole boxful of ones that hadn't sold that he would let go for cheap. In the stack she found a purple one with kittens that wasn't too bad. Very Japanese, which was also very fresh this year. And only a hundred yuan for phone and three hundred minutes.

He took the flat plastic sheet from her and dropped it in a pot of boiling water big enough to make dumplings. The hinges embedded in the sheet were made of plastic with molecular memory, and when they got hot they bent and the plastic folded into a rough cell phone shape. He fished the phone out of the water with tongs, let it sit for a moment, and then pushed all the seams together so they snapped. "Wait about an hour for it to dry before you use it," he said and handed her the warm phone.

"An *hour*," she said. "I need it now. I need a job."

He shrugged. "Probably okay in half an hour," he said.

She bought a newspaper and scallion pancake from a street food vendor, sat on a curb, and ate while her phone dried. The paper had some job listings, but it also had a lot of listings from recruiters. ONE MONTH BONUS PAY! BEST JOBS! and NUMBER ONE JOBS! START BONUS! People scowled at her for sitting on the curb. She looked like a farmer but what else was she supposed to do? She checked listings on her new cell phone. Online there were a lot more listings than in the paper. It was a good sign. She picked one at random and called.

The woman at the recruiting office was a flat-faced southerner with buckteeth. Watermelon-picking teeth. But she had a manicure and a very nice red suit. The office was not so nice. It was small and the furniture was old. Jieling was groggy from a night spent at a hotel on the edge of the city. It had been cheap but very loud.

The woman was very sharp in the way she talked and had a strong accent that made it hard to understand her. Maybe Fujian, but Jieling wasn't sure. The recruiter had Jieling fill out an application.

"Why did you leave home?" the recruiter asked.

"To get a good job," Jieling said.

"What about your family? Are they alive?"

"My mother is alive. She is remarried," Jieling said. "I wrote it down."

The recruiter pursed her lips. "I can get you an interview on Friday," she said.

"Friday!" Jieling said. It was Tuesday. She had only three hundred yuan left out of the money she had brought. "But I need a job!"

The recruiter looked sideways at her. "You have made a big gamble to come to Shenzhen."

"I can go to another recruiter," Jieling said.

The recruiter tapped her lacquered nails. "They will tell you the same thing," she said.

Jieling reached down to pick up her bag.

"Wait," the recruiter said. "I do know of a job. But they only want girls of very good character."

Jieling put her bag down and looked at the floor. Her character was fine. She was not a loose girl, whatever this woman with her big front teeth thought.

"Your Mandarin is very good. You say you graduated with high marks from high school," the recruiter said.

"I liked school," Jieling said, which was only partly not true. Everybody here had terrible Mandarin. They all had thick southern accents. Lots of people spoke Cantonese in the street.

"Okay. I will send you to ShinChi for an interview. I cannot get you an interview before tomorrow. But you come here at eight AM and I will take you over there."

ShinChi. New Life. It sounded very promising. "Thank you," Jieling said. "Thank you very much."

But outside in the heat, she counted her money and felt a creeping fear. She called her mother.

Her stepfather answered, *"Wei."*

"Is Ma there?" she asked.

"Jieling!" he said. "Where are you!"

"I'm in Shenzhen," she said, instantly impatient with him. "I have a job here."

"A job! When are you coming home?"

He was always nice to her. He meant well. But he drove her nuts. "Let me talk to Ma," she said.

"She's not here," her stepfather said. "I have her phone at work. But she's not there, either. She went to Beijing last weekend and she's shopping for fabric now."

Her mother had a little tailoring business. She went to Beijing every few months and looked at clothes in all the good stores. She didn't buy in Beijing; she just remembered. Then she came home, bought fabric, and sewed copies. Her stepfather had been born in Beijing and Jieling thought that was part of the reason her mother had married him. He was more like her mother than her father had been. There was nothing in particular wrong with him. He just set her teeth on edge.

"I'll call back later," Jieling said.

"Wait, your number is blocked," her stepfather said. "Give me your number."

"I don't even know it yet," Jieling said and hung up.

The New Life company was in a huge, modern-looking building with a lot of windows. Inside it was full of reflective surfaces and very clean. Sounds echoed in the lobby. A man in a very smart gray suit met Jieling and the recruiter, and the recruiter's red suit looked cheaper, her glossy fingernails too red, her buckteeth exceedingly large. The man in the smart gray suit was short and slim and very southern looking. Very city.

Jieling took some tests on her math and her written characters and got good scores.

To the recruiter, the human resources man said, "Thank you, we will send you your fee." To Jieling he said, "We can start you on Monday."

"Monday?" Jieling said. "But I need a job now!" He looked grave. "I . . . I came from Baoding, in Hebei," Jieling explained. "I'm staying in a hotel, but I don't have much money."

The human resources man nodded. "We can put you up in our guest house," he said. "We can deduct the money from your wages when you start. It's very nice. It has television and air-conditioning, and you can eat in the restaurant."

It was very nice. There were two beds. Jieling put her backpack on the one nearest the door. There was carpeting, and the windows were covered in gold drapes with a pattern of cranes flying across them. The television got stations from Hong Kong. Jieling didn't understand the Cantonese, but there was a button on the remote for subtitles. The movies had lots of violence and more sex than mainland movies did— like the bootleg American movies for sale in the market. She wondered how much this room was. Two hundred yuan? Three hundred?

Jieling watched movies the whole first day, one right after another.

On Monday she began orientation. She was given two pale green uniforms, smocks and pants like medical people wore, and little caps and two pairs of white shoes. In the uniform she looked a little like a model worker—which is to say that the clothes were not sexy and made her look fat. There were two other girls in their green uniforms. They all watched a DVD about the company.

New Life did biotechnology. At other plants they made influenza vaccine (on the screen were banks and banks of chicken eggs), but at this plant they were developing breakthrough technologies in tissue culture. It showed many men in suits. Then it showed a big American store and explained how they were forging new exportation ties with the biggest American corporation for selling goods, Wal-Mart. It also showed a little bit of an American movie about Wal-Mart. Subtitles explained how Wal-Mart was working with companies around the world to improve living standards, decrease CO_2 emissions, and give people low prices. The voice narrating the DVD never really explained the breakthrough technologies.

One of the girls was from way up north; she had a strong northern way of talking.

"How long are you going to work here?" the northern girl asked. She looked as if she might even have some Russian in her.

"How long?" Jieling said.

"I'm getting married," the northern girl confided. "As soon as I make enough money, I'm going home. If I haven't made enough money in a year," she went on, "I'm going home anyway."

Jieling hadn't really thought she would work here long. She didn't know exactly what she would do, but she figured that a big city like Shenzhen was a good place to find out. This girl's plans seemed very . . . country. No wonder southern Chinese thought northerners had to wipe the pigshit off their feet before they got on the train.

"Are you Russian?" Jieling asked.

"No," said the girl. "I'm Manchu."

"Ah," Jieling said. Manchu like Manchurian. Ethnic Minority. Jieling had gone to school with a boy who was classified as Manchu, which meant that he was allowed to have two children when he got married. But he had looked Han Chinese like everyone else. This girl had the hook nose and the dark skin of a Manchu. Manchu used to rule China until the Communist Revolution (there was something in between with Sun Yat-sen but Jieling's history teachers had bored her to tears). Imperial and countrified.

Then a man came in from human resources.

"There are many kinds of stealing," he began. "There is stealing of money or food. And there is stealing of ideas. Here at New Life, our ideas are like gold, and we guard against having them stolen. But you will learn many secrets, about what we are doing, about how we do things. This is necessary as you do your work. If you tell our secrets, that is theft. And we will find out." He paused here and looked at them in what was clearly intended to be a very frightening way.

Jieling looked down at the ground because it was like watching someone overact. It was embarrassing. Her new shoes were very white and clean.

Then he outlined the prison terms for industrial espionage. Ten, twenty years in prison. "China must take its place as an innovator on the world stage and so must respect the laws of intellectual property," he intoned. It was part of the modernization of China, where technology was a new future—Jieling put on her I-am-a-good-girl face. It was like politics class. Four modernizations. Six goals. Sometimes when she was a little girl, and she was riding behind her father on his bike to school, he would pass a billboard with a saying about traffic safety and begin to recite quotes from Mao. *The force at the core of the revolution is the people!* He would tuck his chin in when he did this and use a very serious voice, like a movie or like opera. *Western experience for Chinese uses.* Some of them she had learned from him. *All reactionaries are paper tigers!* she would chant with him, trying to make her voice deep. *Be resolute, fear no sacrifice, and surmount every difficulty to win victory!* And then she would start giggling and he would glance over his shoulder and grin at her. He had been a Red Guard when he was young, but other than this, he never talked about it.

After the lecture, they were taken to be paired with workers who would train them. At least she didn't have to go with the Manchu girl, who was led off to shipping.

She was paired with a very small girl in one of the culture rooms. "I am Baiyue," the girl said. Baiyue was so tiny, only up to Jieling's shoulder, that her green scrubs swamped her. She had pigtails. The room where they worked was filled with rows and rows of what looked like wide drawers. Down the center of the room was a long table with petri dishes and trays and lab equipment. Jieling didn't know what some of it was and that was a little nerve-racking. All up and down the room, pairs of girls in green worked at either the drawers or the table.

"We're going to start cultures," Baiyue said. "Take a tray and fill it with those." She pointed to a stack of petri dishes. The bottom of each dish was filled with gelatin. Jieling took a tray and did what Baiyue did. Baiyue was serious but not at all sharp or superior. She explained that what they were doing was seeding the petri dishes with cells.

"Cells?" Jieling asked.

"Nerve cells from the electric ray. It's a fish."

They took swabs and Baiyue showed her how to put the cells on in a zigzag motion so that most of the gel was covered. They did six trays full of petri dishes. They didn't smell fishy. Then they used pipettes to put in feeding solution. It was all pleasantly scientific without being very difficult.

At one point everybody left for lunch but Baiyue said they couldn't go until they got the cultures finished or the batch would be ruined. Women shuffled by them and Jieling's stomach growled. But when the lab was empty Baiyue smiled and said, "Where are you from?"

Baiyue was from Fujian. "If you ruin a batch," she explained, "you have to pay out of your paycheck. I'm almost out of debt and when I get clear"— she glanced around and dropped her voice a little—"I can quit."

"Why are you in debt?" Jieling asked. Maybe this was harder than she thought; maybe Baiyue had screwed up in the past.

"Everyone is in debt," Baiyue said. "It's just the way they run things. Let's get the trays in the warmers."

The drawers along the walls opened out, and inside the temperature was kept blood-warm. They loaded the trays into the drawers, one back and one front, going down the row until they had the morning's trays all in.

"Okay," Baiyue said, "that's good. We'll check trays this afternoon. I've got a set for transfer to the tissue room but we'll have time after we eat."

Jieling had never eaten in the employee cafeteria, only in the guest house restaurant, and only the first night because it was expensive. Since then she had been living on ramen noodles and she was starved for a good meal. She smelled garlic and pork. First thing on the food line was a pan of steamed pork buns, fluffy white. But Baiyue headed off to a place at the back where there was a huge pot of congee—rice porridge—kept hot. "It's the cheapest thing in the cafeteria," Baiyue explained, "and you can eat all you want." She dished up a big bowl of it—a lot of congee for a girl her size—and added some salt, vegetables, and boiled peanuts. "It's pretty good, although usually by lunch it's been sitting a little while. It gets a little gluey."

Jieling hesitated. Baiyue had said she was in debt. Maybe she had to eat this stuff. But Jieling wasn't going to have old rice porridge for lunch. "I'm going to get some rice and vegetables," she said.

Baiyue nodded. "Sometimes I get that. It isn't too bad. But stay away from anything with shrimp in it. Soooo expensive."

Jieling got rice and vegetables and a big pork bun. There were two fish dishes and a pork dish with monkeybrain mushrooms but she decided she could maybe have the pork for dinner. There was no cost written on anything. She gave her *danwei* card to the woman at the end of the line, who swiped it and handed it back.

"How much?" Jieling asked.

The woman shrugged. "It comes out of your food allowance."

Jieling started to argue but across the cafeteria, Baiyue was waving her arm in the sea of green scrubs to get Jieling's attention. Baiyue called from a table. "Jieling! Over here!"

Baiyue's eyes got very big when Jieling sat down. "A pork bun."

"Are they really expensive?" Jieling asked.

Baiyue nodded. "Like gold. And so good."

Jieling looked around at other tables. Other people were eating the pork and steamed buns and everything else.

"Why are you in debt?" Jieling asked.

Baiyue shrugged. "Everyone is in debt," she said. "Just most people have given up. Everything costs here. Your food, your dormitory, your uniforms. They always make sure that you never earn anything."

"They can't do that!" Jieling said.

Baiyue said, "My granddad says it's like the old days, when you weren't allowed to quit your job. He says I should shut up and be happy. That they take good care of me. Iron rice bowl."

"But, but, but," Jieling dredged the word up from some long-forgotten class, "that's *feudal!*"

Baiyue nodded. "Well, that's my granddad. He used to make my brother and me kowtow to him and my grandmother at Spring Festival." She frowned and wrinkled her nose. Country customs. Nobody in the city made their children kowtow at New Year's. "But you're lucky," Baiyue said to Jieling. "You'll have your uniform debt and dormitory fees, but you haven't started on food debt or anything."

Jieling felt sick. "I stayed in the guest house for four days," she said. "They said they would charge it against my wages."

"Oh." Baiyue covered her mouth with her hand. After a moment, she said, "Don't worry, we'll figure something out." Jieling felt more frightened by that than anything else.

Instead of going back to the lab they went upstairs and across a connecting bridge to the dormitories. Naps? Did they get naps?

"Do you know what room you're in?" Baiyue asked.

Jieling didn't. Baiyue took her to ask the floor auntie, who looked up Jieling's name and gave her a key and some sheets and a blanket. Back down the hall and around the corner. The room was spare but really nice. Two bunk beds and two chests of drawers, a concrete floor. It had a window. All of the beds were taken except one of the top ones. By the window under the desk were three black boxes hooked to the wall. They were a little bigger than a shoe box. Baiyue flipped open the front of each one. They had names written on them. "Here's a space where we can put your battery." She pointed to an electrical extension.

"What are they?" Jieling said.

"They're the battery boxes. It's what we make. I'll get you one that failed inspection. A lot of them work fine," Baiyue said. "Inside there are electric ray cells to make electricity and symbiotic bacteria. The bacteria breaks down garbage to feed the ray cells. Garbage turned into electricity. Anti-global-warming. No greenhouse gas. You have to feed scraps from the cafeteria a couple of times a week or it will die, but it does best if you feed it a little bit every day."

"It's alive?" Jieling said.

Baiyue shrugged. "Yeah. Sort of. Supposedly if it does really well, you get credits for the electricity it generates. They charge us for our electricity use, so this helps hold down debt."

The three boxes just sat there looking less alive than a boom box.

"Can you see the cells?" Jieling asked.

Baiyue shook her head. "No, the feed mechanism doesn't let you. They're just like the ones we grow, though, only they've been worked on in the tissue room. They added bacteria."

"Can it make you sick?"

"No, the bacteria can't live in people." Baiyue said. "Can't live anywhere except in the box."

"And it makes electricity?"

Baiyue nodded.

"And people can buy it?"

She nodded again. "We've just started selling them. They say they're going to sell them in China but really, they're too expensive. Americans like them, you know, because of the no-global-warming. Of course, Americans buy anything."

The boxes were on the wall between the beds, under the window, pretty near where the pillows were on the bottom bunks. She hadn't minded the cells in the lab, but this whole thing was too creepy.

Jieling's first paycheck was startling. She owed 1,974 RMB. Almost four months' salary if she never ate or bought anything and if she didn't have a dorm room. She went back to her room and climbed into her bunk and looked at the figures. Money deducted for uniforms and shoes, food, her time in the guest house.

Her roommates came chattering in a group. Jieling's roommates all worked in packaging. They were nice enough, but they had been friends before Jieling moved in.

"Hey," called Taohua. Then seeing what Jieling had. "Oh, first paycheck."

Jieling nodded. It was like getting a jail sentence.

"Let's see. Oh, not so bad. I owe three times that," Taohua said. She passed the statement on to the other girls. All the girls owed huge amounts. More than a year.

"Don't you care?" Jieling said.

"You mean like little Miss Lei Feng?" Taohua asked. Everyone laughed and Jieling laughed, too, although her face heated up. Miss Lei Feng was what they called Baiyue. Little Miss Goody-Goody. Lei Feng, the famous do-gooder soldier who darned his friend's socks on the Long March. He was nobody when he was alive, but when he died, his diary listed all the anonymous good deeds he had done and then he became a hero. Lei Feng posters hung in elementary schools. He wanted to be "a revolutionary screw that never rusts." It was the kind of thing everybody's grandparents had believed in.

"Does Baiyue have a boyfriend?" Taohua asked, suddenly serious.

"No, no!" Jieling said. It was against the rules to have a boyfriend and Baiyue was always getting in trouble for breaking rules. Things like not having her trays stacked by five PM although nobody else got in trouble for that.

"If she had a boyfriend," Taohua said, "I could see why she would want to quit. You can't get married if you're in debt. It would be too hard."

"Aren't you worried about your debt?" Jieling asked.

Taohua laughed. "I don't have a boyfriend. And besides, I just got a promotion so soon I'll pay off my debt."

"You'll have to stop buying clothes," one of the other girls said. The company store did have a nice catalog you could order clothes from, but they were expensive. There was debt limit, based on your salary. If you were promoted, your debt limit would go up.

"Or I'll go to special projects," Taohua said. Everyone knew what special projects was, even though it was supposed to be a big company secret. They were computers made of bacteria. They looked a lot like the boxes in the dormitory rooms. "I've been studying computers," Taohua explained. "Bacterial computers are special. They do many things. They can detect chemicals. They are *massively* parallel."

"What does that mean?" Jieling asked.

"It is hard to explain," Taohua said evasively.

Taohua opened her battery and poured in scraps. It was interesting that Taohua claimed not to care about her debt but kept feeding her battery. Jieling had a battery now, too. It was a reject—the back had broken so that the metal things that sent the electricity back out were exposed and if you touched it wrong, it could give you a shock. No problem, since Jieling had plugged it into the wall and didn't plan to touch it again.

"Besides," Taohua said, "I like it here a lot better than at home."

Better than home. In some ways yes, in some ways no. What would it be like to just give up and belong to the company. Nice things, nice food. Never rich. But never poor, either. Medical care. Maybe it wasn't the worst thing. Maybe Baiyue was a little . . . obsessive.

"I don't care about my debt," Taohua said, serene. "With one more promotion, I'll move to cadres housing."

Jieling reported the conversation to Baiyue. They were getting incubated cells ready to move to the tissue room. In the tissue room they'd be transferred to a protein-and-collagen grid that would guide their growth—line up the cells to approximate an electricity-generating system. The tissue room had a weird, yeasty smell.

"She's fooling herself," Baiyue said. "Line girls never get to be cadres. She might get onto special projects, but that's even worse than regular line work because you're never allowed to leave the compound." Baiyue picked up a dish, stuck the little volt reader into the gel, and rapped the dish smartly against the lab table: *rap*. The needle on the volt gauge swung to indicate that the cells had discharged electricity. That was the way they tested the cells: A shock made them discharge, and the easiest way was to knock them against the table.

Baiyue could sound very bitter about New Life. Jieling didn't like the debt, it scared her a little. But really, Baiyue saw only one side of everything. "I thought you got a pay raise to go to special projects," Jieling said.

Baiyue rolled her eyes. "And more reasons to go in debt, I'll bet."

"How much is your debt?" Jieling asked.

"Still seven hundred," Baiyue said. "Because they told me I had to have new uniforms." She sighed.

"I am so sick of congee," Jieling said. "They're never going to let us get out of debt." Baiyue's way was doomed. She was trying to play by the company's rules and still win. That wasn't Jieling's way. "We have to make money somewhere else," Jieling said.

"Right," Baiyue said. "We work six days a week." And Baiyue often stayed after shift to try to make sure she didn't lose wages on failed cultures. "Out of spec," she said and put it aside. She had taught Jieling to keep the "out of specs" for a day. Sometimes they improved and could be shipped on. It wasn't the way the supervisor, Ms. Wang, explained the job to Jieling, but it cut down on the number of rejects, and that, in turn, cut down on paycheck deductions.

"That leaves us Sundays," Jieling said.

"I can't leave compound this Sunday."

"And if you do, what are they going to do, fire you?" Jieling said.

"I don't think we're supposed to earn money outside of the compound," Baiyue said.

"You are too much of a good girl," Jieling said. "Remember, *it doesn't matter if the cat is black or white, as long as it catches mice.*"

"Is that Mao?" Baiyue asked, frowning.

"No," Jieling said, "Deng Xiaoping, the one after Mao."

"Well, he's dead, too," Baiyue said. She rapped a dish against the counter and the needle on the voltmeter jumped.

Jieling had been working just over four weeks when they were all called to the cafeteria for a meeting. Mr. Cao from human resources was there. He was wearing a dark suit and standing at the white screen. Other cadres sat in chairs along the back of the stage, looking very stern.

"We are here to discuss a very serious matter," he said. "Many of you know this girl."

There was a laptop hooked up and a very nervous-looking boy running it. Jieling looked carefully at the laptop, but it didn't appear to be a special projects computer. In fact, it was made in Korea. He did something and an ID picture of a girl flashed on the screen.

Jieling didn't know her. But around her she heard noises of shock, someone sucking air through their teeth, someone else breathing softly *Ai-yah*.

"This girl ran away, leaving her debt with New Life. She ate our food, wore our clothes, slept in our beds. And then, like a thief, she ran away." The human resources man nodded his head. The boy at the computer changed the image on the big projector screen.

Now it was a picture of the same girl with her head bowed, and two policemen holding her arms.

"She was picked up in Guangdong," the human resources man said. "She is in jail there."

The cafeteria was very quiet.

The human resources man said, "Her life is ruined, which is what should happen to all thieves."

Then he dismissed them. That afternoon, the picture of the girl with the two policemen appeared on the bulletin boards of every floor of the dormitory.

On Sunday, Baiyue announced, "I'm not going."

She was not supposed to leave the compound, but one of her roommates had female problems—bad cramps—and planned to spend the day in bed drinking tea and reading magazines. Baiyue was going to use her ID to leave.

"You have to," Jieling said. "You want to grow old here? Die a serf to New Life?"

"It's crazy. We can't make money dancing in the plague-trash market."

"I've done it before," Jieling said. "You're scared."

"It's just not a good idea," Baiyue said.

"Because of the girl they caught in Guangdong. We're not skipping out on our debt. We're paying it off."

"We're not supposed to work for someone else when we work here," Baiyue said.

"Oh, come on," Jieling said. "You are always making things sound worse than they are. I think you like staying here being little Miss Lei Feng."

"Don't call me that," Baiyue snapped.

"Well, don't act like it. New Life is not being fair. We don't have to be fair. What are they going to do to you if they catch you?"

"Fine me," Baiyue said. "Add to my debt!"

"So what? They're going to find a way to add to your debt no matter what. You are a serf. They are the landlord."

"But if—"

"No but if," Jieling said. "You like being a martyr. I don't."

"What do you care," Baiyue said. "You like it here. If you stay you can eat pork buns every night."

"And you can eat congee for the rest of your life. I'm going to try to do something." Jieling slammed out of the dorm room. She had never said harsh things to Baiyue before. Yes, she had thought about staying here. But was that so bad? Better than being like Baiyue, who would stay here and have a miserable life. Jieling was not going to have a miserable life, no matter where she stayed or what she did. That was why she had come to Shenzhen in the first place.

She heard the door open behind her and Baiyue ran down the hall. "Okay," she said breathlessly. "I'll try it. Just this once."

The streets of Shenzhen were incredibly loud after weeks in the compound. In a shop window, she and Baiyue stopped and watched a news segment on how the fashion in Shenzhen was for sarongs. Jieling would have to tell her mother. Of course her mother had a TV and probably already knew. Jieling thought about calling, but not now. Not now.

She didn't want to explain about New Life. The next news segment was about the success of the People's Army in Tajikistan. Jieling pulled Baiyue to come on.

They took one bus, and then had to transfer. On Sundays, unless you were lucky, it took forever to transfer because fewer buses ran. They waited almost an hour for the second bus. That bus was almost empty when they got on. They sat down a few seats back from the driver. Baiyue rolled her eyes. "Did you see the guy in the back?" she asked. "Party functionary."

Jieling glanced over her shoulder and saw him. She couldn't miss him in his careful polo shirt. He had that stiff party-member look.

Baiyue sighed. "My uncle is just like that. So *boring*."

Jieling thought that to be honest, Baiyue would have made a good revolutionary, back in the day. Baiyue liked that kind of revolutionary purity. But she nodded.

The plague-trash market was full on a Sunday. There was a toy seller making tiny little clay figures on sticks. He waved a stick at the girls as they passed. "Cute things!" he called. "I'll make whatever you want!" The stick had a little Donald Duck on it.

"I can't do this," Baiyue said. "There's too many people."

"It's not so bad," Jieling said. She found a place for the boom box. Jieling had brought them to where all the food vendors were. "Stay here and watch this," she said. She hunted through the food stalls and bought a bottle of local beer, counting out from the little hoard of money she had left from when she'd come. She took the beer back to Baiyue. "Drink this," she said. "It will help you be brave."

"I hate beer," Baiyue said.

"Beer or debt," Jieling said.

While Baiyue drank the beer, Jieling started the boom box and did her routine. People smiled at her but no one put any money in her cash box. Shenzhen people were so cheap. Baiyue sat on the curb, nursing her beer, not looking at Jieling or at anyone until finally Jieling couldn't stand it any longer.

"C'mon, *meimei*," she said.

Baiyue seemed a bit surprised to be called little sister but she put the beer down and got up. They had practiced a routine to an M.I.A. song, singing and dancing. It would be a hit, Jieling was sure.

"I can't," Baiyue whispered.

"Yes you can," Jieling said. "You do good."

A couple of people stopped to watch them arguing, so Jieling started the music.

"I feel sick," Baiyue whimpered.

But the beat started and there was nothing to do but dance and sing. Baiyue was so nervous, she forgot at first, but then she got the hang of it. She kept her head down and her face was bright red.

Jieling started making up a rap. She'd never done it before and she hadn't gotten very far before she was laughing and then Baiyue was laughing, too.

> *Wode meimei hen haixiude*
> *Mei ta shi xuli*
> *tai hen xiuqi—*

> My little sister is so shy
> But she's pretty
> Far too delicate—

They almost stopped because they were giggling but they kept dancing and Jieling went back to the lyrics from the song they had practiced.

When they had finished, people clapped and they'd made thirty-two yuan.

They didn't make as much for any single song after that, but in a few hours they had collected 187 yuan. It was early evening and night entertainers were showing up—a couple of people who sang opera, ac-robats, and a clown with a wig of hair so red it looked on fire, stepping stork-legged on stilts waving a rubber Kalashnikov in his hand. He was all dressed in white. Uncle Death, from cartoons during the plague.

Some of the day vendors had shut down, and new people were showing up who put out a board and some chairs and served sorghum liquor, clear, white, and 150 proof. The crowd was starting to change, too. It was rowdier. Packs of young men dressed in weird combinations of clothes from plague markets—vintage Mao suit jackets and suit pants and peasant shoes. And others, veterans from the Tajikistan conflict, one with an empty trouser leg.

Jieling picked up the boom box and Baiyue took the cash box. Outside the market it wasn't yet dark.

"You are amazing," Baiyue kept saying. "You are such a special girl!"

"You did great," Jieling said. "When I was by myself, I didn't make anything! Everyone likes you because you are little and cute!"

"Look at this! I'll be out of debt before autumn!"

Maybe it was just the feeling that she was responsible for Baiyue, but Jieling said, "You keep it all."

"I can't! I can't! We split it!" Baiyue said.

"Sure," Jieling said. "Then after you get away, you can help me. Just think, if we do this for three more Sundays, you'll pay off your debt."

"Oh, Jieling," Baiyue said. "You really are like my big sister!"

Jieling was sorry she had ever called Baiyue little sister. It was such a country thing to do. She had always suspected that Baiyue wasn't a city girl. Jieling hated the countryside. Grain spread to dry in the road and mother's-elder-sister and father's-younger-brother bringing all the cousins over on the day off. Jieling didn't even know all those country ways to say aunt and uncle. It wasn't Baiyue's fault. And Baiyue had been good to her. She was rotten to be thinking this way.

"Excuse me," said a man. He wasn't like the packs of young men with their long hair and plague clothes. Jieling couldn't place him but he seemed familiar. "I saw you in the market. You were very fun. Very lively."

Baiyue took hold of Jieling's arm. For a moment Jieling wondered if maybe he was from New Life, but she told herself that was crazy. "Thank you," she said. She thought she remembered him putting ten yuan in the box. No, she thought, he was on the bus. The party functionary. The party was checking up on them. Now that was funny. She wondered if he would lecture them on Western ways.

"Are you in the music business?" Baiyue asked. She glanced at Jieling, who couldn't help laughing, snorting through her nose.

The man took them very seriously, though. "No," he said. "I can't help you there. But I like your act. You seem like girls of good character."

"Thank you," Baiyue said. She didn't look at Jieling again, which was good because Jieling knew she wouldn't be able to keep a straight face.

"I am Wei Rongyi. Maybe I can buy you some dinner?" the man asked. He held up his hands. "Nothing romantic. You are so young, it is like you could be daughters."

"You have a daughter?" Jieling asked.

He shook his head. "Not anymore," he said.

Jieling understood. His daughter had died of the bird flu. She felt embarrassed for having laughed at him. Her soft heart saw instantly that he was treating them like the daughter he had lost.

He took them to a dumpling place on the edge of the market and ordered half a kilo of crescent-shaped pork dumplings and a kilo of square beef dumplings. He was a cadre, a middle manager. His wife had lived in Changsha for a couple of years now, where her family was from. He was from the older generation, people who did not get divorced. All around them, the restaurant was filling up, mostly with men stopping after work for dumplings and drinks. They were a little island surrounded by truck drivers and men who worked in the factories in the outer city—tough, grimy places.

"What do you do? Are you secretaries?" Wei Rongyi asked.

Baiyue laughed. "As if!" she said.

"We are factory girls," Jieling said. She dunked a dumpling in vinegar. They were so good! Not congee!

"Factory girls!" he said. "I am so surprised!"

Baiyue nodded. "We work for New Life," she explained. "This is our day off, so we wanted to earn a little extra money."

He rubbed his head, looking off into the distance. "New Life," he said, trying to place the name. "New Life . . ."

"Out past the zoo," Baiyue said.

Jieling thought they shouldn't say so much.

"Ah, in the city. A good place? What do they make?" he asked. He had a way of blinking very quickly that was disconcerting.

"Batteries," Jieling said. She didn't say bio-batteries.

"I thought they made computers," he said.

"Oh yes," Baiyue said. "Special projects."

Jieling glared at Baiyue. If this guy gave them trouble at New Life, they'd have a huge problem getting out of the compound.

Baiyue blushed.

Wei laughed. "You are special project girls, then. Well, see, I knew you were not just average factory girls."

He didn't press the issue. Jieling kept waiting for him to make some sort of move on them. Offer to buy them beer. But he didn't, and when they had finished their dumplings, he gave them the leftovers to take back to their dormitories and then stood at the bus stop until they were safely on their bus.

"Are you sure you will be all right?" he asked them when the bus came.

"You can see my window from the bus stop," Jieling promised. "We will be fine."

"Shenzhen can be a dangerous city. You be careful!"

Out the window, they could see him in the glow of the streetlight, waving as the bus pulled away.

"He was so nice." Baiyue sighed. "Poor man."

"Didn't you think he was a little strange?" Jieling asked.

"Everybody is strange now," Baiyue said. "After the plague. Not like when we were growing up."

It was true. Her mother was strange. Lots of people were crazy from so many people dying. Jieling held up the leftover dumplings. "Well, anyway. I am not feeding this to my battery," she said. They both tried to smile.

"Our whole generation is crazy," Baiyue said.

"We know everybody dies," Jieling said. Outside the bus window, the streets were full of young people, out trying to live while they could.

They made all their bus connections as smooth as silk. So quick, they were home in forty-five minutes. Sunday night was movie night, and all of Jieling's roommates were at the movie so she and Baiyue could sort the money in Jieling's room. She used her key card and the door clicked open.

Mr. Wei was kneeling by the battery boxes in their room. He started and hissed, "Close the door!"

Jieling was so surprised she did.

"Mr. Wei!" Baiyue said.

He was dressed like an army man on a secret mission, all in black. He showed them a little black gun. Jieling blinked in surprise. "Mr. Wei!" she said. It was hard to take him seriously. Even all in black, he was still weird Mr. Wei, blinking rapidly behind his glasses.

"Lock the door," he said. "And be quiet."

"The door locks by itself," Jieling explained. "And my roommates will be back soon."

"Put a chair in front of the door," he said and shoved the desk chair toward them. Baiyue pushed it under the door handle. The window was open, and Jieling could see where he had climbed on the desk and left a footprint on Taohua's fashion magazine. Taohua was going to be pissed. And what was Jieling going to say? If anyone found out there was a man in her room, she was going to be in very big trouble.

"How did you get in?" she asked. "What about the cameras?" There were security cameras.

He showed them a little spray can. "Special paint. It just makes things look foggy and dim. Security guards are so lazy these days no one ever checks things out." He paused a moment, clearly disgusted with the lax morality of the day. "Miss Jieling," he said. "Take that screwdriver and finish unscrewing that computer from the wall."

Computer? She realized he meant the battery boxes.

Baiyue's eyes got very big. "Mr. Wei! You're a thief!"

Jieling shook her head. "A corporate spy."

"I am a patriot," he said. "But you young people wouldn't understand that. Sit on the bed." He waved the gun at Baiyue.

The gun was so little it looked like a toy and it was difficult to be afraid, but still Jieling thought it was good that Baiyue sat.

Jieling knelt. It was her box that Mr. Wei had been disconnecting. It was all the way to the right, so he had started with it. She had come to feel a little bit attached to it, thinking of it sitting there, occasionally zapping electricity back into the grid, reducing her electricity costs and her debt. She sighed and unscrewed it. Mr. Wei watched.

She jimmied it off the wall, careful not to touch the contacts. The cells built up a charge, and when they were ready, a switch tapped a membrane and they discharged. It was all automatic and there was no knowing when it was going to happen. Mr. Wei was going to be very upset when he realized that this wasn't a computer.

"Put it on the desk," he said.

She did.

"Now sit with your friend."

Jieling sat down next to Baiyue. Keeping a wary eye on them, he sidled over to the bio-battery. He opened the hatch where they dumped garbage in them, and tried to look in as well as look at them. "Where are the controls?" he asked. He picked it up, his palm flat against the broken back end where the contacts were exposed.

"Tap it against the desk," Jieling said. "Sometimes the door sticks." There wasn't actually a door. But it had just come into her head. She hoped that the cells hadn't discharged in a while.

Mr. Wei frowned and tapped the box smartly against the desktop.

Torpedinidae, the electric ray, can generate a current of two hundred volts for approximately a minute. The power output is close to one kilowatt over the course of the discharge and while this won't kill the average person, it is a powerful shock. Mr. Wei stiffened and fell, clutching the box and spasming wildly. One . . . two . . . three . . . four . . . Mr. Wei was still spasming. Jieling and Baiyue looked at each other. Gingerly, Jieling stepped around Mr. Wei. He had dropped the little gun. Jieling picked it up. Mr. Wei was still spasming. Jieling wondered if he was going to die. Or if he was already dead and the electricity was just making him jump. She didn't want him to die. She looked at the gun and it made her feel even sicker so she threw it out the window.

Finally Mr. Wei dropped the box.

Baiyue said, "Is he dead?"

Jieling was afraid to touch him. She couldn't tell if he was breathing. Then he groaned and both girls jumped.

"He's not dead," Jieling said.

"What should we do?" Baiyue asked.

"Tie him up," Jieling said. Although she wasn't sure what they'd do with him then.

Jieling used the cord to her boom box to tie his wrists. When she grabbed his hands he gasped and struggled feebly. Then she took her pillowcase and cut along the blind end, a space just wide enough that his head would fit through.

"Sit him up," she said to Baiyue.

"You sit him up," Baiyue said. Baiyue didn't want to touch him.

Jieling pulled Mr. Wei into a sitting position. "Put the pillowcase over his head," she said. The pillowcase was like a shirt with no armholes, so when Baiyue pulled it over his head and shoulders, it pinned his arms against his sides and worked something like a straitjacket.

Jieling took his wallet and his identification papers out of his pocket. "Why would someone carry their wallet to a break-in?" she asked. "He has six ID papers. One says he is Mr. Wei."

"Wow," Baiyue said. "Let me see. Also Mr. Ma. Mr. Zhang. Two Mr. Lius and a Mr. Cui."

Mr. Wei blinked, his eyes watering.

"Do you think he has a weak heart?" Baiyue asked.

"I don't know," Jieling said. "Wouldn't he be dead if he did?"

Baiyue considered this.

"Baiyue! Look at all this yuan!" Jieling emptied the wallet, counting. Almost eight thousand yuan!

"Let me go," Mr. Wei said weakly.

Jieling was glad he was talking. She was glad he seemed like he might be all right. She didn't know what they would do if he died. They would never be able to explain a dead person. They would end up in deep debt. And probably go to jail for something. "Should we call the floor auntie and tell her that he broke in?" Jieling asked.

"We could," Baiyue said.

"Do not!" Mr. Wei said, sounding stronger. "You don't understand! I'm from Beijing!"

"So is my stepfather," Jieling said. "Me, I'm from Baoding. It's about an hour south of Beijing."

Mr. Wei said, "I'm from the government! That money is government money!"

"I don't believe you," Jieling said. "Why did you come in through the window?"

"Secret agents always come in through the window?" Baiyue said and started to giggle.

"Because this place is counter-revolutionary!" Mr. Wei said.

Baiyue covered her mouth with her hand. Jieling felt embarrassed, too. No one said things like "counter-revolutionary" anymore.

"This place! It is making things that could make China strong!" he said.

"Isn't that good?" Baiyue asked.

"But they don't care about China! Only about money. Instead of using it for China, they sell it to America!" he said. Spittle was gathering at the corner of his mouth. He was starting to look deranged. "Look at this place! Officials are all concerned about *guanxi*!" Connections. Kickbacks. *Guanxi* ran China, everybody knew that.

"So, maybe you have an anti-corruption investigation?" Jieling said. There were lots of anti-corruption investigations. Jieling's stepfather said that they usually meant someone powerful was mad at their brother-in-law or something, so they accused him of corruption.

Mr. Wei groaned. "There is no one to investigate them."

Baiyue and Jieling looked at each other.

Mr. Wei explained, "In my office, the Guangdong office, there used to be twenty people. Special operatives. Now there is only me and Ms. Yang."

Jieling said, "Did they all die of bird flu?"

Mr. Wei shook his head. "No, they all went to work on contract for Saudi Arabia. You can make a lot of money in the Middle East. A lot more than in China."

"Why don't you and Ms. Yang go work in Saudi Arabia?" Baiyue asked.

Jieling thought Mr. Wei would give some revolutionary speech. But he just hung his head. "She is the secretary. I am the bookkeeper." And then in a smaller voice, "She is going to Kuwait to work for Mr. Liu."

They probably did not need bookkeepers in the Middle East. Poor Mr. Wei. No wonder he was such a terrible secret agent.

"The spirit of the revolution is gone," he said, and there were real, honest-to-goodness tears in his eyes. "Did you know that Tiananmen Square was built by volunteers? People would come after their regular job and lay the paving of the square. Today people look to Hong Kong."

"Nobody cares about a bunch of old men in Beijing," Baiyue said.

"Exactly! We used to have a strong military! But now the military is too worried about their own factories and farms! They want us to pull out of Tajikistan because it is ruining their profits!"

This sounded like a good idea to Jieling, but she had to admit, she hated the news so she wasn't sure why they were fighting in Tajikistan anyway. Something about Muslim terrorists. All she knew about Muslims was that they made great street food.

"Don't you want to be patriots?" Mr. Wei said.

"You broke into my room and tried to steal my—you know that's not a computer, don't you?" Jieling said. "It's a bio-battery. They're selling them to the Americans. Wal-Mart."

Mr. Wei groaned.

"We don't work in special projects," Baiyue said.

"You said you did," he protested.

"We did not," Jieling said. "You just thought that. How did you know this was my room?"

"The company lists all its workers in a directory," he said wearily. "And it's movie night, everyone is either out or goes to the movies. I've had the building under surveillance for weeks. I followed you to the market today. Last week it was a girl named Pingli, who blabbed about everything, but she wasn't in special projects.

"I put you on the bus; I've timed the route three times. I should have had an hour and fifteen minutes to drive over here and get the box and get out."

"We made all our connections," Baiyue explained.

Mr. Wei was so dispirited he didn't even respond.

Jieling said, "I thought the government was supposed to help workers. If we get caught, we'll be fined and we'll be deeper in debt." She was just talking. Talking, talking, talking too much. This was too strange. Like when someone was dying. Something extraordinary was happening, like your father dying in the next room, and yet the ordinary things went on, too. You made tea, your mother opened the shop the next day and sewed clothes while she cried. People came in and pretended not to notice. This was like that. Mr. Wei had broken into their room with a gun and they were explaining about New Life.

"Debt?" Mr. Wei said.

"To the company," she said. "We are all in debt. The company hires us and says they are going to pay us, but then they charge us for our food and our clothes and our dorm and it always costs more than we earn. That's why we were doing rap today. To make money to be able to quit." Mr. Wei's glasses had tape holding the arm on. Why hadn't she noticed that in the restaurant? Maybe because when you are afraid you notice things. When your father is dying of the plague, you notice the way the covers on your mother's chairs need to be washed. You wonder if you will have to do it or if you will die before you have to do chores.

"The Pingli girl," he said, "she said the same thing. That's illegal."

"Sure," Baiyue said. "Like anybody cares."

"Could you expose corruption?" Jieling asked.

Mr. Wei shrugged, at least as much as he could in the pillowcase. "Maybe. But they would just pay bribes to locals and it would all go away."

All three of them sighed.

"Except," Mr. Wei said, sitting up a little straighter. "The Americans. They are always getting upset about that sort of thing. Last year there was a corporation, the Shanghai Six. The Americans did a documentary on them and then Western companies would not do business. If they got information from us about what New Life is doing . . ."

"Who else is going to buy bio-batteries?" Baiyue said. "The company would be in big trouble!"

"Beijing can threaten a big exposé, tell the *New York Times* newspaper!" Mr. Wei said, getting excited. "My Beijing supervisor will love that! He loves media!"

"Then you can have a big show trial," Jieling said.

Mr. Wei was nodding.

"But what is in it for us?" Baiyue said.

"When there's a trial, they'll have to cancel your debt!" Mr. Wei said. "Even pay you a big fine!"

"If I call the floor auntie and say I caught a corporate spy, they'll give me a big bonus," Baiyue said.

"Don't you care about the other workers?" Mr. Wei asked.

Jieling and Baiyue looked at each other and shrugged. Did they? "What are they going to do to you anyway?" Jieling said. "You can still do a big exposé. But that way we don't have to wait."

"Look," he said, "you let me go, and I'll let you keep my money."

Someone rattled the door handle.

"Please," Mr. Wei whispered. "You can be heroes for your fellow workers, even though they'll never know it."

Jieling stuck the money in her pocket. Then she took the papers, too.

"You can't take those," he said.

"Yes I can," she said. "If after six months, there is no big corruption scandal? We can let everyone know how a government secret agent was outsmarted by two factory girls."

"Six months!" he said. "That's not long enough!"

"It better be," Jieling said.

Outside the door, Taohua called, "Jieling? Are you in there? Something is wrong with the door!"

"Just a minute," Jieling called. "I had trouble with it when I came home." To Mr. Wei she whispered sternly, "Don't you try anything. If you do, we'll scream our heads off and everybody will come running." She and Baiyue shimmied the pillowcase off of Mr. Wei's head. He started to stand up and jerked the boom box, which clattered across the floor. "Wait!" she hissed and untied him.

Taohua called through the door, "What's that?"

"Hold on!" Jieling called.

Baiyue helped Mr. Wei stand up. Mr. Wei climbed onto the desk and then grabbed a line hanging outside. He stopped a moment as if trying to think of something to say.

"A revolution is not a dinner party, or writing an essay, or painting a picture, or doing embroidery," Jieling said. It had been her father's favorite quote from Chairman Mao. ". . . it cannot be so refined, so leisurely and gentle, so temperate, kind, courteous, restrained, and magnanimous. A revolution is an insurrection, an act by which one class overthrows another."

Mr. Wei looked as if he might cry and not because he was moved by patriotism. He stepped back and disappeared. Jieling and Baiyue looked out the window. He did go down the wall just like a secret agent from a movie, but it was only two stories. There was still the big footprint in the middle of Taohua's magazine and the room looked as if it had been hit by a storm.

"They're going to think you had a boyfriend," Baiyue whispered to Jieling.

"Yeah," Jieling said, pulling the chair out from under the door handle. "And they're going to think he's rich."

* * *

It was Sunday, and Jieling and Baiyue were sitting on the beach. Jieling's cell phone rang, a little chime of M.I.A. hip-hop. Even though it was Sunday, it was one of the girls from New Life. Sunday should be a day off, but she took the call anyway.

"Jieling? This is Xia Meili? From packaging. Taohua told me about your business? Maybe you could help me?"

Jieling said, "Sure. What is your debt, Meili?"

"Thirty-eight hundred RMB," Meili said. "I know it's a lot."

Jieling said, "Not so bad. We have a lot of people who already have loans, though, and it will probably be a few weeks before I can make you one."

With Mr. Wei's capital, Jieling and Baiyue had opened a bank account. They had bought themselves out, and then started a little loan business where they bought people out of New Life. Then people had to pay them back with a little extra. They each had jobs—Jieling worked for a company that made toys. She sat each day at a table where she put a piece of specially shaped plastic over the body of a little doll, an action figure. The plastic fit right over the figure and had cutouts. Jieling sprayed the whole thing with red paint and when the piece of plastic was lifted, the action figure had a red shirt. It was boring, but at the end of the week, she got paid instead of owing the company money.

She and Baiyue used all their extra money on loans to get girls out of New Life. More and more loans, and more and more payments. Now New Life had sent them a threatening letter saying that what they were doing was illegal. But Mr. Wei said not to worry. Two officials had come and talked to them and had showed them legal documents and had them explain everything about what had happened. Soon, the officials promised, they would take New Life to court.

Jieling wasn't so sure about the officials. After all, Mr. Wei was an official. But a foreign newspaperman had called them. He was from a newspaper called *The Wall Street Journal* and he said that he was writing a story about labor shortages in China after the bird flu. He said that in some places in the West there were reports of slavery. His Chinese was very good. His story was going to come out in the United States tomorrow. Then she figured officials would have to do something or lose face.

Jieling told Meili to call her back in two weeks—although hopefully in two weeks no one would need help to get away from New Life—and wrote a note to herself in her little notebook.

Baiyue was sitting looking at the water. "This is the first time I've been to the beach," she said.

"The ocean is so big, isn't it?"

Baiyue nodded, scuffing at the white sand. "People always say that, but you don't know until you see it."

Jieling said, "Yeah." Funny, she had lived here for months. Baiyue had lived here more than a year. And they had never come to the beach. The beach was beautiful.

"I feel sorry for Mr. Wei," Baiyue said.

"You do?" Jieling said. "Do you think he really had a daughter who died?"

"Maybe," Baiyue said. "A lot of people died."

"My father died," Jieling said.

Baiyue looked at her, a quick little sideways look, then back out at the ocean. "My mother died," she said.

Jieling was surprised. She had never known that Baiyue's mother was dead. They had talked about so much but never about that. She put her arm around Baiyue's waist and they sat for a while.

"I feel bad in a way," Baiyue said.

"How come?" Jieling said.

"Because we had to steal capital to fight New Life. That makes us capitalists."

Jieling shrugged.

"I wish it was like when they fought the revolution," Baiyue said. "Things were a lot more simple."

"Yeah," Jieling said, "and they were poor and a lot of them died."

"I know." Baiyue sighed.

Jieling knew what she meant. It would be nice to . . . to be sure what was right and what was wrong. Although not if it made you like Mr. Wei.

Poor Mr. Wei. Had his daughter really died?

"Hey," Jieling said, "I've got to make a call. Wait right here." She walked a little down the beach. It was windy and she turned her back to protect the cell phone, like someone lighting a match. "Hello," she said, "hello, Mama, it's me. Jieling."

Aka St. Mark's Place

Richard Bowes

Over the last twenty years Richard Bowes has published five novels, the most recent of which is From the Files of the Time Rangers. *The novel* Minions of the Moon *won a Lambda Award.*

His stories have appeared in The Magazine of Fantasy & Science Fiction, SCI FICTION, *and elsewhere. The novella "Streetcar Dreams" won a World Fantasy Award. His story "There's a Hole in the City" won the* storySouth *2006 Million Writers Award for Fiction. His most recent short-fiction collection* Streetcar Dreams and Other Midnight Fancies *was published by PS Publishing in England in 2006.*

Recent and forthcoming stories will be in Electric Velocipede #10 *and* Subterranean *magazine, and* Horror: The Best of the Year, 2006, The Coyote Road: Trickster Tales, *and* So Fey *anthologies.*

Richard Bowes has lived for most of his life in Manhattan. Several of his recent stories have taken place downtown in the Greenwich Village and East Village of his youth, places that have changed drastically over the past thirty years but that live on, forever memorialized by Bowes's vivid imagination.

Part One

Later in life Judy used other names. But she was Judy Finch when she was growing up on St. Mark's Place, which is itself a kind of alias for the three blocks of 8th Street between Third Avenue and Tompkins Square Park.

In the spring of '65 she was fifteen and had what she thought of as her first real boyfriend. Judy was light-haired and blue-eyed. The boy who called himself Ray Light had dark hair, brown eyes, was almost a year older and a bit taller. But their hair was the same length and some days, without planning it, they dressed almost identically.

Sitting on a neighborhood stoop one sunny day they blended into each other, his head resting on her shoulder, her denim-clad legs draped over his, one passing their last cigarette to the other.

Ray Light was not his real name. He'd chosen it just after running away from home. When he talked about that, Judy saw him sitting on the edge of a loading dock in Ohio, waiting for a guy, any guy, to start him on his way to New York City. She thought that being able to do this was another sign that they were in love.

The thin, jumpy man who picked him up, before getting down to business, asked his name. Instead of boring Jonathan Duncan, which he'd been called since birth, out came Ray Light. Later it occurred to both Ray and Judy that this had been prophecy.

Ray came from a very nice suburb of Cincinnati. His family hadn't expected a son who had long hair and wanted to paint, to dance, to play music. What he wanted to do varied from day to day.

When he talked about this, Judy thought his plans were kind of hopeless. She had some idea how these things worked. Her father was the conceptual sculptor Jason Finch. Her mother was the essayist and critic Anna Muir. She was going to study acting.

Ray lived with a guy he called the Man who locked Ray out of his loft on 4th Street every morning as he went to work and let him back in when he came home. When she thought about his situation, something deep inside Judy ached.

Ray had just said, "I'm going to ask the Man to lend me the money to buy a guitar," when she looked up and found this other kid standing there waiting for them to notice him.

"You got a light," the kid asked and wiggled an unlighted Camel. Ray handed him matches and looked right into his face. Judy gave him the once-over.

He lighted up with a little flourish, handed back the book of matches, and said, "The name's BD." They told him their first names. He said he'd just moved into the neighborhood and wanted to know where he could hear music. They told him there were hootenannies in Washington Square and folk rock in little cafés in the East and West Village.

When he asked, "Is there someplace I can score grass?" they both shook their heads, and when he didn't walk away they got up and did just that.

Later they compared notes and both knew immediately that this kid was from the halfway house. His institutional haircut, white T-shirt, sneakers, and jeans were like a uniform.

The halfway house on St. Mark's Place near First Avenue was a place for teenage boys whose parents were enmeshed in the legal system or in the hospital or somehow couldn't or wouldn't take care of them. They followed a type—white, skinny, a little in shock—and they got held there until they could finish high school and go on to college or more likely go into the army. Vietnam was just starting to heat up.

"Is he a nark?" Judy wondered.

"If he's not in the halfway house, he's got one hell of a cover," said Ray.

They walked by Judy's place. Her father's studio occupied the ground floor of a building on the south side of St. Mark's near the corner of Second Avenue. The first floor had once been a barn when it was a tradesman's house, and a horse and cart were kept there.

The barn doors had long ago been cemented shut and had windows cut into them. Her father used it as his studio.

Her mother was away a lot. She was in Madison that week leading a seminar on the works of Kate Chopin. Because her father's studio was too crowded to give him the needed space, he had started to spend a lot of his time upstairs in the living room. He'd rolled up the rug to expose the gleaming parquet floor and had a row of bricks toppled like dominoes in an S-formation. He was working out the exact shape and dynamics of the fallen bricks. There were scrapes on the floor. The building had been bought with her mother's money.

Today Jack Moore from the Museum of Modern Art was there, smoking a cigarette and sipping a scotch. He smiled and said hello to Judy and nodded to Ray.

Jason Finch was forty and looked thirty. He wore a denim work shirt and work boots. When he worked with bricks, with electric wiring, with pipes like in his last piece, Jason Finch always began to act and sound like a blue-collar worker, a union man doing what he got paid to do.

"Hey," he said to Judy while scribbling notes on the back of an envelope. "Did you do that science paper?"

"I finished it in study period and handed it in," she said though she hadn't and Jack Moore, with his cop's face and drinker's nose, chuckled.

"We're going to watch TV," she said. Her father nodded vaguely. One rule bound Judy and Ray's time in the house. She couldn't have him in her room with the door closed.

Ray let her take the lead. They kissed long and hard, as on the screen an actor dressed like a mailman talked to a clown who spoke by holding up voice balloons with words written on them. She switched channels and in another city in the late afternoon, a bunch of boys in three-button jackets and narrow ties and girls in short skirts and long hair danced like it was Saturday night.

The two of them danced a little, giggled and ground against each other. Her father and the critic laughed in the living room.

Another rule limited their time together. Ray had to leave a little before six to be home for the Man. Judy found this tragic and romantic. She usually walked him over to 4th Street.

That day he wanted to leave a little early and chose to take a roundabout route. Usually Ray never wanted to go near the halfway house. That evening he insisted they walk down St. Mark's Place.

Against a brick wall in the twilight, neighborhood boys—some still in parts of their Catholic school uniforms—played handball, Ukrainians against Poles.

Across the street kids from the halfway house leaned on the railings in front of their building and watched. They didn't even speak to each other, much less form teams of their own. Each stood apart from the others and watched the passersby. Behind them, in the ground-floor windows, Judy could see lights on in the dining hall. Ray glanced their way casually but Judy knew he was looking for BD.

The Man lived down on 4th Street between Bowery and Second Avenue on the top floor of a loft building that was still mostly factories. Judy, when she'd first met Ray a couple of months before, would go by there at night and look up at the lights in the windows. That evening they kissed and hugged a few doors down from the place where he lived.

"You were looking for BD," she said.

"I think he's a spotter," Ray told her.

"What?"

"Someone who looks for runaways," he said, gave her one last kiss, and went inside to ring the bell and be allowed upstairs.

Judy stared after him not breathing. She'd never heard him refer to himself as a runaway. For a moment when he'd said it, she'd seen an image of a figure running down the middle of a highway late at night, headlights blasting past him in both directions. And she knew that was his image of himself.

Walking along thinking about that, Judy let herself float on the surface of the city, on the deep smoke of a Ukrainian sausage factory, on a tall woman in tights, a dance skirt, and straight black hair carrying dry cleaning in one hand and a trumpet case in the other, on fire engines blasting up the avenue and the feel of a stray evening sea breeze that hadn't yet picked up city soot and grease.

She was on St. Mark's Place, walking past the Dom, the big old Polish Wedding Hall, when someone said, "Hi." And there was BD right in front of her with a cigarette in his mouth.

Later it occurred to Judy that he could have followed them to where Ray lived and then doubled around to casually encounter her there.

"You're going to be late for dinner," she said indicating the halfway house.

"As long as I'm on time for lights-out they don't care," he said not missing a beat nor in any way surprised that she knew where he lived.

They stood for a moment amid the Slavs and Spanish who came out of the rumbling subway and off buses on their way home from work, students and poets and shambling winos and a pair of old hookers with minds like confetti walking to their beats up on 14th Street. The man who called himself Mr. William Shakespeare, and who dressed in a velvet doublet and red tights, went past them speaking blank verse to himself.

BD said, "You live around here?" and she nodded vaguely in the direction of her house. "With your parents?"

The way he asked made her feel for him a bit. She said, "Mostly with my father, right now."

"What does he do?"

"These days he's mostly a bricklayer."

"That's good work," he said. "My father worked delivering the *Daily News*. He got sick and died and I had a choice of living with family I don't like or coming here."

Judy was surprised that he spoke better than she'd heard him do earlier and that he told her about himself like that. Afterward she would never trust him. But right then, she said good-bye and once indoors thought quite a few times about how his nose was just a little flattened and his T-shirt read in washed-out letters POLICE ATHLETIC LEAGUE GOLDEN GLOVES.

She attended the Quaker high school on Stuyvesant Park, eight blocks up Second Avenue from where she lived. When she came out of there at the end of the day, Ray stood across the street.

He had one foot up behind him and leaned against the antique iron spiked fence that ran around the park, smoking a Marlboro, glancing at passersby. Seeing him in that hustler pose it struck her for the first time how lost he looked.

She crossed the street and took his arm as they walked through Stuyvesant Park. She thought about how he always waited for her to take the lead and imagined this was what he did with the Man.

"That guy BD isn't in the halfway house," he said. "I went by there this morning and asked, and no one had heard of him.

"I knew I was taking a risk. One of the counselors spoke to me. Acted like he thought I'd come in looking for shelter. He's queer. Told me they took runaways. Tried to stop me from leaving and to drag me into the showers before I got away." Judy saw it all as he spoke.

They went arm in arm past the Eastern rite church and strange little stores that shipped packages to Eastern Europe, and stayed on the other side of 10th Street from the gang of psycho, speeding Italian kids that hung around that corner.

He was shaking. They sat on a bench in the St. Mark's in the Bowery churchyard and she held him. "They know I'm here. This morning when I left the house I saw BD, whoever he is, right down the street. They're going to try and take me back home. My parents will institutionalize me."

Ray didn't want to hang around the neighborhood that afternoon. So he and Judy walked in a wide loop over to Greenwich Village, through Washington Square, past coffeehouses and Italian clubs, down streets lined with buildings full of sweatshops, past garages and places you could buy live chickens to kill.

All the way, he talked about what he was going to do. He'd tell the Man what happened, get as much cash as possible, and split. He'd call her when he was on his way and maybe she could meet him and they'd say good-bye.

It was like the center of her world was about to disappear. She offered to hide him in her house, to get her parents' friends to help him.

But he refused. She saw Ray reflected in a mirror wearing just a bathrobe and with his head shaved standing in what looked like a hospital or prison corridor. It was the first time Judy had seen his future. They both knew this was what was going to happen to him.

Both were crying and it was almost dark when they set foot on his block. Nothing was happening: A woman pushed a baby carriage, a super hauled trash to the curb, a couple of drag queens sashayed toward the Club 86 near Second Avenue.

They walked to his door and he turned to kiss her. "I've never known anybody like you. You're part of me. You can see what I'm thinking. You're the only reason I've stayed here."

The door to the building opened and a guy who had been waiting in the hallway came out and grabbed Ray. The car must have been right around the corner because it appeared and stopped directly behind them. The men were big but they didn't hurt anybody. Two of them cuffed Ray and carried him despite his yelling and thrashing to the backseat of the car.

The third blocked Judy from interfering. Deflected her hands, booted aside her kicks. "You shithead," she screamed.

"Now, miss, you shouldn't talk like that," he said and grinned very hard. Then he turned and jumped in the backseat and they tore off down the street.

Judy ran after the car, tried to remember the license but couldn't. She felt Ray's rage and fear. His face was shoved into the seat, his pants got yanked down. A needle was stuck in his butt.

After that he slipped like water through her fingers as she stood on the corner and tried to hold him in her mind and heart. For an instant she had a glimpse, a vision, of three figures against a background of what looked like Technicolor amoebas writhing under a huge microscope.

Judy became aware that a background noise was a man screaming, "I'll kill you sons of bitches! Bring him back! He's radiant! He's the future!"

People on the street who had barely noticed the abduction stared up at the building. She looked and saw a guy with wild hair and eyes, leaning out his window staring at where the car had gone. Judy knew this was the Man and hated him with everything she had in her.

She ran home wanting to lock herself in her room and her mother was there. So were Randolph Crain and Evelyn Killeen, an old married couple, stage actors whom Judy had always liked.

Her father was down in the studio and there was the sound of an electric saw. Her mother was standing on the stairs telling him to come up because they had guests and it was rude. Randolph and Evelyn were saying they understood. And Judy went past them with her hands over her face, ran upstairs, and slammed the bathroom door.

Her mother tried to talk her out. "Honey, I know I've been away and you felt abandoned. But tell me what's wrong so I can help you."

"I'm not your child!" she yelled.

Her father tried next, all quiet emotion as befit an honest working-man. "Judy, tell me who it was that hurt you."

"You couldn't see the one I love when he was in front of you!"

It was Evelyn Killeen who came so silently to the door that Judy didn't know she was there until she spoke. "You lost your young man, honey." Her voice was uncannily youthful. "I read that in you when you rushed past me just now."

Some years later Judy found exactly those lines when she read for the part of Norah, the older sister, in the 1930s romantic comedy *September Fancy*.

That night, though, bundled up in her bathrobe, she told her story to all of them amid tears and hiccups.

Later she heard her mother downstairs in the living room say clearly, "You let her hang around where she could get kidnapped."

Then her father mumbled something unclear. And her mother said, "Your family. They're deranged enough. Your parents told me I was unfit to be a mother."

"*My* parents! Your old man looked like something out of the wax museum."

"His money was good enough to buy this damn place."

The next morning when Judy was on her way to school, her father was heading out the door at the same time as if by coincidence. And, like it was the most normal thing imaginable, he walked to school with her.

And she was so lonely because Ray wasn't there that she let him do that.

BD was on the corner of Second Avenue. The sight of him angered Judy so much that she told her father who he was and how she knew he had turned Ray in.

That afternoon her mother came to the school and took her daughter out of study hall. She had packed two suitcases and said Judy was going on a little vacation with Randolph and Evelyn at their house out in Bucks County.

She was too surprised and distraught to properly protest. Next came her parents' divorce, then a move with her mother to Cambridge, Massachusetts, after which she found herself in school in Vermont. It was a couple of years before she heard from Ray, and even longer before she got more than a glimpse of St. Mark's Place.

Part Two

In the fall of 1968, BD was calling himself Bobby Danton. He liked simple cover names that were easy to remember. He was back in the city where he'd been born and raised, and working the East Village where he had worked before.

BD was twenty-three, looked a couple of years younger, and could, if necessary, shave close, wear a shy smile, and pass for nineteen or even eighteen. It was a handy talent in his line of work.

His hair was only down to his ears. He was growing a beard and mustache both because he had been here before and needed to hide his face and because it was hip.

His stash of grass was top grade and he was generous with it. The employer had rented him an apartment in a third-story walk-up on 7th Street around the corner from Tompkins Square Park.

One Monday morning that October, he was having a little morning-after toss in bed with Rachel, a waitress from Stanley's bar on St. Mark's. They'd met the night before. He did some grunting, she moaned, and the noise attracted the attention of Marlene, his six-year-old German shepherd, who scratched at the door and barked three times.

When he came back from giving Marlene food and water and promising her a good long walk, Rachel was sitting up and lighting a joint. She was a singer. This morning she looked a little older than he'd guessed. "Your dog's a jealous bitch," she said but smiled nicely.

Aside from the big, secondhand bed, the room contained nothing but a used dresser with a lamp on it and a night table with a clock and a radio. "You don't go in for decoration," she observed, looking around and toking. "Most guys would put up a poster, maybe have a record or two lying around. This is what the artists call austerity."

He remembered that Rachel, with her curly dark hair and ripe body, was also an artist's model. In fact that's what had first made him interested in her at Stanley's. "You know Jason Finch?" he asked. "He does sculpture."

"Jason doesn't come around much anymore. All the artists are up at Max's Kansas City. The Warhol crowd, too. Last year Warhol rented the Dom, that old Polish Wedding Hall upstairs from Stanley's.

"He called the place the Exploding Plastic Inevitable. The Velvet Underground and Nico and all his other freaks were all over the place. Then, poof, he lost interest and they all went uptown. We still got plenty of freaks, just not those ones. How do you know Jason?"

He wanted to say, *I knew his daughter,* but recognized that would be stupid. Part of BD's cover was that he studied architecture at Cooper Union. So he said, "We talked about him in class."

She nodded and pulled her stuff together, got up, and went into the bathroom. She was heftier than he liked, a little older. But beer and gin and grass and a hit or two of hash laced with opium had smoothed the way.

While he waited for his guest to depart, he scratched Marlene's ears the way he'd learned she liked and listened to mandolins and guitars on a distant stereo and car horns blasting on the street outside.

Thinking about Judy Finch reminded him of his last tour in the neighborhood. Back then BD was twenty and just finished with his hitch in the army. The halfway house where he'd ended up when his family had dissolved one day had been good preparation for barracks society. He'd learned how to keep a proper distance, to protect his privacy.

College didn't interest him. When he stopped by the house, a counselor who had known him when he was a resident said a private detective agency was looking for someone they could use for under-cover work.

That was BD's job the day he was trailing Jonathan Duncan. Little Johnny had changed his name to Ray and started living with a chicken hawk. He was sitting on a stoop making out with what looked like his twin but turned out to be a girl. They had an aura BD could still feel but couldn't describe even to himself. He was surprised they hadn't drawn a crowd.

When Rachel had gone, BD slipped a camera into his jacket pocket, clipped the leash onto Marlene's collar, and left for work.

It was a beautiful morning with a lingering chill in the shadows and warmth in the sun. She was almost prancing at the end of her leash. He had inherited Marlene from another agent. They got along well and walking her was a great cover for being out and around.

On Avenue A, just inside the gates of Tompkins Square Park, was a lithe girl with vacant green eyes in a ballet skirt, halter, sandals, and maybe nothing else. She called herself Krazy Kid and he'd seen her a couple of nights before at a loft party on Avenue C.

"Hey, dog man," she said.

He gave Marlene a sit command and she allowed herself to be pet-
ted. "How come your parents named you Krazy Kid?" he asked and the
girl laughed quietly. He guessed that she was, maybe, sixteen and he
didn't even know her real name and had no reason to believe that anyone was looking for her.

All he knew was that she was sweet and the guy he had seen her
hanging on to was a scumbag. He liked to imagine himself rescuing
people.

For the last couple of years while his face faded from local memory,
his employers, Guardian Lamp Investigations ("Lost and runaway children our specialty and our mission"), had him out on loan to a private-
eye firm in the Upper Midwest.

The last place he'd worked was Madison, where his name was
Danny Bremmer and he was a clean-cut army deserter, a simple boy
from Erie, Pennsylvania, hiding out because he didn't want to go to
'Nam. One crash pad passed him along to the next like he was a sacred
relic, and kids got snatched up and returned to their families in his
wake.

The yellow pages ad for the Midwest firm was a drawing of a figure
in what might almost have been a cop's uniform shining a flashlight
into an alley where a teary-eyed, scared little girl huddled. In fact, the
last runaway child he'd helped return (to a family of wealthy aluminum
manufacturers terrified of scandal) was a seventeen-year-old, three-
hundred-pound blob of fat with an insatiable appetite for methedrine
and for whores who'd sit on his face.

When Krazy Kid said good-bye to the German shepherd and then
to him, he went to the dog run and let Marlene off the leash. She
bounded forward, stopped, seemed to watch a slightly stubby dog
with some Doberman in him.

A little farther down the fence, staring through the dogs and trees
and iron lampposts of this ragged-assed old-fashioned park, looking
like he was gazing into the navel of the universe and was not pleased
by what he saw, was a skinny black man with gray hair. He was dressed
in ratty pin-striped dress pants and a turtleneck jersey. On his head was

a broken-down velvet Borsalino that must once have belonged to a pimp.

BD guessed that at one time Chambliss had been that man. Right now, though, what he did mainly was deal, shoot junk, and climb fire escapes to break into the apartments of people who went to work during the day.

BD moved down the fence, keeping his eye on Marlene like that was his concern. When he was close, Chambliss—without shifting his gaze, without moving his mouth—said, "That one you was interested in? Calls herself Aurora?"

Marlene was racing in an improvised pack up a dirt mound and down the other side. A woman called, "Regal!" to the Doberman mix.

Chambliss said, "She's in a political commune on Avenue B and Sixth Street, southeast corner. There's some commie dyke runs it. They got pictures on the windows of Chairman Mao. I seen Aurora out shopping at the bodega around the corner. She does that every morning."

A group of kids barefoot and in tatters came by ringing cowbells and chanting "Hare Krishna." A police cruiser sped across 9th Street with its cherry-top flashing. The kids all screamed, *"Pig"* and gave the cops the finger.

Chambliss said, "I gave you the lead. You owe me twenty."

"Friday." BD just breathed the word but compared with the other man's voice it felt like he was shouting. That was company policy; Chambliss got paid for the week on Friday.

Chambliss was silent for a long moment but BD knew he was going to speak again. He listened to the chants fading, to distant sirens, to the occasional yip and snarl from the dog run.

Then he heard, "I hear some queer dude last night was asking about undercovers. Says he knew one was working the neighborhood a few years back disguised as a halfway house boy, calling himself BD. Wants to know what became of him."

BD always kept a twenty folded thin in his pocket. He had it in his hand as Chambliss pushed away from the fence. The black man seemed as if he might have something more to add.

Before BD could ask what that was, Marlene, bothered by Regal the Doberman mutt, took a bite out of his shoulder as the two of them began snapping and snarling. The mutt's owner yelled her protest. As BD looked that way, Chambliss ambled past, his hands hung at his sides. When he snapped up the twenty it was too fast for a human eye to follow.

BD's living room had a sofa and chair from the Goodwill, a telephone, and not much more. Late that afternoon BD sat on the couch with his feet resting on the chair and talked to his boss. He rolled a joint as he spoke.

"Aurora Sun?" he said. "Formerly Marilyn Friedberg of Greenwich, Connecticut? She's living at Ninety-three Avenue B. I started charting her daily routine this morning.

"Yeah, I'm sure. She's stopped washing her hair and wearing dresses but it's her. The photos are on their way up to you."

BD paused, twirled the joint in his fingers, and said, "I got a question. About an old case from early sixty-five. You remember a queer rich kid named Jonathan Duncan who called himself Ray Light? We put a snatch on him, returned him to the bosom of his family. I've got reason to think the little freak is back."

Marlene was stretched out on the floor. She raised her head and BD scratched her ears as his boss searched the files. It turned out that as far as Guardian Lamp Investigations knew nobody was looking for Jonathan Duncan. The boss wondered if BD had fond memories or something.

That made BD angrier than he expected to be. He said, "I don't feel a lot of sympathy for a spoiled fag who had some queen supporting him and had a girlfriend on the side and a rich family spends thousands of dollars to make him come home and be rich along with them again. It was my job to return him. And I did it. I just wonder if he's back here and trying to fuck up our operation."

Again he listened to his supervisor. "I am sticking to business and not letting things get personal," he said. "Aurora will be packed for shipping by Wednesday. Thursday at the latest."

After he hung up and fired the joint BD thought of Ray Light and Judy Finch on the stoop. He remembered how he'd risked blowing his cover for no reason at all when he went up and asked them for a match.

Later, on the day they'd planned to do the snatch, he'd tailed the two of them, called in his location from pay phones as they sat on benches with her holding him, traveled arm in arm in a wide arc through the city. He forgot to breathe sometimes watching them.

Then they turned back toward 4th Street and he knew they were headed to the spot where the snatch was set to go down. For a moment he wanted to catch up and warn them, to be part of what they were and run off with them.

Instead he made the call and Ray Light got taken off the street, right on schedule. The next morning Judy's father walked her to school. The day after that she was gone.

That had been his first assignment. He was a lot more professional now and nothing like that had happened since. Tuesday he was up early staking out the address on Avenue B, confirming what Chambliss had said about Aurora Sun's morning schedule.

By that evening the Friedbergs had seen the photos of a barefoot waif in an oversize muumuu and confirmed that this was their daughter. The snatch was set up for the next morning. It was all going very smoothly.

He started drinking that night at the Annex opposite the north corner of Tompkins Square Park. There he met some people he kind of knew and ended up at a crash pad where the air was so full of pot and incense smoke that it felt like you needed to part it like beaded curtains. Something had been added to the grass. The walls were moving.

Then he saw what appeared to be Ray Light looking just as he had the day he got snatched. With Light was a crowd of very thin, pale, and amused people. They wavered in the candlelight, stared at him, and made kissing mouths.

BD watched as Ray stepped forward. Only when the figure was right in front of him did he realize it was actually Judy Finch.

"How's it going, BD," she asked. She was taller than he remembered and much thinner.

"The name's Bobby Danton," he said.

"Cut the shit, BD," she replied and smiled. "You've been asking about me. You want to know where I went? After you kidnapped Ray and then starting hanging around in front of our house, my parents thought I was going to be snatched. They were getting divorced and to keep me safe I got sent to an all-girl school in fucking Vermont. Two and a half years of subzero hard time. Thanks to you."

She spoke in a loud clear voice that everyone around could hear over the music. Later he found out she was studying acting. The pupils of her eyes were like pinpricks.

"Doing a lot of meth?" he asked.

"Uh-huh. Another thing you need to answer for. Brought up in the East Village and the most I'd done was a couple of tokes of grass and a sip or two of Daddy's booze. One semester at school and I had an extreme speed need."

She took out a matchbook, stuck it in his shirt pocket, and said, "This is Ray Light's number. He always talks about that vision you had of our future. You need to call him." By the time he could react, she and everyone with her were gone.

A few years before when they had snatched Ray Light, BD was around the corner in a phone booth. He'd just made the call that set the operation in motion. The car with the kid facedown in the backseat sped right past him.

For an instant it was as if he were in Ray's head. In that moment he saw three figures: one in denim and short hair, one in leathers, one in flowing robes. They stood on a stage amid bright light and flowing color. He knew the three were Ray and Judy and him.

The next morning BD and Marlene watched from a block away as Aurora walked to the local bodega. He gave the signal and a woman from Guardian Lamp came up behind Aurora while a man suddenly stepped in her way. She didn't even yell when they hustled her into the car that rolled up the street.

Then someone appeared and snapped a picture of them. A woman shouted, "Kidnapping pigs!"

"Nazis!" yelled a man and threw a beer bottle against the front window as the car jumped a light and sped away.

"Hey, dog man," said a familiar voice. BD turned and someone took his picture. Krazy Kid and her sleaze of a boyfriend were there. She spat at him. The boyfriend had a camera. He took another shot. BD went at them. Marlene snarled. They ran but not before getting one last shot of him and his dog.

When he got home, someone waited across the street and watched him go in the front door. BD packed everything he owned into two suitcases. He looked out the front windows and saw a couple of guys standing in doorways on the block. He called Guardian Lamp.

"Someone talked," said the boss.

"Chambliss," said BD. The whole thing was a setup. He should have known that when Chambliss said someone was looking for him.

"You trusted him too fucking much," said the boss. "I'll send a car around to pick you up. We got stuff to discuss."

The issue of *The East Village Other* with pictures of BD on the front pages and "Undercover Cop" in headlines hadn't yet hit the street and been reprinted in hippie enclaves everywhere. But BD knew that his career was over.

He waited downstairs in the front hall. When the car pulled up, he came out the door of his building. Someone stepped up to him saying, "Press. I'd like to talk to you." But Marlene with one growl and an aborted lunge took care of that.

No one else came near them. He put his luggage in the trunk and got in the backseat with the dog. He wondered how he'd take care of her.

Somebody shouted, "That's him!" as the car pulled away. Someone took a picture of him. He took the matchbook with Ray Light's phone number out of his pocket.

BD remembered something about what Judy had called his vision. He knew that the three figures were Ray Light, Judy Finch, and him. But he hadn't been able to tell which one of them he was.

Part Three

Early in 1971, a couple of days after his band, Lord of Light, played the Fillmore East, Ray Light was interviewed in a booth at the Odessa, the blowsy old Ukrainian Restaurant on Tompkins Square Park. Judy had taken him there when they were kids. He sat facing the front window so he could keep an eye on Marlene, who sat next to the parking meter where she'd been tied.

"It's been awhile since you've been in New York," said the rock critic for *The Village Voice*. This was a second-stringer—not Bangs or Goldstein. But then Ray was still young and his group was an opening act at the Fillmore—not the headliner or even the number two band.

The critic made statements instead of asking questions. He had hair that came down like a curtain to his shoulders without a curl or twist but with some gray strands.

Ray saw him as a failed PhD candidate who'd blown out his frontal lobes in the battle for cosmic consciousness. Not someone with whom he could make contact.

He said, "It's been almost six years. I lived here until my family had me kidnapped. This is where I met my soul mate. And the private eye who snatched me."

He planted this information in each interview. His bright smile gave it an eerie quality. Judy had taught him that trick.

"You were sixteen when you were returned to your family," said the interviewer.

The guy had done his homework and Ray believed this was going well. "They opened up my mind back there," he said. "Shock treatment is better than acid."

"You were close to Phillip Marcy, the playwright."

Ray frowned for a moment like he was trying to think how best to put this. "I mostly called him the Man. Close? Well, he kept me hand-cuffed to his bed a few times. Recently we were in touch. In lots of ways he was a monster. But he taught me stuff."

The reporter raised an eyebrow, seemed interested but a bit uneasy about asking what kind of stuff got taught.

Ray Light told him, "The Man said that if you don't make your own story out of your life, someone will make his story out of your life. I guess he couldn't take his own advice."

Ray had known the Man was going to jump before he did. He had gleaned that from a kid in Seattle months earlier. They'd linked minds when the other recognized him on the street. Later in a hotel room, Ray caught in the other's memory a picture of himself in *Rolling Stone* alongside a brief article on the suicide of Phillip Marcy.

He hadn't thought much about the Man but after that vision, he talked about their time together in an interview in the *San Francisco Or-acle*. When it came out, he sent it to the Man, then called him up and said he had a song, "Spangles, Bondage, and Speed," that he wanted them to sing onstage. Not at the Fillmore but maybe at Max's or On-dine in a midnight show.

The Man refused. Ray insisted. Ray spoke about him on the radio. When the Man jumped, the article in *Rolling Stone* was accompanied by a picture of Ray.

Now the Man was part of Ray's story. A legend was being built. As the tour progressed there were whispers, and someone had nicknamed the group "Ray of Dark Light."

The interview was winding down and Ray indicated he had an ap-pointment. The reporter said, "This was fascinating," but seemed anx-ious to get away, which was perfect.

Marlene danced on her leash when he returned to her. She had been the first thing that had gotten taken away from BD when he ar-rived begging to become part of the vision of the three of them that he'd once seen.

A couple of nights before, Ray had stood in the wings of the Fillmore East and looked through a peephole at the crowd filtering into the seats that soared up the roof of the old movie house.

Here Joplin had shouted and moaned as the red and yellow plasma of Joshua Light Show exploded on the screen behind her and the packed balconies screamed back. Now Joplin was gone. Tonight's main act was not going to fill the theater and there was a rumor the Fillmore was closing. The crown was in the street. Nobody knew who'd be the next king or queen.

The sound check had been done. The emcee was warming up the crowd. His drummer and bass player, steady guys who kept to themselves, waited behind him in the wings.

Judy came up beside him and put her hand on his arm, smiling. She could play keyboards and sing backup like Emmylou Harris. BD appeared carrying a tambourine and looking as if he still couldn't figure out what had happened to him.

"And now the Fillmore East is proud to present, Elektra recording artists Lord of Light."

There was good applause and some cheers as they made their entrance. The audience saw what Ray had picked out of BD's mind years before. Ray wore black leather from head to toe. The first song would be "Dollar a Day Boy," about the girl who loved him and the cop who busted him. The girl now had a blond crew cut and a Marlboro in her mouth. In silk robes and hair to his waist the ex-cop moved like he was in a trance.

The trio paused and looked out at the audience. In that moment Ray linked with another consciousness. And in it he caught a glimpse of his future.

That glimpse was what had him standing at the eastern end of St. Mark's Place on a February evening in a light, cold rain. He faced Tompkins Square and watched the lights come on.

In the neighborhood around the park there were patches of black where streetlamps were broken, storefronts boarded up, buildings abandoned. It had always been a gritty neighborhood. Now speed and junk ruled and graffiti sprouted everywhere: death heads and Black Panther symbols, swastikas and cult signs.

People mourned the death of the East Village. Ray knew the good part was just starting. This time and place needed its own myths and he was prepared to provide them.

Hendrix's gift while he lived was to stand on a stage amid the smoke and reverb and for a solid hour enfold ten thousand minds inside his own.

Ray could touch the consciousness of a few people. Among those were certain ones like Judy and BD who could see not just his past but his future.

He had once asked a guru, a Jungian analyst in Taos who had done much mescaline, about this gift. The old woman had looked right through him and said, "You are a diver in the gestalt sea where there is no then or now or will be. The ones you find there know you entirely."

Shock treatment and drugs had sharpened his ability to find these people. But lately what they showed him was small. He had few hints of what lay beyond the Fillmore performance and was afraid that his gift was gone.

Then on Friday night someone in the audience showed Ray himself all alone and in a spotlight in front of a huge iron gate. The gate was black and decorated with gargoyle heads with red and green moving eyes. His expression was desperate, possessed, and he sang into a hand mike. Singing at the Gates of Hell was how he thought of it.

The vision chilled and mesmerized him. He had to find out how he'd come to be at the gates and what would happen next. It bothered Ray that Judy and BD were not with him there.

All he knew was that the one he'd touched was a woman, that her name was Rainier though it had once been different, and that she thought of herself as a witch and prophet. After the show and for the night and day afterward he searched for her and hoped she hadn't gone back to Westchester or Queens.

Judy still had contacts in the neighborhood. One of them was Chambliss. He brought the word on Sunday morning, murmured to them while they waited to cross Second Avenue. "Woman says she'll meet you right after dark in Tompkins Square Park on the Avenue B side. Don't bring nobody. She'll take you where you can talk." The folded twenties disappeared into his pocket.

It was so obviously a trap that Judy and Ray laughed and made plans. At some point BD was called in. That night right on schedule Ray crossed Avenue A and walked into the park.

Marlene began to growl before he sensed Rainier's presence. He saw her under a streetlamp, a woman in her thirties wearing a long black dress and shawl. She kept her distance but looked at him wide-eyed and gestured for him to follow her through the almost empty park.

Over the years he wondered if his visions were self-fulfilling prophecies. But he missed them acutely when they dried up. To find what else this woman could show him he was willing to do to her things as bad as had ever been done to him.

She stayed about fifty feet ahead, walking rapidly and glancing back. As she reached the gates on Avenue B, he called to her to slow down. She turned toward him and so didn't see the van with its headlights off as it rolled up behind her and braked.

The rear door of the van opened as Ray released Marlene, who sprang forward snarling. Judy jumped out of the driver's seat and BD came out of the back to make a perfect snatch.

The Goosle

Margo Lanagan

Margo Lanagan lives in Sydney, Australia, and works as a contract technical writer. She has published three collections of speculative short stories: White Time, Black Juice, *and* Red Spikes. *Her stories have won two World Fantasy Awards, two Ditmar Awards, four Aurealis Awards, and a Michael L. Printz Honor, and have been shortlisted for many other awards, including a Nebula, a Hugo, and the James Tiptree Jr. Award. Lanagan taught at Clarion South in 2005 and in 2007. She has also published poetry, and fiction for junior readers and teenagers. She maintains a blog at www.amongamidwhile.blogspot.com.*

Lanagan often twists Australian myth and children's tales into something new, making them uniquely her own—as she does in this vicious follow-up to a well-known fairy tale.

There," said Grinnan as we cleared the trees. "Now, you keep your counsel, Hanny-boy."

Why, that is the mudwife's house, I thought. Dread thudded in me. Since two days ago among the older trees when I knew we were in my father's forest, I'd feared this.

The house looked just as it did in my memory: the crumbling, glittery yellow walls, the dreadful roof sealed with drippy white mud. My tongue rubbed the roof of my mouth just looking. It is crisp as wafer biscuit on the outside, that mud. You bite through to a sweetish sand inside. You are frightened it will choke you, but you cannot stop eating.

The mudwife might be dead, I thought hopefully. So many are dead, after all, of the black.

But then came a convulsion in the house. A face passed the window hole, and there she was at the door. Same squat body with a big face snarling above. Same clothing, even, after all these years, the dress trying for bluishness and the pinafore for brown through all the dirt. She looked just as strong. However much bigger I'd grown, it took all my strength to hold my bowels together.

"Don't come a step nearer." She held a red fire-banger in her hand, but it was so dusty—if I'd not known her I'd have laughed.

"Madam, I pray you," said Grinnan. "We are clean as clean—there's not a speck on us, not a blister. Humble travellers in need only of a pig hut or a chicken shed to shelter the night."

"Touch my stock and I'll have you," she says to all his smoothness. "I'll roast your head in a pot."

I tugged Grinnan's sleeve. It was all too sudden—one moment walking wondering, the next on the doorstep with the witch right there, talking heads in pots.

"We have pretties to trade," said Grinnan.

"You can put your pretties up your poink-hole where they belong."

"We have all the news of long travel. Are you not at all curious about the world and its woes?"

"Why would I live here, tuffet-head?" And she went inside and slammed her door and banged the shutter across her window.

"She is softening," said Grinnan. "She is curious. She can't help herself."

"I don't think so."

"You watch me. Get us a fire going, boy. There on that bit of bare ground."

"She will come and throw her bunger in it. She'll blind us, and then—"

"Just make and shut. I tell you, this one is as good as married to me. I have her heart in my hand like a rabbit-kitten."

I was sure he was mistaken, but I went too, because fire meant food and just the sight of the house had made me hungry. While I fed the fire its kindling I dug up a little stone from the flattened ground and sucked the dirt off it.

Grinnan had me make a smelly soup. Salt fish, it had in it, and sea celery and the yellow spice.

When the smell was strong, the door whumped open and there she was again. Ooh, she was so like in my dreams, with her suddenness and her ugly intentions that you can't guess. But it was me and Grinnan this time, not me and Kirtle. Grinnan was big and smart, and he had his own purposes. And I knew there was no magic in the world, just trickery on the innocent. Grinnan would never let anyone else trick me; he wanted that privilege all for himself.

"Take your smelly smells from my garden this instant!" the mudwife shouted.

Grinnan bowed as if she'd greeted him most civilly. "Madam, if you'd join us? There is plenty of this lovely bull-a-bess for you as well."

"I'd not touch my lips to such mess. What kind of foreign muck—"

Even I could hear the longing in her voice that she was trying to shout down.

There before her he ladled out a bowlful—yellow, splashy, full of delicious lumps. Very humbly—he does humbleness well when he needs to, for such a big man—he took it to her. When she recoiled he placed it on the little table by the door, the one that I ran against in my clumsiness when escaping, so hard I still sometimes feel the bruise in my rib. I remember, I knocked it skittering out the door, and I flung it back meaning to trip up the mudwife. But instead I tripped up Kirtle, and the wife came out and plucked her up and bellowed after me and kicked the table onto the path, and ran out herself with Kirtle like a tortoise swimming from her fist and kicked the table aside again—

Bang! went the cottage door.

Grinnan came laughing quietly back to me.

"She is ours. Once they've et your food, Hanny, you're free to eat theirs. Fish-and-onion pie tonight, I'd say."

"Eugh."

"Jealous, are we? Don't like old Grinnan supping at other pots, hnh?"

"It's *not* that!" I glared at his laughing face. "She's so ugly, that's all. So old. I don't know how you can even think of—"

"Well, I am no primrose myself, golden boy," he says. "And I'm grateful for any flower that lets me pluck her."

I was not old and desperate enough to laugh at that joke. I pushed his soup bowl at him.

"Ah, bull-a-bess," he said into the steam. "Food of gods and seducers."

When the mudwife let us in, I looked straight to the corner, and the cage *was still there!* It had been repaired in places with fresh-plaited withes, but it was still of the same pattern. Now there was an animal in it, but the cottage was so dim . . . a very thin cat, maybe, or a ferret. It rippled slowly around its borders, and flashed little eyes at us, and smelled as if its own piss were combed through its fur for pomade. I never smelled that bad when I lived in that cage. I ate well, I remember; I fattened. She took away my leavings in a little cup, on a little dish, but there was still plenty of me left.

So that when Kirtle freed me I *lumbered* away. As soon as I was out of sight of the mud house I stopped in the forest and just stood there blowing from the effort of propelling myself, after all those weeks of sloth.

So that Grinnan when he first saw me said, *Here's a jubbly one. Here's a cheesecake. Wherever did you get the makings of those round cheeks?* And he fell on me like a starving man on a roasted mutton leg. Before too long he had used me thin again, and thin I stayed thereafter.

He was busy at work on the mudwife now.

"Oh my, what an array of herbs! You must be a very knowledgeable woman. And hasn't she a lot of pots, Hansel! A pot for every occasion, I think."

Oh yes, I nearly said, *including head boiling, remember?*

"Well, you are very comfortably set up here, indeed, madam." He looked about him as if he'd found himself inside some kind of enchanted palace, instead of in a stinking hovel with a witch in the middle of it. "Now, I'm sure you told me your name—"

"I did not. My name's not for such as you to know." Her mouth was all pruny and she strutted around and banged things and shot him sharp looks, but I'd seen it. We were in here, weren't we? We'd made it this far.

"Ah, a guessing game!" says Grinnan delightedly. "Now, you'd have a good strong name, I'm sure. Bridda, maybe, or Gert. Or else something fiery and passionate, such as Rossavita, eh?"

He can afford to play her awhile. If the worse comes to the worst, he has the liquor, after all. The liquor has worked on me when nothing else would, when I've been ready to run, to some town's wilds where I could hide—to such as that farm wife with the worried face who beat off Grinnan with a broom. The liquor had softened me and made me sleepy, made me give in to the old bugger's blandishments; next day it had stopped me thinking with its head pain, further than to obey Grinnan's grunts and gestures.

How does yours like it? said Gadfly's red-haired boy viciously. *I've heard him call you "honey," like a girl-wife; does he do you like a girl, face-to-face and lots of kissing? Like your boy-bits, which they is so small, ain't even there, so squashed and ground in?*

He calls me Hanny, because Hanny is my name. Hansel.

Honey is your name, eh? said the black boy—a boy of black skin from naturalness, not illness. *After your honey hair?*

Which they commenced patting and pulling and then held me down and chopped all away with Gadfly's good knife. When Grinnan saw me he went pale, but I'm pretty sure he was trying to cut some kind of deal with Gadfly to swap me for the red-hair (with the *skin like milk, like freckled milk,* he said), so the only thing it changed, he did not come after me for several nights until the hair had settled and I did not give off such an air of humiliation.

Then he whispered, *You were quite handsome under that thatch, weren't you? All along.* And things were bad as ever, and the next day he tidied off the stragglier strands, as I sat on a stump with my poink-hole thumping and the other boys idled this way and that, watching, warping their faces at each other and snorting.

The first time Grinnan did me, I could imagine that it didn't happen. I thought, I had that big dump full of so much nervous earth and stones and some of them must have had sharp corners and cut me as I passed them, and the throbbing of the cuts gave me the dream, that the old man had done that to me. Because I was so fearful, you know, frightened of everything coming straight from the mudwife, and I put fear and pain together and made it up in my sleep. The first time I could trick myself, because it was so terrible and mortifying a thing, it could not be real. It could not.

I have watched Grinnan a long time now, in success and failure, in private and on show. At first I thought he was too smart for me, that I was trapped by his cleverness. And this is true. But I have seen others laugh at him, or walk away from his efforts easily, shaking their heads. Others are cleverer.

What he does to me, he waits till I am weak. Half asleep, he waits till. I never have much fight in me, but dozing off I have even less.

Then what he does—it's so simple I'm ashamed. He bares the flesh of my back. He strokes my back as if that is all he is going to do. He goes straight to the very oldest memory I have—which, me never having told him, how does he know it?—of being sickly, of my first mother bringing me through the night, singing and stroking my back, the oldest and safest piece of my mind, and he puts me there, so that I am sodden with sweetness and longing and nearly-being-back-to-a-baby.

And then he proceeds. It often hurts—it *mostly* hurts. I often weep. But there is a kind of bargain goes on between us, you see. I pay for the first part with the second. The price of the journey to that safe, sweet-sodden place is being spiked in the arse and dragged kicking and biting my blanket back to the real and dangerous one.

Show me your boy-thing, the mudwife would say. *Put it through the bars.*

I won't.

Why not?

You will bite it off. You will cut it off with one of your knives. You will chop it with your ax.

Put it out. I will do no such thing. I only want to wash it.

Wash it when Kirtle is awake, if you so want me clean.

It will be nice, I promise you. I will give you a nice feeling, so warm, so wet. You'll feel good.

But when I put it out, she exclaimed, *What am I supposed to do with that?*

Wash it, like you said.

There's not enough of it even to wash! How would one get that little peepette dirty?
I put it away, little shred, little scrap I was ashamed of.

And she flung around the room awhile, and then she sat, her face all red crags in the last little light of the banked-up fire. *I am going to have to keep you forever!* she said. *For years before you are any use to me. And you are expensive! You eat like a pig! I should just cook you up now and enjoy you while you are tender.*

I was all wounded pride and stupid. I didn't know what she was talking about. *I can do anything my sister can do, if you just let me out of this cage. And I'm a better woodchopper.*

Woodchopper! she said disgustedly. *As if I needed a woodchopper!* And she went to the door and took the ax off the wall there, and tested the edge with one of her horny fingertips, and looked at me in a very *thoughtful* way that I did not much like.

Sometimes he speaks as he strokes. *My Hanny,* he says, very gentle and loving like my mother, *my goosle, my gosling, sweet as apple, salt as sea.* And it feels as if we are united in yearning for my mother and her touch and voice.

She cannot have gone forever, can she, if I can remember this feeling so clearly? But, ah, to get back to her, so much would have to be undone! So much would have to un-happen: all of Grinnan's and my wanderings, all the witch-time, all the time of our second mother. That last night of our first mother, our real mother, and her awful writhing and the noises and our father begging, and Kirtle weeping and needing to be taken away—that would have to become a nightmare, from which my father would shake me awake with the news that the baby came out just as Kirtle and I did, just as easily. And our mother would rise from her bed with the baby; we would all rise into the baby's first morning, and begin.

It is very deep in the night. I have done my best to be invisible, to make no noise, but now the mudwife pants, *He's not asleep.*

Of course he's asleep. Listen to his breathing.

I do the asleep-breathing.

Come, says Grinnan. *I've done with these, bounteous as they are. I want to go below.* He has his ardent voice on now. He makes you think he is barely in control of himself, and somehow that makes you, somehow that flatters you enough to let him do what he wants.

After some uffing and puffing, *No,* she says, very firm, and there's a slap. *I want that boy out of here.*

What, wake him so he can go and listen at the window?

Get him out, she says. *Send him beyond the pigs and tell him to stay.*

You're a nuisance, he says. *You're a sexy nuisance. Look at this! I'm all misshapen and you want me herding children.*

You do it, she says, rearranging her clothing, *or you'll stay that shape.*

So he comes to me and I affect to be woken up and to resist being hauled out the door, but really it's a relief of course. I don't want to hear or see or know. None of that stuff I understand, why people want to sweat and pant and poke bits of themselves into each other, why anyone would want to do more than hold each other for comfort and stroke each other's back.

Moonlight. Pigs like slabs of moon, like long, fat fruit fallen off a moon-vine. The trees tall and brainy all around and above—*they* never sweat and pork; the most they do is sway in a breeze, or crash to the ground to make useful wood. The damp smell of night forest. My friends in the firmament, telling me where I am: two and a half days north of the ford with the knotty rope; four and a half days north and a bit west of "Devilstown," which Grinnan called it because someone made off in the night with all the spoils *we'd* made off with the night before.

I'd thought we were the only ones not back in their beds! he'd stormed on the road.

They must have come very quiet, I said. *They must have been accomplished thieves.*

They must have been sprites or devils, he spat, *that I didn't hear them, with* my ears.

We were seven and a half days north and very very west of Gadfly's camp, where we had, as Grinnan put it, *tried the cooperative life for a while*. But those boys, *they were a gang of no-goods*, Grinnan says now. Whatever deal he had tried to make for Freckled-Milk, they laughed him off, and Grinnan could not stand it there having been laughed at. He took me away before dawn one morning, and when we stopped by a stream in the first light he showed me the brass candlesticks that Gadfly had kept in a sack and been so proud of.

And what'll you use those for? I said foolishly, for we had managed up until then with moon and stars and our own wee fire.

I did not take them to use them, Hanny-pot, he said with glee. *I took them because he loved and polished them so.* And he flung them into the stream, and I gasped—and Grinnan laughed to hear me gasp—at the sight of them cutting through the foam and then gone into the dark cold irretrievable.

Anyway, it was new for me still, there beyond the mudwife's pigs, this knowing where we were—though I had lost count of the days since Ardblarthen when it had come to me how Grinnan looked *up* to find his way, not down among a million tree roots that all looked the same, among twenty million grass stalks, among twenty million million stones or sand grains. It was even newer how the star pattern and the moon movements had steadied out of their meaningless whirling and begun to tell me whereabouts I was in the wide world. All my life I had been stupid, trying to mark the things around me on the ground, leaving myself trails to get home by because every tree looked the same to me, every knoll and declivity, when all the time the directions were hammered hard into their system up there, pointing and changing-but-never-completely-changing.

So if we came at the cottage from this angle, whereas Kirtle and I came from the front, that means . . . but Kirtle and I wandered so many days, didn't we? I filled my stomach with earths, but Kirtle was piteous weeping all the way, so hungry. She would not touch the earth; she watched me eating it and wept. I remember, I told her, *No wonder you are thirsty! Look how much water you're wasting on those tears!* She had brown hair,

I remember. I remember her pushing it out of her eyes so that she could see to sweep in the dark cottage—the cottage where the mudwife's voice is rising, like a saw through wood.

The house stands glittering and the sound comes out of it. My mouth waters; they wouldn't hear me over that noise, would they?

I creep in past the pigs to where the blobby roof edge comes low. I break off a blob bigger than my hand; the wooden shingle it was holding slides off, and my other hand catches it soundlessly and leans it against the house. The mudwife howls; something is knocked over in there; she howls again and Grinnan is grunting with the effort of something. I run away from all those noises, the white mud in my hand like a hunk of cake. I run back to the trees where Grinnan told me to stay, where the woman's howls are like mouse squeaks and I can't hear Grinnan, and I sit between two high roots and I bite in.

Once I've eaten the mud I'm ready to sleep. I try dozing, but it's not comfortable among the roots there, and there is still noise from the cottage—now it is Grinnan working himself up, calling her all the things he calls me, all the insults. *You love it,* he says, with such deep disgust. *You filth, you filthy cunt.* And she *oh*'s below, not at all like me, but as if she really does love it. I lie quiet, thinking, Is it true, that she loves it? That I do? And if it's true, how is it that Grinnan knows, but I don't? She makes noise, she agrees with whatever he says. *Harder, harder,* she says. *Bang me till I burst. Harder!* On and on they go, until I give up waiting—they will never finish!

I get up and go around the pigsty and behind the chicken house. There is a poor field there, pumpkins gone wild in it, blackberry bushes foaming dark around the edges. At least the earth might be softer here. If I pile up enough of this floppy vine, if I gather enough pumpkins around me—

And then I am holding not a pale baby pumpkin in my hand, but a pale baby skull.

Grinnan and the mudwife bellow together in the house, and something else crashes broken.

The skull is the colour of white mud, but hard, inedible—although when I turn it in the moonlight I find tooth marks where someone has tried.

The shouts go up high—the witch's loud, Grinnan's whimpering.

I grab up a handful of earth to eat, but a bone comes with it, long, white, dry. I let the earth fall away from it.

I crouch there looking at the skull and the bone, as those two finish themselves off in the cottage.

They will sleep now—but I'm not sleepy anymore. The stars in their map are nailed to the inside of my skull; my head is filled with dark clarity. When I am sure they are asleep, I scoop up a mouthful of earth, and start digging.

Let me go and get the mudwife, our father murmured. *Just for this once.*

I've done it twice and I'll do it again. Don't you bring that woman here! Our mother's voice was all constricted, as if the baby were trying to come up her throat, not out her nethers.

But this is not like the others! he said, desperate after the following pain. *They say she knows all about children. Delivers them all the time.*

Delivers them? She eats them! said our mother. *It's not just this one. I've two others might catch her eye, while I feed and doze. I'd rather die than have her near my house, that filthy bag.*

So die she did, and our new brother or sister died as well, still inside her. We didn't know whichever it was. *Will it be another little Kirtle-child?* our father had asked us, bright-eyed by the fire at night. *Or another baby woodcutter, like our Hans?* It had seemed so important to know. Even when the baby was dead, I wanted to know.

But the whole reason! our father sobbed. *Is that it could not come out, for us to see!* Which had shamed me quiet.

And then later, going into blackened towns where the only way you could tell man from woman was by the style of a cap, or a hair ribbon draggling into the dirt beneath them, or a rotted pinafore, or worst by the amount of shrunken scrag between an unclothed person's legs—why, then I could see how small a thing it was not to know the little one's sex. I could see that it was not important at all.

When I wake up, they are at it again with their sexing. My teeth are stuck to the inside of my cheeks and lips by two ridges of earth. I have to break the dirt away with my finger.

What was I thinking, last night? I sit up. The bones are in a pile beside me; the skulls are in a separate pile—for counting, I remember. What I thought was: Where did she *find* all these children? Kirtle and I walked for days, I'm sure. There was nothing in the world but trees and owls and foxes and that one deer. Kirtle was afraid of bats at night, but I never saw even one. And we never saw people—which was what we were looking for, which was why we were so unwise when we came upon the mudwife's house.

But what am I going to do? What was I planning, piling these up? I thought I was only looking for all Kirtle's bits. But then another skull turned up and I thought, Well, maybe this one is more Kirtle's size, and then skull after skull—I dug on, crunching earth and drooling and breathing through my nose, and the bones seemed to rise out of the earth at me, seeking out the moon the way a tree reaches for the light, pushing up thinly among the other trees until it finds light enough to spread into, seeking out *me*, as if they were thinking, Here, finally, is someone who can do something for us.

I pick up the nearest skull. Which of these is my sister's? Even if there were just a way to tell girls' skulls from boys'! Is hers even here? Maybe she's still buried, under the blackberries where I couldn't go for thorns.

Now I have a skull in either hand, like someone at a market weighing one cabbage against another. And the thought comes to me: Something is different. Listen.

The pigs. The mudwife, her noises very like the pigs'. There is no rhythm to them; they are random grunting and gasping. And I—

Silently I replace the skulls on the pile.

I haven't heard Grinnan this morning. Not a word, not a groan. Just the woman. The woman and the pigs.

The sunshine shows the cottage as the hovel it is, its saggy sides propped, its sloppy roofing patched with mud splats simply thrown from the ground. The back door stands wide, and I creep up and stand right next to it, my back to the wall.

Wet slaps and stirrings sound inside. The mudwife grunts—she sounds muffled, desperate. Has he tied her up? Is he strangling her? There's not a gasp or word from him. That *thing* in the cage gives off a noise, though, a kind of low baying. It never stops to breathe. There is a strong smell of shit. Dawn is warming everything up; flies zoom in and out the doorway.

I press myself to the wall. There is a dip in the doorstep. Were I brave enough to walk in, that's where I would put my foot. And right at that place appears a drop of blood, running from inside. It slides into the dip, pauses modestly at being seen, then shyly hurries across the step and dives into hiding in the weeds below.

How long do I stand there, looking out over the pigsty and the chicken house to the forest, wishing I were there among the trees instead of here clamped to the house wall like one of those gargoyles on the monks' house in Devilstown, with each sound opening a new pocket of fear in my bowels? A fly flies into my gaping mouth and out again. A pebble in the wall digs a little chink in the back of my head, I'm pressed so hard there.

Finally, I have to know. I have to take one look before I run, otherwise I'll dream all the possibilities for nights to come. She's not a witch; she can't spell me back; I'm thin now and nimble; I can easily get away from her.

So I loosen my head, and the rest of me, from the wall. I bend one knee and straighten the other, pushing my big head, my popping eyes, around the doorpost.

I only meant to glimpse and run. So ready am I for the running, I tip outward even when I see there's no need. I put out my foot to catch myself, and I stare.

She has her back to me, her bare, dirty white back, her baggy arse and thighs. If she weren't doing what she's doing, that would be horror enough, how everything is wet and withered and hung with hair, how everything shakes.

Grinnan is dead on the table. She has opened his legs wide and eaten a hole in him, in through his soft parts. She has pulled all his innards out onto the floor, and her bare bloody feet are trampling the shit out of them, her bare shaking legs are trying to brace themselves on the slippery carpet of them. I can smell the salt fish in the shit; I can smell the yellow spice.

That devilish moan, up and down it wavers, somewhere between purr and battle-yowl. I thought it was me, but it's that shadow in the cage, curling over and over itself like a ruffle of black water, its eyes fixed on the mess, hungry, hungry.

The witch pulls her head out of Grinnan for air. Her head and shoulders are shiny red; her soaked hair drips; her purple-brown nipples point down into two hanging rubies. She snatches some air between her red teeth and plunges in again, her head inside Grinnan like the bulge of a dead baby, but higher, forcing higher, pummelling up inside him, *fighting* to be un-born.

In my travels I have seen many wrongnesses done, and heard many others told of with laughter or with awe around a fire. I have come upon horrors of all kinds, for these are horrible times. But never has a thing been laid out so obvious and ongoing in its evil before my eyes and under my nose and with the flies feasting even as it happens. And never has the means to end it hung as clearly in front of me as it hangs now, on the wall, in the smile of the mudwife's ax edge, fine as the finest nail paring, bright as the dawn sky, the only clean thing in this foul cottage.

I reach my father's house late in the afternoon. How I knew the way, when years ago you could put me twenty paces into the trees and I'd wander lost all day, I don't know; it just came to me. All the loops I took, all the mistakes I made, all laid themselves down in their places on the world, and I took the right way past them and came here straight, one sack on my back, the other in my arms.

When I dreamed of this house it was big and full of comforts; it hummed with safety; the spirit of my mother lit it from inside like a sacred candle. Kirtle was always here, running out to greet me all delight.

Now I can see the poor place for what it is, a plague-ruin like so many that Grinnan and I have found and plundered. And tiny—not even as big as the witch's cottage. It sits in its weedy quiet and the forest chirps around it. The only thing remarkable about it is that I am the first here; no one has touched the place. I note it on my star map—there *is* safety here, the safety of a distance greater than most robbers will venture.

A blackened boy-child sits on the step, his head against the doorpost as if only very tired. Inside, a second child lies in a cradle. My father and second mother are in their bed, side by side just like that lord and lady on the stone tomb in Ardblarthen, only not so neatly carved or richly dressed. Everything else is exactly the same as Kirtle and I left it. So sparse and spare! There is nothing of value here. Grinnan would be angry. *Burn these bodies and beds, boy!* he'd say. *We'll take their rotten roof if that's all they have.*

"But Grinnan is not here, is he?" I say to the boy on the step, carrying the mattock out past him. "Grinnan is in the ground with his ladylove, under the pumpkins. And with a great big pumpkin inside him, too. And Mrs. Pumpkin-Head in his arms, so that they can sex there underground forever."

I take a stick and mark out the graves: Father, Second Mother, Brother, Sister—and a last big one for the two sacks of Kirtle-bones. There's plenty of time before sundown, and the moon is bright these nights, don't I know it. I can work all night if I have to; I am strong enough, and full enough still of disgust. I will dig and dig until this is done.

I tear off my shirt.

I spit in my hands and rub them together.

The mattock bites into the earth.

Shira

Lavie Tidhar

Lavie Tidhar grew up on a kibbutz in Israel, lived in Israel and South Africa, traveled widely in Africa and Asia, and has lived in London for a number of years. He currently lives in Vanuatu, an island-nation in the South Pacific. He is the winner of the 2003 Clarke-Bradbury Prize (awarded by the European Space Agency), is the editor of the anthology A Dick & Jane Primer for Adults, *and is the author of the novella "An Occupation of Angels." His stories appear in* SCI FICTION, Strange Horizons, ChiZine, Fantasy Magazine, Postscripts, Clarkesworld Magazine, *and many others, and in translation in seven languages.*

Tidhar's alternate history provocatively removes one of the flashpoints of world politics in order to imagine a better future for all.

Shira n. (Hebrew: שִׁירָה)

1. Singing; Poetry; (Biblical) Song
2. A contemporary girl's name

Nur remembered a paragraph from one of Tirosh's poems, from the single book he published, two years before the twentieth century came to an end: "The morning rises: another train station. The skies are a dark blue and the streetlamps are lit; people, like the sunken chests of ancient treasures, sit in their depths. It is too early to begin a rescue operation: for a short while, before the sun rises, we are alone." She didn't like the imagery, did not find in it the originality required to make the poem anything other than minor, but still . . . she thought about it now, because in his way Tirosh had captured, in the poem, a certain essence of what it meant to travel alone.

Damascus Station had an official name that was not used; for the city's residents, at least, it had only one name, a linguistic combination that made those few who protected the language grow angry every time it was used: Dimashq-*Central*. Through the station's transparent dome the sky appeared almost purple, and the cold air-conditioned atmosphere raised expectations for another day of *khamsin*. Nur thought she'd be glad not to be in the city during the heat wave but now, before boarding the train, a ticket in her hand and a small, friendly suitcase following her devoutly, she no longer knew how she felt.

Even at such an early hour of the morning there were people at the station, and a few shops were open. Nur bought the morning edition of *Al-Iktissadiya* and then, on her way to the platform, discovered a small branch of Steimatzky. She had once read that one of the first branches of Steimatzky, that conglomerate of Hebrew booksellers, was in Damascus, in the early years of the twentieth century, an interesting fact without much practical use, one of the many she had collected at the university. Still, something in the historical connection attracted her, and on the spur of the moment she entered the shop.

Unlike the large bookshops in the city centre, this one was in effect a hole in the wall, dark in the way of secondhand bookshops and with the same dry smell in the air. An employee who seemed no more than eighteen napped behind a counter, and the shop was otherwise empty. Nur went straight to the poetry shelves. The books appeared not used but merely old, as if they had been sitting on the shelves for a very long time without buyers or readers. But most of the poetry was modern, a poetry-of-After, and Nur was never able to get excited over modern Hebrew poetry. Poetry of the end of the twentieth century, of the fin de siècle, was her interest, and within it her dissertation focused on that unknown poet, Lior Tirosh, whose only book, *Remnants of God*, she had found by chance in the flea market of Damascus and of which she had not since seen another copy. If only she could use the database of the Hebrew Library in Jerusalem . . . but of course, the Small Holocaust prevented that years ago.

She left the shop without a book and went to platform eighteen, the terminal for Haifa. The train was a many-eyed silver bullet. Dark windows seemed to her like mirrorshades. She found her carriage and climbed onboard.

At this early hour the number of passengers travelling to Haifa was small. Nur sat by herself in a seat by the window and waited for her journey to start.

The suitcase followed her to the train and now waited politely by her feet. Nur motioned for it to come closer and took out the book. It was this book that pushed her to go to this city, which she had never before visited. A book no one knew but her, or so it had seemed since she found it, while working on the completion of her thesis, "On the Vision of the Small Holocaust in the Work of Lior Tirosh."

Remnants of God. The title, as ostentatious as it was, seemed to her merely a sign of youth, the sophomore title of a young—though talented—poet. Nur had found it in Ismail Emporium, a secondhand bookshop by the university. A slim volume in hardcover, and the date, in Roman numerals as ostentatious as the title, was MCMXCVIII. The name of the poet was unfamiliar to her, and the mark of the year—was that really a first edition, a poetry book from before the Small Holocaust?—made her shiver, and bargain almost angrily with the bookseller. Ismail, in the end, gave her the book almost for free—"Who buys Hebrew poetry, who? Only your crowd at the university, and you don't have money anyhow"—and Nur took it to her small room in the university buildings and began to read the poems.

They were a mixed assemblage. Many of the poems formed a sort of travel journal, with date-marks from Europe and Africa. Tirosh travelled a lot while writing the poems, and wrote about the places he'd been. There were also some love poems, and some poems in a more surrealist style. The poems of a young poet: He was not a Yehuda Amichai or a Dan Pagis, but he had promise.

She kept returning to the poem that was, perhaps, the silliest, "Little God," but that nevertheless successfully combined for her two of the subjects that had preoccupied Tirosh in all of his poems:

> In the skies the weather forecast was written with a
> spit-wet finger
> On the radio the winds blew from station to station
> Little God sat on a rock, catching yellow fish.
> The weatherman said to expect a heat wave
> Little God took off his clothes
> Jumped in the water, amongst the yellow fish he swam
> His little penis piercing the water layers without resistance.
> The sea danced to the sounds of sunset
> The winds calmed down, gone home to sleep
> Perhaps watch a film
> Little God stayed alone in the water

Happy among the yellow fish
Soon he may come out
Develop lungs grow hands
Stand erect, maybe even
Dress.

The poem showed Tirosh's continuous engagement with the question of the existence of God, of the struggle between religion and the science he seemed to have believed in. The combination of God and evolutionary theory in a poem that drew on an English Nonsense tradition for its purpose was of little significance, perhaps, but interesting for Nur. In another poem he wrote: "God is a teacher in Malawi / Had hardly finished High School / He doesn't know what are vibrations / Or who is Neil Armstrong / But knows when to punish and when to reward."

The doors closed with an exhalation of air, the suitcase retreated behind Nur's legs and hid there, and the train was on its way, passing out of the transparent dome of Damascus Station, its face towards the distant sea. Nur put the book on her knees and watched the streets of Damascus wake. Tall office buildings hid the sun. The streets began to fill with people. There was a tension rising inside her, a reluctance to leave her city behind. Nur did not like to travel; she liked to read. And perhaps, she thought, returning to the subject that had occupied her in the last few months, perhaps that was why she liked Tirosh: He travelled, she felt, for her sake.

More than the other poems, however, it was the obviously political writing that interested Nur. Despite their small number they had a power, a combination of passion and anger, on the one hand the desire to get involved—and on the other, it seemed to her that the poet had wanted to stand with his arms crossed and say, *Not playing*, an image that never failed to make her smile.

One of his quieter poems was "I, Jonathan":

In Sweden, the Arab–Israeli conflict is reduced to the
    television screen.
In Sweden, it is cold, the last of the Vikings emigrated to
    Valhalla many years ago.
In Sweden, it is cold and quiet.
Magdalena rolls on the tongue the foreign words:
"Shalom," "Home," "The Western Wall"
Outside the snow falls, oblivious.
The descendants of the Vikings do not want to fight.
Neither do I.
From here everything seems blurry,
Like a dream
(like a violent video movie,
Like an original story by the Brothers Grimm)
It is cold and quiet and peaceful
And I tire of metaphors,
Tire of death.
The Vikings will no longer set out to conquer new lands.
Not anymore.
Magdalena is restless
She wants to go out, drink, dance.
I, a descendant of Absalom and David,
Still hear the King's battle cry
The crying of his son in the oak.
And, in the distance, Jonathan
Looking for love
Who would go time after time
To seek his death on the battlefields.

Nur stretched her legs and settled deeper into the book. From here everything seems blurry, Tirosh had written, and though Nur would have preferred the poem without the lines that immediately followed, the forced similes of movie and story, the clear language, and the final metaphor attracted her in their simplicity. She could have written her entire thesis on these poems without a qualm, but it was the cycle of poems that closed the book, with its cryptic notes and hints of the future, that called her at last from the depths of the past and caused her to sit on the empty train at this hour in the early morning, on her way to distant Al-Khaifa.

Nur opened the book on page seventy-one and began to read that last, strange poem . . .

Tirosh once wrote a cycle of haikus about his trip through Europe. "The Mediterranean waves / in a temper / after two months of parting," she remembered (Tirosh did not pay much attention to the number of syllables, regrettably, and the poems were not true haiku), and looked through the window: The Mediterranean looked calm and inviting, a distant flash of bright light was probably the enormous golden dome of the Baha'i temple, and the green mountain in the distance was likely the forested Carmel. She put her face to the window and gazed, fascinated, at the approaching city. Haifa, whom some called the Replacement City, was busy with erected mosques and synagogues and churches, but soon the train was past the religious quarter and into the city proper: Nur grew up in a neighbourhood whose residents were mostly descendants of the first *aliyah* to Syria after the Small Holocaust and now, in the slow journey through the city, the many signs that advertised new books in Hebrew brought her an unexpected pleasure.

The train slowed and finally stopped underneath a different dome, at a platform that announced itself energetically as the International Terminal. Nur rose and stretched, and the suitcase ran excitedly across the aisle like a rabbit released into freedom. Together they got off the train, and Nur found herself before a crowd of strangers, all but one calling names that weren't her own.

"Nur? Nur Husseini?" A woman in a summery dress approached her, hand outstretched. "You're Nur? From Damascus University?"

"Shulamit?"

"*Nu*, so who would I be, Golda Meir?" The woman winked at her and Nur laughed.

"Very nice to meet you."

"You, too. Are you hungry? Do you want to stop and drink something before we go back to the flat? Don't worry, I prepared the guest room and a whole pile of poetry books I want your opinion on. How was the journey? Did you bring newspapers?"

Nur said that no, she wasn't hungry, that she would be glad to go straight to the flat, that she was grateful for the hospitality and would be happy to read the poetry books, that the journey was fine and that if Shulamit wanted a paper she brought with her a copy of *Al-Iktissadiya*, which she hadn't read and was not going to anymore.

Without noticing, while talking, Nur found herself in the complex network of the Carmelit, Haifa's ancient subway, made simple under Shulamit's guidance, and then they were no longer inside the Carmelit but outside, in the cool air of the mountain Nur had seen from the train, and the Mediterranean was spread below them like the map of another world.

"Welcome to Haifa," Shulamit said.

Her flat was on the third floor of an apartment block built, so she said to Nur, in the last years before the Small Holocaust. At this point, upon using the term, she stopped and looked at Nur with an examining gaze. "It is hard for my generations to use those words, at least in public," she said. "If you talk to people in the street, you'll see we hardly ever refer to the destruction knowingly. People say 'Before' or 'After,' without saying what."

Nur nodded; it was the habit in the neighbourhood where she grew up, and at the university, which many Palestinians attended. Of course, she thought now, sitting on Shulamit's flowery sofa with her face to the small balcony and to the breeze blowing in from the Mediterranean Sea, the problem was with the expression itself: *the Small Holocaust*, as if it were not important enough, painful enough, as if the event were almost insignificant. People did not know what to call the wound that had erupted in their history, did not know how to define in words what had happened, and instead denied its existence with their silence. There were those among the orthodox Jews who called the event "the Third Destruction," and the academics still referred to it as "the Small Holocaust," but to most people there was no name for the event that brought with it such devastation—but also led to the growth of a new and unexpected flower: peace.

Tirosh, who chased peace without success between the pages of his slim book, refused to identify with one side or another; Tirosh's criticism, Nur thought, was of human nature itself. "There are words I do not like," he once wrote, "especially 'inevitable,' when coupled with 'war.'"

More lines rose in her mind. "What, after all, has happened," Tirosh wrote in his poem "Shalom, Friend," whose title itself, so Nur argued in her thesis, ridiculed a collective ritual of mourning, "the prime minister was murdered / It isn't the first political assassination in history;

> And I, I don't belong to the children crying in the Square,
> More to those who smoke marijuana on the beach
> In Malawi, perhaps those who
> Wander in an acid trip
> (Hebrew is not a suitable language for writing
> About drugs). People here prefer television,
> News and terror attacks.

She wondered what it was like, growing up in the world Before. In her world, the world that came After, television and terror attacks were things that belonged to another time, and the news in *Al-Iktissadiya* tended to the economic and scientific alongside large parts devoted to entertainment and even, here and there, to literature. In fact, the editor of one of the networks, whom she met at some book launch about a month before, had already expressed interest in publishing her thesis. She told this now to Shulamit, who returned from the small kitchen carrying on a tray a carafe of lemonade full of *nana*—mint—two tall glasses, and a plateful of cookies. "From the shop," she said and poured Nur a glass of lemonade. "I still remember my grandfather baking us cookies, but I didn't inherit his cooking ability, or the interest.

"I'm sure your work will have plenty of readers," she added. "I read the copy you sent me and it seemed interesting, a little esoteric for my taste maybe, but interesting. What are you going to do first?"

Nur sipped the cold drink and smiled. She had liked Shulamit almost immediately, and felt much calmer now than she had as she was leaving Damascus. "I thought I'd start in the New National Library, try and find something in the archives that still hadn't been through sorting and scanning. Then the Book Museum, the Haifa Museum, the National Museum, do the same thing, and then look in the secondhand bookshops—if there is one place where I can find something new by Tirosh, or even information about the man himself, it would be here."

Shulamit nodded. "A good plan," she said. "I'll arrange a few meetings for you—there's a collector of poetry books I know who might be able to help, and I thought you could also go out of town, there's the archive in Akra and some others." A smile framed her face; Nur thought it was a pleasant face, open and comforting, and the thought raised in her a smile in reply.

"It will be a lot of work for you to find anything," Shulamit said.

"I know," Nur said. "But the chase is part of the fun."

Shulamit nodded in agreement, and they sat comfortably and drank lemonade, and discussed poetry.

At the end it took Nur less than seven hours to find the start of the thread in the maze, and it happened by chance, not in a dusty archive but at the dinner table.

"I invited a few people to meet you," Shulamit said. "I hope that's all right? I thought you could rest a little, I'll order dinner from the Indian restaurant on the corner—these are all interesting people, and they all really want to meet you."

Nur said that as far as she was concerned it was perfectly fine, and that she'd be happy to meet Shulamit's friends. After a two-hour rest in the guest room—which was indeed comfortably prepared for her, and was airy and spacious besides—she washed, and admitted to herself that she did not feel bad at all. The morning doubts had passed and in their place an expectation remained, accompanied by an unexpected feeling of confidence. In the coming days, she felt with a certainty that surprised her, she would meet Tirosh: It was as though he waited for her, somewhere in the twisting streets of the city that sprawled below.

First to appear was Keren Nevoh, about forty, pretty, a lecturer on the Renaissance at Haifa University. She switched between Hebrew and a Lebanese Arabic that Nur found hard to understand. Eduard Ab-dallah—"But call me Eddie"—was thin and tall and talked enthusiastically about the mining initiatives in the asteroid belt. The last two guests appeared together. Shiri and Michal Livnat, identical rings on their fingers, holding hands. Michal explained with a shy smile that they had just returned from their honeymoon in Turkey. Shiri, it turned out, was a young poetess who worked in a combination of light sculpture and spoken poetry; while Michal, the quieter of the two women, was a project manager for a medium-size wetware company in Tel Aviv.

Keren volunteered to go with Shulamit to get the food and Nur remained to talk with Eddie, Shiri, and Michal.

"So what's your thesis about?" Shiri asked. "Shulamit was pretty mysterious when I asked. She didn't volunteer too many details." She looked at Nur expectantly, and Nur felt sudden embarrassment. She didn't talk much about Tirosh's work and now, with an audience of listening Israelis, was unsure what to say. She explained about finding the book, about her interest in the years that came Before. About Tirosh's political poems, and about his other poems also, the few love poems and the travel journal that read like a lyrical diary. She discovered in herself a confidence while she spoke, a passion for the subject that had never left her. She almost didn't notice the passage of time, and was surprised when Shulamit and Keren returned, laden with food.

"Did you tell them about 'Song of Myself'?" Shulamit asked. "Tell them, tell them. It's fascinating." As she spoke she prepared the table, laying plates heaped with food on the tablecloth.

"Isn't that the title of a poem by Walt Whitman?" Shiri asked.

Shulamit nodded in agreement. "Yes, yes, this Tirosh liked to quote. The entire poem is some kind of an attempt to rewrite Whitman in Hebrew. In my opinion," she said, and looked at Nur, who laughed and said that she was right, Tirosh was heavily influenced by Whitman in the poem, but he combined in it a larger number of references to other works than in any of his other poems. "For instance," she said, "the Haggadah, the Bible, and other Hebrew poets from that period, like Yehuda Amichai and Chana Senesh."

"What's the poem about?" Eddie asked, and his expression seemed bothered, as if he was trying to remember something he had forgotten.

"That's it, that in Nur's opinion Tirosh is talking in the poem about the Small Holocaust," Shulamit said with an undecipherable look.

"I don't understand," Michal said. "It was written Before, wasn't it? So, what, you're saying he predicted the future?"

" 'And lest I forget you, Jerusalem'?" Nur quoted. She felt a tightness in her throat, and the atmosphere in the room changed, became attentive, almost tense. " 'The city is built on a thousand years of shit and death, a Troy of / holy destruction, a bastard daughter to a multitude of religions / worshipping death.' " The food sat on the plates. " 'I let the dead bury the dead / in large mounds of dust / let the living take care each of himself / All are the same in sleep and in death / each man and his unique oblivion disappear in a final *aktzia* / into the darkness of memory.' "

She fell silent, played with a fork nervously.

"Go on," Michal said. She held on to Shiri's hand like a shield. "Please."

"I don't understand," Keren said. "Just because he writes like this about Jerusalem, it doesn't mean . . ." She turned her head to Shulamit, who sat at the head of the table, as if asking for help.

"He wrote more than that," Shulamit said. "I don't remember how it goes, Nur . . . ?"

Nur made herself put the fork down on the table. " 'Let the sun rise,' " she quoted, feeling sweat now despite the cool breeze blowing in from the sea, " 'Let the atom bombs fall in a splendorous bounty of cataclysmic mushrooms, / let the morning shine on a brave, new world, / let the nuclear fallout spread like a sea of shibboleths.' " She skipped several lines and said, quietly, " 'let us fade like a blessed match, that burned and consumed hearts.' "

"The Small Holocaust wasn't nuclear," Eddie said. "But I see what you mean. He wrote as if one was the product of the other. As if some kind of holocaust had to, even *should have*, taken place."

Nur nodded without words, grateful for his understanding. Shiri smiled. " 'Let the sun rise,' " she said, "that's Rotblit's 'Song of Peace,' isn't it?"

"Yes," Shulamit said. "And that last line is from Senesh. I said he liked to quote." She stretched in her seat and began to serve food. "Keren, toss the salad, will you? Eat, eat, before it gets cold."

Nur and Eddie stood on the balcony and looked at the city's lights. The sounds of conversations and traffic and competing music emanated from below.

"The entire meal something's been bothering me," Eddie said. "Like I've already come across this name once. Lior Tirosh. I have no idea how, it's not as if I read much poetry, not to say in Hebrew, but I know I came across it somewhere."

He fell silent and looked at the view. "It's different in space," he said suddenly. "In the halfway point between Earth and Mars there are two days of weightlessness, and then you can float in perfect silence and look out on the entire universe. It can change people's perspective." He laughed. "Even though most of us remain the same, whether we're in space or not."

Nur, who enjoyed the food and felt much better when the conversation moved from her work to other subjects, looked at the slopes of the Carmel and said, "Things aren't bad here, either."

Eddie laughed. "Your Tirosh, he didn't sound like a happy person, from what you quoted."

"He cared," Nur said. "That's what I like about him. The poetry sometimes fails, sometimes he can't say exactly what he means. But he cares. Besides"—she shrugged and smiled— "of all the travelling and the marijuana he writes about, it sounds to me like he didn't particularly suffer."

She tried not to rise to Eddie's comment about recognising Tirosh's name. Did not want to be disappointed so soon into her journey, but she felt the stirrings of excitement taking root in her heart.

"If I remember," Eddie said, "I'll call you straightaway and let you know."

Nur raised her wineglass in salute, and Eddie raised his grape juice against her.

"Cheers," he said.

"*L'chaim*," Nur said, and they both laughed.

Eddie called when Nur and Shulamit sat down with their coffee in the morning.

"I remembered," he said in victory. "I knew I recognised the name from somewhere."

"Where from?" Nur asked. She felt peaceful, since last night she was convinced that the contact would come, and now was not surprised.

Eddie sounded embarrassed. "Look, I have a friend who would know a lot more than me. I spoke to him and he'd be glad to meet you." He gave her the address, in Hachalutz Street, in the old quarter of Hadar.

"Thanks," Nur said, turning to Shulamit with a question in her eyes. Shulamit shrugged and whispered, "Haven't a clue."

Eddie hung up—hurriedly, Nur thought—and she got up and put her coffee on the table. There was no point waiting; she decided to leave immediately and meet Eddie's mysterious friend.

Shulamit wished her luck and gave her a map of the Carmelit, and in a short time Nur had left the apartment and walked to the nearest station. She found her way to Hachalutz Street Station and there, surrounded by the smells of frying falafel, shawarma, and roasted eggplant which made her suddenly hungry, she walked up the street in search of the address, which turned out to be an apartment above a darkened bookshop that looked as if it had never been opened.

She rang the bell. "Mr. Katz?"

She waited, heard slow steps coming down hidden stairs.

The door opened slowly.

Mr. Katz was small of stature, with short silver hair and a dignified expression, like that of a lecturer on tenure.

"Nur?" He didn't wait for an answer but began climbing back up the stairs. Nur looked at Mr. Katz's back moving away, painfully slow. As they said in the neighbourhood . . . *nu*. She shrugged and smiled to herself and followed him up the stairs.

"Tea? Coffee?"

Mr. Katz's apartment was a temple of books. Old books hid in glass cabinets, were piled on the floor in between, sat in boxes, winked behind flowerpots, rested on the windowsill, and on the walls . . . there were yellowing posters there: of monsters and spaceships, djinns and bronzed Amazonian warriors, weird creatures and the views of strange, other worlds . . .

"Mr. Katz?" Nur didn't know what to say. "You're not a poetry collector, are you?"

"Poetry?" Mr. Katz turned and faced her. "Poetry?" The hand that held the coffee spoon shook. "My dear, I have not read poetry since I was forced, at the age of eight, to recite Bialik's 'To a Bird' in front of the whole class. No, Ms. Husseini"— he stretched as high as he could—"I collect science fiction."

"I don't understand," Nur said. They sat by a table laden with books and drank coffee. Nur bit on a cookie. "Eddie said you'd know about Lior Tirosh."

"Lior Tirosh," Mr. Katz said excitedly. "Of course. You say he wrote poetry, too? Interesting. Very interesting. I'm very glad to meet another person who's interested in Tirosh. Fascinating."

"You say he also wrote science fiction?" Nur asked. She didn't know whether to laugh or cry; she didn't know what to expect, but . . . she refused to admit to herself that she was disappointed.

Mr. Katz's hand reached under the table and returned with an ancient-looking magazine; he laid it gently before Nur. "*Groteska* number forty-eight," he said fondly. "The longest-running magazine in the history of Israeli science fiction." He said it with the importance reserved for lecturers on the ages of the Enlightenment or ancient Greece. "The only one to come out both Before and After. Sixty-one volumes, a mixture of translated and original fiction." He smiled, as if to himself. "And, of course, Tirosh's stories."

Nur opened the pages of the magazine. The table of contents included, among story titles such as "War in Zero-g," "The Wolfmen of Tel Hannan," and "The Passion Knights of the Purple Planet" (to which, she noticed, was attached a detailed illustration), a story titled "Where All the Waters Meet" and next to it, in small letters, the name of the author: Lior Tirosh.

Nur felt dizzy. Up until now she had expected to find it had all been a mistake, that there were two people called Lior Tirosh, and that here was simply the wrong one. But she recognised the title of the story as a line from T. S. Eliot's poem "Marina." In hands that had become suddenly greedy she turned the pages until she reached the story. She read it, the coffee cooling beside her, a lone cookie floating on the murky liquid.

The story told of an escaped convict, a murderer, who arrives by spaceship at a solar system where, in a giant asteroid belt revolving around the sun, lives a race of beelike creatures. The queen of the aliens is telepathic, and in her conversations with the hero she is revealed to him not as a ruler but as a sex slave, her only role that of producing offspring. The human hero and the alien queen fall in love and try to escape. They fail, and the hero remains, as a punishment, in eternal sleep on a wandering asteroid, doomed to meet his lover only in dreams, in the place where, as Eliot wrote, all the waters meet.

Nur discovered her throat was dry. "How many stories did he write?" she whispered.

"I never counted," Mr. Katz said apologetically. "He appears in about half the volumes of *Groteska,* in all the volumes of *Scanners in the Dark* and *The New Adventures of Captain Yuno,* in one or two issues of *The Tenth Dimension* and of *Travels Through Space and Time* . ... I'm afraid you'll need to go over them one by one. It's also worth checking the other magazines, and there were also some original anthologies." He stood up. "The apartment is yours," he said. "I have to go open the shop. If I don't have a choice I might even sell something."

He smiled, wished her luck, and turned to the stairs.

Nur remained alone in the apartment, surrounded by books like walls.

She didn't know what she was looking for. A hint as to Tirosh's activity, perhaps, who seemed to have abandoned the writing of poetry after the publication of his first book and turned instead to writing stories that found a home only in the yellowing pages of the science-fiction and fantasy magazines. An ex-boyfriend had tried to interest her in science fiction once, and gave her the al-Qaeda series of an American writer called Asimov, as well as some of the books from the Egyptian New Wave, but she had never been interested in that kind of writing: She preferred poetry, and autobiographies.

Tirosh, she discovered, was indeed productive. His stories returned again and again to the subjects dealt with in his poetry, and if he did not document the places where he had been then he did the places that existed elsewhere, in his imagination. He returned again and again to human nature, to war and peace, addiction and pain, God and religion, the need for belief and for absolution.

She moved her chair as the shadows migrated across the room, and read. Occasionally she prepared a cup of coffee. And read. Hours passed, and with them the day.

The room had turned almost entirely dark, and rain began to fall outside, when she found the story. She turned on the light. And read.

It appeared in volume thirteen of *Groteska* and was called, simply, "Shira."

In the story, Nur read, a woman wanders across the Middle East, restless and without direction. In a secondhand bookshop in Damascus she finds an old Hebrew poetry book whose title is *Remnants of God*. The poems awaken in her something she does not understand, and on the spur of the moment she goes on a train journey towards Israel. A kind of holocaust has taken place in Israel's past; Tirosh avoided describing it in detail, but hinted that Jerusalem no longer existed, and that the nature of its destruction and the amount of pain it had caused brought, after a few years, a peace born of shared victimhood, creating in this way a new Middle East that collectively mourned Jerusalem.

In the story, the heroine arrives in Haifa—which Tirosh called "the Replacement City"—and on a dark and moonless night meets a strange man who may or may not be the author of the collection of poems she found. They spend the night together, and in the morning the mysterious lover is gone. The ending was left ambiguous on purpose, the story ending the way it began, at a train station in the beginning—or perhaps the end of—a journey, leaving more questions than answers.

Nur felt herself disappearing inside Tirosh's fiction, and shook herself with effort. She thought about the maze he had created for her, of the route she followed . . . became lost in? "In your subjective time," Tirosh wrote in *Remnants of God*, "like a tourist in Daedalus's maze, I am lost. Still charmed, looking in all directions. Not yet knowing that the thread is missing. And that you are built into the maze, and that there are no exits and no entrances." As if in response to the weight of the words in her head, light steps sounded climbing the stairs and she looked to the door with relief, expecting Mr. Katz's lined face. She was about to call his name.

But the face that appeared in the open door was not Mr. Katz's. The man who stood in the doorway was of an average height, with dark, curly hair that had begun receding across his forehead. He had a nice smile, and he looked at her for a long moment with a gaze that made her blush.

"What's the story?" he asked.

The question, with its dual meaning, made her smile.

He smiled back. Lines had began to collect at the corners of his eyes, but the eyes themselves were clear and scrutinised her for a length of time. On the spur of the moment she rose and moved towards him, pulling him into the room through the open door. Nur, she whispered to herself. What are you doing? But in her heart she knew that the only way out of the maze is to walk it, until reaching the end.

" 'Venus rises from the sea,' " he said, and leaned towards her. " 'Perfect every time she is revealed / Born anew into an old photograph.' " He knelt by Nur's side and held her hand. " 'She brings with her the scent of salt,' " he whispered, the smile retreating to the corners of his mouth, " 'of drowned ships and ancient time / Venus calls in foreign tongues / cries only she understands.' "

" 'She brings with her many things,' " Nur whispered, the words of the poem rising in her mind. " 'But mainly memories / no matter, she will hold, calm, stroke . . .' " She fell quiet, looking into the eyes of the stranger before her.

His face was close to hers. His breath was warm, and he smelled of aftershave, and a little of sweat. " 'The clocks move slower, tonight,' " he said.

"Who . . . ?" Nur said. She didn't know what to say, what to ask. She looked into his eyes; he had long lashes and eyes that were sometimes green, sometimes brown. He shook his head, a no without words.

" 'What do you teach me,' " he said into the stillness of her face, his lips close, so close she could almost feel, taste them. " 'To hold hands in a crowd / your voice in the dark against my body, the nature / of thoughts is that they pass, I can't / commemorate you, in poem or / story or image / or memory / for its nature is to pass to fade to die . . .' "

" 'And finally forget you,' " Nur whispered. " 'Perhaps that composition called synesthesia, where the senses mix and merge, and sound becomes movement becomes taste/scent becomes touch/look.' " She bent close to him, unable to remove her gaze from his face. " 'All the things that needed saying have been said.' "

" 'And a confusion of the senses, you said,' " he whispered, and leaned to kiss her, " 'is the most beautiful hell . . .' "

Nur tasted his lips. She held him, passed her fingers through his hair.

She undressed him slowly, stopping to breathe his body into her, to taste his naked skin, to preserve him in her mind.

" 'I try to explain to myself the movement of the moon in water,' " he spoke into her shoulder and she shivered and pulled harder at his shirt, almost tearing it, " 'in the darkness your nipples were coloured dark, and your lips had the taste of light to them.' " He kissed her neck slowly. " 'Outside the rain fell, and in your movement of undressing there was the movement of the moon in water, your eyes drowned in flame . . .' "

Nur held him. "No words," she said.

He smiled, and they kissed. "No words," he agreed. The rain knocked on the window.

> Already, your reflection fades.
> Your image (breaking in the shop windows, in the fountains,
> In the Seine) disappears. The same moon shines on both of us
> In two different places.
> Your name is missing from all the telephone directories.

She woke up in Shulamit's guest room. The sun shone through the window, and Nur felt as if she had woken up from a long dream, a dream that lasted months and years.

By the side of the bed was her creased copy of *Remnants of God*. She opened it.

In an unclear handwriting it said, "We'll always have Haifa." She laughed and threw the book on the bed.

In the living room, Shulamit welcomed her with a coffee.

"*Nu*, did you find your man in the end?" she asked.

Nur smiled. "Maybe I just stopped looking," she said.

"The morning rises," Tirosh wrote. "Another train station." Nur stood on the Damascus platform of the Haifa train station, the suitcase at her feet like a loyal puppy.

The train arrived at the station and the doors opened. Nur climbed onboard and sat by the window, and waited for her journey to start.

The Passion of Azazel

Barry N. Malzberg

Barry N. Malzberg's latest collection of essays on science fiction, Breakfast in the Ruins, *was published in the spring of 2007; the book conflates his 1982 classic* Engines of the Night *and all of the essays published since. His collection* In the Stone House *was published in 2000; several of his 1970s science-fiction novels have been reissued within the past half decade.*

*Malzberg's body of work includes a fair number of novels (*The Cross of Fire*) and short stories concerned with religion, but "The Passion of Azazel" is only the third work that has dealt with the Judaic. (Two 1970s short stories appear in Jack Dann's anthology* More Wandering Stars.*) He has been publishing science fiction and fantasy for more than forty years; his first story, "We're Coming Through the Windows" (*Galaxy *magazine, August 1967), was sold on January 11, 1967. With a fetching smile and an indescribable moué, Malzberg further notes that these last years of his seventh decade are becoming, unsurprisingly, a tortuous slog.*

With his inimitable cynic's eye, Malzberg portrays a regular guy who decides to take control of his nightmares in an imaginative way, with results he certainly was not expecting.

*And the High Priest shall take two goats . . . one as an offering and the other as a scapegoat
. . . And he shall kill the goat which is the offering and sprinkle its blood . . . and he shall lay
his hands on the head of the scapegoat and confess upon it all of the iniquities of the Children
of Israel and the goat shall be sent to the wilderness with a man who is in waiting . . .*
　　　　　　　　　　　　　　　　　　　　　　　　　　　　—LEVITICUS

*The High Priest dispatched the scapegoat to the wilderness, where it was driven off a
rocky cliff until its bones shattered like a potter's vessel . . . and the face of the High Priest
when he left the Holy of Holies . . . was like the lightning bolts emanating from
the radiance of the heavenly host . . .*
　　　　　　　　　　　　　　　　　　—MUSSAF PRAYER, DAY OF ATONEMENT

I believe you had a previous life as a scapegoat." The hypnotherapist's eyes were brooding but filled with sincerity and profoundly abstracted as if she were retreating into some inaccessible, entombed place. "Of course that is quite a daring assumption, Schmuel. Still, you are so convincing. Your recurrent nightmares of falling, of being hurled from mountains to rock, carrying the sins of your community. The memories that emerged during your hypnotic regression. This goes beyond the Orthodoxy you were raised with, beyond the usual Freudian interpretation of 'falling dreams' as sexual repression or anxiety. Of course"— with a little smile—"isn't Orthodoxy simply institutionalized sexual repression and anxiety? But we won't discuss that now." She returned to her more serious tone. "A daring assumption," she repeated.

The knowledge, long deflected, was shocking. Schmuel the scapegoat! But a relief, too. Recognition. Meeting the enemy and discovering your oldest friend. Could this explain the flashbacks, the night sweats, the depression, the riotous, collapsing images of falling, the helplessness, the sheer animal passivity of that descent, the shattering of bone? "If this is so," the hypnotist continued, "it would explain a great deal. Perhaps it would explain everything. Reincarnation is not charlatanry, you know. There is explicit scientific evidence, an impressive body of research that grows all the time."

She did not have to convince me.

In the beginning was the Word and the Word was with God and the Word was God. And the Word was built from letters. Hebrew letters. The seventy-two letters of God's Name. And from those letters, everything. The heavens and the earth. Mountains, rocks, trees. Mosquitoes, fish, human beings. Goats.

So here is Schmuel, six years after the regression, at another crucial point of his beleaguered and circumstance-laden life, just shy of rabbinical ordination, drowning in a sea of Hebrew letters—

I am spending less and less time in the Yeshiva classroom, less and less time studying the minutiae of religious laws governing kosher food and kosher sex, ritual handwashing and penitential fasting. Seeking more satisfying solutions, I am struggling to manipulate Hebrew letters in the back room of an arts and crafts shop on East Broadway under the watchful eye and sage tutelage of the wizened Rabbi Bentov. I am attempting to construct a golem. A golem in the form of a goat. Made of Hebrew letters, combinations of the letters in God's Name. I will only construct the purest, most authentic golem—not constructed out of clay, with merely a few Hebrew letters engraved on its forehead, but the more difficult task of making the goat from nothing but the letters themselves.

So can a golem be made in the form of a goat? Yes, according to the ancient Kabbalists. But can I trust them? Working at this, poring over the Sefer Yetzirah on East Broadway in an unusual divination of construction and dedication, I cannot answer, have no way of being sure. But then again, how can one be sure of anything, from divine revelation to divine retribution? But I know I must try to make this golem— this thing that has fascinated and called to me since the first time I ever heard the word *golem* from my rabbinic father, thundering in one of his sermons against "today's irresponsible celebrities who demean Kabbalah by making it no more than a machine to manufacture good-luck charms and golems." What is a golem, I had asked later. And had been thunderously told that I was too young and ignorant to understand, that a person may not study Kabbalah until he has mastered Bible, Talmud, commentaries, and Jewish law. Which only whetted my interest even more.

The golem, I had discovered upon peering through my father's library when he was sleeping, was a creature in the image of a man, constructed from mystical permutations and combinations of Hebrew letters, animate in its last stages and potentially dangerous—although, according to several renowned historians, the stories of destructive golems were likely the product of anti-Semitic lore. Some Kabbalists, I later learned, had also made animal golems. Practice makes perfect? Were they like scientists who must experiment on mice and monkeys before experimenting on a human being? No, I found out. The animals were to become sacrifices. Goats were a favorite.

Young Schmuel, his little mouth open and his eyes round in the forbidden library, has transmogrified into Schmuel the soon-to-be-rabbi, the incipient Kabbalist, immersed in the terrifying and wondrous synergy of experience and history, symbol and reality. The journey from scapegoat to creator of goats. From tormented dreams to ferocious *pilpul*, to murmured incantations and esoteric combinations of Hebrew letters.

"Why do you want to make a goat?" asks Rabbi Bentov yet again. "If you do not plan to sacrifice it, what is the point? The ancients sometimes created human golems to help them with tasks such as drawing water from a well or protecting the village from attack. Today I get mostly rabbinical students who have other ideas, equally practical. They usually want to make a female golem. For marriage. You know how congregations prefer to hire married rabbis so their wives can bake kugels and organize sisterhood meetings. Why a goat?"

I could explain if I wanted to. But I do not want to. No one, not even my esteemed Kabbalistic instructor, can know about my memories, my real motives.

Schmuel on the hypnotist's couch, that fateful day, meeting himself for the first time—

Hebrew chanting. "Please Lord, I have sinned, I have transgressed . . . Forgive my iniquities, as it is written, For this day of Yom Kippur shall atone for you." The true and ineffable four-letter Name of God is uttered, mysterious and austere. And a resounding wave of voices, "Blessed be the Name of His glorious kingdom forever and ever."

I am hovering above the Temple of Jerusalem, looking down at a man dressed in white vestments. A priest. The High Priest. Surrounded by other priests, the Temple Mount thronged with thousands of worshippers, pilgrims from all over Israel.

I move closer and suddenly I am on all fours. Something is hanging from the foot of my spine. A tail. My hands and feet are hooves and my legs are covered with white fur. I am a goat. A he-goat. There is another goat next to me. My brother. We suckled together, we grazed together, and we were taken together to stand beside this High Priest on this holiest day of the year. I call to him and my voice is a bleat. He understands and bleats back.

We have been uneasy since we were wrenched from the bosom of our mother and the meadow of grass and flowers and led through the mountainous terrain of Israel to Jerusalem. Days of walking in the heat, with only occasional stops for hay and water. Where were we going? And why? We could not bear to look at one another, because our fear was mirrored in each other's eyes, and there was no escaping it. Better to pretend we were merely being transferred to greener pastures.

But no pasture, no meadow, instead a stone courtyard spattered with blood, an altar, a sharp silver object wielded by the priest in white. I do not understand. I do not recognize these things.

The priest pulls my brother away. Oh, no, no! They are holding my brother down, he is crying for me to help him, but they are restraining me. Let me go, I want my brother, but they pull me away as the gleaming thing, the long silver thing, sharp, sharp, is near his throat, and—stop them! His throat is cut, his head tumbles to the ground, his legs are still kicking, and, improbably, his horn in the dirt is still trying to butt its way to freedom, but he is dead. Even as a goat, I know this. I know terror and I know death.

The blood is running into a basin. The priest is dipping his finger in the blood, he is sprinkling it around. Then they lead me forward. I know what lies in store. I struggle and bite the restraints. I try to butt them with my horns. But they are stronger and I am pushed ahead to the murderous priest and his blood-spattered vestments. I am crying, begging God to have mercy on me, to save me on this holiest day of the year. I have not sinned. I do not deserve to die.

The priest approaches. He lays his hands on my head. A gentle gesture, a bene-diction, and I briefly calm. Have my prayers been heard? His hands rest on my head as he again engages in the Confession. The people of Israel have sinned. Transgressed . . . Forgive . . . The people fall prostrate, blessing the Name again. Then the priest turns to a man who has been waiting on the side. "Take him away."

I am led away. I have been saved! In my jubilation, I push aside the picture of my brother in his final death throes, push away my questions about the God who spared me but killed him. I am alive. The only thought that is important now, I am alive.

We are climbing a mountain steeper than any I trod in my journey toward Jerusalem. I am thirsty, my tongue dry as the sand, hard and cold as the stones un-derfoot. I try to lie down, but the man forces me up, dragging me forward. I stumble, my legs giving way, but he pulls again and I move ahead, pain and fatigue burning my thighs.

We are almost at the top of the cliff. Suddenly, he cuts the rope and I am free! He moves behind me and I collapse gratefully, relief crowding out the pain, the terror. Gray numbness overtaking me, I lie down and—

And there is pain. Red, searing pain. A sound as wind singing. It is the whirring of a whip as it lashes my hindquarters, the agony building until I must run away from it. I stumble, scramble to my feet, hurtling ahead to the top of the cliff, the whip land-ing again and again, as I surge forward, my lungs screaming, no longer allowing my legs the luxury of stumbling, so I run, forward, forward—

And then I am airborne, catapulting downward, my heart exploding with merciless knowledge as the blood bursts forth, and I tumble toward the ravine, and—

You will not get away with this, Lord, You, your priests, your people, your Torah—

And then the impact. The shattering of bones. The silence.

Vengeance is mine, saith the Lord.
Vengeance is mine, saith the goat.

"Call me Azazel," says my goat.

The incantations finally complete, the letters still swirling, my newly formed goat has risen to his feet. He is white and bearded, a visage wholly becoming an Orthodox goat. He bleats but his words have a distinctly human aspect. "Let us go to the Yeshiva together and we will take them by storm."

Rabbi Bentov steps forward, pride in his student's accomplishment trumped by consternation. "What have you done? You used the wrong spell. Animals can't speak, except for—"

"If you bring up the story of Balaam's donkey, I will butt you with my horns. Are you comparing me to that ass?" Rabbi Bentov backs away. "And that is exactly the point," Azazel continues, "to speak. To utter words. In the beginning was the Word—"

Rabbi Bentov holds up his hands. "But what will you do? I am responsible for anything that happens. I have taught Schmuel everything he knows about making a golem."

Azazel kicks his hoof impatiently. "You are responsible for everything and nothing. Come, Schmuel, we have work to do." He turns tail and trots away, with me in pursuit. We leave Rabbi Bentov gesticulating helplessly, muttering prayers and Kabbalistic incantations.

Off we go, Azazel and I, into the welter of East Broadway. I am no less surprised than the disconcerted Rabbi Bentov. Can golems talk? Can golems dispute, order, direct, pontificate? These are questions for the theoreticians, for the rabbi himself, but not for Schmuel or Azazel, who has not stopped talking since we left the arts and crafts store.

"Consider the Israelites," Azazel says. He has become chatty, confidential. "Not a goat but a golden calf. Isn't that interesting? The goats have gotten short shrift in the Bible, let me tell you. Moses was praised for rescuing a lamb, not a goat. It was a ram who jumped onto the altar to save Isaac from slaughter, and Jacob did genetic engineering on sheep. Even the disgusting litany of prescribed sacrifices consists of mostly cows and sheep with very few goats—except for those who are tossed off cliffs. But"—he winks—"even though the goat has been neglected and scarcely worthy even of being victimized by atrocities, we do corner the market on the holiest day of the year. The most important sacrifice. Now, what do you think of that?"

On and on. He seems more interested in venting his indignation at the ignominious treatment of his (our?) species, his (my!) brethren than responding to my feeble attempts to interject with such practical questions as how we will walk the long distance to the rabbinical school, and what we are planning to do once we get there. He keeps up his pace of walking, as of speaking, stopping only to offer commentary about the neighborhood and its inhabitants. "Isn't it interesting how New Yorkers keep to themselves? No one greets us, no one waves hello—humans are the rudest, the most self-absorbed species. I know some of us"— he nudges me and winks conspiratorially, we are after all brothers—"don't always mind our manners, but this is terribly disturbing." I note that he does not refer to me as his creator but as his equal—perhaps correctly, after all, I have been a fellow goat in my last incarnation. Perhaps he even was my unfortunate brother, slaughtered just hours before my own death.

"Disturbing," Azazel prattles on, "because their utter self-centeredness bespeaks their utter inconsideration for any species but their own. Pardon me," Azazel calls to an obviously *frum* lady with a large wig, black stockings, and a long dress, pushing a double stroller with shopping bags dangling from the handles and a crying infant in each seat, a toddler clinging to her arm. So preoccupied is she with her children she appears oblivious to the talking goat and his partner. "Excuse me," Azazel calls again and this time she stops, as if the sight finally registers. Her *frum* mouth opens in a little O of astonishment and contemplation as she drops her shopping bags and grabs her toddler. He is gesticulating rapturously in our direction. "Nice boy," Azazel comments as we start off again, leaving the woman pointing and shouting in Yiddish. "Got to get them when they're young. Before they start studying and preaching and praying. When they're old geezers it's too late, they deserve to be shoved off some cliff."

I am panting, as much from the effects of *hearing* him as from the physical exertion of keeping up with the four-legged Azazel. He has the advantage, he knows it, and he's wickedly flaunting his superior ambulation. I grab him by the tail.

He pirouettes, an elegant, almost dainty maneuver, and I narrowly avoid being butted by his horns.

"I just want to slow down," I say, still panting.

"Did they give you a chance to stop and catch your breath when you were on your way to the cliff?" he demands. He winks again, an overused mannerism that's becoming increasingly annoying. "Ha, got you now!"

"Why are you treating me like this?" I ask in a plaintive voice. I hear the little whine of the supplicant, the victim.

"Just because you suffered, you think you deserve to be coddled and pampered? We all suffer, friend. You chose to create me, now you have to listen to me. Or why did you create me anyway?"

Why indeed. I had thought—ridiculously, I now realize—that I would find companionship, simpatico. My goat and I would compare notes about what it is like to be a goat, to suffer at the hands of human beings. I could share the trauma of my memories, receive his warm, nuzzled consolation. But apparently he has an agenda of his own, and I now know that one can never account for one's creation, that the very act of creation is the act of self-abnegation, of self-destruction. Goat or human, the end must be accounted for in the beginning.

These are philosophical reflections of some import, but they do not concern me so much as the state of my feet as I try to keep up with Azazel. Somehow, the *frum* lady appears to be pursuing us and keeping up with our lightning pace—nothing short of remarkable, as she is weighed down by wigs and children and packages and by sexual repression and anxiety (tip-of-the-yarmulke to the hypnotist). But here she is, her wig only slightly disarranged, her babies still crying, her toddler still laughing and pointing.

We seem to be moving uptown, to Washington Heights, to the rabbinical school, through streets replete with old men and boom-box-wielding teens and gaudy clothing on racks, Spanish and Hebrew and German and Yiddish competing for purchase. Cheerfully, Azazel thrusts a horn into the clothing rack as sweaters and slacks tumble onto the sidewalk, the owner cursing in Spanish. "See"—his face assumes a goatlike smirk—"does he notice me? Only when his sales rack falls—and my, how angry he gets. But it is nothing compared to what the rabbis will do when we teach them a lesson."

We? I feel sick. My mouth is dry, the mouth that uttered Kabbalistic incantations. My hands are shaking, the hands that formed the Hebrew letters that birthed Azazel. Waves of sickness overtake me as I contemplate what he might have in mind for the rabbis. The Yeshiva looms within sight, seen through the haze, the traffic, the disorder of Pinehurst Avenue, an unhappy edifice lurking by the river, and only then does the impact and circumstance of our journey come upon me. Exactly what am I to do? I will introduce Azazel to the Rosh Yeshiva—the dean of the rabbinical school—and I know that only then will the true purpose of the golem be revealed . . . but it is unclear what I intend to happen. The proximity to the Hudson River and the beckoning Jersey Palisades is disconcerting. Will the astonished rabbi be conveyed to the Jersey Palisades and thrown off a cliff? Will Azazel himself become a Jersey-bound golem, seeking rocky ascent on those shiny rungs of grass and stone, then a quick fall? Will he want me to jump to my fate yet again? I shudder. Surely I cannot know any of this; I am merely the vessel of vengeance, the agent of reconstruction: agent of the golem goat, I can only witness this last and terrible reparation. Or so I would hope. For at the heart of this speculation is a vast and consuming emptiness, once disguised as mastery, now in its truer incarnation as terror but beyond the possibility of answer.

The school beckons. The Rosh Yeshiva is standing at its entrance, a volume of Talmud in one hand, a prayer book in the other. A frown tugs at the panels of his face, rippling through his beard: "So you have decided to grace us with your presence? Three weeks, and you don't come to class, you don't call, you don't write, you don't visit. I hear you fancy yourself a Kabbalist." (He has heard? And from whom?)

Azazel tugs at my hand. "Would you look at that? You show up with a goat and instead of marveling, he complains you're cutting classes. The pettiness of human beings, especially rabbis, cannot be fathomed."

"What do you have to say for yourself?" the Rosh Yeshiva asks me. "Please say it quickly. I have a class to teach."

I clear my throat, an uncomfortable noise, rather like a bleat. I open my mouth but before I can say anything, Azazel leaps in. "Teach, teach, teach, class, class, class. Don't you rabbis ever think about anything other than the Torah? The law? The teachings?"

The Rosh Yeshiva seems to notice my goat for the first time. "Schmuel, what kind of farce is this? Take that animal away."

I am about to say that I created the goat but as usual, Azazel is faster than I and infinitely more talkative. "*That animal*, is this what you just called me?"

"And stop putting words in its mouth," the Rosh Yeshiva continues. "I don't know what magic you're using, sleight of hand, ventriloquism, to make it talk but it is very disrespectful—"

Azazel rises on his hind legs with indignation. "*He* is not putting words in *my* mouth! I can speak for myself thank you very much, and we have some business to transact, you and I. Liberation, my friend. And you will be the first liberated."

The Rosh Yeshiva draws himself up to his full height, which isn't very tall, and folds his arms, the Talmud and prayer book against his chest. "There is no greater liberation than Torah study," he says stiffly.

"Ask *her*," Azazel replies, winking fetchingly at the *frum* lady, who has apparently been following us and has just arrived.

The Rosh Yeshiva's face wears a terrible expression. "She is a lady. She has no place in a men's Yeshiva."

Azazel tap-dances from hoof to hoof. "Do you hear him?" he asks me. Then he turns to the *frum* lady. "Liberation, right? Tell him how liberated you are. Free to follow your dreams. Free to jump off a cliff and fly, right?"

The babies are still crying, the toddler is crowing and pointing, straining against his mother's grasp. "Please, Moishy," she begs her son, ignoring the goat and clutching the child. "Be good."

"Oh, but he is good, better than all of you," Azazel says, cavorting on the sidewalk.

"We have to go home, Moishy," she says, beseeching more than telling. But Moishy has his own ideas. He breaks free, shakes off his mother's pleading hand, and leaps onto Azazel's back. "Play, play," he crows.

"And the child shall lead them!" Azazel shouts. "Follow your leader, Rabbi!"

"I won't go!" the Rosh Yeshiva shouts back. "This is a travesty. This is"— he waves his hands wildly—"this is an outrage, an abomination."

By now, rabbinical students are pouring out of the building, gaping at the scene unfolding on the steps of the Yeshiva. A few eye me cautiously, and I can almost hear them thinking, That Schmuel, he always was a strange one, wasn't he?

"You will come with me." Azazel's voice has taken on a distinctly menacing tone.

"Please climb down, Moishy," the *frum* lady implores her child. He chortles and claps his hands, then throws his arms around Azazel's neck. "Play," he says again.

"A fitting leader," Azazel says in a voice suddenly casual, nonchalant. "So follow your leader, Rabbis."

The Rosh Yeshiva is about to protest when Azazel butts him— gently but firmly—with his horn. "Schmuel, you know what you must do if he refuses to go."

But Schmuel has become irrelevant, overshadowed by the more powerful goat—no doubt the brother, who has come to take revenge not only on the priests and assembled masses but also on his sibling who could not save him from slaughter. Irrelevant, I am struck silent. Inert.

"You know what to do," Azazel repeats. He gazes at me and in that moment we are suckling together, grazing side by side, we are stumbling toward Jerusalem, and the High Priest—another rabbi—is tearing us asunder. Across the sword, our eyes meet and the words begin to fall quick and full from my mouth. My fingers are moving rapidly, forming Hebrew letters in the air.

The Rosh Yeshiva's beard lengthens and whitens, his hands fall to the sidewalk, his feet become hooves, a tail sprouts from his hindquarters. He opens his mouth to speak but all that comes out is a bleat. I look around and my fellow students are also on all fours, the bleating thunderous against the now silent New York streets. White goats with black yarmulkes or black hats perched at odd angles atop their tufty heads, black jackets and pants hanging awkwardly over their furry forms. A great multitude of rabbinic goats.

And they stampede in their numbers along Pinehurst to Fort Washington Avenue, then onto the George Washington Bridge. Cars screech to a halt, horns blare, police sirens scream, but the goats continue their stampede, and suddenly, there are more, thousands of goats, some with black hats and sidelocks, some with colorful crocheted yarmulkes, all following the procession of Azazel, with little Moishy riding akimbo, shouting lustily. Then me, the humble servant-creator, the terrified servant-creator. Then the *frum* lady, huffing and puffing to catch up with her precious little boy, her shopping bags long gone, her infants still crying. And behind us, the streaming, bleating multitudes.

Across the bridge, into New Jersey, up the Palisades Interstate Parkway to the State Lookout.

To the cliff. The rocky cliff.

I feel even sicker than I did before. Azazel may be long-winded, he may be irreverent, he may be nasty, but just how nasty? How far will he carry the quest for revenge? I start to expostulate, to reason, to plead, but he silences me by butting me with his horns. He turns to face the multitude, who have stopped just short of the cliff, swaying uneasily as they look down.

"Hear O Israel," he proclaims, and miraculously he is heard throughout the crowd, to the very last, most junior rabbinic student. "For centuries you have prayed for the rebuilding of the Temple and the restoration of the rituals, you have devoted your lives to studying the book that spawned the torture. You have served oppression, you have worshipped evil. You have sinned. You have transgressed. You have committed iniquity. You will bear your sins."

He butts the Rosh Yeshiva, pushing him forward to the edge of the cliff. In and out of the crowd he weaves, his horns working deftly, as he prods and pokes and drives the herd to the edge. "Now, then!"

The Rosh Yeshiva falls first, followed by throngs of goats, a blizzard of fur and hooves and beards and tails and black jackets and sidelocks, the air rent with terror and entreaty.

"Now, Schmuel, now!" And he looks at me without so much as a twinkle of humor, Azazel and I in the communion of brothers. And in that moment, as our souls unite, I see my fingers once again forming letters in the air, my mouth moving frenetically, the incantations frantically tumbling as fast as the goats themselves.

And before the goats reach the rocky bottom they rise, a great white cloud of jubilation, a burst of hallelujah. Blessed be the Kingdom of Truth forever and ever. Higher and higher they go, until they are indistinguishable from the white clouds billowing across the sky, until they are the tail of a comet streaking into the night.

"Come on, Schmuel!" And I grab the hand of the *frum* lady, hoist the double stroller, and leap, the babies now silently sleeping. Azazel leaps with Moishy still gleefully clinging to his neck. As we are airborne we rise together. We fly amid the clouds, we soar, we swoop, we ascend in a whirlwind beyond the clouds, beyond the firmament, to the truest liberation, to the lightning bolts and radiance of the heavenly host.

The Lagerstätte

Laird Barron

Laird Barron was born in Alaska, where he raised and trained huskies for many years. He migrated to the Pacific Northwest in the mid-1990s and began to concentrate on writing poetry and fiction. He currently resides in Olympia, Washington, where he is working on a number of projects.

His award-nominated work has appeared in SCI FICTION *and* The Magazine of Fantasy & Science Fiction, *and has been reprinted in* The Year's Best Fantasy and Horror, Year's Best Fantasy 6, *and* Horror: The Best of the Year, 2006.

Barron has, in a relatively short time, achieved a well-deserved reputation for writing powerful horror stories and novellas. "The Lagerstätte" is a bit different from his usual—but still quite dark.

October 2004

Virgil acquired the cute little blue-and-white-pin-striped Cessna at an auction; this over Danni's strenuous objections. There were financial issues; Virgil's salary as department head at his software development company wasn't scheduled to increase for another eighteen months and they'd recently enrolled their son Keith in an exclusive grammar school. Thirty grand a year was a serious hit on their rainy-day fund. Also, Danni didn't like planes, especially small ones, which she asserted were scarcely more than tin, plastic, and balsa wood. She even avoided traveling by commercial airliner if it was possible to drive or take a train. But she couldn't compete with love at first sight. Virgil took one look at the four-seater and practically swooned, and Danni knew she'd had it before the argument even started. Keith begged to fly and Virgil promised to teach him, teased that he might be the only kid to get his pilot's license before he learned to drive.

Because Danni detested flying so much, when their assiduously planned weeklong vacation rolled around, she decided to boycott the flight and meet her husband and son at the in-laws' place on Cape Cod a day late, after wrapping up business in the city. The drive was only a couple of hours—she'd be at the house in time for Friday supper. She saw them off from a small airport in the suburbs, and returned home to pack and go over last-minute adjustments to her evening lecture at the museum.

How many times did the plane crash between waking and sleeping?

There was no way to measure that; during the first weeks the accident cycled through a continuous playback loop, cheap and grainy and soundless like a closed-circuit security feed. They'd recovered pieces of fuselage from the water, bobbing like cork—she caught a few moments of news footage before someone, probably Dad, killed the television.

They threw the most beautiful double funeral courtesy of Virgil's parents, followed by a reception in his family's summer home. She recalled wavering shadowbox lights and the muted hum of voices, men in black hats clasping cocktails to the breasts of their black suits, and severe women gathered near the sharper, astral glow of the kitchen, faces gaunt and cold as porcelain, their dresses black, their children underfoot and dressed as adults in miniature; and afterward, a smooth descent into darkness like a bullet reversing its trajectory and dropping into the barrel of a gun.

Later, in the hospital, she chuckled when she read the police report. It claimed she'd eaten a bottle of pills she'd found in her mother-in-law's dresser and curled up to die in her husband's closet among his Little League uniforms and boxes of trophies. That was simply hilarious because anyone who knew her would know the notion was just too goddamned melodramatic for words.

March 2005

About four months after she lost her husband and son, Danni transplanted to the West Coast, taken in by a childhood friend named Merrill Thurman, and cut all ties with extended family, peers, and associates from before the accident. She eventually lost interest in grieving just as she lost interest in her former career as an entomologist; both were exercises of excruciating tediousness and ultimately pointless in the face of her brand-new, freewheeling course. All those years of college and marriage were abruptly and irrevocably reduced to the fond memories of another life, a chapter in a closed book.

Danni was satisfied with the status quo of patchwork memory and aching numbness. At her best, there were no highs, no lows, just a seamless thrum as one day rolled into the next. She took to perusing self-help pamphlets, treatises on Eastern philosophy, and trendy art magazines; she piled them in her room until they wedged the door open. She studied Tai Chi during an eight-week course in the decrepit gym of the crosstown YMCA. She toyed with an easel and paints, attended a class at the community college. She'd taken some drafting in college. This was helpful for the technical aspects, the geometry of line and space; the actual artistic part proved more difficult. Maybe she needed to steep herself in the bohemian culture—a cold-water flat in Paris, or an artist commune, or a sea shanty on the coast of Barbados.

Oh, but she'd never live alone, would she?

Amid this reevaluation and reordering came the fugue, a lunatic element that found genesis in the void between melancholy and nightmare. The fugue made familiar places strange; it wiped away friendly faces and replaced them with beekeeper masks and reduced English to the low growl of the swarm. It was a disorder of trauma and shock, a hybrid of temporary dementia and selective amnesia. It battened to her with the mindless tenacity of a leech.

She tried not to think about its origins, because when she did she was carried back to the twilight land of her subconscious; to Keith's fifth birthday party; her wedding day with the thousand-dollar cake, and the honeymoon in Niagara Falls; the Cessna spinning against the sun, streaking downward to slam into the Atlantic; and the lush corruption of a green-black jungle and its hidden cairns—the bones of giants slowly sinking into the always hungry earth.

The palace of cries where the doors are opened with blood and sorrow. The secret graveyard of the elephants. The bones of elephants made a forest of rib cages and tusks, dry riverbeds of skulls. Red ants crawled in trains along the petrified spines of behemoths and trailed into the black caverns of empty sockets. Oh, what the lost expeditions might've told the world!

She'd dreamed of the Elephants' Graveyard off and on since the funeral and wasn't certain why she had grown so morbidly preoccupied with the legend. Bleak mythology had interested her when she was young and vital and untouched by the twin melanomas of wisdom and grief. Now such morose contemplation invoked a primordial dread and answered nothing. The central mystery of her was impenetrable to casual methods. Delving beneath the surface smacked of finality, of doom.

Danni chose to endure the fugue, to welcome it as a reliable adversary. The state seldom lasted more than a few minutes, and admittedly it was frightening, certainly dangerous; nonetheless, she was never one to live in a cage. In many ways the dementia and its umbra of pure terror, its visceral chaos, provided the masochistic rush she craved these days—a badge of courage, the martyr's brand. The fugue hid her in its shadow, like a sheltering wing.

May 6, 2006

(D. L. Session 33)

Danni stared at the table while Dr. Green pressed a button and the wheels of the recorder began to turn. His chair creaked as he leaned back. He stated his name, Danni's name, the date and location.

—How are things this week? he said.

Danni set a slim metal tin on the table and flicked it open with her left hand. She removed a cigarette and lighted it. She used matches because she'd lost the fancy lighter Merrill got her as a birthday gift. She exhaled, shook the match dead.

—For a while, I thought I was getting better, she said in a raw voice.

—You don't think you're improving? Dr. Green said.

—Sometimes I wake up and nothing seems real; it's all a movie set, a humdrum version of *This Is Your Life!* I stare at the ceiling and can't shake this sense I'm an imposter.

—Everybody feels that way, Dr. Green said. His dark hands rested on a clipboard. His hands were creased and notched with the onset of middle age; the cuffs of his starched lab coat had gone yellow at the seams. He was married; he wore a simple ring and he never stared at her breasts. Happily married, or a consummate professional, or she was nothing special. A frosted window rose high and narrow over his shoulder like the painted window of a monastery. Pallid light shone at the corners of his angular glasses, the shiny edges of the clipboard, a piece of the bare plastic table, the sunken tiles of the floor. The tiles were dented and scratched and bumpy. Fine cracks spread like tendrils. Against the far walls were cabinets and shelves and several rickety beds with thin rails and large, black wheels.

The hospital was an ancient place and smelled of mold and sickness beneath the buckets of bleach she knew the custodians poured forth every evening. This had been a sanatorium. People with tuberculosis had gathered here to die in the long, shabby wards. Workers loaded the bodies into furnaces and burned them. There were chutes for the corpses on all of the upper floors. The doors of the chutes were made of dull, gray metal with big handles that reminded her of the handles on the flour and sugar bins in her mother's pantry.

Danni smoked and stared at the ceramic ashtray centered exactly between them, inches from a box of tissues. The ashtray was black. Cinders smoldered in its belly. The hospital was "no smoking," but that never came up during their weekly conversations. After the first session of him watching her drop the ashes into her coat pocket, the ashtray had appeared. Occasionally she tapped her cigarette against the rim of the ashtray and watched the smoke coil tighter and tighter until it imploded the way a demolished building collapses into itself after the charges go off.

Dr. Green said, —Did you take the bus or did you walk?

—Today? I walked.

Dr. Green wrote something on the clipboard with a heavy golden pen. —Good. You stopped to visit your friend at the market, I see.

Danni glanced at her cigarette where it fumed between her second and third fingers.

—Did I mention that? My Friday rounds?

—Yes. When we first met. He tapped a thick, manila folder bound in a heavy-duty rubber band. The folder contained Danni's records and transfer papers from the original admitting institute on the East Coast. Additionally, there was a collection of nearly unrecognizable photos of her in hospital gowns and bathrobes. In several shots an anonymous attendant pushed her in a wheelchair against a blurry backdrop of trees and concrete walls.

—Oh.

—You mentioned going back to work. Any progress?

—No. Merrill wants me to. She thinks I need to reintegrate professionally, that it might fix my problem, Danni said, smiling slightly as she pictured her friend's well-meaning harangues. Merrill spoke quickly, in the cadence of a native Bostonian who would always be a Bostonian no matter where she might find herself. A lit major, she'd also gone through an art-junkie phase during grad school, which had wrecked her first marriage and introduced her to many a disreputable character as could be found haunting the finer galleries and museums. One of said characters became ex-husband the second and engendered a profound and abiding disillusionment with the fine-arts scene entirely. Currently, she made an exemplary copy editor at a rather important monthly journal.

—What do you think?

—I liked being a scientist. I liked to study insects, liked tracking their brief, frenetic little lives. I know how important they are, how integral, essential to the ecosystem. Hell, they outnumber humans trillions to one. But, oh my, it's so damned easy to feel like a god when you've got an ant twitching in your forceps. You think that's how God feels when He's got one of us under His thumb?

—I couldn't say.

—Me neither. Danni dragged heavily and squinted. —Maybe I'll sell Bibles door-to-door. My uncle sold encyclopedias when I was a little girl.

Dr. Green picked up the clipboard. —Well. Any episodes—fainting, dizziness, disorientation? Anything of that nature?

She smoked in silence for nearly half a minute. —I got confused about where I was the other day. She closed her eyes. The recollection of those bad moments threatened her equilibrium. —I was walking to Yang's grocery—it's about three blocks from the apartments. I got lost for a few minutes.

—A few minutes.

—Yeah. I wasn't timing it, sorry.

—No, that's fine. Go on.

—It was like before. I didn't recognize any of the buildings. I was in a foreign city and couldn't remember what I was doing there. Someone tried to talk to me, to help me—an old lady. But I ran from her instead. Danni swallowed the faint bitterness, the dumb memory of nausea and terror.

—Why? Why did you run?

—Because when the fugue comes, when I get confused and forget where I am, people frighten me. Their faces don't seem real. Their faces are rubbery and inhuman. I thought the old lady was wearing a mask, that she was hiding something. So I ran. By the time I regained my senses, I was near the park. Kids were staring at me.

—Then?

—Then what? I yelled at them for staring at me. They took off.

—What did you want at Yang's?

—What?

—You said you were shopping. For what?

—I don't recall. Beets. Grapes. A giant zucchini. I don't know.

—You've been taking your medication, I presume. Drugs, alcohol?

—No drugs. Okay, a joint occasionally. A few shots here and there. Merrill wants to unwind on the weekends. She drinks me under the table—Johnnie Walker and Manhattans. Tequila if she's seducing one of the rugged types. Depends where we are. She'd known Merrill since forever. Historically, Danni was the strong one, the one who saw Merrill through two bad marriages, a career collapse, and bouts of deep clinical depression. Funny how life tended to put the shoe on the other foot when one least expected.

—Do you visit many different places?

Danni shrugged. —I don't—oh, the Candy Apple. Harpo's. That hole-in-the-wall on Decker and Gedding, the Red Jack. All sorts of places. Merrill picks; says it's therapy.

—Sex?

Danni shook her head. —That doesn't mean I'm loyal.

—Loyal to whom?

—I've been noticing men and . . . I feel like I'm betraying Virgil. Soiling our memories. It's stupid, sure. Merrill thinks I'm crazy.

—What do *you* think?

—I try not to, Doc.

—Yet the past is with you. You carry it everywhere. Like a millstone, if you'll pardon the cliché.

Danni frowned.

—I'm not sure what you mean—

—Yes, you are.

She smoked and looked away from his eyes. She'd arranged a mini gallery of snapshots of Virgil and Keith on the bureau in her bedroom, stuffed more photos in her wallet, and fixed one of Keith as a baby on a keychain. She'd built a modest shrine of baseball ticket stubs, Virgil's moldy fishing hat, his car keys, though the car was long gone, business cards, canceled checks, and torn-up Christmas wrapping. It was sick.

—Memories have their place, of course, Dr. Green said. —But you've got to be careful. Live in the past too long and it consumes you. You can't use fidelity as a crutch. Not forever.

—I'm not planning on forever, Danni said.

August 2, 2006

Color and symmetry were among Danni's current preoccupations. Yellow squash, orange baby carrots, an axis of green peas on a china plate; the alignment of complementary elements surgically precise upon the starched white tablecloth—cloth white and neat as the hard white fabric of a hospital sheet.

Their apartment was a narrow box stacked high in a cylinder of similar boxes. The window sashes were blue. All of them a filmy, ephemeral blue like the dust on the wings of a blue emperor butterfly; blue over every window in every cramped room. Blue as dead salmon, blue as ice. Blue shadows darkened the edge of the table, rippled over Danni's untouched meal, its meticulously arrayed components. The vegetables glowed with subdued radioactivity. Her fingers curled around the fork; the veins in her hand ran like blue-black tributaries to her fingertips, ran like cold iron wires. Balanced on a windowsill was her ant farm, its inhabitants scurrying about the business of industry in microcosm of the looming cityscape. Merrill hated the ants and Danni expected her friend to poison them in a fit of revulsion and pique. Merrill wasn't naturally maternal and her scant reservoir of kindly nurture was already exhausted on her housemate.

Danni set the fork upon a napkin, red gone black as sackcloth in the beautiful gloom, and moved to the terrace door, reaching automatically for her cigarettes as she went. She kept them in the left breast pocket of her jacket alongside a pack of matches from the Candy Apple.

The light that came through the glass and blue gauze was muted and heavy even at midday. Outside the sliding door was a terrace and a rail; beyond the rail, a gulf. Damp breaths of air were coarse with smog, tar, and pigeon shit. Eight stories yawned below the wobbly terrace to the dark brick square. Ninety-six feet to the fountain, the flagpole, two rusty benches, and Piccolo Street where winos with homemade drums, harmonicas, and flutes composed their symphonies and dirges.

Danni smoked on the terrace to keep the peace with Merrill, straight-edge Merrill, whose poison of choice was Zinfandel and fast men in nice suits, rather than tobacco. Danni smoked Turkish cigarettes that came in a tin she bought at the wharf market from a Nepalese expat named Mahan. Mahan sold coffee, too, in shiny black packages, and decorative knives with tassels depending from brass handles.

Danni leaned on the swaying rail and lighted the next to the last cigarette in her tin and smoked as the sky clotted between the gaps of rooftops, the copses of wires and antennas, the static snarl of uprooted birds like black bits of paper ash turning in the Pacific breeze. A man stopped in the middle of the crosswalk. He craned his neck to seek her out from amid the jigsaw of fire escapes and balconies. He waved and then turned away and crossed the street with an unmistakably familiar stride, and was gone.

When her cigarette was done, she flicked the butt into the empty planter, one of several terra-cotta pots piled around the corroding barbecue. She lighted her remaining cigarette and smoked it slowly, made it last until the sky went opaque and the city lights began to float here and there in the murk, bubbles of iridescent gas rising against the leaden tide of night. Then she went inside and sat very still while her colony of ants scrabbled in the dark.

May 6, 2006

(D. L. Session 33)

Danni's cigarette was out; the tin empty. She began to fidget. —Do you believe in ghosts, Doctor?

—Absolutely. Dr. Green knocked his ring on the table and gestured at the hoary walls. —Look around. Haunted, I'd say.

—Really?

Dr. Green seemed quite serious. He set aside the clipboard, distancing himself from the record. —Why not. My grandfather was a missionary. He lived in the Congo for several years, set up a clinic out there. Everybody believed in ghosts—including my grandfather. There was no choice.

Danni laughed. —Well, it's settled. I'm a faithless bitch. And I'm being haunted as just desserts.

—Why do you say that?

—I went home with this guy a few weeks ago. Nice guy, a graphic designer. I was pretty drunk and he was pretty persuasive.

Dr. Green plucked a pack of cigarettes from the inside pocket of his white coat, shook one loose, and handed it to her. They leaned toward each other, across the table, and he lighted her cigarette with a silvery Zippo.

—Nothing happened, she said. —It was very innocent, actually.

But that was a lie by omission, was it not? What would the good doctor think of her if she confessed her impulses to grasp a man, any man, as a point of fact, and throw him down and fuck him senseless, and refrained only because she was too frightened of the possibilities? Her cheeks stung and she exhaled fiercely to conceal her shame.

—We had some drinks and called it a night. I still felt bad, dirty, somehow. Riding the bus home, I saw Virgil. It wasn't him; he had Virgil's build and kind of slouched, holding on to one of those straps. Didn't even come close once I got a decent look at him. But for a second, my heart froze. Danni lifted her gaze from the ashtray. —Time for more pills, huh?

—Well, a case of mistaken identity doesn't qualify as a delusion. Danni smiled darkly.

—You didn't get on the plane and you lived. Simple. Dr. Green spoke with supreme confidence.

—Is it? Simple, I mean.

—Have you experienced more of these episodes—mistaking strangers for Virgil? Or your son?

—Yeah. The man on the bus, that tepid phantom of her husband, had been the fifth incident of mistaken identity during the previous three weeks. The incidents were growing frequent; each apparition more convincing than the last. Then there were the items she'd occasionally found around the apartment—Virgil's lost wedding ring gleaming at the bottom of a pitcher of water; a trail of dried rose petals leading from the bathroom to her bed; one of Keith's crayon masterpieces fixed by magnet on the refrigerator; each of these artifacts ephemeral as dew, transitory as drifting spider thread; they dissolved and left no traces of their existence. That very morning she'd glimpsed Virgil's bomber jacket slung over the back of a chair. A sunbeam illuminated it momentarily, dispersed it among the moving shadows of clouds and undulating curtains.

The Lagerstätte · 263

—Why didn't you mention this sooner?

—It didn't scare me before.

—There are many possibilities. I hazard what we're dealing with is survivor's guilt, Dr. Green said. —This guilt is a perfectly normal aspect of the grieving process.

Dr. Green had never brought up the guilt association before, but she always knew it lurked in the wings, waiting to be sprung in the third act. The books all talked about it. Danni made a noise of disgust and rolled her eyes to hide the sudden urge to cry.

—Go on, Dr. Green said.

Danni pretended to rub smoke from her eye. —There isn't any more.

—Certainly there is. There's always another rock to look beneath. Why don't you tell me about the vineyards. Does this have anything to do with the *Lagerstätte*?

She opened her mouth and closed it. She stared, her fear and anger tightening screws within the pit of her stomach. —You've spoken to Merrill? Goddamn her.

—She hoped you'd get around to it, eventually. But you haven't and it seems important. Don't worry—she volunteered the information. Of course I would never reveal the nature of our conversations. Trust in that.

—It's not a good thing to talk about, Danni said. —I stopped thinking about it.

—Why?

She regarded her cigarette. Norma, poor departed Norma whispered in her ear, *Do you want to press your eye against the keyhole of a secret room? Do you want to see where the elephants have gone to die?*

—Because there are some things you can't take back. Shake hands with an ineffable enigma and it knows you. It has you, if it wants.

Dr. Green waited, his hand poised over a brown folder she hadn't noticed before. The folder was stamped in red block letters she couldn't quite read, although she suspected ASYLUM was at least a portion.

—I wish to understand, he said. —We're not going anywhere.

—Fuck it, she said. A sense of terrible satisfaction and relief caused her to smile again. —Confession is good for the soul, right?

August 9, 2006

In the middle of dressing to meet Merrill at the market by the wharf when she got off work, Danni opened the closet and inhaled a whiff of damp, moldering air and then screamed into her fist. Several withered corpses hung from the rack amid her cheery blouses and conservative suit jackets. They were scarcely more than yellowed sacks of skin. None of the desiccated, sagging faces was recognizable; the shade and texture of cured squash, each was further distorted by warps and wrinkles of dry-cleaning bags. She recoiled and sat on the bed and chewed her fingers until a passing cloud blocked the sun and the closet went dark.

Eventually she washed her hands and face in the bathroom sink, staring into the mirror at her pale, maniacal simulacrum. She skipped makeup and stumbled from the apartment to the cramped, dingy lift that dropped her into a shabby foyer with its rows of tarnished mailbox slots checkering the walls, its low, grubby light fixtures, a stained carpet, and the sweet-and-sour odor of sweat and stagnant air. She stumbled through the security doors into the brighter world.

And the fugue descended.

Danni was walking from somewhere to somewhere else; she'd closed her eyes against the glare and her insides turned upside down. Her eyes flew open and she reeled, utterly lost. Shadow people moved around her, bumped her with their hard elbows and swinging hips; an angry man in brown tweed lectured his daughter and the girl protested. They buzzed like flies. Their miserable faces blurred together, lit by some internal phosphorus. Danni swallowed, crushed into herself with a force akin to claustrophobia, and focused on her watch, a cheap windup model that glowed in the dark. Its numerals meant nothing, but she tracked the needle as it swept a perfect circle while the world spun around her. The passage, an indoor–outdoor avenue of sorts. Market stalls flanked the causeway, shelves and timber beams twined with streamers and beads, hemp rope and tie-dye shirts and pennants. Light fell through cracks in the overhead pavilion. The enclosure reeked of fresh salmon, salt water, sawdust, and the compacted scent of perfumed flesh.

—*Danni*. Here was an intelligible voice amid the squeal and squelch. Danni lifted her head and tried to focus.

—*We miss you*, Virgil said. He stood several feet away, gleaming like polished ivory.

—What? Danni said, thinking his face was the only face not changing shape like the flowery crystals in a kaleidoscope. —What did you say?

—*Come home*. It was apparent that this man wasn't Virgil, although in this particular light the eyes were similar, and he drawled. Virgil grew up in South Carolina, spent his adult life trying to bury that drawl, and eventually it emerged only when he was exhausted or angry. The stranger winked at her and continued along the boardwalk. Beneath an Egyptian cotton shirt, his back was almost as muscular as Virgil's. But, no.

Danni turned away into the bright, jostling throng. Someone took her elbow. She yelped and wrenched away and nearly fell.

—Honey, you okay? The jumble of insectoid eyes, lips, and bouffant hair coalesced into Merrill's stern face. Merrill wore white-rimmed sunglasses that complemented her vanilla dress with its wide shoulders and brass buttons, and her elegant vanilla gloves. Her thin nose peeled with sunburn. —Danni, are you all right?

—Yeah. Danni wiped her mouth.

—The hell you are. C'mon. Merrill led her away from the moving press to a small open square and seated her in a wooden chair in the shadow of a parasol. The square hosted a half dozen vendors and several tables of squawking children, overheated parents with flushed cheeks, and senior citizens in pastel running suits. Merrill bought soft ice cream in tiny plastic dishes and they sat in the shade and ate the ice cream while the sun dipped below the rooflines. The vendors began taking down the signs and packing it in for the day.

—Okay, okay. I feel better. Danni's hands had stopped shaking.

—You do look a little better. Know where you are?

—The market. Danni wanted a cigarette. —Oh, damn it, she said.

—Here, sweetie. Merrill drew two containers of Mahan's foreign cigarettes from her purse and slid them across the table, mimicking a spy in one of those 1970s thrillers.

—Thanks, Danni said as she got a cigarette burning. She dragged frantically, left hand cupped to her mouth so the escaping smoke boiled and foamed between her fingers like dry-ice vapors. Nobody said anything despite the NO SMOKING signs posted on the gate.

—Hey, what kind of bug is that? Merrill intently regarded a beetle hugging the warmth of a wooden plank near their feet.

—It's a beetle.

—How observant. But what kind?

—I don't know.

—What? You don't know?

—I don't know. I don't really care, either.

—Oh, please.

—Fine. Danni leaned forward until her eyeballs were scant inches above the motionless insect. —Hmm. I'd say a *Spurious exoticus minor*, closely related to, but not to be confused with, the *Spurious eroticus major*. Yep.

Merrill stared at the beetle, then Danni. She took Danni's hand and gently squeezed. —You fucking fraud. Let's go get liquored up, hey?

—Hey-hey.

May 6, 2006

(D. L. Session 33)

Dr. Green's glasses were opaque as quartz.

—The *Lagerstätte*. Elucidate, if you will.

—A naturalist's wet dream. Ask Norma Fitzwater and Leslie Runyon, Danni said and chuckled wryly. —When Merrill originally brought me here to Cali, she made me join a support group. That was about, what? A year ago, give or take. Kind of a twelve-step program for wannabe suicides. I quit after a few visits—group therapy isn't my style and the counselor was a royal prick. Before I left, I became friends with Norma, a drug addict and perennial houseguest of the state penitentiary before she snagged a wealthy husband. Marrying rich wasn't a cure for everything, though. She claimed to have tried to off herself five or six times, made it sound like an extreme sport.

—A fascinating woman. She was pals with Leslie, a widow like me. Leslie's husband and brother fell off a glacier in Alaska. I didn't like her much. Too creepy for polite company. Unfortunately, Norma had a mother-hen complex, so there was no getting rid of her. Anyway, it wasn't much to write home about. We went to lunch once a week, watched a couple of films, commiserated about our shitty luck. Summer camp stuff.

—You speak of Norma in the past tense. I gather she eventually ended her life, Dr. Green said.

—Oh, yes. She made good on that. Jumped off a hotel roof in the Tenderloin. Left a note to the effect that she and Leslie couldn't face the music anymore. The cops, brilliant as they are, concluded Norma made a suicide pact with Leslie. Leslie's corpse hasn't surfaced yet. The cops figure she's at the bottom of the bay, or moldering in a wooded gully. I doubt that's what happened, though.

—You suspect she's alive.

—No, Leslie's dead under mysterious and messy circumstances. It got leaked to the press that the cops found evidence of foul play at her home. There was blood or something on her sheets. They say it dried in the shape of a person curled in the fetal position—somebody mentioned the flash shadows of victims in Hiroshima. This was deeper, as if the body had been pressed hard into the mattress. The only remains were her watch, her diaphragm, her *fillings*, for Christ's sake, stuck to the coagulate that got left behind like afterbirth. Sure, it's bullshit, urban legend fodder. There were some photos in the *Gazette*, some speculation among our sorry little circle of neurotics and manic depressives.

—Very unpleasant but, fortunately, equally improbable.

Danni shrugged. —Here's the thing, though. Norma predicted everything. A month before she killed herself, she let me in on a secret. Her friend Leslie, the creepy lady, had been seeing Bobby. He visited her nightly, begged her to come away with him. And Leslie planned to.

—Her husband, Dr. Green said. —The one who died in Alaska.

—The same. Trust me, I laughed, a little nervously, at this news. I wasn't sure whether to humor Norma or get the hell away from her. We were sitting in a classy restaurant, surrounded by execs in silk ties and Armani suits. Like I said, Norma was loaded. She married into a nice Sicilian family; her husband was in the import–export business, if you get my drift. Beat the hell out of her, though; definitely contributed to her low self-esteem. Right in the middle of our luncheon, between the lobster tails and the éclairs, she leaned over and confided this thing with Leslie and her deceased husband. The ghostly lover.

Dr. Green passed Danni another cigarette. He lighted one of his own and studied her through the blue exhaust. Danni wondered if he wanted a drink as badly as she did.

—How did you react to this information? Dr. Green said.

—I stayed cool, feigned indifference. It wasn't difficult; I was doped to the eyeballs most of the time. Norma claimed there exists a certain quality of grief, so utterly profound, so tragically pure, that it resounds and resonates above and below. A living, bleeding echo. It's the key to a kind of limbo.

—The *Lagerstätte*. Dr. Green licked his thumb and sorted through the papers in the brown folder. —As in the Burgess Shale, the La Brea Tar Pits. Were your friends amateur paleontologists?

—*Lagerstätten* are 'resting places' in the Deutsch, and I think that's what the women meant.

—Fascinating choice of mythos.

—People do whatever it takes to cope. Drugs, kamikaze sex, religion, anything. In naming, we seek to order the incomprehensible, yes?

—True.

—Norma pulled this weird piece of jagged gray rock from her purse. Not rock—a petrified bone shard. A fang or a long, wicked rib splinter. Supposedly human. I could tell it was old; it reminded me of all those fossils of trilobites I used to play with. It radiated an aura of antiquity, like it had survived a shift of deep geological time. Norma got it from Leslie and Leslie had gotten it from someone else; Norma claimed to have no idea who, although I suspect she was lying; there was definitely a certain slyness in her eyes. For all I know, it's osmosis. She pricked her finger on the shard and gestured at the blood that oozed on her plate. Danni shivered and clenched her left hand. —The scene was surreal. Norma said: *Grief is blood, Danni. Blood is the living path to everywhere. Blood opens the way.* She said if I offered myself to the *Lagerstätte*, Virgil would come to me and take me into the house of dreams. But I wanted to know whether it would really be him and not . . . an imitation. She said, *Does it matter?* My skin crawled as if I were waking from a long sleep to something awful, something my primal self recognized and feared. Like fire.

—You believe the bone was human.

—I don't know. Norma insisted I accept it as a gift from her and Leslie. I really didn't want to, but the look on her face, it was intense.

—Where did it come from? The bone.

—The *Lagerstätte*.

—Of course. What did you do?

Danni looked down at her hands, the left with its jagged white scar in the meat and muscle of her palm, and deeper into the darkness of the earth. —The same as Leslie. I called them.

—You called them. Virgil and Keith.

—Yes. I didn't plan to go through with it. I got drunk, and when I'm like that, my thoughts get kind of screwy. I don't act in character.

—Oh. Dr. Green thought that over. —When you say called, what exactly do you mean?

She shrugged and flicked ashes into the ashtray. Even though Dr. Green had been there the morning they stitched the wound, she guarded the secret of its origin with a zeal bordering on pathological.

Danni had brought the weird bone to the apartment. Once alone, she drank the better half of a bottle of Maker's Mark and then sliced her palm and made a doorway in blood. She slathered a vertical seam, a demarcation between her existence and the abyss, in the plaster wall at the foot of her bed. She smeared Virgil's and Keith's initials and sent a little prayer into the night. In a small clay pot she'd bought at a market, she shredded her identification, her (mostly defunct) credit cards, her Social Security card, a lock of her hair, and burned the works with the tallow of a lamb. Then, in the smoke and shadows, she finished getting drunk off her ass and promptly blacked out.

Merrill wasn't happy; Danni had bled like the proverbial stuck pig, soaked through the sheets into the mattress. Merrill decided her friend had horribly botched another run for the Pearly Gates. She had brought Danni to the hospital for a bunch of stitches and introduced her to Dr. Green. Of course Danni didn't admit another suicide attempt. She doubted her conducting a black-magic ritual would help matters, either. She said nothing, simply agreed to return for sessions with the good doctor. He was blandly pleasant, eminently nonthreatening. She didn't think he could help, but that wasn't the point. The point was to please Merrill and Merrill insisted on the visits.

Back home, Merrill confiscated the bone, the ritual fetish, and threw it in the trash. Later, she tried like hell to scrub the stain. In the end she gave up and painted the whole room blue.

A couple of days after that particular bit of excitement, Danni found the bone at the bottom of her sock drawer. It glistened with a cruel, lusterless intensity. Like the monkey's paw it had returned, and that didn't surprise her. She folded it into a kerchief and locked it in a jewelry box she'd kept since first grade.

All these months gone by, Danni remained silent on the subject.

Finally, Dr. Green sighed. —Is that when you began seeing Virgil in the faces of strangers? These doppelgängers? He smoked his cigarette with the joyless concentration of a prisoner facing a firing squad. It was obvious from his expression that the meter had rolled back to zero.

—No, not right away. Nothing happened, Danni said. —Nothing ever does, at first.

—No, I suppose not. Tell me about the vineyard. What happened there?

—I . . . I got lost.

—That's where all this really begins, isn't it? The fugue, perhaps other things.

Danni gritted her teeth. She thought of elephants and graveyards. Dr. Green was right, in his own smug way. Six weeks after Danni sliced her hand, Merrill took her for a day trip to the beach. Merrill rented a convertible and made a picnic. It was nice, possibly the first time Danni felt human since the accident, the first time she'd wanted to do anything besides mope in the apartment and play depressing music.

After some discussion, they chose Bolton Park, a lovely stretch of coastline way out past Kingwood. The area was foreign to Danni, so she bought a road map pamphlet at a gas station. The brochure listed a bunch of touristy places. Windsurfers and bird-watchers favored the area, but the guide warned of dangerous riptides. The women had no intention of swimming; they stayed near a cluster of great big rocks at the north end of the beach—below the cliff with the steps that led up to the posh houses, the summer homes of movie stars and advertising executives, the beautiful people.

On the way home, Danni asked if they might stop at Kirkston Vineyards. It was a hole-in-the-wall, only briefly listed in the guidebook. There were no pictures. They drove in circles for an hour tracking the place down—Kirkston was off the beaten path, a village of sorts. There was a gift shop and an inn, and a few antique houses. The winery was fairly large and charming in a rustic fashion, and that essentially summed up the entire place.

Danni thought it was a cute setup; Merrill was bored stiff and did what she always did when she'd grown weary of a situation—she flirted like mad with one of the tour guides. Pretty soon, she disappeared with the guy on a private tour.

There were twenty or thirty people in the tour group—a bunch of elderly folks who'd arrived on a bus and a few couples pretending they were in Europe. After Danni lost Merrill in the crowd, she went outside to explore until her friend surfaced again.

Perhaps fifty yards from the winery steps, Virgil waited in the lengthening shadows of a cedar grove. That was the first of the phantoms. Too far away for positive identification, his face was a white smudge. He hesitated and regarded her over his shoulder before he ducked into the undergrowth. She knew it was impossible, knew that it was madness, or worse, and went after him anyway.

Deeper into the grounds she encountered crumbled walls of a ruined garden hidden under a bower of willow trees and honeysuckle vines. She passed through a massive marble archway, so thick with sap it had blackened like a smokestack. Inside was a sunken area and a clogged fountain decorated with cherubs and gargoyles. There were scattered benches made of stone slabs, and piles of rubble overrun by creepers and moss. Water pooled throughout the garden, mostly covered by algae and scum; mosquito larvae squirmed beneath drowned leaves. Ridges of broken stone and mortar petrified in the slop and slime of that boggy soil and made waist-high calculi among the freestanding masonry.

Her hand throbbed with a sudden, magnificent stab of pain. She hissed through her teeth. The freshly knitted pink slash, her Freudian scar, had split and blood seeped so copiously her head swam. She ripped the sleeve off her blouse and made a hasty tourniquet. A grim, sullen quiet drifted in, a blizzard of silence. The bees weren't buzzing and the shadows in the trees waxed red and gold as the light decayed.

Virgil stepped from behind stalagmites of fallen stone, maybe thirty feet away. She knew with every fiber of her being that this was a fake, a body double, and yet she wanted nothing more than to hurl herself into his arms. Up until that moment, she didn't realize how much she'd missed him, how achingly final her loneliness had become.

Her glance fell upon a gleaming wedge of stone where it thrust from the water like a dinosaur's tooth, and as shapes within shapes became apparent, she understood this wasn't a garden. It was a graveyard.

Virgil opened his arms—

—I'm not comfortable talking about this, Danni said. —Let's move on.

August 9, 2006

Friday was karaoke night at the Candy Apple.

In the golden days of her previous life, Danni had a battalion of friends and colleagues with whom to attend the various academic functions and cocktail socials as required by her professional affiliation with a famous East Coast university. Bar-hopping had seldom been the excursion of choice.

Tonight, a continent and several light-years removed from such circumstances, she nursed an overly strong margarita while up on the stage a couple of drunken women with big hair and smeared makeup stumbled through that old Kenny Rogers standby, "Ruby, Don't Take Your Love to Town." The fake redhead was a receptionist named Sheila, and her blond partner, Delores, a vice president of human resources. Both of them worked at Merrill's literary magazine and they were partying off their second and third divorces, respectively.

Danni wasn't drunk, although mixing her medication with alcohol wasn't helping matters; her nose had begun to tingle and her sensibilities were definitely sliding toward the nihilistic side. Also, she seemed to be hallucinating again. She'd spotted two Virgil look-alikes between walking through the door and her third margarita; that was a record, so far. She hadn't noticed either of the men enter the lounge; they simply appeared.

One of the mystery men sat among a group of happily chattering yuppie kids; he'd worn a sweater and parted his hair exactly like her husband used to before an important interview or presentation. The brow was wrong, though, and the smile way off. He established eye contact and his gaze made her prickle all over because this simulacrum was so very authentic; if not for the plastic sheen and the unwholesome smile, he was the man she'd looked at across the breakfast table for a dozen years. Eventually he stood and wandered away from his friends and disappeared through the front door into the night. None of the kids seemed to miss him.

The second guy sat alone at the far end of the bar. He was much closer to the authentic thing; he had the nose, the jaw, even the loose way of draping his hands over his knees. However, this one was a bit too rawboned to pass as *her* Virgil; his teeth too large, his arms too long. He stared across the room, too-dark eyes fastened on her face, and she looked away and by the time she glanced up again he was gone.

She checked to see if Merrill noticed the Virgil impersonators. Merrill blithely sipped her Corona and flirted with a couple of lawyer types at the adjoining table. The suits kept company with a voluptuous woman who was growing long in the tooth and had piled on enough compensatory eye shadow and lipstick to host her own talk show. The woman sulked and shot dangerous glares at Merrill. Merrill smirked coyly and touched the closer suit on the arm.

Danni lighted a cigarette and tried to keep her expression neutral while her pulse fluttered and she scanned the room with the corners of her eyes like a trapped bird. Should she call Dr. Green in the morning? Was he even in the office on weekends? What color would the new pills be?

Presently, the late-dinner and theater crowd arrived en masse and the lounge became packed. The temperature immediately shot up ten degrees and the resultant din of several dozen competing conversations drowned all but shouts. Merrill had recruited the lawyers (who turned out to be an insurance claims investigator and a CPA—Ned and Thomas, and their miffed associate Glenna, a court clerk—to join the group and migrate to another, hopefully more peaceful watering hole.

They shambled through neon-washed night, a noisy, truncated herd of quasi-strangers, arms locked for purchase against the mist-slick sidewalks. Danni found herself squashed between Glenna and Ned the Investigator. Ned grasped her waist in a slack, yet vaguely proprietary fashion; his hand was soft with sweat, his paunchy face made more uncomely with livid blotches and the avaricious expression of a drowsy predator. His shirt reeked so powerfully of whiskey it might've been doused in the stuff.

Merrill pulled them to a succession of bars and nightclubs and all-night bistros. Somebody handed Danni a beer as they milled in the vaulted entrance of an Irish pub and she drank it like tap water, not really tasting it, and her ears hurt and the evening rapidly devolved into a tangle of raucous music and smoke that reflected the fluorescent lights like coke-blacked miner's lamps, and at last a cool, humid darkness shattered by headlights and the sulfurous orange glow of angry clouds.

By her haphazard count, she glimpsed in excess of fifty incarnations of Virgil. Several at the tavern, solitary men mostly submerged in the recessed booths, observing her with stony diffidence through beer steins and shot glasses; a dozen more scattered along the boulevard, listless nomads whose eyes slid around, not quite touching anything. When a city bus grumbled past, every passenger's head swiveled in unison beneath the repeating flare of dome lights. Every face pressed against the dirty windows belonged to him. Their lifelike masks bulged and contorted with inconsolable longing.

Ned escorted her to his place, a warehouse apartment in a row of identical warehouses between the harbor and the railroad tracks. The building had been converted to a munitions factory during the Second World War, then housing in the latter 1960s. It stood black and gritty; its greasy windows sucked in the feeble illumination of the lonely beacons of passing boats and the occasional car.

They took a clanking cargo elevator to the top, the penthouse as Ned laughingly referred to his apartment. The elevator was a box encased in grates that exposed the inner organs of the shaft and the dark tunnels of passing floors. It could've easily hoisted a baby grand piano. Danni pressed her cheek to vibrating metal and shut her eyes tight against vertigo and the canteen-like slosh of too many beers in her stomach.

Ned's apartment was sparsely furnished and remained mostly in gloom even after he turned on the floor lamp and went to fix nightcaps. Danni collapsed onto the corner of a couch abridging the shallow nimbus of light and stared raptly at her bone-white hand curled into the black leather. Neil Diamond crooned from velvet speakers. Ned said something about his record collection and, faintly, ice cracked from its tray and clinked in glass with the resonance of a tuning fork.

Danni's hand shivered as if it might double and divide. She was cold now, in the sticky hot apartment, and her thighs trembled. Ned slipped a drink into her hand and placed his own hand on her shoulder, splayed his soft fingers on her collar, traced her collarbone with his moist fingertip. Danni flinched and poured gin down her throat until Ned took the glass and began to nuzzle her ear, his teeth clicking against the pearl stud, his overheated breath like smoldering creosote and kerosene, and as he tugged at her blouse strap, she began to cry. Ned lurched above her and his hands were busy with his belt and pants, and these fell around his ankles and his loafers. He made a fist in a mass of her hair and yanked her face against his groin; his linen shirttails fell across Danni's shoulders and he bulled himself into her gasping mouth. She gagged, overwhelmed by the ripeness of sweat and whiskey and urine, the rank humidity, the bruising insistence of him, and she convulsed, arms flailing in epileptic spasms, and vomited. Ned's hips pumped for several seconds and then his brain caught up with current events and he cried out in dismay and disgust and nearly capsized the couch as he scrambled away from her and a caramel gush of half-digested cocktail shrimp and alcohol.

Danni dragged herself from the couch and groped for the door. The door was locked with a bolt and chain and she battered at these, sobbing and choking. Ned's curses were muffled by a thin partition and the low thunder of water sluicing through corroded pipes. She flung open the door and was instantly lost in a cavernous hall that telescoped madly. The door behind her was a cave mouth, the windows were holes, were burrows. She toppled down a flight of stairs.

Danni lay crumpled, damp concrete wedged against the small of her back and pinching the back of her legs. Ghostly radiance cast shadows upon the piebald walls of the narrow staircase and rendered the scrawls of graffiti into fragmented hieroglyphics. Copper and salt filled her mouth. Her head was thick and spongy and when she moved it, little comets shot through her vision. A moth jerked in zigzags near her face, jittering upward at frantic angles toward a naked bulb. The bulb was brown and black with dust and cigarette smoke. A solid shadow detached from the gloom of the landing; a slight, pitchy silhouette that wavered at the edges like gasoline fumes.

Mommy? A small voice echoed, familiar and strange, the voice of a child or a castrato, and it plucked at her insides, sent tremors through her.

—Oh, God, she said and vomited again, spilling herself against the rough surface of the wall. The figure became two, then four and a pack of childlike shapes assembled on the landing. The pallid corona of the brown bulb dimmed. She rolled away, onto her belly, and began to crawl . . .

August 10, 2006

The police located Danni semiconscious in the alley behind the warehouse apartments. She didn't understand much of what they said and she couldn't muster the resolve to volunteer the details of her evening's escapades. Merrill rode with her in the ambulance to the emergency room where, following a two-hour wait, a haggard surgeon determined that Danni suffered from a number of nasty contusions, minor lacerations, and a punctured tongue. No concussion, however. He punched ten staples into her scalp, handed over a prescription for painkillers, and sent her home with an admonishment to return in twelve hours for observation.

After they'd settled safe and sound at the apartment, Merrill wrapped Danni in a blanket and boiled a pot of green tea. Lately, Merrill was into feng shui and Chinese herbal remedies. It wasn't quite dawn and so they sat in the shadows in the living room. There were no recriminations, although Merrill lapsed into a palpable funk; hers was the grim expression of guilt and helplessness attendant to her perceived breach of guardianship. Danni patted her hand and drifted off to sleep.

When Danni came to again, it was early afternoon and Merrill was in the kitchen banging pots. Over bowls of hot noodle soup Merrill explained she'd called in sick for a couple of days. She thought they should get Danni's skull checked for dents and rent some movies and lie around with a bowl of popcorn and do essentially nothing. Tomorrow might be a good day to go window-shopping for an Asian print to mount in their pitifully barren entryway.

Merrill summoned a cab. The rain came in sheets against the windows of the moving car and Danni dozed to the thud of the wipers, trying to ignore the driver's eyes upon her from the rearview. He looked unlike the fuzzy headshot on his license fixed to the visor. In the photo his features were burnt teak and warped by the deformation of aging plastic.

They arrived at the hospital and signed in and went into the bowels of the grand old beast to radiology. A woman in a white jacket injected dye into Danni's leg and loaded her into a shiny, cold machine the girth of a bread truck and ordered her to keep her head still. The technician's voice buzzed through a hidden transmitter, repulsively intimate as if a fly had crawled into her ear canal. When the rubber jackhammers started in on the steel shell, she closed her eyes and saw Virgil and Keith waving to her from the convex windows of the plane. The propeller spun so slowly, she could track its revolutions.

—The doctor says they're negative. The technician held photographic plates of Danni's brain against a softly flickering pane of light. —See? No problems at all.

The crimson seam dried black on the bedroom wall. The band of black acid eating plaster until the wall swung open on smooth, silent hinges. Red darkness pulsed in the rift. White leaves crumbled and sank, each one a lost face. A shadow slowly shaped itself into human form. The shadow man regarded her, his hand extended, approaching her without moving his shadow legs.

Merrill thanked the woman in the clipped manner she reserved for those who provoked her distaste, and put a protective arm over Danni's shoulders. Danni had taken an extra dose of tranquilizers to sand the rough edges. Reality was a taffy pull.

Pour out your blood and they'll come back to you, Norma said and stuck her bleeding finger in her mouth. Her eyes were cold and dark as the eyes of a carrion bird. Bobby and Leslie coupled on a squeaking bed. Their frantic rhythm gradually slowed and they began to melt and merge until their flesh rendered to a sticky puddle of oil and fat and patches of hair. The forensics photographers came, clicking and whirring, eyes deader than the lenses of their cameras. They smoked cigarettes in the hallway and chatted with the plainclothes about baseball and who was getting pussy and who wasn't; everybody had sashimi for lunch, noodles for supper, and took work home and drank too much. Leslie curdled in the sheets and her parents were long gone, so she was already most of the way to being reduced to a serial number and forgotten in a cardboard box in a storeroom. Except Leslie stood in a doorway in the grimy bulk of a nameless building. She stood, hip-shot and half silhouetted, naked and lovely as a Botticelli nude. Disembodied arms circled her from behind, and large, muscular hands cupped her breasts. She nodded, expressionless as a wax death masque, and stepped back into the black. The iron door closed.

Danni's brain was fine. No problems at all.

Merrill took her home and made her supper. Fried chicken; Danni's favorite from a research stint studying the migration habits of three species of arachnids at a southern institute where grits did double duty as breakfast and lunch.

Danni dozed intermittently, lulled by the staccato flashes of the television. She stirred and wiped drool from her lips, thankfully too dopey to suffer much embarrassment. Merrill helped her to bed and tucked her in and kissed her good night on the mouth. Danni was surprised by the warmth of her breath, her tenderness; then she was heavily asleep, floating facedown in the red darkness, the amniotic wastes of a secret world.

August 11, 2006

Merrill cooked waffles for breakfast; she claimed to have been a "champeen" hash-slinger as an undergrad, albeit Danni couldn't recall that particular detail of their shared history. Although food crumbled like cardboard on her tongue, Danni smiled gamely and cleared her plate. The fresh orange juice in the frosted glass was a mouthful of lye. Merrill had apparently jogged over to Yang's and picked up a carton the exact instant the poor fellow rolled back the metal curtains from his shop front, and Danni swallowed it and hoped she didn't drop the glass because her hand was shaking so much. The pleasant euphoria of painkillers and sedatives had drained away, usurped by a gnawing, allusive dread, a swell of self-disgust and revulsion.

The night terrors tittered and scuffled in the cracks and crannies of the tiny kitchen, whistled at her in a pitch only she and dogs could hear. Any second now, the broom closet would creak open and a ghastly figure shamble forth, licking lips riven by worms. At any moment the building would shudder and topple in an avalanche of dust and glass and shearing girders. She slumped in her chair, fixated on the chipped vase, its cargo of wilted geraniums drooping over the rim. Merrill bustled around her, tidying up with what she drily attributed as her latent German efficiency, although her mannerisms suggested a sense of profound anxiety. When the phone chirped and it was Sheila reporting some minor emergency at the office, her agitation multiplied as she scoured her little address book for someone to watch over Danni for a few hours.

Danni told her to go, she'd be okay—maybe watch a soap and take a nap. She promised to sit tight in the apartment, come what may. Appearing only slightly mollified, Merrill agreed to leave, vowing a speedy return.

Late afternoon slipped over the city, lackluster and overcast. Came the desultory honk and growl of traffic, the occasional shout, the off-tempo drumbeat from the square. Reflections of the skyline patterned a blank span of wall. Water gurgled, and the disjointed mumble of radio or television commentary came muffled from the neighboring apartments. Her eyes leaked and the shakes traveled from her hands into the large muscles of her shoulders. Her left hand ached.

A child murmured in the hallway, followed by scratching at the door. The bolt rattled. She stood and looked across the living area at the open door of the bedroom. The bedroom dilated. Piles of jagged rocks twined with coarse brown seaweed instead of the bed, the dresser, her unseemly stacks of magazines. A figure stirred amid the weird rocks and unfolded at the hips with the horrible alacrity of a tarantula. *You filthy whore*. She groaned and hooked the door with her ankle and kicked it shut.

Danni went to the kitchen and slid a carving knife from its wooden block. She walked to the bathroom and turned on the shower. Everything seemed too shiny, except the knife. The knife hung loosely in her fingers; its blade was dark and pitted. She stripped her robe and stepped into the shower and drew the curtain. Steam began to fill the room. Hot water beat against the back of her neck, her spine and buttocks as she rested her forehead against the tiles.

What have you done? You filthy bitch. She couldn't discern whether that accusing whisper had bubbled from her brain or trickled in with the swirling steam. *What have you done?* It hardly mattered now that nothing was of any substance, of any importance besides the knife. Her hand throbbed, bleeding. Blood and water swirled down the drain.

Danni. The floorboards settled and a tepid draft brushed her calves. She raised her head and a silhouette filled the narrow door, an incomprehensible blur through the shower curtain. Danni dropped the knife. She slid down the wall into a fetal position. Her teeth chattered, and her animal self took possession. She remembered the ocean, acres of driftwood littering a beach, Virgil's grin as he paid out the tether of a dragonhead kite they'd bought in Chinatown. She remembered the corpses hanging in her closet, and whimpered.

A hand pressed against the translucent fabric, dimpled it inward, fingers spread. The hand squelched on the curtain. Blood ran from its palm and slithered in descending ladders.

—Oh, Danni said. Blearily, through a haze of tears and steam, she reached up and pressed her bloody left hand against the curtain, locked palms with the apparition, giddily cognizant this was a gruesome parody of the star-crossed lovers who kiss through glass. —Virgil, she said, chest hitching with sobs.

—You don't have to go, Merrill said and dragged the curtain aside. She too wept, and nearly fell into the tub as she embraced Danni and the water soaked her clothes, and quantities of blood spilled between them, and Danni saw her friend had found the fetish bone, because there it was, in a black slick on the floor, trailing a spray of droplets like a nosebleed. —You can stay with me. Please stay, Merrill said. She stroked Danni's hair, hugged her as if to keep her from floating away with the steam as it condensed on the mirror, the small window, and slowly evaporated.

May 6, 2006

(D. L. Session 33)

—Danni, do you read the newspapers? Watch the news? Dr. Green said this carefully, giving weight to the question.

—Sure, sometimes.

—The police recovered her body months ago. He removed a newspaper clipping from the folder and pushed it toward her.

—Who? Danni did not look at the clipping.

—Leslie Runyon. An anonymous tip led the police to a landfill. She'd been wrapped in a tarp and buried in a heap of trash. Death by suffocation, according to the coroner. You really don't remember.

Danni shook her head. —No. I haven't heard anything like that.

—Do you think I'm lying?

—Do you think I'm a paranoid delusional?

—Keep talking and I'll get back to you on that, he said, and smiled.
—What happened at the vineyard, Danni? When they found you, you
were quite a mess, according to the reports.

—Yeah. Quite a mess, Danni said. She closed her eyes and fell back
into herself, fell down the black mine shaft into the memory of the garden, the *Lagerstätte*.

Virgil waited to embrace her.

Only a graveyard, an open charnel, contained so much death. The
rubble and masonry were actually layers of bones; a reef of calcified
skeletons locked in heaps; and mummified corpses; enough withered
faces to fill the backs of a thousand milk cartons, frozen twigs of arms
and legs wrapped about their eternal partners. These masses of ossified
humanity were cloaked in skeins of moss and hair and rotted leaves.

*Norma beckoned from the territory of waking dreams. She stood upon the precipice
of a rooftop. She said, Welcome to the* Lagerstätte. *Welcome to the secret graveyard
of the despairing and the damned. She spread her arms and pitched backward.*

Danni moaned and hugged her fist wrapped in its sopping rags. She
had come unwittingly, although utterly complicit in her devotion, and
now stood before a terrible mystery of the world. Her knees trembled
and folded.

Virgil shuttered rapidly and shifted within arm's reach. He smelled
of aftershave and clove, the old, poignantly familiar scents. He also
smelled of earthiness and mold, and his face began to destabilize, to
buckle as packed dirt buckles under a deluge and becomes mud.

Come and sleep, he said in the rasp of leaves and dripping water. His
hands bit into her shoulders and slowly, inexorably drew her against
him. His chest was icy as the void, his hands and arms iron as they
tightened around her and laid her down in the muck and the slime. His
lips closed over hers. His tongue was pliant and fibrous and she
thought of the stinking brown rot that carpeted the deep forests.
Other hands plucked at her clothes, her hair; other mouths suckled her

neck, her breasts, and she thought of misshapen fungi and scurrying centipedes, the ever-scrabbling ants, and how all things that squirmed in the sunless interstices crept and patiently fed.

Danni went blind, but images streamed through the snarling wires of her consciousness. *Virgil and Keith rocked in the swing on the porch of their New England home. They'd just finished playing catch in the backyard; Keith still wore his Red Sox jersey, and Virgil rolled a baseball in his fingers. The stars brightened in the lowering sky and the streetlights fizzed on, one by one. Her mother stood knee-deep in the surf, apron strings flapping in a rising wind. She held out her hands. Keith, pink and wrinkled, screamed in Danni's arms, his umbilical cord still wet. Virgil pressed his hand to a wall of glass. He mouthed, I love you, honey.*

I love you, Mommy, Keith said, his wizened infant's face tilted toward her own. Her father carefully laid out his clothes, his police uniform of twenty-six years, and climbed into the bathtub. We love you, girlie, Dad said and stuck the barrel of his service revolver into his mouth. Oh, quitting had run in the family, was a genetic certainty given the proper set of circumstances. Mom had drowned herself in the sea, such was her grief. Her brother, he'd managed to kill himself in a police action in some foreign desert. This gravitation to self-destruction was ineluctable as her blood.

Danni thrashed upright. Dank mud sucked at her, plastered her hair and drooled from her mouth and nose. She choked for breath, hands clawing at an assailant who had vanished into the mist creeping upon the surface of the marsh. Her fingernails raked and broke against the glaciated cheek of a vaguely female corpse; a stranger made wholly inhuman by the slow, steady vise of gravity and time. Danni groaned. Somewhere, a whippoorwill began to sing.

Voices called for her through the trees; shrill and hoarse. Their shouts echoed weakly, as if from the depths of a well. These were unmistakably the voices of the living. Danni's heart thudded, galvanized by the adrenal response to her near-death experience and, more subtly, an inchoate sense of guilt, as if she'd done something unutterably foul. She scrambled to her feet and fled.

Oily night flooded the forest. A boy cried, *Mommy, Mommy!* Amid the plaintive notes of the whippoorwill, Danni floundered from the garden, scourged by terror and no small regret. By the time she found her way in the dark, came stumbling into the circle of rescue searchers and their flashlights, Danni had mostly forgotten where she'd come from or what she'd been doing there.

Danni opened her eyes to the hospital, the dour room, Dr. Green's implacable curiosity.

She said, —Can we leave it for now? Just for now. I'm tired. You have no idea.

Dr. Green removed his glasses. His eyes were bloodshot and hard, but human after all. —Danni, you're going to be fine, he said.

—Am I?

—Miles to go before we sleep, and all that jazz. But yes, I believe so. You want to open up, and that's very good. It's progress.

Danni smoked.

—Next week we can discuss further treatment options. There are several medicines we haven't looked at; maybe we can get you a dog. I know you live in an apartment, but service animals have been known to work miracles. Go home and get some rest. That's the best therapy I can recommend.

Danni inhaled the last of her cigarette and held the remnants of fire close to her heart. She ground the butt into the ashtray. She exhaled a stream of smoke and wondered if her soul, the souls of her beloved, looked anything like that. Uncertain of what to say, she said nothing. The wheels of the recorder stopped.

Gladiolus Exposed

Anna Tambour

Anna Tambour lives in Australia with a large family of other species, including one man. Her collection Monterra's Deliciosa & Other Tales *and novel* Spotted Lily *are Locus Recommended Reading List selections. Her site, Anna Tambour and Others, is at www.annatambour.net. If you are (or are not) enthused by dung beetles, raw quince, sea squirts, anarchic ants, or if you need to consult the Onuspedia ("An expert is someone who always makes sure of spelling"), see Medlar Comfits, her blog at http://medlarcomfits.blogspot.com.*

As you can tell from her bio, Tambour has eclectic interests. As does her narrator in this tale of obsession and discontent. ·

The weekend at Thoreau's Retreat was Katie's idea. Wilder Benn & Ho had just picked up the account. She was elaborately casual when she pitched this togetherness jaunt to me. It's free, she said, and it might be "sorta fun in a perverted way." "I'm perverted," I laughed.

The ads for Thoreau's Retreat offer a Revive the Mood "Two nights' accommodation for two. Complimentary nonalcoholic Vermont-grown champagne, resident sensei on call 24/7. Complimentary pocket guides to Vermont wildlife, use of Zeiss Conquest binoculars so you can spot, without disturbing, our natural wonders such as the Great Spangled Fritillary Butterfly and the rare Stinkpot Turtle; and a host of surprises."

Thoreau's Retreat is conveniently close to Killington, a fact left out of the literature. After Killington, Katie talked a bit as I drove. *What stinks? the promotionals? ads? Thoreau's Retreat?* I didn't answer, as that would have been interrupting.

I had my own theory about that come-on Thoreau quote next to the rates in the brochure—"*Why should we be in such desperate haste to succeed?*"—but I kept my thoughts to myself. Katie does not appreciate comments from people who don't know anything, unless they are in a focus group.

As soon as we arrived, there was a clash of shoe wear. Katie's calves won't tolerate flats, and her feet are naturally pointed. The looks I got were worse than those directed at her, as if I'd bound her into those high heels. I like them, but my taste is only a coincidence. She ignored the scorn but lost her above-all-this composure when the unpaved grounds sucked down her stilettos. The Revive the Mood Special didn't come with complimentary Dr. Zen shoes.

As to the romantic atmosphere supplied by the sight of other guests, I had forgotten how much even people of wealth can, left au naturel, age to resemble black-and-white films. The gray-and-white, ultra-wrinkled couple checking in before us offended me. "What's your excuse?" I wanted to yell, but because of Katie, I behaved myself.

We had to walk from the carpark through the commons to our cabin, which welcomed us with a rag rug, two rocking chairs, art over the bed in the shape of the largest picture I've ever seen of an asparagus spear, tastefully shot, captioned in faux nineteenth-century handwriting, "THINGS DO NOT CHANGE. WE CHANGE."—HENRY DAVID THOREAU, and the pièce de résistance of surprises: a jar of Metamucil cookies. The bathroom romanced us with a toilet, douche, stand-up shower, Japanese-style straight-sided cube of a tub, and a notice about the evils of laundering. The toilet had no paper seal to break. I dreaded the bed, but it was the saving grace of the place. Katie flopped on it with a historical romance, grimly determined to last out the weekend, but in no way wanting to compromise herself by experiencing more than she had to. Lucky for her, she didn't have to dread the resort's idea of food. It was no worse than her usual. I drove to Killington, where I got a pizza made by someone who thinks that ketchup is Italian. By the time I got back, Katie had found out that Thoreau's Retreat offers no decadent room service, so she was waiting for me to lead her on another expedition over the grass to the "Commons Lodge," her heels aerating the soil, me helping to pull her free at each step. I sat with her in the restaurant while she ate. Despite and because of her condition, she stuffed herself full of celery root *au jus*.

I won't tell you what Thoreau's Retreat offers in the way of small-screen adult entertainment. For once, I went to bed before ten o'clock. Katie was asleep before eight. Horrorville it was, but two days without decent food wouldn't kill me, and the weekend was a good idea. I felt a twinge of nostalgia for a time when I considered walking in the mountains to be exercise. Now a break for forty-eight hours was good for me, as it was so rare, and we needed to have time together enforced upon us, otherwise it never seemed to happen.

The next morning at dawn (the quiet woke me) I was taking the mountain air, perfuming it with a contraband Cohiba while I picked wildflowers for my pregnant wife, when a sparkle of dew caught my eye, and I noticed the gladiolus—not some flopsy yellow common garden flower, but a *gladiolus*, commonly called the "body" of the three-part bone. The sternum or "breastbone" as it is commonly known. I laid it on my hand and it looked as if the bone were formed for me: exactly the length of my wrist crease to the tip of my middle finger.

Bones, like the salt-and-pepper granite stones in Vermont, rise to the surface of fields each spring when the ground thaws. Sunlight glinted in the sharply defined facet for the third costal cartilage. The convex curve of the lateral border of the gladiolus faced the sky, two facets rising free of the earth.

My mouth flooded with cigar juice as my fingers nosed the ground all around what I estimated to be the dimensions of the whole sternum. Then as delicately as I could, I dug with the tips of my fingers in the sodden but surprisingly hard ground—under the gladiolus, that broad blade of middle section, till it looked like a bridge over a valley. A fist-size rock had to be pried from the sticky soil before I could get to the manubrium. (The articular surface for the clavicle emerged, surprisingly for such dense bone, as a complex splinter surrounded by dark clumps of soil salted with frustratingly bonelike pieces of quartz.) The knees of my weekend chinos were so stained by this time that they would have made a homeless person blush. My fingertips felt abused, my nails looked disgraceful, and my back was sending urgent messages to my brain. Time was passing, though, so in a spirit of no rest for the wicked, I tackled the other end of the bone, the delicate xiphoid process . . . and spat a cigar stub that looked like a wad of cud when I pulled just wrong and snapped the delicate filliped point.

From my first sight of that tiny pool of dew in the bone facet, I knew this to be not the normal bones that pop out in thaws: cattle, sheep, and deer. That glimmering facet made my heart race. A human breastbone is unmistakable, and anatomy was my favorite subject in med school, however much I love urology. I knew as soon as the gladiolus was exposed in all its length that it had belonged to either a small adult male or a female about the size of Katie.

What finally lay on the palm of my hand—stretching from my wrist crease to the top of my middle finger—was the breastbone itself, the sternum. The body of it was a perfect gladiolus, but both ends of the sternum were damaged—the superior end intriguing as hell; the inferior, a blunt accusation.

Ever since scaring myself as a kid with stories I read by flashlight, I've fantasized about finding someone, and here a someone was. Odd to find this, but then I suppose in real life it isn't skulls that people "find," but bones that the average person would never know were human. How many people in, say, Brattleboro, let alone Killington or Thoreau's Retreat, would know a human bone from wildlife? I felt a frisson at the thought of finding this before it was stepped on by an ignorant hiker. Chakra charts don't teach diddly about bones.

I dug till my fingers said they'd sue me, and then I had to leave. With no tools, I couldn't dig deep, nor far. I found no other bones, though I expected to find at least the tip of a rib. And I had hoped to find an answer to the mystery of the shattered manubrium, one of the toughest bones to fracture in the human body. I held my breath when I found a bit of metal. A bullet . . . But once I cleaned it with spit, the bit was only a pebble that I had mistaken for something important because it was time to go. Although I was in sight of the resort, the actual site was featureless, so I pushed the dirt back into the hole I'd made so it would all look like a marmot or some such's rooting around for food, and I hid my Piaget under the fist-size stone that I planted in the middle of the site.

In the five-minute walk down to our cabin, I remembered the flowers, but it was too late to pick new ones. Instead I swept into the Commons Room and spotted a crystal bowl of crocuses. Perfect, so I took it. If you know what you're doing and don't explain, you can do anything.

Katie was conveniently asleep when I got back. I placed the bowl by the bed and went to our bathroom where I wish my dentist could have seen how gentle and effective a cleaning can be. I used my toothbrush and Katie's whitening toothpaste.

Job completed, the manubrium was intellectually appealing, although aesthetically flawed. I couldn't look at the xiphoid process because it annoyed me. But the gladiolus was simply beautiful. I dried the sternum on my towel, rolled it in my clean shirt, and packed it in my suitcase while Katie snored—and I remembered to change my slacks just before she woke, just in time for brunch.

She didn't object when I said that we needed to leave by two o'clock. I said that I had forgotten about a case I had to check on at Mount Sinai, but I really wanted to get home because being so close to the bone site frustrated me. I needed equipment better than my fingers and some Thoreau's Retreat Commons Room spoon. And I didn't want to have to think, on my next dig, whether Katie would be awake.

Monday morning I was back at the clinic, and she was back at the agency. She rang me at eleven o'clock.

"Tell me all you know about incontinence pads." The first time she'd ever shown an interest.

A typical month—we didn't see much of each other, and there was no way I could get right back to the site. First, I had a rushed week, then it was off to England, to Freeman Hospital Newcastle Upon Tyne, where Haslam's "Imaging in Loin Pain Best Practice" would have had me seeking him out during coffee at another time, and David Tolley's Stuart Lecture, "The Changing Face of Urology—Are We Prepared?" was not obvious. As to my own paper, the topic of urological forensics is a well without end of fascination; but I wished yet again, as I presented my findings, that Katie's verve were mine when it comes to communication.

But I had to get back to Vermont. Katie was by this time obsessed by Etheria (latest focus-group fave name, Katie said). She wanted me on tap, but not at hand.

Finally, I left work at seven PM one Friday, in a rented Land Rover. I slept somewhere as downmarket as Vermont goes, where I was unlikely to meet a bottle of anything de-alcoholed. Before dawn, I set out with the gear that I bought along the way: a collapsible shovel and a metal detector.

Not being a Daniel Boone sort, I had thought I would never find the place again without the metal detector, but I knew it even in the moon-distorted light, and through the haze of pain I felt when I twisted my ankle between two rocks while I focused not down, but ahead. *Approaching . . . almost . . . there.* Logically, I should have known that I would recognize the spot, considering the number of times I had dreamed the find over the past weeks.

I didn't expect my watch to be as ruined as it looked, but I'd already claimed it on insurance.

When I began to dig, the only sounds I heard were owl calls.

By the time I had dug a hole big enough to bury a Yeti, the garbage truck was hoeing down its breakfast in Thoreauland.

I found nothing but bittersweet-chocolate-colored dirt and enough quartz pebbles to light Hansel and Gretel's walk to the wicked witch of Mars. I unearthed nothing else. No ribs, vertebrae, skull, no bullet, bit of iron, wooden cosh—no implement or agent of death; and not even a sliver of shattered bone.

Yet even the telltale heart had an explanation.

I hadn't told Katie about the bone before, and didn't plan to tell her. She is conventional about things like insurance and laws, and she would have expected me to alert someone. *I don't know. The authorities,* she would have said.

And then I would have given up the precious thing for no reason, and it would be officiously boxed and lost, buried where no thaw would ever expose it.

A couple of weeks passed, busy as ever for both of us, but one Friday we were both able to knock off work by six for a little romantic dinner at a place I thought she'd like.

"Feel like going back to Thoreau's Retreat?" I asked.

"As paying guests?"

"I guess so," I said. I abhor wasting money. "What's wrong? They too cheap to give you another weekend for research?"

"We lost the account."

"Oh," I said. I knew she'd feel bad about it, so I changed the subject. "What happened to Etheria?"

"Etheria?" Her fork split an asparagus spear down the middle. Her brow would have creased, if it could have, as she separated a sliver of cheese from the vegetable as carefully as if she were boning a fish.

I couldn't watch her eat. I hoped the baby wouldn't come out looking like it had spent its time in her dieting for life.

"The incontinence pads," I said.

She dropped her fork and knife on the white expanse of plate. "Do you have to do that?"

At that point in our relationship, our chemical attraction was something we could remember, but she didn't choose to and she made it hard for me to put that attraction above the way she feels about my work, conveniently forgetting how we met. *Why is what I do, of the two of us, the unmentionable?*

She was at five months then, and a couple of weeks later suffered a miscarriage. I wasn't surprised, but she was. It was incredibly tough. She'd planned for that baby. We both had. All the emotional capital she'd sunk into it. We almost split up after that but were so busy, it was easier not to.

In that post-expecting period of adjustment we made time to make some resolutions together.

1. We would try to rediscover each other again;
2. She would try not to be patronizing about my work; and
2a. I would quit smoking the cigars that she said she smelled on my breath.

During the next stage in our relationship, Katie and I stayed home in the evenings and watched movies together. I found the gladiolus invaluable as an aid. I used to sit with it. The facets for the third, fourth, and fifth costal cartilages fit my fingers so perfectly, the gladiolus felt like part of an intimate garment. As I touched the hand-warmed bone, I imagined what had happened. All sorts of lives and deaths danced as the movies played. Greta Garbo and Robert Taylor Camilled in black and white, to the happy tears of Katie while I fondled the bone. *The English Patient*, something that would previously have had me crawling the walls or snoring in relief, played all the way through while I dreamed with my eyes open, sternum in hand. *Thelma & Louise* drove cross-country while the bone submerged itself in flesh, grew attachments, developed a life and personality, found an accident waiting to happen, or a murderer. Katie could put anything on, even *Fried Green Tomatoes*, and I sat through it, rapt.

But she found a new annoyance to complain about.

"Where'd you get that hideous bone?"

I'd already planned what I would say if she asked. "An anatomy kit."

"Can't you use a rubber ball?"

I said I liked the bone. It reminded me of med school.

She came home one day with a squeezy in the supposed shape of a brain, a stupid promotional that I can't imagine why she thought I hadn't seen. It insulted me as much as if I had proposed a name for that disposable urinary collection device that she of all people had as an account.

She began to work late again and through the weekend, and so did I.

We rarely met, but when I was in her presence, I found that touching the bone soothed me. I could tolerate her presence.

One evening while she was watching, a few drops from my glass of water fell on the bone, magnifying a section. When I wiped it dry, light fell upon it in just such a way that I noticed something I hadn't seen before, but I wasn't sure of what I saw. The next day I was able to confirm. The anterior surface of the gladiolus was shallowly adorned with the faintest and finest of carvings—a Victorian monogram, scrolling frills, the finest of lines. Only five millimeters in diameter, I couldn't make out the letters under any power of magnification because they were both too fanciful and too patchy; but I think there were three (and one of them was an L or a J) surrounded by a garland of flowers (forget-me-nots?). I cursed the cleaning I had done, so harsh I almost missed this.

The mystery of no other bones was now partly solved, though new mysteries leapt into my mind with the swiftness of bandits leaping upon a lonely Victorian coach.

The monogram could only have been carved by an expert, I am sure. A skilled engraver. This confirmed some theories I had wanted to firm up.

The more I felt along the gladiolus, the more I knew that its size was exactly Katie's. I hadn't thought of her sexually for some time, but now I was drawn to the wide space between her breasts. Her aversion to fat revealed far more of her now than when we met. The attachments of the muscles of her third costal cartilage were so visible that in some lights, they were shadowed as if they had no epidermal cover. She loved her muscles showing, so I could gaze there (when we were together) to my heart's content (and imagine it at other times). When she was in the mood, as she sometimes still was, I could run my fingertips along her flesh. At those times, we were more powerfully aligned than ever before. I imagined her gladiolus, undressed and gleaming, curving seductively from damp earth . . .

I wasn't obsessed or anything. The bone stayed home. Too risky to carry with me—nosy security, luggage loss, the off chance that I'd leave it in my hotel bed during some red-eye packing rush. Anyway, during a conference, I thought about the paper I'd deliver, and then about how I was. When I got home, sometimes Katie was home, too. But always, the bone was there to greet me.

One night I came home about five AM from a conference in Vienna. Katie was in bed. Vienna had been bad. I'd had twenty-two hours to think about how boring I was, how I wished that Katie could sell my ideas. I undressed and got into my side, reaching for the bone on my night table, but my table was bare. It took me shining her light in her face to wake her up.

I had to ask three times before she woke sufficiently to understand. "Sorry, the cleaner threw it out," she said. She flicked off her light and pulled the sheet over her head.

I can't express sufficiently how *bad* I felt. *Bereaved*. Breathless. Heart-sick. I moved my pillow so I could see better. I needed to wake Katie up enough to make love. I looked down at the shape of her face under the sheet. She was very still.

Too still to be asleep.

Cleaner, my ass! She was holding her breath, the bitch. As Poe said, "Years of love have been forgot, in the hatred of a minute."

Daltharee

Jeffrey Ford

Jeffrey Ford lives in New Jersey with his wife and two sons. He teaches literature and writing at Brookdale Community College. His most recent novel, The Girl in the Glass, *won the Edgar Allan Poe Award. His short novel* The Cosmology of the Wider World *was published in 2005 and his second collection of short stories,* The Empire of Ice Cream, *in 2006. He has recently had stories published in the anthology* The Coyote Road: Trickster Tales *and in the Datlow-edited issue 7 of* Subterranean *magazine and will have a story in the forthcoming anthology* The Starry Rift. *Two of his stories were reprinted in* The Year's Best Fantasy and Horror #19 *and one in* The Year's Best Fantasy and Horror #20.*

Ford is able to move among science fiction, fantasy, and horror with great ease—as is ably demonstrated by this little tale that steps a bit into each.

You've heard of bottled cities, no doubt—society writ minuscule and delicate beyond reason: toothpick-spired towns, streets no thicker than thread, pinprick faces of the citizenry peering from office windows smaller than sequins. Hustle, politics, fervor, struggle, capitulation, wrapped in a crystal firmament, stoppered at the top to keep reality both in and out. Those microscopic lives, striking glass at the edge of things, believed themselves gigantic, their dilemmas universal.

Our research suggested that Daltharee had many multistoried buildings carved right into its hillsides. Surrounding the city there was a forest with lakes and streams, and all of it was contained within a dome, like a dinner beneath the lid of a serving dish. When the inhabitants of Daltharee looked up they were prepared to not see the heavens. They knew that the light above, their Day, was generated by a machine, which they oiled and cared for. The stars that shone every sixteen hours when Day left darkness behind were simple bulbs regularly changed by a man in a hot-air balloon.

They were convinced that the domed city floated upon an iceberg, which it actually did. There was one door in the wall of the dome at the end of a certain path through the forest. When opened, it led out onto the ice. The surface of the iceberg extended the margin of one of their miles all around the enclosure. Blinding snows fell, winds constantly roared in a perpetual blizzard. Their belief was that Daltharee

drifted upon the oceans of an otherwise frozen world. They prayed for
the end of eternal winter, so they might reclaim the continents.

And all of this: their delusions, the city, the dome, the iceberg, the
two quarts of water it floated upon, were contained within an old gallon glass milk bottle, plugged at the top with a tattered handkerchief
and painted dark blue. When I'd put my ear to the glass, I'd heard, like
the ocean in a seashell, fierce gales blowing.

Daltharee was not the product of a shrinking ray as many of these
pint-size metropolises are. And please, there was no magic involved. In
fact, once past the early stages of its birth it was more organically
grown than shaped by artifice. Often, in the origin stories of these
diminutive places, there's a deranged scientist lurking in the wings.
Here, too, we have the notorious Mando Paige, the inventor of sub-
microscopic differentiated cell division and growth. What I'm referring to was Paige's technique for producing super-miniature human
cells. From the instant of their atomic origin, these parcels of life were
beset by enzymatic reaction and electric stunting the way tree roots
are tortured over time to create a bonsai. Paige shaped human life in
the form of tiny individuals. They landscaped and built the city, laid
roads, and lurched in a sleepwalking stupor induced by their creator.

Once the city in the dome was completed, Paige introduced more
of the crumb-size citizenry through the door that opened onto the iceberg. Just before closing that door, he set off a device that played an
A flat for approximately ten seconds, a preordained spur to consciousness, which brought them all awake to their lives in Daltharee. Seeding the water in the gallon bottle with crystal ions, he soon after
introduced a chemical mixture that formed a slick, unmelting icelike
platform beneath the floating dome. He then introduced into the atmosphere fenathol nitrate, silver iodite, anamidian betheldine, to initi-
ate the frigid wind and falling snow. When all was well within the
dome, when the iceberg had sufficiently grown, when winter ruled, he
plugged the gallon bottle with an old handkerchief. That closed system of winter, with just the slightest amount of air allowed in through
the cloth, was sustainable forever, feeding wind to snow and snow to

302 · JEFFREY FORD

cold to claustrophobia and back again in an infinite loop. The Daltha-
reens made up the story about a frozen world to satisfy the unknown.
Paige manufactured three more of these cities, each wholly different
from the others, before laws were passed about the imprisonment of
humanity, no matter how minute or unaware. He was eventually, himself, imprisoned for his crimes.

We searched for a method to study life inside the dome but were
afraid to disturb its delicate nature, unsure whether simply removing
the handkerchief would upset a brittle balance between inner and outer
universes. It was suggested that a very long, exceedingly thin probe that
had the ability to twist and turn by computational command could be
shimmied in between the edge of the bottle opening and the cloth of
the handkerchief. This probe, like the ones physicians used in the twentieth and twenty-first centuries to read the hieroglyphics of the bowel,
would be fitted out with both a camera and a microphone. The device
was adequate for those cities that didn't have the extra added boundary
of a dome, but even in them, how incongruous, a giant metal snake just
out of the blue, slithering through one's reality. The inhabitants of these
enclosed worlds were exceedingly small but not stupid.

In the end it was my invention that won the day—a voice-activated
transmitter the size of two atoms was introduced into the bottle. We
had to wait for it to work its way from the blizzard atmosphere,
through the dome's air filtration system, and into the city. Then we had
to wait for it to come in contact with a voice. At any point a thousand
things could have gone wrong, but one day, six months later, who
knows how many years that would be in Dalthareen time, the machine
transmitted and my receiver picked up conversations from the domed
city. Here's an early one we managed to record that had some interesting elements:

"I'm not doing that now. Please, give me some room . . . ," she said.

There is a long pause filled with the faint sound of a utensil clink-
ing a plate.

"I was out in the forest the other day," he said.

"Why?" she asked.

"I'm not sure," he told her.

"What do you do out there?" she asked.

"I'm in this club," he said. "We got together to try to find the door in the wall of the dome."

"How did that go?" she asked.

"We knew it was there and we found it," he said. "Just like in the old stories . . ."

"Blizzard?"

"You can't believe it," he said.

"Did you go out in it?"

"Yes, and when I stepped back into the dome, I could feel a piece of the storm stuck inside me."

"What's that supposed to mean?" she said.

"I don't know."

"How did it get inside you?" she asked.

"Through my ears," he said.

"Does it hurt?"

"I was different when I came back in."

"Stronger?"

"No, more something else."

"Can you say?"

"I've had dreams."

"So what," she said. "I had a dream the other night that I was out on the Grand Conciliation Balcony, dressed for the odd jibbery, when all of a sudden a little twisher rumbles up and whispers to me the words— 'Elemental Potency.' What do you think it means? I can't get the phrase out of my head."

"It's nonsense," he said.

"Why aren't *your* dreams nonsense?"

"They are," he said. "The other night I had this dream about a theory. I can't remember if I saw it in the pages of a dream magazine or someone spoke it or it just jumped into my sleeping head. I've never dreamed about a theory before. Have you?"

"No," she said.

"It was about living in the dome. The theory was that since the dome is closed things that happen in the dome only affect other things in the dome. Because the size of Daltharee is as we believe so minuscule compared to the rest of the larger world, the repercussions of the acts you engage in in the dome will have a higher possibility of intersecting each other. If you think of something you do throughout the day as an act, each act begins a chain reaction of mitigating energy in all directions. The will of your own energy, dispersed through myriad acts within only a morning, will beam, refract, and reflect off the beams of others' acts and the walls of the closed system, barreling into each other and causing sparks at those locations where your essence meets itself. In those instances, at those specific locations, your will is greater than the will of the dome. What I was then told was that a person could learn a way to act at a given hour—a quick series of six moves—that send out so many ultimately crisscrossing intentions of will that it creates a power mesh capable in its transformative strength of bending reality to whim."

"You're crazy," she said.

There is a slight pause here, the sound of wind blowing in the trees.

"Hey, whatever happened to your aunt?" he asked.

"They got it out of her."

"Amazing," he said. "Close call . . ."

"She always seemed fine, too," she said. "But swallowing a knitting needle? That's not right."

"She doesn't even knit, does she?"

"No," she said.

"Good thing she didn't have to pass it," he said. "Think about the intersecting beams of will resulting from that act."

She laughed. "I heard the last pigeon died yesterday."

"Yeah?"

"They found it in the park, on the lawn amid the Moth trees."

"In all honesty, I did that," he said. "You know, not directly, but just by the acts I went through yesterday morning. I got out of bed, had breakfast, got dressed, you know . . . like that. I was certain that by midday that bird would be dead."

"Why'd you kill it?" she asked.

There's a pause in the conversation here filled up by the sound of machinery in the distance just beneath that of the wind in the trees.

"Having felt what I felt outside the dome, I considered it a mercy," he said.

"Interesting . . . ," she said. "I've gotta get going. It looks like rain."

"Will you call me?" he asked.

"Eventually, of course," she said.

"I know," he said. "I know."

Funny thing about Paige, he found religion in the latter years of his life. After serving out his sentence, he renounced his crackpot Science and retreated to a one-room apartment in an old boardinghouse on the edge of the great desert. He courted an elderly woman there, a Mrs. Trucy. I thought he'd been long gone when we finally contacted him. After a solid fifteen years of recording conversations, it became evident that the domed city was failing—the economy, the natural habitat were both in disarray. A strange illness had sprung up amid the population, an unrelenting, fatal insomnia that took a dozen of them to Death each week. Nine months without a single wink of sleep. The conversations we recorded then were full of anguish and hallucination.

Basically, we asked Paige what he might do to save his own created world. He came to work for us and studied the problem full-time. He was old then, wrinkles and flyaway hair in strange, ever-shifting formations atop his scalp, eyeglasses with one ear loop. Every time he'd make a mistake on a calculation or a technique, he'd swallow a thumbtack. When I asked if the practice helped him concentrate he told me, "No."

Eventually, on a Saturday morning when no one was at the lab but himself and an uninterested security guard, he broke into the vault that held the shrinking ray. He started the device up, aimed it at the glass milk bottle containing Daltharee, and then sat on top of the bottle, wearing a parachute. The ray discharged, shrinking him. He fell in among the gigantic folds of the handkerchief. Apparently he managed to work his way down past the end of the material and leap into the blizzard, out over the dome of the city. No one was there to see him slowly descend, dangerously buffeted by the insane winds. No one noticed him slip through the door in the dome.

Conversations came back to us eventually containing his name. Apparently he'd told them the true nature of the dome and the bottle it resided in. And then after some more time passed, there came word that he was creating another domed city inside a gallon milk bottle from the city of Daltharee. Where would it end, we wondered, but it was not a thought we enjoyed pursuing as it ran in a loop, recrossing itself, reiterating its original energy in ever-diminishing reproductions of ourselves. Perhaps it was the thought of it that made my assistant accidentally drop the milk bottle one afternoon. It exploded into a million dark blue shards, dirt and dome and tiny trees spread across the floor. We considered studying its remains, but instead, with a shiver, I swept it into a pile and then into the furnace.

A year later, Mrs. Trucy came looking for Mando. She insisted upon knowing what had become of him. We told her that the law did not require us to tell her, and then she pulled a marriage certificate out of her purse. I was there with the Research General at the time, and I saw him go pale as a ghost upon seeing that paper. He told her Mando had died in an experiment of his own devising. The wrinkles of her gray face torqued to a twist and sitting beneath her pure silver hair, her head looked like a metal screw. Three tears squeezed out from the corners of her eyes. If Mando died performing an experiment, we could not be held responsible. We would, though, have to produce the body for her as proof that he'd perished. The Research General told her we were conducting a complete investigation of the tragedy and would contact her in six weeks with the results and the physical proof—in other words, Mando's corpse.

My having shoveled Daltharee into the trash without searching for survivors or mounting even a cursory rescue effort was cause for imprisonment. My superior, the Research General, having had my callous act take place on his watch, was also liable. After three nerve-racking days, I conceived of a way for us to save ourselves. In fact it was so simple it astounded me that neither one of us, scientific minds though we be, didn't leap to the concept earlier. Using Mando's own process for creating diminutive humanity, we took his DNA from our genetic files, put it through a chemical bath to begin the growth process, and then tortured the cells into tininess. We had to use radical enzymes to speed the process up given we only had six weeks. By the end of week five we had a living, breathing Mando Paige, trapped under a drinking glass in our office. He was dressed in a little orange jumpsuit, wore black boots, and was in the prime of his youth. We studied his attempts to escape his prison with a jeweler's loupe inserted into each eye. We thought we could rely on the air simply running out in the glass and him suffocating.

Days passed and Paige hung on. Each day I'd spy on his meager existence and wonder what he must be thinking. When the time came and he wasn't dead, I killed him with a cigarette. I brought the glass to the very edge of the table, bent a plastic drinking straw, shoved the longer end of it up into the glass, and then caught it fairly tightly against the table edge. As for the part that stuck out, I lit a cigarette, inhaled deeply and then blew the smoke up into the glass. I gave him five lungfuls. The oxygen displacement was too much, of course.

Mrs. Trucy accepted our story and the magnified view of her lover's diminutive body. We told her how he bravely took the shrinking ray for the sake of Science. She remarked that he looked younger than when he was full-size and alive, and the Research General told her, "As you shrink, wrinkles have a tendency to evaporate." We went to the funeral out in the desert near her home. It was a blazingly hot day. She'd had his remains placed into a thimble with some tape across the top, and this she buried in the red sand.

Later, as the sun set, the Research General and I ate dinner at a ramshackle restaurant along a dusty road right outside of Mateos. He had the pig knuckle with sauerkraut and I had the chicken croquettes with orange gravy that tasted brown.

"I'm so relieved that asshole's finally dead," whispered the Research General.

"There's dead and there's dead," I told him.

"Let's not make this complicated," he said. "I know he's out there in some smaller version of reality, he could be filling all available space with smaller and smaller reproductions of himself, choking the ass of the universe with pages and pages of Mando Paige. I don't give a fuck as long as he's not here."

"He is here," I said, and then they brought the martinis and the conversation evaporated into reminiscence.

That night as I stood out beneath the desert sky having a smoke, I had a sense that the cumulative beams generated by the repercussions of my actions over time, harboring my inherent will, had reached some far-flung boundary and were about to turn back on me. In my uncomfortable bed at the Hacienda Motel, I tossed and turned, drifting in and out of sleep. It was then that I had a vision of the shrinking ray, its sparkling blue emission bouncing off a mirror set at an angle. The beam then travels a short distance to another mirror with which it collides and reflects. The second mirror is positioned so that it sends the ray back at its own original source. The beam strikes and mixes with itself only a few inches past the nozzle of the machine's barrel. And then I see it in my mind—when a shrinking ray is trained upon itself, its diminutive-making properties are canceled twice, and as it is a fact that when two negatives are multiplied they make a positive, this process makes things bigger. As soon as the concept was upon me, I was filled with excitement and couldn't wait to get back to the lab the next day to work out the math and realize an experiment.

It was fifteen years later—the Research General had long been fired—when Mando Paige stepped out of the spot where the shrinking ray's beam crossed itself. He was blue and yellow and red and his hair was curly. I stood within feet of him and he smiled at me. I, of course, couldn't let him go—not due to any law but my own urge to finish the job I'd started at the outset. As he stepped back toward the ray, I turned it off, and he was trapped, for the moment, in our moment. I called for my assistants to surround him, and I sent one to my office for the revolver I kept in my bottom drawer. He told me that one speck of his saliva contained four million Daltharees. "When I fart," he said, "I set forth Armadas." I shot him and the four assistants and then automatically acid-washed the lab to destroy the Dalthareen plague and evidence of murder. No one suspected a thing. I found a few cities sprouting beneath my fingernails last week. There were already rows of domes growing behind my ears. My blood no doubt is the manufacturer of cities, flowing silver through my veins. Crowds behind my eyes, commerce in my joints. Each idea I have is a domed city that grows and opens like a flower. I want to tell you about cities and cities and cities named Daltharee.

Jimmy

Pat Cadigan

Pat Cadigan has twice won the Arthur C. Clarke Award for best·science-fiction novel of the year. She lives in gritty, urban North London with her husband, the Original Chris Fowler, and her son Rob.

Although primarily known as a science-fiction writer (she's one of the original cyberpunks), she also writes fantasy and horror·stories, which have been collected in Patterns, Dirty Work, *and* Home by the Sea.

She has written twelve books, including two nonfiction and one young adult. Her next novel, Reality Used to Be a Friend of Mine, *will appear Real Soon.*

In "Jimmy," Cadigan perfectly captures what a pain it was to be an eleven-year-old during the early 1960s. But her eponymous character has an even worse time of it.

The day JFK got shot, things got *really* crazy for Jimmy Streubal. For me, too—hell, for everybody—but mostly for Jimmy.

It wasn't like things weren't already screwy for him. He had this really messed-up family situation. When his parents were together, they used to have the kind of fights that the neighbors called the police about. After they got divorced, legend had it the custody fight was back-asswards—his mother tried to force his father to take him and vice versa. In those days, the scandal of having divorced parents in a small town was bad enough but when neither of them wanted you, it was like going around with the word TRASH tattooed on your forehead.

But it was even worse than that for Jimmy. He had a lot of relatives on both sides of the family—aunts, uncles, all kinds of cousins, and grandparents—and none of them wanted him any more than his parents did.

Social Services was *forced to intervene,* as my mother put it. She worked in the admitting office at the local hospital and she knew everybody in Social Services, including Jimmy's social worker, Mrs. Beauvais. Because there were so many Streubals and Streubal in-laws in town, my mother told me, Mrs. Beauvais was under orders to get one of them to take Jimmy. The county had only one group home for orphaned or unwanted boys but it was over thirty miles away and filled to twice its official capacity with kids who were worse off. The state's

foster-family subsidy was good enough that she could usually talk a re-
luctant relative into a ninety-day trial period. Unfortunately, Jimmy
never lasted that long. Four or five weeks later, Mrs. Beauvais would get
a call telling her to come and get him *now*. All she could do was take
Jimmy back to her office and call the next relative on the list.

My mother didn't normally share this kind of information with me,
but Jimmy and I had been friends since kindergarten and she wanted
me to know the facts rather than the gossip. So she swore me to se-
crecy, promising to kill me if I let anything slip (in those days, if your
parents loved you, they threatened your life at least once a week).

I dutifully vowed not to say a word. I didn't tell her that I had already heard the same thing, generously embellished, from Mrs. Beauvais's niece, who sat behind me and served as the class distributor of
any gossip worth repeating. Big problems in a small town: If you had
any, there wasn't a hope in hell of keeping them quiet. Nor did I mention that I had heard even more detailed information from Jimmy himself. Neither my mother nor Mrs. Beauvais's niece knew, for example,
that he was always evicted before anyone called the Social Services office; when Mrs. Beauvais arrived, she would find him waiting out on
the sidewalk, regardless of the weather or time of day (or night), with
a note listing all of his sins and general shortcomings pinned to his
shirt.

"My mom said I stole from her purse," Jimmy told me. "My dad
claimed I smoked his cigarettes and sneaked out at night when I was
supposed to be in bed."

"Where did you go?" I asked him.

"Dunno. He never said." Jimmy wrinkled his nose. "Just out somewhere, getting into trouble and he couldn't control me."

"Jeez."

"Uz," Jimmy added, grinning a little. If you split the syllables between two kids, it didn't count as swearing.

"Did you ever ask him?"

"Ask him what—where I went? Are you kidding? You think I
wanted a fat lip?" He ran a hand over his crew cut. Jimmy always had

crew cuts, even in the coldest weather. On the first day of school in first grade, the teacher swore she saw lice in his hair so every few weeks, Mrs. Beauvais dragged him to the barber to have clippers run over his head. His hair was so short that it was hard to tell what color it was. I didn't think it was fair but Jimmy said it was better than getting his head scrubbed with disinfectant shampoo.

"That stuff smells funny," he said. "Like you oughta wash floors with it, not your hair, and if it gets in your eyes, it stings worse than anything. I got some in my mouth once and I couldn't taste anything else for days."

It was an odd friendship, Jimmy and me—a boy and a girl, the class troublemaker and the straight-A student. It started, as I said, back in kindergarten. I first noticed Jimmy because he was actually doing something wrong: He was over at the small sink in the corner where Miss Campbell had us all wash our hands after finger-painting, and he was filling a paper cup with water and pouring it into the trash can, over and over again.

I remember this so vividly that even now I can close my eyes and see it like a clip from a movie—an indie production shot on a budget, *The Chant of Jimmy Streubal,* maybe. I can see Jimmy moving from the small white sink to the trash can, also white, round-topped with a swing door, and slightly taller than he was, and back again with an expression of deep concentration on his face, a little man with a mission.

I remember the other kids standing around watching in horrified anticipation of what would happen when Miss Campbell finally looked up from whatever she was engaged in and saw what he was doing; this was so far off the misbehavior scale that no one could imagine what sort of punishment Jimmy was in for.

Most of all, I remember that I understood immediately what he was doing: He wanted to know how many cups of water it would take to fill the trash can all the way to the top. This was something I had wondered about myself and I had even contemplated trying the same thing to find out. Ultimately, I had decided against it, as it seemed to be the sort of thing that would make Miss Campbell scream and yell and call your mother. As it turned out, I was right but that was no fun. Fun would have been Jimmy telling us exactly how many cups it took and Miss Campbell writing it on the board for him, not to mention getting to see a trash can full of water, instead of what actually happened.

Strangely, that's the one thing I can't remember—what happened when Jimmy got caught, or even how he got caught. Whether one of the kids finally got tired of waiting for the storm and called out, *Miss Campbell, look what Jimmy's doing!* or whether Miss Campbell herself suddenly realized there was too much running-water noise and turned to see what fresh hell her teaching degree had visited on her now, I have forgotten completely.

I've also forgotten exactly how Jimmy was punished for this stupendous transgression but shortly after that, we became friends. We didn't talk about the Trash Can Incident until a few years later when, after confirming I'd been right about his intentions, I asked him how many cups of water he thought it would have taken.

"At first, I thought maybe a hundred," he told me, his voice thoughtful and serious. "But I was just a little kid, I didn't even really know what a hundred meant. Now I know it would have taken a lot more and I would have had to pour a lot faster—water was leaking out all over the floor."

That surprised me—I didn't remember any water on the floor. Just Jimmy pouring cup after cup into that white trash can. I asked him if that was when all the trouble had first started, with one very bad morning in kindergarten.

"Nah," he said, "it had already started at home. The kids next door were playing with matches one day and they set their room on fire. They told their parents I did it and everyone believed them. I couldn't even tie my own shoes let alone light a match but everyone believed them anyway."

In a properly aligned universe, Jimmy would have been throwing rocks at me, putting spiders in my desk, spitting in my hair when my back was turned, and extorting my lunch money out of me. He didn't actually do anything like that to me or anyone else but for some reason, everyone was sure he did. I couldn't figure it out; Jimmy said it was his lot in life. His *karma*, he called it. I had to look that one up, something that didn't happen very often even when I was ten years old. It didn't occur to me to wonder how Jimmy would know about something like that. I just figured he was as brainy as I was and hiding it. No one would have believed he was really smart—if he'd ever gotten an A or even a B, everyone would have accused him of cheating. Kids like Jimmy weren't smart and they weren't talented. They couldn't be— otherwise their parents would have wanted them. Wouldn't they?

Big problems in a small town; messy questions with neat answers.

Where were you when you heard Kennedy got shot? had a neat answer for everybody. I was in school—just another day in fifth grade—but Jimmy wasn't there. Thrown out again, I thought; he was always absent when someone threw him out. This time it was his aunt Linda. Mrs. Barnicle (I swear to God, that was really her name) raised her eyebrows at his empty desk and then got this look like she smelled something bad. That was how she always looked at Jimmy and I hated her for it. I don't think she knew that she was doing it, which made me hate her even more.

As if she sensed something, she looked over at me, her expression changing to puzzled and then disapproving, and I realized I had been scowling at her with that same bad-smell expression on my own face. If I didn't cut it out, I was going to get the chair—the wooden chair in the far corner. You'd get exiled to it for chewing gum, passing notes, answering back, or other high crimes, and if you didn't sit completely still, it let out a god-awful squealing noise. I had never sat there; Jimmy, of course, had done more time in it than anyone else in the class, maybe more than everyone else combined. It never squealed when he sat in it, which seemed to annoy Mrs. Barnicle more than if he had made it sing "The Star-Spangled Banner."

I looked away from her quickly and started sorting my books and papers, hoping she wouldn't decide to come over and ask me if there was something I'd like to share with her and the rest of the class. Fortunately, the Moran twins went up to her with a complicated question about a math problem we'd had for homework. I kept my head down. With any luck, she would forget all about me.

The day progressed unremarkably. Judy LeBlanc got caught with a Beatles magazine and was sent to the chair for the rest of the day, Beatlemania being the bane of Mrs. Barnicle's existence. Judy cried steadily if quietly for the first half hour; she was afraid she wouldn't get the magazine back and so were the rest of us. She had promised to show it to us at recess and obviously that wasn't going to happen now. Disappointment hung over us like an indoor cloud.

Then someone called Mrs. Barnicle out of the classroom and when she came back, she looked as if she'd been hit over the head with a baseball bat. I don't remember what she said, not the exact words. I just remember disbelief and shock, and an echo of the feeling I'd had when my father had died, a sense that all the things that were supposed to be steady and permanent were actually no more substantial or enduring than soap bubbles.

I automatically turned to look at Jimmy. His empty desk sat there as if it were anyone else's, as if it belonged to a kid who just happened to be sick today and not someone whose aunt was kicking him out. As if everything were really quite normal and it wasn't a world where the president had just been assassinated.

Assassinated. That was the word Mrs. Barnicle used. She said it over and over and it was so scary, not even the biggest loudmouth jerks in the class sniggered at it.

They let us out early. On my way home, I passed people crying on the street. Grown-ups crying in public, as if JFK had been someone they'd known personally. Maybe it was Kennedy or maybe it was the tenor of the times, or maybe it was both. Whatever it was, I can't imagine it happening now; but then, it made everything even scarier and more messed-up. My mother was still at work, unreachable except in an emergency, and since I had neither been shot nor done the shooting, this didn't qualify. Even if she had been home, she would have been glued to the news and telling me to be quiet. Didn't matter to me—I wanted Jimmy, not my mother. Jimmy knew about messed-up things. I hurried home, changed out of my school clothes, and went to look for him.

His aunt Linda lived four blocks away from our apartment building, which wasn't *quite* outside the boundary my mother had told me I was confined to when she wasn't home. As a latchkey kid, I was under strict orders not to *roam the streets,* something my mother considered both dangerous and disgraceful. Personally, I didn't see the harm in going for a walk but after discovering the hard way that she somehow always found out when I disobeyed—secret mother radar? superpowers?—I did as I was told. The only person who didn't make fun of me for this was Jimmy, which I thought was above and beyond the call of friendship. Hell, I made fun of *myself* for it.

I walked over to Jimmy's aunt's house wishing it weren't too cold to ride my bike—otherwise I could have been over there and back in under fifteen minutes. Less if his cousins were outside, because then I wouldn't have to ring the doorbell and talk to his aunt. You could never depend on an adult for a straight answer in a situation like this anyway and Linda Valeri wasn't the most approachable person in town. Chances were she'd just yell *Mind your own business!* and slam the door in my face. His cousins, on the other hand, would fall all over themselves to tell me where he was just to show off how much they knew.

The afternoon sky was graying up so that the day looked colder than it really was. I remember that and I remember I could almost smell snow in the air. Six days to Thanksgiving and it hadn't snowed but a couple of times; what was left from that wouldn't have made a decent-size snowman. I was thinking about how early it got dark, how it would be like midnight by six o'clock, which was when my mother got home from work. I had to find Jimmy before then because I wasn't supposed to be out after dark, especially not on a school night. Then I turned the corner onto his aunt's street and walked right into the middle of his latest crisis.

All three of Jimmy's cousins were outside in front of the house along with his aunt Linda. She had been crying and still was a little, dabbing at her reddened eyes and nose with a wad of tissues about twice the size of a softball. She was talking to two people standing with their backs to me: a woman in an expensive tweed coat and a turquoise velvet hat and a tall skinny guy in a trench coat. A big boat of an Oldsmobile and a little red VW were parked nose-to-nose at the curb, or sort of nose-to-nose—the VW had one tire up on the curb. I was thinking the Olds looked familiar when one of Jimmy's cousins suddenly yelled, "Hey, I bet *she* knows—*she's* his girlfriend!"

All three adults turned to see who *she* was, Jimmy's aunt glaring as if I had killed Kennedy and the other two looking like they thought I could catch the person who had.

"Hello? Little girl?" said the woman, bending down a little with a slightly desperate smile. This was Jimmy's social worker, Mrs. Beauvais, I realized, and I stepped back, wondering if it was too late to run. "What's your name, dear?"

"She lives in one of those big blocks on Water Street," Jimmy's aunt said. From the tone in her voice, you'd have thought she was talking about maggots.

Mrs. Beauvais tossed her an irritated glance and turned back to me, her smile becoming more desperate. "It's okay, dear, you're not in trouble."

The tall skinny man next to her rolled his eyes; when he realized I had seen him, he gave me a big thousand-watt, pleading smile of his own. "Well, of *course* she knows she's not in trouble, Jean-Marie," he said, his voice going all gooey. "We just want to ask you if you know where Jimmy Streubal is. Are you really his girlfriend?"

"*No!*" I said hotly, looking daggers at Jimmy's cousins. If the adults hadn't been around, I'd have punched them out for that slander. They knew it, too; they made faces at me behind Mrs. Beauvais's back.

"We're just friends. I gotta go home—"

"No, please, wait a minute—at least tell us your name," said Mrs. Beauvais, also going all gooey now. "It's so nice for us to meet a friend of Jimmy's."

I was probably the only one they had ever met, I thought, as I told her who I was.

"Oh, you're *Janet's* daughter!" Mrs. Beauvais exclaimed as if this was the most wonderful thing she had ever heard. "I know your mother *very* well, I see her whenever I'm at the hospital—"

"The hospital?" Jimmy's aunt snapped, stepping forward. "Oh my God, you mean her mother's a nurse?"

"No, she works in the admitting office," Mrs. Beauvais said, still sounding utterly delighted. "And a lovely person she is—"

"Oh, *that's* just *great.*" I thought Jimmy's aunt was going to spit with disgust. "She'll know all our private business and so will this little shit here—"

Mrs. Beauvais straightened up instantly. "I have warned you before—do *not* use that language *about* children *in front of* children, *especially* your own, or Jimmy won't be the only child going into care tonight."

Jimmy's aunt stared at her openmouthed—she needed a dentist *bad*, I thought—then turned to look at her daughters now lined up on the sidewalk next to her. Their faces were so terror-stricken that I forgot I wanted to punch them out. I tried to will Jimmy's aunt to bend down, gather them into her arms, and tell them they didn't have to be afraid. Instead, she turned back to Mrs. Beauvais. "You got someplace to take them, you go right ahead, lady. I need a rest and I can't get a babysitter."

All three girls burst into loud tears. It was all I could do not to cry with them.

"Oh, for Christ's sake, shut up!" Jimmy's aunt shouted, dabbing at her eyes with the enormous tissue wad. "You're not goin' nowhere, they don't got nobody to take care of you. Now shut up before I give you something to cry about!" This only made them cry louder. Mrs.

Beauvais turned to the skinny guy, who went over to the girls and tried to comfort them.

Naturally, they thought he was trying to take them away. Screaming at the tops of their lungs, they ran into the house and slammed the door. Even then we could still hear them wailing and sobbing. I looked around, wondering why the neighbors weren't coming out to see what was going on, and then remembered about Kennedy. They'd all be glued to their TV sets. Besides, they were probably used to hearing Linda Valeri's kids cry.

"Oh, what are *you* lookin' so upset for?" she asked the skinny guy, who was pinching the bridge of his nose like he had a bad headache. "*You* don't have to live with that—*I* do."

"Mrs. Valeri—" he started.

"Don't *Mrs. Valeri* me, you—you—" She hesitated, as if she'd been about to say something and then caught herself. "You *social worker.* You never mind about them *or* my brother's kid. We've got *real* problems now. Kennedy's been shot, probably by some Communist! This time next week we could have Russian tanks rolling down Main Street, unless they just drop the bomb on us. You gonna take my kids away then?"

Mrs. Beauvais and the skinny guy looked at each other for a moment; then she turned to me with a pained look that was trying to be a smile. "Sweetheart, an awful lot has happened today and it's got everyone so upset they're saying things they don't mean—"

If she was talking about Jimmy's aunt, she was a lousy judge of character, I thought, but I didn't say anything.

"—but right now, I'm very, very worried about Jimmy because nobody seems to know where he is." She stared into my face as if she really expected me to solve all her problems.

"Well, he wasn't in school today," I offered.

She nodded patiently. "Yes, we know that now. His aunt Linda said Jimmy left the house this morning just like always so she thought he *was* in school. When he didn't come home with his cousins, she called to see if he was with me. Now we're all very concerned—"

"Include me out," said Jimmy's aunt. "That kid can take care of himself just fine."

"Please, Mrs. Valeri—" said the skinny guy.

"Don't Mrs. Valeri me!"

He looked like he wanted to say something; instead, he turned his back and moved away a couple of feet. What did she want him to call her, I wondered—Aunt Linda? Your Majesty? At least none of us had to call her Mommy; inside the house, Jimmy's cousins were still wailing and sobbing.

"There, you hear that?" Jimmy's aunt said, gesturing with the wad of tissues. "That's *my* night shot to shit. Smooth move, Ex-Lax, thanks for nothin'. You're so worried about Jimmy, go look for him. I did what I was supposed to do. I told you to come and get him after school. It's not my fault if he took off. All I can say is, I just better see a check for the last month and a half or I'll sue you *and* the city." She marched into the house and slammed the door behind her. A moment later we could hear her screeching at the kids, who began crying louder than ever.

Mrs. Beauvais seemed to sag all over, even her face, as if she were deflating. Then the skinny guy touched her arm and nodded toward me. She squared her shoulders and made herself smile. "I have an idea," she said, trying to sound cheerful. "Why don't you help me look for Jimmy? We'll drive around in my car."

I looked at the big Oldsmobile. "I'd have to ask my mother but she's still at work, and I'm not supposed to call her there unless it's an emergency."

"That's no problem, *I'll* call her," said the social worker airily. "There's a pay phone in the candy store up the street, we'll call her from there."

"Well . . . I guess," I said dubiously. First it was *"I'll* call her" and in the next breath it was *"We'll* call her"? Sounded like a classic double cross to me. But even if it wasn't, I didn't think this was going to go over very well. It had the feel of something that was supposed to be a good deed but would somehow end up backfiring and getting me into trouble.

The skinny guy bent down so we were eye-to-eye. "Look, Jimmy might have been intending to go straight to school when he left his aunt's house this morning and then had an accident or something. He could be lying hurt somewhere, unable to call for help and hoping that someone, anyone would come looking for him. I bet he doesn't even know what happened to the president."

I shifted uncomfortably from one foot to the other, imagining myself lying unseen all day in a ditch with a broken leg or worse without anyone knowing it. The fact that there were no ditches where even a mouse could have lain unseen all day between my house and school didn't matter.

"Good girl." The social worker was ushering me toward her car quickly, before I could think of an argument. "Hop in, we'll drive to the store."

I pulled away from her. Getting into someone's car without permission? Unthinkable, even if I got permission afterward.

"Please," Mrs. Beauvais said wearily. "It'll take me a half hour to walk all the way there, make the call, and walk back again. That's a half hour when we could be looking for Jimmy and it'll be dark soon."

I gave in, hoping that somehow my mother either wouldn't find out or would make an exception to the rule this one time. Like if Jimmy really were lying hurt somewhere and would have died if I hadn't gone looking for him with his social worker. Nobody would punish a kid for saving someone's life, I thought.

The guy behind the counter at the candy store was watching a little black-and-white TV with the sound turned down low. Every minute or so, he changed the channel, which meant he had to fiddle with the antenna. A lady came out from the back room and asked him what was happening now. Then they'd both look at the skinny guy and say something like, "Can you believe it? What's this country coming to?" The skinny guy nodded and said something similar, all the while glancing over at Mrs. Beauvais, who was on the pay phone with my mother. Getting her permission for me to drive around with her and look for Jimmy was taking a lot longer than I'd thought it would.

Not a good sign—the longer it took, the more trouble I would probably be in later, whether we found Jimmy or not. Hoping I wouldn't have to talk to my mother myself, I stayed by the counter with the skinny guy, who had told me he was Mrs. Beauvais's assistant.

The conversation went on and on; I couldn't imagine what they were saying to each other and I didn't want to. The candy-store guy had flipped around the dial six or seven times when Mrs. Beauvais suddenly looked up and beckoned to me, pointing at the receiver. My heart sank but I went over anyway.

"—absolutely right, Janet, I *don't* know what it's like to bring up a child as a single parent," she was saying. "But you've known me for years and I would hope you know that I would never let any harm come to a child in my care. There is absolutely no danger and if I thought there were—"

Long pause. Mrs. Beauvais patted my shoulder reassuringly and then held on to it to keep me from walking away.

"I highly doubt that anyone would think anything bad about you *or* your daughter just because they saw her in my car, and if anyone ever did say anything, you have my assurance that I would correct them—"

Pause again.

"Well, then, how about just until four thirty? No matter what, I will drive her home at four thirty on the dot." Pause. "Yes, I promise. Four thirty *on the dot*. Yes, she's right here—" Mrs. Beauvais put her hand over the receiver and held it out to me. I took it from her, thinking that JFK had been lucky to have a quick death.

"Hi, Mom," I said miserably.

"Why does Social Services think you know where that boy is?" she demanded. "Where on earth would they get an idea like that?"

"I don't know," I said even more miserably.

"However you managed to get involved in this, you'd better be home at four thirty *on the dot*. Because I'm going to call the house at four thirty-five and you'd better answer by the third ring."

"I will—"

She went on but the social worker took the phone away from me and talked over her, thanking her profusely for allowing me to help a child who through no fault of his own was in trouble and what a day this was with one thing and another, isn't it just awful what happened and again, thank you *so, so much.* I was pretty sure my mother was still talking when Mrs. Beauvais hung up and turned to me with a bright, professional smile. "I guess we'd better get a move on if I'm going to get you home on time."

"Four thirty on the dot," I reminded her. My mother was going to kill me.

"Where are you two going to look first?" the skinny guy asked Mrs. Beauvais as we left the store.

"Well, where do *you* think we should look?" she asked me brightly. "Is there any special place Jimmy likes to go that only he knows about and nobody else does?"

I wanted to laugh in her face. If only Jimmy knew about it and nobody else, then I wouldn't know about it, either. Then I thought of the embankment and the area under the Fifth Street Bridge.

"Maybe," I said. "There's this place where we go sledding when it snows." I looked down at her feet. She was wearing boots but they had heels and looked dressy and expensive. "It's over by the playground. The one near the bridge."

"That's where we'll be," she told the skinny guy.

"I'll go uptown, then," he said and headed for his VW. I almost called after him not to bother—Jimmy never went uptown if he had a choice—but Mrs. Beauvais was stuffing me back into the front seat of the Oldsmobile like she was afraid I'd change my mind.

Back then, the Fifth Street Bridge was one of the longer bridges in that part of the county. It connected the main part of town with the more suburban south side, stretching over the railroad tracks that went to and from the state capital and, parallel to the tracks, the Nashua River, which in those days wasn't so much a river as a waste runoff from the paint factory and a couple of paper mills. You could tell how good business was by the color of the water—bright red, ink blue, puke green, or milk of magnesia white were all signs of an economic upturn, more so if there was a particularly bad stench.

Mrs. Beauvais parked the car across the street from the playground and peered through the windshield, worried. "Do you think Jimmy is *on* the bridge?" I knew she was looking at the concrete arches on the near side. The more daring high school boys showed off by walking all the way up and over them. Occasionally, the fire department would have to come out and rescue someone who'd reached the top and then lost his nerve, and everyone knew someone who knew someone who had seen the kid who had fallen off and splattered all over the road, although no one seemed to know exactly when this grisly event had occurred. I knew Mrs. Beauvais was wondering if Jimmy planned to walk over.

"No," I said, "he's not *on* the bridge. He's under it."

She looked at me, horrified. "But it's *dangerous* down there. The railroad tracks—he could get run over by a train. Or he could fall in the river—God only knows what would happen to him if he did!"

I shrugged. Getting hit by a train seemed to be a lot more difficult than avoiding it—it wasn't like a train could sneak up on you, after all, you could hear it coming for miles, which gave you plenty of time to get out of the way. The river we gave a much wider berth. It was generally accepted among kids that if you stuck your finger in the Nashua, all the flesh would dissolve off it, leaving the naked bone. But that was pretty easy to avoid, too—you just stayed far away from the water's edge. Not hard to do—there was a lot of land under the bridge, overgrown and wild, a jungle in the middle of town.

As if Mrs. Beauvais caught a sense of my thoughts, she said, "You know, sweetheart, sometimes bad people hide down there. Tramps passing through, criminals on the run from the police. If Jimmy ran into someone like that—well, there are people so bad they do that, you know. They hurt kids."

I didn't say anything. I had a vague idea of what she was talking about but as far as I knew, bad people like that didn't hide in the undergrowth beneath bridges—they lurked around outside schools with bags of candy.

"Do you and Jimmy spend a lot of time down there?" she asked, looking into my face seriously.

"Everybody goes sliding here when there's enough snow," I said. "There's a steep part and a part that's not so steep. Sometimes if it's slippery enough you can build up enough speed to go all the way to the tracks, practically."

"That's *very* dangerous," Mrs. Beauvais scolded. "A train could come along at exactly the wrong moment and there'd be nothing left of you."

"Nobody's ever slid *onto* the tracks," I said. "I don't think you could go fast enough."

She sighed heavily and looked toward the bridge again. "You think Jimmy's down there now?"

"I don't know," I said. "We'd have to go down and see. If you want, I'll go down by myself and come back and tell you."

Mrs. Beauvais shook her head so emphatically, the little net veil on her hat wiggled. "Didn't you hear me just tell you it's dangerous? Besides, I don't just want to know where he is. He has to come with me."

"Why?" I asked.

She looked startled at the question. I was startled myself at my sudden and hitherto unsuspected nerve. Never in my life had I ever asked an adult to explain herself.

"His aunt kicked him out, didn't she," I said.

"I'd rather you didn't put it that way," Mrs. Beauvais said and I realized she was embarrassed, which startled me even more.

"Where's he going to go now?"

She tapped her gloved fingers on the steering wheel. "That's a good question. I think Jimmy may have finally run out of relatives."

"Why can't you just *make* his mother take him?" I said. "Isn't it against the law or something for a mother to refuse to take care of her own kid?"

Mrs. Beauvais gave me another startled look. "I'm sorry, that was indiscreet. I shouldn't have said anything about Jimmy," she said in that brisk way grown-ups use when they've done something wrong and a kid bags them right in the act. "It's nothing that concerns you. These are matters that you'll never have to worry about, God willing. Now let's see if we can find Jimmy."

We got out of the car and Mrs. Beauvais followed me over to the easier way down, which wasn't all that easy for her in those boots and her dress and her nice tweed coat. I thought she probably would have had a hard time anyway at her age; I had no idea how old she was but all grown-ups seemed to be too old for everything kids could do. Every time I looked back at her clambering down the uneven slope after me, I was tempted to tell her to forget it, Jimmy probably wasn't down here, it was too cold.

I guess she knew from the look on my face because she kept telling me to keep going, she was doing fine, she had actually been a kid once herself, even if I found that hard to believe. What I found hard to believe was that I would get her back up the hill to the car fast enough so she could drive me home in time for my mother's four thirty-five phone call. How could I have been so stupid, I thought furiously. If I'd been with another kid, it would have been simple: I could just say I had to go home or my mother would kill me and then leave. The other kid wouldn't have blamed me for taking off. But if I left Mrs. Beauvais here, I would somehow end up in worse trouble when my mother found out. And she would find out, because Mrs. Beauvais saw her several times a week. She'd make a point of telling her.

That was grown-ups for you—do them a favor and they'd end up making stuff that should have been simple into something so complicated you ended up in trouble no matter what you did. Maybe that was why Jimmy's life was all messed up, I thought—he'd done some adult a favor once and he'd been paying for it ever since.

Finally we reached the bottom of the hill where the land sloped gently toward the railroad tracks. Mrs. Beauvais stood there for a few moments, swaying on her high-heeled boots, her pocketbook swinging from the crook of her elbow. Jeez, why hadn't she hidden that under the front seat, I wondered as she grabbed my shoulder to steady herself.

"I don't suppose there's an easier way back up?" she asked, puffing a little. I shook my head; I was doomed.

After she caught her breath, we continued down the slope and I led her toward the patch of land directly under the bridge. In the summer, big weeds grew up around the bridge support, overgrowth tall enough to hide in. I had thought most of it would have been gone now, killed off by the cold, but a lot of the thicker stalks were still there, yellow and dry as old corn husks.

"Jimmy?" I called softly, moving ahead of Mrs. Beauvais. "It's me, are you down here?" I glanced back at the social worker picking her way along the frozen ground, both arms out for balance as if she were walking a tightrope or something. I should have made her wait in the car, I thought, watching her pause to frown at her right boot. She'd stepped in something.

Without waiting for her, I plunged into the thickest part of the tall dead weeds close to the bridge support, both arms out in front of me so I wouldn't go face-first into the cement if I tripped. Abruptly, one of the stalks tilted down and hit me right on the bridge of my nose. Tears sprang into my eyes even though it wasn't quite as bad as the time the army brat who lived upstairs from us punched me in the nose. I staggered sideways, my hands grabbing for something, anything. Weeds broke off in my left hand; what felt like several jets of warm, humid air hit my right palm, and then I was sitting on the ground with Jimmy standing over me. He was wearing only a light, threadbare brown plaid shirt and jeans, but he didn't look cold.

"What're you doing here?" His voice sounded tired and old.

"Looking for you." I got up and brushed myself off. "Just like everybody else in town, I think. Well, your social worker and her assistant, anyway. The one who drives the red VW. They made me help them."

I spotted Mrs. Beauvais about twenty feet away, turning around with a desperate, bewildered expression on her face. I waved at her. "Hey, over here!"

Jimmy pulled my arm down. "Don't bother. She can't hear you. Or see you."

I twisted out of his grip. "What are you talking about? She's just right there—" I raised my arm to wave at her again and saw the air in front of me ripple, as if it were shimmering in intense heat.

"Okay, go ahead—wave, yell, yodel for all I care." Jimmy chuckled. "*Can* you yodel?"

I couldn't but I tried waving and yelling some more. Mrs. Beauvais didn't even look in our direction as she stumbled around in her expensive boots.

"Jeez, Jimmy. How are you doing it?"

"I'm not doing anything. *They* are." He jerked his thumb upward. I looked. Instead of the underside of the bridge, there was—

Well, I don't know what it was; I still don't. That might have been because only part of it was visible, as if someone had torn a strip out of the world overhead so it could show through, like a hidden attic between a ceiling and a roof, but I don't think so. It did remind me of an attic but it also made me think of a submarine. Or, strangely, a cross between Mrs. Beauvais's pocketbook, still swinging from the crook of her arm, and the roof of my mouth.

Too weird; I wanted to lower my head but my neck wouldn't move and closing my eyes made me feel dizzy. There was another, worse feeling creeping up on me as well, a strong sense of not mattering, of being so small next to everything else that I might as well not exist. It was horrible and scary but at the same time I also felt oddly relieved to know where I stood in the universe of things. But not happy; definitely not happy.

"Jimmy?" I said weakly.

"I know," he said. "This is my *dharma*."

I'd never heard the word before; it lodged in my brain like a barbed hook. "Who—or what—is up there?" I asked. I thought I saw faint shadows moving in the vaulted darkness. Later, much later, I thought of a church or a cathedral, but it wasn't like that at all.

"I just told you—my dharma. That's what they said, anyway. It means this is how it is for me."

"Oh." I wanted to tell him that my neck wouldn't move but I couldn't remember how to say something like that.

"I don't know if that's really the right word, considering they're doing it to me," Jimmy went on. "Probably doesn't matter—I can't stop it. They're just gonna keep doing anything they want to me."

"What are they doing?" I asked.

Jimmy hesitated. "They're still trying to find a word for that. If they ever do, it'll probably be a bad word. *Really* bad. But what it is, they make me know things."

My neck was starting to hurt. "They tell you stuff?"

"No, they make me know things."

"That's what I meant—they tell you things."

He made a frustrated noise. "*No.* It's not the same thing. I could tell you something but that wouldn't mean you'd *know* it."

"What're you talking about?" I said, getting frustrated myself, both with the argument and not being able to move my head. "If you tell me something, I'll know it."

"Oh, yeah? I can tell you I ran a mile without stopping and got tired but you won't know my feet hurt and my legs were wobbly and my lungs burned like fire. Even if I told you that, too, you still wouldn't *know* it, because it didn't happen to you. Unless I could *make* you know it my way."

"Oh." I managed to get both my hands up behind my neck and started rubbing it, pushing on the base of my skull as I did. After a bit, I could feel my head tilting down again little by little. Finally I was looking straight ahead instead of straight up. Mrs. Beauvais tramped back and forth in front of me and although I could see her mouth opening and closing, I didn't hear her. I didn't hear anything except Jimmy's voice and under that, a soft rushing noise, like when you put a seashell to your ear.

"Is that why you weren't in school today?" I asked. "Because someone was making you know something?"

"I didn't want to," he said. "I tried to run away but I ended up here."

"Have you been here all day?"

"Not exactly here. But all day, yeah."

"Mrs. Beauvais's assistant thought you might be stuck somewhere, like lying hurt in a ditch and unable to call for help. He said you probably didn't even know about what happened to the president."

"Oh, I know," Jimmy said. "I know all about it. I know everything."

"You do?"

"Yeah. They *made* me know."

The pain in his voice made me turn toward him. In the same moment, I suddenly noticed that the daylight was all but completely gone. Everything of the day seemed to rush down on me like an avalanche—Jimmy's empty desk, Mrs. Barnicle, Judy and her Beatles magazine, hearing that Kennedy had been shot, Jimmy's aunt and his cousins, Mrs. Beauvais and her assistant, the phone ringing in our empty apartment with my mother on the other end of the line getting madder and madder. Then I felt Jimmy's hand take hold of mine.

A riot of new images bloomed in my head.

I saw the presidential motorcade from several different angles and people lining the Dallas streets; sunlight gleamed off the shiny cars as JFK smiled and waved until part of his head exploded into red mist; Jackie Kennedy, slim and angular in her refined pink suit and pillbox hat, elegant face twisted in anguish, crawling onto the back of the car, not to get the attention of the bodyguard there but to grab up something that had landed on the trunk—part of her husband's skull. People screaming, sirens screaming, the air itself was screaming, electric with the fear that came with the breaking of the social compact we made not to kill each other.

Only I didn't know about things like *social compact*, not the words, not the concept. Well, yes, I knew but I didn't know that I knew. As brainy as I was, I was still supposed to be safe from knowing that for a long time.

Mrs. Beauvais stumbled across my field of vision looking bewildered and scared. Social worker, social compact worker. Her and her assistant, trying to keep Jimmy within the social compact, trying to catch him when he fell outside of it. But they didn't know about this. Whatever *this* was.

"Jimmy." It was an effort to speak. "Let's go."

"Where?"

"To her. Mrs. Beauvais."

"*You* can. They're not done with me yet. There's more to come."

"How do you know?"

"I just do."

"When will they be done?"

"When they are."

"But what—"

"I just showed you," he said, almost snapping. "I *made* you know some of it. Only a little."

"How?"

"I don't know. Maybe I could because you wanted to know."

Mrs. Beauvais was standing in front of me almost close enough to touch now. The air between us shimmered again. I should reach out and pull her in, I thought.

"You can't," Jimmy said, as if I had spoken aloud. "There's no room for her in here. No room with them. She's too full. Maybe you'd better go now before they make *you* know something."

"You think they would?"

"I dunno. They might. If they do, you could end up like me. Nobody'll want you. And you don't have as many relatives as I do. If your mom doesn't want you, you'll have nowhere to go."

"That wouldn't happen," I said.

Jimmy gave a small, bitter laugh. "You don't know what you're talking about. But I do. They messed me up, making me know things. It's like I've got scars, only they don't show the way normal scars do. People look at me and they know something's wrong. They don't know what, they just know there's something off. They try to figure it out—some think it's a bad smell, I don't wash maybe, or I'm look-ing at them funny, like I don't respect them. Or they can't see *me*, they see someone bad they used to know. Maybe some of them even dream that I do things I haven't done and then think it was real after they wake up."

"What about me? I don't think any of those things," I said. "And what about Mrs. Beauvais? She doesn't, either."

"Yes, she does," Jimmy said. "She holds her nose and forces herself to smile and try to help me because it's her job. But deep down, she thinks I'm bad. As for you—" He hesitated. "Well, there's some people who don't get a rash from poison ivy. You're like one of them." He sighed. "You better go. They're coming back for me."

"I don't want to leave you here," I said.

"You have to. If they come back and see y—"

His voice didn't so much stop as it snapped off like a dry twig. I wasn't going to look up again because I knew if I did I wouldn't be able to look away. But knowing that made it impossible *not* to look. I raised my head.

I'm not sure what I expected to see—monsters that looked like Frankenstein or the Creature from the Black Lagoon or maybe a robot like the one in *The Day the Earth Stood Still.* But they were nothing like any of those, the ones who made Jimmy Streubal know things. They were something I had never seen before, something I knew I would never see again. So I took a good, long, hard look at them, I memo-rized every line and shadow and feature while they looked back at me and did the same. And when I was sure I knew exactly what they looked like, something in my mind clicked, like a switch or a lock, and to this day if I try to describe them even just to myself, no words or gestures will come.

The one thing I can describe, however, is the way they sniffed at me, tasted me, and then gently pushed me away.

I tried to reach for Jimmy—whether to stay with him or pull him with me, I still don't know. It didn't work. The air around me shim-mered and I fell, rolling over and over on the dead weeds in the cold, to stop at the very expensive boots of the very, very surprised Mrs. Beauvais.

She pulled me to my feet and started yelling at me about how I had scared her. I didn't say anything, just waited for her to pause for breath so I could suggest we go back up to her car. Even if four thirty-five was long gone and my mother was probably on her way home, I hoped I might get off a little more lightly if I had to face the music with Mrs. Beauvais beside me.

But she kept yelling and yelling and yelling, and she was holding my shoulder so that her fingers were digging into it harder and harder. I thought she was going to twist my arm off if she didn't scream her own head off first.

I tried to pull away from her but that only made her madder. She started jerking me back and forth and it really hurt. I struggled to get away from her and she was trying to hang on to me and finally I just pushed her as hard as I could.

She went over backward and I started to run away. But she didn't get up and yell some more and I knew something was really wrong. I went back to look. She had hit her head on a rock and there was blood all over the dead grass and her velvet hat, more blood than I had ever seen in my life.

I turned to run and a small movement caught my eye. Over by the bridge, the air was shimmering, as if heat were rising from an unseen fire. For a moment, I had a powerful urge to plunge back into it. But I couldn't leave Mrs. Beauvais lying there, not even if I had killed her.

It seemed to take forever to get up the easy slope. By the time I reached the top, I barely had enough breath left to run to the nearest house for help.

I don't think that I've ever had so many people yelling at me for so long, before or since. Everyone who saw me seemed to feel compelled to yell at me for something, even people I didn't know. Somewhere in all the noise, someone—probably Mrs. Beauvais although it could

have been my mother—convinced the police to conduct a thorough
search of the area under the Fifth Street Bridge. One of the TV news
programs in the capital got wind of it and actually sent out a reporter
and a camera crew, and we saw thirty, maybe forty seconds of every
cop in town poking around the dead weeds under the bridge. One of
them went right past a spot by the bridge support where the air
seemed to wiggle and shimmer like it did when it was very hot, but
that could have been the film or the TV.

Nobody found anything. There was no sign of Jimmy, no sign of
anything, nothing but dead weeds and Mrs. Beauvais's blood. There
was plenty of that.

I was positive she would bleed to death by the time the ambulance
got there. But when they brought her up on the stretcher, she was not
only alive but conscious and talking, insisting that they take me in the
ambulance with her. So she could have me arrested at the hospital for
pushing her down, I thought, but I was wrong about that, too. She told
the ambulance guys on the way in that she had been about to take me
back up to her car so she could drive me home when someone came
out of nowhere and gave her a hard shove that knocked her down and
although she didn't see who did it, it must have been Jimmy. It couldn't
have been anyone else.

They asked me if I'd seen Jimmy do it; I told them no but I don't
think they believed me. Then we got to the hospital emergency room
where my mother was waiting for me and the yelling began again.

I spent Thanksgiving vacation under house arrest. I did a lot of reading
and watched a lot of TV. I saw JFK's funeral and the film of Jack Ruby
killing Lee Harvey Oswald. I didn't see Jimmy.

When school resumed in December, Jimmy's desk was still empty and
it stayed that way. Mrs. Barnicle said he was missing. *Unfortunately missing* was how she put it. Nobody knew where he was.

Even after my house arrest was lifted, my mother threatened me with dire punishments if I should ever show the incredibly bad judgment to go down under the Fifth Street Bridge again. I didn't tell her the threats weren't necessary; I had the odd sense that she felt it was her duty to make them.

Eventually, trains ceased to run on that stretch of track. Environmentalists cleaned up the Nashua River. It looked beautiful but you couldn't have paid most people to go near it anyway.

I had been living in Chicago for ten years when my mother wrote to tell me that the Fifth Street Bridge was to be torn down and replaced with a better structure. She sent newspaper clippings; I read the articles, looked at the photos carefully, but there was nothing to see.

I still wonder why Jimmy didn't come with me out of that strange space under the bridge, whether it was because those . . . beings, whatever they were, wouldn't let him go or whether he was just sick and tired of having to be at odds with the whole world. Either way, I always feel a sense of seriously deep loss when I think of him.

It's not just the loss of Jimmy himself, although he did leave a big hole in my childhood life. I can't help thinking that we lost an opportunity for something—"we" as in people in general. The way Jimmy was being made to know things—I think eventually more people would have been made to know things. Really know them, in the profound and meaningful way that leads to understanding and possibly even—pardon the expression—enlightenment.

But it didn't agree with us. I felt how difficult it was when Jimmy made me know what happened to JFK. It was overwhelming and I shut my mind off from it as best I could, partly because Jimmy wasn't there to help me with it. But mostly because for as long as it was vivid in me, people were angry with me. Jimmy had been right—when you were made to know things in that way, it messed you up with other people.

I still look for Jimmy. I look for that shimmer in the air, like from intense heat. And whenever I see it, I look the other way.

Prisoners of the Action

Paul McAuley and Kim Newman

Paul McAuley's novels have won the Philip K. Dick Memorial Award, the Arthur C. Clarke Award, the John W. Campbell Memorial Award, and the Sidewise Award. His latest novels are Players *and* Cowboy Angels. *His most recent story collection is* Little Machines. *A former scientist, he lives in London; his website can be found at www.omegacom.demon.co.uk.*

Kim Newman was born in Brixton (London), grew up in the West Country, went to university near Brighton, and now lives in Islington (London). His most recent fiction includes Where the Bodies Are Buried, The Man from the Diogenes Club, *and* Secret Files of the Diogenes Club *under his own name, as well as* The Vampire Genevieve *as Jack Yeovil. His nonfiction books include* Ghastly Beyond Belief *(with Neil Gaiman),* Horror: 100 Best Books *and* Horror: Another 100 Best Books *(both with Stephen Jones), and a host of books on film. He is a contributing editor to* Sight & Sound *and* Empire *magazines; has written and broadcast widely on a range of topics; and has scripted radio documentaries, role-playing games, and TV programs. He has won the Bram Stoker Award, the International Horror Guild Award, the British Science Fiction Award, and the British Fantasy Award. His official website can be found at www.johnnyalucard.com.*

McAuley and Newman have collaborated before, most notably while hosting the entertaining and imaginative 2005 Prix Victor Hugo Awards Ceremony in Glasgow, for which they were subsequently nominated for the Hugo (Gernsback) Award for Best Dramatic Presentation, Short Form. "Prisoners of the Action," a novella, is somewhat more serious, but has its amusing moments.

olonel Franklin Dice walked off the ramp of the transport plane on rubbery legs, kit-bag strap biting into his shoulder, and stamped the concrete to get feeling back into his feet. He had been in the air for over a day and a half—going around the world the wrong way to avoid trouble spots in Africa and the Middle East. His flight plan had comprised hops from DC to San Diego, Pearl Harbor, the Philippines, some outcrop-with-an-airstrip-and-a-flag west of Sumatra, and, finally, Great James Island, an atoll in the middle of the Indian Ocean, and debatably part of the Chagos Archipelago.

Dice's first view of the island was a simmering runway, a row of Black Hawk and Little Bird helicopters, and a green fire truck parked on a bone-white coral road. His second was Colonel Stanley Stock, the base commander, steaming toward him, tailed by an anxious knot of officers. A small, trim man in his fifties, pure white hair in a crew cut with high sidewalls, Colonel Stock gave Dice a karate-chop salute, brusquely welcomed him to Great James, and ignored a query about the whereabouts of Captain McAndrews, the officer-in-command of the military police on the island, and Dice's point of contact.

"You may think your investigation is the most important legal action since they found presidential cum on Monica Lewinsky's dress," Stock said, "but I will absolutely not tolerate interference with the day-to-day running of this facility. Forget your letters of authority from that committee of easy-chair generals back in the Pentagon. Out here, my word is law. If you compromise island security in any way, I will have you arrested and put on the next transport out. Is that understood, soldier?"

The man was wound up tight, jaw muscles knotted like a bulldog's, eyes narrowed in a cold, hard, death-ray stare. Dice understood why: In this man's army, getting a rep as a bad commander was worse than being tagged a war criminal.

Stock kept staring, just the way he'd learned from assertiveness tapes. Dice took his time responding, letting a little warm wind pass between them.

"*Colonel* Stock," he said, gently stressing their equivalent rank, "I understand you're proud of your little kingdom and that around here your whim is law. However, as far as I'm concerned, it's at the back end of my list of prime vacation spots. The only reason I'd make a stink if you were to order your vassals to frog-march me back onto this bird is that I'd have to explain to the oversight committee why I came back empty-handed. Let me assure you that it is my express intention to carry out the investigation with minimum fuss and get out of here as swiftly as I can. If that means keeping out of your way, it'll be fine with me . . ."

Stock couldn't suppress a smirk. It was obvious he believed Dice had just rolled over, when in fact Dice was deploying his favorite courtroom tactic. It was simple but effective: He let the hostile witness think he was dismissed and off the hook, then fired the killer question as the boob was halfway out of the box, with relief-sweat popping prematurely on his forehead.

". . . *But,*" he continued, watching the word sink in like a hook, "it is in the nature of things that, sooner or later, we're gonna have to have a conversation about what went down here."

Colonel Stock bristled. "I'm in charge of perimeter security and day-to-day running, no more, no less. As I made it abundantly clear in my report, 'what went down' was nothing to do with me and everything to do with the Frank-Einsteins and their experiments. *They* supervise what goes on in the pits and *they* control access to the POTAs.

If you want to minimize your time here, I suggest you begin *and end* your investigation with the bubblebrains."

POTAs: Prisoners of the Action. The reason why Great James had been turned into a cross between a maximum-security prison and a summer camp for mad scientists; the reason why Dice had been sent halfway around the world.

Dice said, "Colonel, if I never had to talk with you again, I'd consider myself a fortunate man."

Watching Stock process that was like watching a walrus try advanced algebra. The man eventually swallowed as if getting rid of a bad taste and said, "I hope we're on the same page, Colonel."

"We're definitely in the same army. And it's our mutual bad luck that the army needs to know what happened here."

Dice was tempted to goose the base commander further by suggesting that an officer a tad more suspicious and a little less good-natured than himself might wonder why Stock had come at him hot and heavy so early in the day. He was straight off the plane and getting snarled at before the engines had stopped whining. But Colonel Stock was looking past Dice now—case closed!—moving on to greet Jubilee Bliss.

The senator came down the ramp among a posse of aides wearing black suits, shades, and earplugs with coiled flexes that snaked down the backs of the starched collars of their shirts. He'd changed from flight coveralls into a gray silk suit, string tie, and cowboy boots. Groomed, enormous, and slick, he was making an entrance, as if stepping out of a limo for a thousand-dollar-a-plate fund-raiser rather than a transport plane on a godforsaken outcrop. Bliss folded both of his huge hands around Stock's proffered paw, giving a movie-star grin while murmuring platitudes, holding his head up to emphasize his height and minimize his puffy chin while one of his aides crouched to get a heroic image, with the burning sky behind him, on Digi-Beta.

Bliss was Bible Beltway, famous for his world-class abilities in filibustering, pork barreling, and pandering to the unplumbed depths of fundamentalist prejudice. Using influence gained from his work on the president's reelection campaign, he'd finessed himself onto the oversight committee with responsibility for Great James Island, but his visit was more of a scouting mission for the aerospace company located in his state and run by his brother-in-law than an investigation into means and practice. Joining him in the photo op was Rose-of-Mary, his twenty-four-year-old daughter. A Christian girl—rock singer and advocate of premarital virginity, she had backed her father's last campaign with a triple-platinum album, *Do What Daddy Says*. She looked like an alarmingly thin white-blond angel and had given everyone on the flight silver armbands that signified support of her cause. Dice's was in his pocket, but most of the crew had tied the things somewhere about their persons for the duration of the flight.

The Bliss Pack allowed themselves to be led around the side of the plane, to where a line of Humvees and Jeeps were waiting. As soon as the senator and Rose-of-Mary hove into their view, a small military band started to blow the hell out of something by Sousa, most of the notes snatched away in the fierce hot salt wind.

Dice wondered where Captain McAndrews had gotten to. Surely he couldn't be the lone cyclist who'd just appeared out of the heat-haze, wobbling at a slow but steady pace across the concrete apron toward the plane. When a couple of the senator's black suits broke away to intercept this possible kamikaze, the cyclist stood on his pedals and, with a surprising burst of speed, swerved around the aides, zoomed under the plane's wing, and braked neatly in front of Dice.

Dice's first thought was that the apparition was a Sikh, but what seemed like a turban was actually a puffed-up watch cap threaded through with shiny strands. With his ragged blue uniform, deep tan, gray beard, and over-regulation-length hair, the newcomer was a ringer for Ben Gunn. Dice considered telling him that he could come out of the jungle because World War Two was over and—guess what?—we won. The hermit straightened his back and snapped off a precise salute, then pulled a black lump from the wicker basket slung in front of his handlebars and thrust it into Dice's hands.

"With the compliments of Her Most Ancient and Awful Majesty the Queen, may Gawd bless Her and keep Her, sah!"

It was another watch cap, layers of tinfoil lining the wool.

The man leaned closer and said, in a confidential voice, "For the preservation of your precious brain waves."

Dice guessed this must be one of the victims of the infamous Great James Syndrome: crazy as a soup sandwich, but no threat to life and limb.

"Who do I have to thank?" he asked.

"No thanks needed, American soldier-johnny," the man said. "Wear it in good health, though. And think of England."

His gaze was ice blue and keen, but fixed beyond Dice as if he were expecting a cavalry regiment to charge out of the sea in support of one lone attorney in uniform. Tendrils of his untrimmed beard wavered in the hot wind like sea anemone tentacles. He saluted again and pedaled off, making a wide, wobbling circle around the band.

The convoy of Humvees and Jeeps sped off, carrying away Colonel Stock, Senator Bliss, the virginal Rose-of-Mary, and all the aides and officers. The musicians halted in midmarch and began to pack up their instruments. Many were non-regulation-issue, soldered-together affairs of tubes, bells, and keys: Rube Goldberg devices more like amusing industrial sculpture than brass-band kit. There was a tired old joke that military justice—Dice's field—was to the civilian variety as marching bands were to the New York Philharmonic. Dice had a chill premonition that on Great James, the gulf between anything at all and its counterpart in the ordinary world was vast, cool, and unsympathetic.

A loading crew in coveralls or shorts moved up the ramp past Dice, trampling a litter of discarded strips of silver cloth. A truck backed up, ready to receive the plane's cargo. Two hundred yards away, a Little Bird helicopter lifted straight into the air, its downdraft sending white sand shooting across the runway as it turned and headed toward the sparkling blue sea. And a tall blond man, bareheaded in camouflage fatigues, drove up in a Jeep, jumped out, and saluted.

"Colonel Dice, sir," he said, "Sergeant Timothy Haines, sir."

Haines had a Chicago accent and a Boy Scout's enthusiasm.

Dice sloughed his kit bag and returned the salute. "I arranged to be met by Captain McAndrews, Sergeant."

"Captain McAndrews is currently indisposed, sir. Colonel Stock put me in charge of base security, pending his recovery."

"When did this happen?"

Dice had talked to McAndrews on an encrypted satellite phone only twelve hours ago, while the plane was refueling at Manila. He had sounded sharp, focused, and cautious.

"Just this morning, sir. Captain Mac's orderly found him painting equations on the walls of his room. With his own excrement."

"You better take me to see him."

"Sorry, sir, but that won't be possible right now. Right now he's in quarantine, and in any case far too . . . discomposed, to entertain visitors."

"Really. How about I talk to one of his doctors?"

"Of course, sir. But they'll all tell you the same thing: that he's one sick bunny rabbit."

Haines slung Dice's kit bag into the back of the Jeep and asked if he had any other luggage.

"I plan to spend as little time here as possible," Dice said, climbing into the shotgun seat.

Haines took the wheel and fired up the Jeep. "I hope your plan holds, sir."

The sergeant noticed that Dice had the madman's woolly hat in his lap.

"I see you got your welcome-to-paradise tea cozy from Bomber Brown."

"That beachcomber is Peter Brown? *Wing Commander* Brown?"

Great James was sovereign British territory and officially an RAF base, commanded by a senior British officer who had nothing at all to do with running the place except signing off orders he wasn't authorized to read.

"He's mostly harmless, sir. Everything is relative, of course, especially here, but you can safely ignore him."

"On this rock, with nothing to occupy his mind, I guess it's little wonder he's gone stir crazy. Especially given the, um, current attrition rate."

"Sir, permission to speak frankly?"

"By all means, Sergeant."

"If you're worried about compromising security, I'm fully up to speed with every aspect of what you're here to investigate. Plus, it's hard to keep secrets in this place—even the lowliest hump has a good idea of what's happening. Currently, we have two hundred thirty-eight persons, seven point three three percent of total base population, incapacitated by what you call GJS, Great James Syndrome, and we call Island Fever. Captain Mac is the latest victim, a very severe case, but well within the statistical spread. An unknown number of other personnel, possibly one hundred percent, suffer from minor effects but are able to carry out their duties. Affliction with full-blown Fever appears to follow a lunar cycle, peaking at each full moon."

"Like the Wolf Man," mused Dice.

"I have graphs I could show you," said Haines, his gaze just a little too bright.

"The Pentagon has graphs, too, Sergeant. If I may speak frankly, I'm pleased we can speak plainly, because we have a lot to talk about. But first, I want you to drive me to the nearest shower."

They passed Wing Commander Brown, yawing alarmingly on his old-fashioned bike. They passed the fire truck, its ladder extended at a forty-five-degree angle into the grove of palm trees. Swaying at the top was an enlisted man, picking coconuts and dropping them to the ground, where two other grunts collected them in a wheelbarrow under the watchful gaze of a female MP. The coconut handlers wore only footgear, khaki shorts, and huge, padded, elbow-length gauntlets.

Dice said, "Is that what passes for punishment detail here?"

"Not as crazy as it looks, sir. And supervision is necessary. The Brits did a lot of atmospheric testing here back in the 1950s. The coconuts are radioactive. They have to be harvested before they fall, in case someone is tempted to eat them."

"I see. We wouldn't want anyone getting a bellyful of radioactive coconut milk and becoming a superhero. 'Blessed with the proportionate skull thickness of a coconut, young Billy Barker dons a hairy cape and fights crime as Coco-Man.' "

"I believe the army is more worried about men getting radiation poisoning and dying, sir."

"All this and the POTAs, too. No wonder people are going crazy here."

At the officers' quarters, in the bleak, fiercely air-conditioned room he'd been allocated, Dice took advantage of the shower and the first plumbed-in latrine he'd seen in three continents. Refreshed, relieved, and shaved, with clean skivvies under his funky uniform, Dice found Haines leaning against the wall outside his room, reading a James Lee Burke novel. The sergeant shut the book and slipped it into his back pocket, muttering, "Page one twenty, third paragraph down, second sentence in, third word."

Dice took that onboard. Haines definitely had a touch of Island Fever.

"I think I should visit the prisoner now," said Dice.

"Of course, sir. Which one, sir?"

"Private Montori, unless you've caught her collaborators. In which case, I'll gratefully shake your hand, recommend you for field promotion, and ask you to drive me back to the airstrip before that transport leaves."

"I was thinking of the victim, sir. The POTA."

"Take me to Montori, Sergeant. I'll tell you who or what else I need to see after that."

They had to drive halfway around the circumference of the island to reach the brig. Named in 1694 by explorers so far out from Portsmouth that Captain George Holland didn't know James II had been deposed, Great James had once been an idyllic, textbook coral atoll, a scattering of islets, coconut palms, and white beaches in a rough circle about ten miles across, with reefs full of fish in the inner lagoon and a barricade of outer reefs stretching into the open ocean. Until the mid-1950s it had supported a small, indigenous population of Ilois, Creole-speaking descendants of escaped slaves from French Africa and seafaring Indians. The natives had been moved out when Prime Minister Anthony Eden decided to use their home as a test ground for prototypes of a battlefield nuclear weapon. The program was abandoned a few years later when the British were persuaded to engage in joint UK–US ops, and Great James had become part of the Cold War front line, in everything but name a USAF base. Most of the islets were concreted over and joined by causeways and bridges. A runway two miles long was built to support long-range bombers, and a harbor blasted out of the reef. Silos were sunk and ICBMs pointed well to the north of Afghanistan, targeting military facilities in Turkmenistan and Kazakhstan, then pulled out and scrapped after one of the SALT agreements. B-52s had used the field as a staging post in the Afghan and Iraq wars. Now the island housed the Prisoners of the Action, POTAs, twenty enemy survivors of that nightmare remake of *Invasion of the Saucer Men*—a *lot* less funny than the original—which every media outlet in the States had to be dissuaded from calling an alien invasion or a War of the Worlds.

After fifty years of military rule, Great James was a stark place, miles of flat concrete blinding in tropical sun (Dice's sunglasses were in the top drawer of the desk in the den of his house in Alexandria), studded with bunkers, laboratories, hangars, junkyards full of rusting vehicles, firing pits, and experimental kit. There was a recreation area, with baseball and basketball and tennis courts, and a miniature golf course. And there was the prison compound: not the facility where the POTAs were kept—those were the former missile silos two miles around the curve of the island—but the place where servicemen and -women accused of crimes against military discipline were penned, along with the 238 cases of severe Great James Syndrome. Neat ranks of open-sided tents were pitched inside a double fence of razor wire, with coils of barbed wire between, guard towers on each corner, and the original guardhouse, a long, low L-shaped building a little like a civilian motel, to one side.

Private Montori was at the far end of the guardhouse's jail block, in the only occupied cell. Two MPs in white helmets, both hard-faced women, guarded her door. Chalked on the corridor wall nearby were designs that could have been theorems, a complicated tic-tac-toe variant, or a folk-art mural from a culture Dice didn't recognize. Though the guards were as stock-still as the redcoats outside Buckingham Palace, Dice saw smudges of chalk on their pressed khakis and wondered if they had been taking turns to add to the design.

He handed his sidearm to one of the soldier girls and let her see that his slim, leather document case—a graduation present from his mother to "My son, the lawyer"—contained nothing but papers and photographs. Haines gave a nod, and the second MP unlocked the door with a key on a long chain fixed to her belt, stood aside so Dice could step in, then shut the door behind him.

The prisoner, wearing baggy green coveralls and looking far plainer and much more ordinary than in her infamous photographs, was sitting on her cot, knitting something that was beginning to take the shape of a multicolored squid. She saw Dice's bars, stood, and saluted.

He returned the salute and told her to sit down.

"I already told them I don't need a lawyer, sir."

She was very young and tightly wound, shoulders hunched defensively, hands clutching her knitting to her chest, muscles jumping in her face, but her gaze was hard and defiant.

Dice leaned against the wall and folded his arms, tried to look as unthreatening as possible, and told the woman, "My name is Franklin Dice, Private Montori. I'm a lawyer, yes, but I'm not your lawyer. I've come here to find out what happened, and I was hoping that you and I could have a friendly off-the-record talk."

Montori's expression became even more guarded. "You sound like you're some kind of cop. Maybe I should see a lawyer after all."

Dice gave her his best smile. "It's a little early for that, Private. Between you and me and the wall, it isn't even clear that a crime has been committed, let alone whether you should be accused of anything."

"Maybe that's true, sir, but I reckon I'm definitely under arrest."

"As I understand it, you're under observation. What we have to do right now is work out where we go from here. But I can only do that if you help me."

"Begging your pardon, sir, but they aren't going to let me go anywhere," Montori said with flat finality, and started clacking her needles again without taking her gaze from Dice's face. Five balls of different-colored wool were being worked together, around strips of foil from candy wrappers.

Dice wondered if she was trying to improve on Wing Co Brown's design for protective headgear.

Private Christine Montori. Chris Montori.

This month, she was one of the most famous faces on the planet. And not in a bubbly, trivial Britney Spears sort of way.

She was from one of those mountain places in flyover country where "this girl's army" had seemed a better career path than getting married to one of her cousins and dropping a bunch of two-headed babies before she was old enough to vote. A week ago, no one born outside the county had heard of her hometown. Now it was under siege by the world's media, and her fellow citizens had declared that they were behind her 100 percent. Their pastor had just hosted a celebratory Klan-style burning of *X-Files* DVD box sets and L. Ron Hubbard books, and there was talk of a march on the White House to protest the witch hunt against their fairest daughter for something that as far as they were concerned wasn't a crime at all, and her unconstitutional incarceration on a rock halfway around the world.

That something was torture of the enemy. Or at least, accessory to torture.

What Private Christine Montori had done was pose for pictures next to one of the Prisoners of the Action, smiling as if she'd just been elected Gangbang Queen at the County Fair. Although it was still classified information, journalists had begun to catch on that it was almost impossible to get a good image of the POTAs on anything that relied on pixels rather than silver nitrate or color-dye film stock. Everything electronic, from a cellular phone to a top-of-the-line DV camera, pictured the Prisoners of the Action as nothing more than grayish blurs, ghosts. Christine Montori was just plain unlucky that her still-unidentified partner in crime, snapping away with a cheap disposable camera that used good old-fashioned Kodak film, had come up with clear, pristine, funny-yet-terrifying images of one of the alien invaders. She was unluckier still that, despite standing orders against passing any images of anything at all on Great James to civilians, the camera had been smuggled off the island to a journalist who'd turned it into the biggest scoop since the Zapruder movie.

The iconic photograph showed Christine Montori in combat fatigue pants and cap, bare-chested, tummy sucked in, tits stuck out, with guns in both hands, one aimed at the ceiling, one pointed at the smallest and topmost of the POTA's three spheres that was all too easy to call a head. Her black bra was wound around the head-lump like a cartoon baby's bonnet. Below it, three filmy apertures that weren't eyes were wide open, surrounded by cilia as erect as mascaraed lashes, seeming to stare in terror and panic. There were greasy holes in its bubbly torso, with vivid purple interiors. Dice understood all the Prisoners had them, but anyone who didn't know would assume they were wounds.

The POTA did have an actual wound, in fact, but that was hard to make out from the pictures that flashed around the world. Thoughtfully, the unknown snapper had taken detail shots and, a subpoena later, they were in the folder Dice had been given in DC. Below the three apertures that weren't eyes was a larger, triangular aperture that wasn't a mouth. The POTAs didn't ingest food in any way their captors had been able to record. The "mouth" was an ovoid cave leading to three peanut-size lumps made of crystalline sections of the single vast molecule from which each POTA was woven. It was theorized, not entirely in a jocular manner, that this ingress might be some kind of sex organ, which raised the horrible probability that the next occupant of this "secure hospital" cell would be some stupid soldier boy who tried to fuck the thing. At least that wasn't Montori's kick.

Until the pictures appeared, none of the geniuses in charge of the POTAs—frustrated at getting nothing useful out of their captives and no doubt suffering from various degrees of Island Fever, their experimental, security, and containment procedures growing increasingly sloppy—seemed to have noticed what had been done. The aperture had been stuffed full of a substance that turned out to be common sea salt, of which Great James had an unlimited supply, and then sewn shut: not with surgical sutures from a medical kit or the kind of regular needle and thread someone like Montori might have access to for uniform repairs, but with thick, black twine.

Mouth filled with salt, and sewn shut.

That was horribly familiar. Like every other island where slaves had fetched up, Great James had once incubated its own version of voodoo, though Dice's working assumption was that the tradition had been reimported by some GI from Louisiana or the Caribbean. Pins in dolls. Teterodotoxin jabs to make mindless slaves. Frenzied dances. Papa Legba, Baron Samedi, and Erzulie Freda. What had been done to the Prisoner was what a voodoo practitioner did to a zombie when it had outlived its usefulness and needed to be put back in the grave again for good.

So far, only Private Montori had been fingered for the crime, if that was what it was. But she'd had associates. Dice had been sent to find out who they were.

He unzipped his document case, took a detail blowup from the folder, and held it in front of Montori's face. "Let's try a few easy questions, Private. Nothing difficult, nothing you haven't been asked before. If you can provide answers, I can promise it will do you a great deal of good."

She scowled at him, her needles still clacking away.

Dice said, "You don't believe me, and I can understand why, but it happens to be true. It's why I've been sent here. I know that what happened wasn't your idea, that you were tricked into helping out. So how about taking a look at this?"

The POTA wasn't in this slice of the image, which included the edge of an observation window. The shutterbug had snapped his own reflection. A dark-skinned male in a white robe and a black top hat, camera and hands covering most of his face.

Captain McAndrews's initial investigation had yielded three possible suspects: privates Walter Garrett, Shaq Fuqua, and Tozer Dinkley. All three, like Montori, worked maintenance at the pits where the POTAs were held. All three had been interviewed at length by Captain McAndrews; all three had denied any involvement and produced stand-up alibis.

Montori didn't even bother to look at the photo.

"I respectfully decline to answer, Colonel."

"Taken as read, Private. No one wants to rat on their bunkies. But look a little closer and tell me who *this* is?"

Behind the photographer, nearly out of frame, was another party. Precisely, the sleeve of another party. White, not fatigue or camo green.

Montori blinked. Dice knew McAndrews hadn't shown her this detail because it had emerged only after digital enhancement. He thought she was genuinely surprised. But then she shook her head and clacked her needles a little faster.

Dice said, "That isn't one of your bunkies, is it? Could it be one of the scientists? If it is, you see, I can't help but wonder if you were co-opted into one of their experiments."

Montori had jabbed herself with one of her needles. Blood trickled into her knitted squid, soaking through the weave stitch by stitch as if purposefully.

Her mouth worked; words emerged reluctantly, as if forced out under torture. "I . . . respectfully . . . decline . . ."

"Was it an experiment, Christine? Or should we call it a ritual?"

Dice spent another ten minutes trying to cajole her into opening up, but she wouldn't answer any of his questions and grew more and more agitated, although she never once stopped knitting.

At last, when he was sure that he had pushed her as far as he could, he told her, "You're upset, Christine. It isn't surprising, in the circumstances. What I want you to do now is think about what I just showed you, and think about this: If someone ordered you to do what you did, you aren't under orders now. I will see you later, we will talk again." He rapped on the cell door; when the MP opened it, Montori held up her work and stared straight at Sergeant Haines.

"Six hundred and ninety-four," she said.

"Well done," Haines said, and tossed in a package of cigarettes, which bounced ignored on Montori's cot.

Her needles began clacking again. Dice looked at Haines.

"Stitches since the door was opened," the sergeant explained, as if this was something that had to be checked and recorded.

The door was shut and locked; Dice holstered his Beretta.

"Why is she allowed knitting needles? She could have someone's eye out with those things. Or her own."

"It keeps her calm, sir. She's under observation, twenty-four seven."

"She has a bad case of Island Fever, doesn't she?"

"As bad as it gets, sir."

"Bring in Garrett, Fuqua, and Dinkley. Put them in individual cells, tell them I'm going to talk to them, and tell them who I am and why I'm here."

"You're aware, sir, that they have already been interrogated?"

"I'm aware. Bring them in, individual cells, tell 'em who and why, leave them to stew. When you've arranged that, you can take me to see the scene of the crime."

An officer was waiting outside—a suntanned woman with untidy blond hair, studying the ground to one side of her shoes like a shy teenager trying at once not to attract the attention of a boy she liked while getting a full ogle of him. "Lieutenant Shane, sir," she said with nervous abruptness and stuck out her hand, as if expecting it to be kissed by Casanova.

Dice shook her limp, damp paw.

Haines said, "If Private Montori had a lawyer, sir, it would be Lieutenant Shane."

"This is well outside my area of expertise, Colonel," said Shane.

"It's outside anyone's area of expertise, Lieutenant."

"Anne-Louise," she said, inappropriately. "Most of my cases fall into the she-said-I-could-rape-her or he-was-asking-for-a-broken-head categories. This is, um, out of this world."

"Well, we don't know that, do we, Lieutenant? It comes under what I guess we should call inappropriate speculation. I don't care whether the POTAs are from Mars or Missouri. All I care about is what was done to one of them here, how it happened, and who did it. Have you talked to Private Montori? Have you advised her to shut up?"

Lieutenant Shane twisted the toe of one shoe behind the heel of the other. "She won't talk to anyone."

"Is that because she's crazy or crazy-smart?"

"It's all . . . *foof*," said Lieutenant Shane, waving her hand butterfly-style, sticking out her lower lip and blowing a directed blast of air up to shift her fringe. Thirty years old going on twelve, staring at him with lovesick puppy eyes. "Foof and folly-faraw."

Dice, taken aback, said, "No kidding."

After the Action was over, the military took possession of the surviving aggressors. The POTAs. After all, the military had won the war; they were goddamn *entitled*. No one in the Pentagon was about to admit they were out of their depth. Within a few days, interrogators who'd wasted years learning how to bellow, "Where's your secret chemical weapon dump?" in seventeen Mideastern and Asian languages were demoted to glorified prison wardens, and Intelligence moved in. Spook debriefers did no better with the Prisoners than anyone else, but took longer about it and used up more electricity.

After everyone despaired of getting conventional answers out of the POTAs, the White House did what they probably should have done in the first place and called for scientists. Frank-Einsteins and bubblebrains in Colonel-Stock-speak. Of course, since the president and his aides were calling the shots, they didn't trawl universities for whitecoats who might have the first idea about where to start. Instead, they went straight to the pharm and biotech corporations that had contributed to their campaign funds. If they couldn't get intel from the POTAs, they might at least stumble across commercial applications that could line the pockets of everyone involved. A little reverse engineering and, who knew, the whole crapshoot might pay for itself with a zero point energy propulsion unit or some other piece of far-future indistinguishable-from-magic technology. Eventually, the sellout scientists from Big Tobacco, Big Oil, Big Pharm, and what no one these days called the Military-Industrial Complex got fed up and brought in resentful, envious, poverty-stricken ex-classmates from the universities who'd been trying to get on Great James ever since it had become the POTAs' prison. Experts in disciplines with obscure names: xenobiology, cryptozoology. Self-styled geniuses who'd spent years of hermetic study compiling dictionaries of dolphin language or decoding the semiotics of bee-dances. There'd even been a science-fiction writer along for the ride.

Months passed. A year. The Action subsided into the basement of the nation's memory and the public's famously short-term attention span moved on to new distractions: earthquakes, political scandals, movie-star romances and divorces, pop-star pregnancies, the jump-the-shark fourth season of a Fox series. Until the Montori scandal erupted, the whole show had employed just one single, solitary public relations officer, whose job had been to keep the journos drunk, drugged, and fucked back on Diego Garcia, the nearest thing to an R&R facility in the archipelago. The pap pack took tours of picturesque coral reefs and lightly rewrote pdf press releases about "ongoing research," "flawless security," and limp human interest stories.

Meanwhile, a few results from the labor-intensive and horribly expensive studies trickled in. The POTAs were found to be each woven from a single molecule of triple-stranded buckyball tougher than diamond, doped with heavy metals, and bristling with catalytic sites. They secreted, or excreted, impacted crystalline versions of the same molecule, spindly shards that bonded to anything, be it stone or flesh, worked in so deep they could not be removed. There had been many casualties among those who had encountered the Prisoners after they had crashed. These crystals might be shit or might be babies. No one knew. Like viruses, it was hard to tell if the Prisoners were organic or inorganic, live or dead. When one was sliced up by an X-ray laser, every piece remained active and wriggling, like so many lizards' tails; allowed to reunite, they fused into a single ball that gradually resumed the correct shape, three spheres of diminishing size balanced one on top of the other.

Similar experiments suggested that nothing short of the ground zero of a nuclear explosion could destroy the Prisoners: Kinetic weapons sliced through them with no effect; they deflected the shock waves of explosions, withstood vacuum or Mariana Trench pressures, immersion in liquid helium or molten lead. And they were all linked in some undetermined way. Hurt one, and the rest reacted in identical fashion, like the twins in *The Corsican Brothers* or—and this struck sparks—the victim of the curse and the doll into which voodoo pins were stuck.

Most research quickly foundered in a quicksand of theory and countertheory. It wasn't even a given that the Prisoners, prized wriggling out of the jagged wrecks of their croissant-shaped shells like the soft parts of so many limpets, were the actual enemy. They could as easily be engines, hood ornaments, or Pet Rocks.

The shells were on Great James, too, baffling a whole other crew of aerospace grant-guzzlers and naval aviation boys. Whether or not the POTAs were the pilots, the shells were destructive—after the attack on Washington, DC, Dice had seen slices cut out of national monuments to prove it, and row after row of dead people with crystal shrapnel shot through them—but if they followed any battle plan or system, it was hard to tell. Their formations had moved fast and cut random swaths through cities, but they might as easily have been mowing a lawn as fighting a war, rearranging the world to suit some arbitrary aesthetic impulse. Plenty of folk would disagree, especially those with crystal working through their bodies like cancer. Plenty of folk said it didn't matter whether the POTAs were culpable or not; they should be put down just to be on the safe side.

Meanwhile, on this remote base protected by half the Pacific Fleet, the two research teams that studied either the POTAs or their shells worked away to not much point. They'd gotten up softball teams that played each other on weekends, but otherwise they had no contact, and jealously guarded their theories from each other. Dice suspected each camp liked to dribble hints of far-reaching results to the other, just to keep up the buzz of envy and resentment. The supposed nerds in the silos regularly thrashed the flight-specialist fighter jocks at softball, which did little for the free and fair exchange of scientific information.

The Pentagon didn't much mind. The POTAs were contained and the pretense that useful work was being done could be kept up forever. It seemed unlikely that any of their deep secrets would easily be uncovered: where they came from, whether they were a failed one-off attack or a first wave, whether or not they were intelligent. Great James was a profitable boondoggle, a pump-primer for funds that could be siphoned off and used elsewhere.

And then came the first recorded case of Great James Syndrome.

The POTAs were kept in missile pits, and despite the five-hundred-ton concrete and steel caps, their escape-artist potential was an endless source of worry. As long as they were safely contained, it didn't matter if anyone ever found out anything useful. But if even one escaped, everyone in the Pentagon down to the ten-man team that kept the Coke machines refilled could kiss their fat service pensions good-bye. The POTAs couldn't be caged; they oozed between bars or mesh like tar. The missile pits were a good short-term solution, but there was a strong possibility that sooner or later one of the POTAs would squeeze through a crack or crevice. And then an NCO with too much time on his hands invented a shackle that fitted and restrained their blobby bodies.

Corporal Flavors was a farmboy from Ohio with an education that had ended at high school and no particular aptitude for mathematics until, after a few days' guard duty at the pits, his mind kinked in an unexpected direction and he hit on an unexpected principle of knot theory as basic as the wheel. Suddenly, commercial and military applications were back on the menu. In the army, one school of thought had it that a patent on the Flavors Lock could bring in more money than the invention of milk cartons (Corporal Flavors hadn't even *considered* patenting his doohickey, and a squadron of lawyers decided that the army could lay claim to it because it was invented on army time, with army matériel). More cautious souls pointed out that it could cause major, unpredictable, seismic shifts in national security, not to mention the global economy. After all, anyone with five pieces of metal, a drill, and some wire could whip up a Flavors Lock in twenty minutes and turn an ordinary safe into Fort Knox. And while the army was trying to decide whether to patent the doohickey and declare financial independence from the federal government, or melt every known Flavors Lock and drop the corporal into the ocean, Great James was seized by an unprecedented outbreak of creativity as more and more of its personnel succumbed to Island Fever.

Pretty soon, the Flavors Lock was just the first entry in a bulging catalog of one-off wonders, fruits of misapplied, unfathomable genius, and neat gadgets that could change the world if only someone could figure out how to duplicate them. Squads of scientists had been driven crazy, trying and failing. Senator Jubilee Bliss had a cunning plan to change all of that.

"Poppin' a cap in mah bitch's head, bitch talk back—the bitch be dead!"

The surveillance center rattled with the aggressive thump of rap music, fed through an open-air Tannoy rigged up to blast back at the small white civilian who was chanting along with the words, squirming around in his swivel chair as if competing in the Special Hip-Hop Olympics.

When he caught sight of Dice and Haines in the doorway, between the two armed guards (one wore a homemade hat, presumably courtesy of Wing Commander Brown), the man shut off his sound system, made a devil's-horn shape with his fingers, and said, "Whassup, mah niggas?"

He wore a silver band tied around his forehead, but Dice assumed he wasn't a true fan of Christian girl-rock.

Haines made introductions. "Dr. Susal, Colonel Dice. Colonel, this is Dr. Susal from the Californian Institute for the Search for Extra-Terrestrial Intelligence."

Dr. Susal grinned more widely than seemed necessary. "Deedy-doody. Scanning the deeps for ping-pings, West Coast styling."

Dice wondered if torturing the prisoner hadn't been displacement activity by people who would rather have been torturing Dr. Susal. Of course, the Einstein's ownership of a white lab coat put him in the ring as a suspect, too. Him, and a round hundred scientists and engineers.

"They aren't Extra-Terrestrial Intelligences," said the other whitecoat in the room—a slim Asian woman who had taken off her airport runway ear defenders when the rap cut out. "At least, not in any accepted sense of the term."

"Moira Wing," explained Haines.

Dice wasn't looking at her, but at the bank of screens behind her.

There they were.

On twenty TVs, seen from high angles, the cloudy blurs of POTAs squatted in their pits like so many bee larvae in their cells.

Haines was telling the room who Dice was and why he was on Great James Island. Dice jerked his attention away from the fuzzy TV pictures to the occupants of the room, cursing his sloppiness—he should have been watching Wing and Susal, looking for telltale twinges and tics when his identity was revealed.

"Here," said Wing. "This'll give you a better idea."

She stepped over to a freestanding control panel, tapped out a code. A section of the wall rolled up. Beyond was thick, one-way leaded glass (the proverbial reflective surface in the pit) and a view down into Silo Three, current home of the alleged victim.

Dr. Susal swiveled away, complaining. He didn't want to look at the prisoner.

"We had it installed so VIPs could eyeball the Prisoners," said Wing. "It's too dangerous to enter the pits unsupervised, and the surveillance cameras . . . Well, it's like looking at the moon through fog with a Christmas cracker magnifying glass. It cost thirty million dollars to cut away a section of blastproof reinforced concrete and install it, so I hope you enjoy the view."

She had a definite accent, and sounded coolly amused.

Dice stepped up to the glass. He had read the reports, seen the photographs, but this was up close and personal.

The window was halfway up the side of the pit. Twenty feet below, the POTA, hobbled by its Flavors Lock, squatted at the bottom of the stark, floodlit pit.

It consisted of three spheres arranged like the snowmen Dice had built as a boy—skirt, torso, head. Its skin was silk-smooth and a uniform deep, dark blue. There were tendrils, especially on the top and bottom spheres, which had once attached to the interior of their shell-ships.

"I'll bust a cap in its ass for you, homes," Susal said, and scooted across the surveillance room in his swivel chair to a computer, typing in a command.

A robot arm attached halfway up the smooth cylindrical wall of the pit came to life and extended mantis-fashion, lowering toward the POTA. Pincers tipped with ceramic and copper spikes opened wide, spanning either side of the POTA's topmost sphere. Susal typed another command. Arcs of lightning flashed, throwing stark shadows across the pit. The POTA deformed, its head-sphere flattening to a thick disk as if ducking away from the pincers.

Dice stepped backward, feeling as if he'd been punched in the stomach. Susal cackled. "Two thousand volts of zap and the cocksucker barely twitches."

"The usual reaction, nothing unexpected," Dr. Wing said, tapping with a forefinger a computer flatscreen that displayed dozens of EEG-style lines, all spiking in various ways at the same point.

Susal pulled down a microphone and said into it, "Oh six twenty-one oh seven, fourteen oh six, GMT. Experiment number seven eight five two one, standard demonstration run, two thousand volts, one-second duration. Standard defensive reaction, no deviation." He tapped at the keyboard and turned to face Dice as beyond the heavy glass window, the arm retracted upward. "I can pepper its hide with a heavy machine gun if you want. VIPs love that. And we've got a chain saw and a leather mask somewhere—could tape you an alien snuff movie, make a fortune on pirate DVD."

"I'll pass," Dice said, watching the POTA's head-sphere slowly resume its shape. It reminded him of a tortoise cautiously reextending its head after a fright.

"Fair enough. It don't snuff properly anyway."

Dice felt nauseated and was trying not to show it. It wasn't so much what had been done to the POTA, though that was bad enough, but the scientists' casual brutalization of whatever it was they had hold of.

He said, "It changed shape. Can it move around at all?"

"Not while restrained," Wing said. "But take off the Flavors Lock and the subject can move around very readily. They bounce by elastically deforming on their lower sphere. Remember Space Hoppers? It looks something like that."

Dice was surprised Wing remembered the 1970s toy. He would have thought she was younger.

She said, "Before the Flavors Lock, the POTAs would sometimes keep on bouncing for hours, picking up momentum, careening off all the walls . . ."

"Trying to escape?"

Wing shrugged. "The movement could be play, fury, a symphony, death throes that last a hundred years, or it could be absolutely meaningless. After one was cut up, the fragments were still able to move in synchrony. The thing I find rather disturbing is that they don't make any noise, moving or still. In fact, they absorb sound waves, like baffles . . ."

"Is why I crank up mah boom box," explained Dr. Susal.

"They can act individually, but if put together in a smallish space they synchronize—each moving exactly like another," said Wing, coming to stand beside Dice. "Pick one up and toss it against a wall, and the others will go, too, like a game of Simon Says. This casts some light on what was called their 'attack formation.' They may not be individuals, but cells of a larger entity—in which case, it is possible that only a small part of the whole thing is in captivity."

"And people say they're not aliens."

"Not me, Colonel Dice," said Wing. "These are *aliens,* in the sense of not being like anything that's ever been measured before. What we don't know is where they're from. Outer space, the deep past or the far future, some kind of parallel universe . . ."

"Something way weirder than alternate histories where Spain didn't sign the Treaty of Utrecht and everyone in America speaks Hebrew," footnoted Susal. "It's a definite maybe far-from-probable pinhole of possibility. Then again, the blue niggas could have come from Fairyland, Cyberspace, or Ronald McDonald's big fat clown ass."

As far as Dice was concerned, the Hollow Earth and Santa's Workshop theories were just as likely—the enemy's point of origin was unknown, but its craft were first logged over Greenland, heading south, moving fast. Textbook UFOs, if not flying saucers.

They did a lot of damage, but were taken down like skeet.

Now the War Crimes Commission in the Hague and cabals of *fromage*-gobbling surrender monkeys in the UN were arguing that as losers in the Action, as *prisoners of war,* the POTAs had the right not to be treated as lab rats. It was a violation of their inalienable if nonhuman rights to be shackled witnesses while pages were torn out of *Dianetics* and stuffed in piss-filled buckets (where *had* the idea that the POTAs were Scientologists come from?) or brassieres tied around their smallest spheres or guns stuck where their earholes would have been if they had or wanted or needed ears. Or have handfuls of salt sewn into their bodies.

Dice turned his back on the huge glass window and the big blue entity behind it, and opened his folder. As briskly as he could, he led Wing and Susal through a list of questions. Thanks to McAndrews's report, he already knew the answers, but he'd been trained in Neuro-Linguistic Programming and paid careful attention to Wing's and Susal's body and eye movements, signifiers of their mental states, as they responded to his interrogation.

Telling him that yes, the POTA in Pit Three, behind the glass, was the very same POTA that had been tortured/humiliated by monster-lover Montori and her merry crew. That the only way into the pit was via a platform and stairs halfway up the wall, or the slab of armored concrete that capped it. That hatchway could be accessed via a side corridor in the surveillance center. The other pits could be accessed only via inspection hatches sealed with locks that could be opened only by turning two different keys at the same time, plus a separate keypad-activated set of electronic bolts. The pits *were* connected by a system that had delivered fresh water from a central source to the sprayheads that had cooled missiles during static firing tests, but that was completely flooded and accessible only by someone wearing scuba gear.

Dice said, "You maintain round-the-clock surveillance? This room is always manned?"

One of the screens blinked off for a few seconds, came back on.

"Righteous, my brutha," said Dr. Susal, eyes wide with fake innocence.

"I'll take that as a yes. So, how come no one was looking when Private Montori was posing for Playmate of the Month?"

"I'll let my colleague, Professor Dr. Wing, take that question," said Dr. Susal.

Dice looked at the woman.

"There were errors in the early days of the program," she said in measured, controlled tones. "They will not be repeated."

"What kind of errors?"

"Human errors."

Dr. Wing was looking at Dice with the calm, slightly bored expression of an expert poker player who could be holding a pair of deuces or a full flush.

Dice said, "People got access to one of your prisoners and spent a lot of time doing weird stuff to it. Specifically, to the Prisoner on the other side of this sheet of glass. Did someone fall asleep? Were they absent from their station?"

"Sometimes people get distracted," Dr. Wing said.

"Or they were bribed. Or they were in on the deal. I'd like to take a look at your duty sheets."

"You're welcome to interview the guards, of course. Unfortunately, several have succumbed to Island Fever since the . . . incident. You'll have to work hard to get sense out of them."

Wing's expression didn't change, but her steady gaze, never looking up or to the side, suggested to Dice that she was lying or stonewalling rather than drawing upon her memory. Hook her up to a lie detector? No, she was the ultra-controlled type who could claim to have shot Lincoln, Kennedy, and J. R. Ewing without making the pens twitch. Dr. Susal was a better bet, if he could get past the man's shuck and jive.

Dice stepped up to the little man and said, "You keep video cameras permanently trained on the Prisoners and on the entrances to their pits."

"Twenty-four seven," Dr. Susal said.

"So why is there no video record of the little party that Private Montori and her associates had themselves in the pit?"

"We fucked up, my man," Dr. Susal said.

"A glitch," Dr. Wing said.

"According to Captain McAndrews's report, someone switched off the cameras," Dice said. "Who has access to the controls?"

"I'm the man, man," Dr. Susal said. "So is my bitch."

"No one else?"

"Anyone who can fuck with my computers," Dr. Susal said. "You know why we don't have Internet access on this rock anymore?"

Dice knew. In the past month, Great James had become the major source of computer viruses, worms, and Internet spam. One particular spam message, the so-called Illuminatus Penis Extension Offer, had driven more than eight thousand recipients into apparently permanent psychosis.

"I believe that he knows the veiled import of your question," said Dr. Wing.

"Of course he knows. He's the Man. The Man always knows. Hey, take a lookee here," Dr. Susal said, spinning around in his chair and scooting it across the floor to a bank of monitors labeled INTERNAL SECURITY. "It's the big white chief, come to preach at us poor bone-chewin' natives."

"Senator Bliss," Sergeant Haines said. "He demanded a full tour of the facility."

"Hail to the Chief," sang Dr. Susal, "he's the Chief, he needs some hail-iiing . . . Hail to the Chief, he's a hail-worthy kind of guy-yyyy."

"You're quite welcome to stay," Dr. Wing told Dice. "I understand that Senator Bliss has stirringly controversial views vis-à-vis our large blue friends."

"I've already heard them," Dice said, and turned for the door.

Too late. Senator Bliss strolled into the surveillance room ahead of his posse of black-suited aides and Colonel Stock. The base commander had acquired a silver armband. Rose-of-Mary stuck to him like a shadow, elfin in a desert sand camo jumpsuit and a black beret with a diamond cross pinned to its peak, her fierce gaze sweeping past Dice and locking onto the POTA.

"Mercy me," she said, her strong, clear voice echoing around the vault of the observation room. "There's no mistaking that monstrous . . . *thing* for anything but the handiwork of the Great Satan. Colonel, are you *quite* sure we're safe?"

"I give you my word," Colonel Stock said indulgently.

"One of my charities cares for orphans whose parents were *horribly* slaughtered by the enemy," Rose-of-Mary said. "They are brought up as good Christian soldiers—they look *so* sweet in their little uniforms.

When I was invited here, I prayed with them, Colonel, on national TV, and pledged to make sure that these filthy things will answer in full for their wickedness. I have brought a vial—"

"Hush, dear," Senator Bliss said. "I want to have a word with Colonel Dice."

"Yes, Daddy," Rose-of-Mary said meekly.

Bliss, two hundred and fifty pounds of political muscle in his two-thousand-dollar gray silk suit, dazzled Dice with his dentistry. "Let me speak plainly, Colonel. I believe you are grossly exceeding your authority by being here. If you have clearance for this facility, you'd better show it to me right now. Colonel Stock, did you give Colonel Dice clearance?"

"That isn't up to me, sir," Colonel Stock said. "Like I told you, this is the preserve of the Frank-Einsteins."

"As I told you on the plane, sir," Dice told Bliss, "I have been given authority by General Rapf, chair of the combined services oversight committee for Great James, to investigate recent shortcomings in security in any manner I see fit."

"And as I informed Colonel Dice, Colonel Stock," Bliss said, his voice a bass purr, "General Rapf will soon be relieved of his responsibility for Great James."

"And then we can all go home," Dice said. "I'm already looking forward to it. But until then, I have a job to do."

"Your typical army hack," Bliss told Stock and his daughter. "Loyal to a fault, the fault being a certain stubbornness. I bet if they told him to paint coal white, he'd give it two coats."

Rose-of-Mary giggled dutifully.

"That's the army way, sir," Colonel Stock agreed.

Senator Bliss said, "Regardless of your status and your duties, Colonel Dice, this is to be a private briefing. So if you don't mind . . ."

Aides took a step forward.

"I'll need to talk to you again, so don't leave town," Dice told the two scientists.

He was no wiser about who had gained access to the POTA along with Chris Montori, or how they had got in, but despite Susal's spot of crude torture, his glimpse of the big blue beast at the heart of the mystery had left him feeling both elated and oddly soothed. As he pushed between the aides toward the exit, Rose-of-Mary was saying, "Colonel, I have a vial of water from the holy river Jordan. I would *greatly* appreciate it if your scientists would study its effect on that monstrous thing . . ."

Lieutenant Shane was waiting outside the entrance to the brig like a fan hoping for a glimpse of her idol, her face lighting up when Dice climbed out of the Jeep.

"Sergeant Haines will let you know if anyone is in need of you," Dice told her.

"I was hoping that we could have a private conference, Colonel."

She'd undone the top three buttons of her fatigues and was suddenly standing too close. She was wearing one of Rose-of-Mary's silver virginity armbands, perhaps ironically. Dice remembered the thirteen-year-old younger sister of one of his school buddies who'd started sending him scent-doused billets-douxs during his first semester at college, and took pity on the woman.

"Stand easy, Lieutenant," he told her. "Until I've determined there's a crime, you don't have any client."

Fortunately, Lieutenant Shane didn't try to follow him into the cell block. The three suspects had been locked in adjoining cells. Dice studied them through the spyholes and turned to Haines.

"Walter Garrett is our man. Turn the other two loose, tell Garrett I'll talk to him in the morning, and keep him under observation."

"If that's what you want, sir."

Haines was sulking.

"How long have you been in the military police, Sergeant?"

"I'm not in the police, sir. As I told you, I was assigned the position by Colonel Stock after Captain Mac got a full-blown case of Island Fever."

"What did you do before that?"

"I worked in Colonel Stock's office, sir. I can type using all ten fingers."

Dice felt suddenly off balance, realizing that he'd made what could have been a fatal assumption about Haines. From now on, he was going to have to question everything. And he was also going to have to confront Colonel Stanley Stock sooner rather than later.

He said, "I guess your stint in the typing pool didn't teach you the difference between a guilty and an innocent man. You put one of each in a cell and leave them, the innocent man frets about what might happen, but the guilty man goes to sleep. See, as far as the guilty man is concerned, the worst has already happened. He's already done the crime, now he's been brought in because of it. How can things get any worse? So, nothing else to do, he goes to sleep . . . like Private Walter Garrett."

Haines smiled. "You know, sir, I had my suspicions about Garrett."

"Because he's a bunky of Montori."

"No, sir. Because he's from New Orleans."

"City of jazz and voodoo. No, they don't call it that there, do they? They call it hoodoo. Wake Garrett up and tell him I'll talk to him tomorrow. He'll probably squeal for a lawyer. If he does, give him Shane. There's nothing she can do for him that will affect my interrogation. Talking of Shane, is there a back way out of this place? I have the feeling that when she sees me again she's liable to try something foolish."

Dice, thirty-six hours in transit and several time zones away from where he felt he should be, was running on nerves and army coffee. Worried that he might slip up again, he planned to catch some sleep and roust Private Garrett in the wee small hours. Have an intense little conversation with him, then talk to Colonel Stock. What else? Jesus, talk to Captain McAndrews's doctors. And try to talk to McAndrews, too; a dollar to a doughnut, his Island Fever wasn't genuine.

First, a short, refreshing catnap. But when Dice reached his chill little room, he discovered a handwritten note propped on top of the drum-tight blanket of his cot. In a neat, slanting hand it read:

> *Colonel Stanley X. Stock requests the pleasure of the company of Colonel*
> *Franklin Clay Dice at a reception and dinner in honor of Senator Jubilee*
> *and Rose-of-Mary Bliss. Officers' Mess, 6 for 6:30. PS. Please be prompt.*
> *PPS. Sidearms to be surrendered at the door.*

Dice groaned. It was six ten. He didn't even have enough time for a cup of coffee.

In the officers' mess, a single long table had been laid with white linen, sparkling crystal and silverware, and arrangements of orchids and ferns that must have flown in on the same plane as Dice. Or perhaps there was a garden hidden somewhere on the island. After only a few hours here, he was beginning to believe anything was possible.

He was seated at the other end of the long table from Colonel Stock and the Bliss Pack. It suited him just fine. He was too tired for small talk, and on the final part of his long journey he'd heard enough from Jubilee Bliss to last him the rest of his life. From the snatches he could hear now, Bliss was still giving Colonel Stock the full benefit of his views about the commercial potential of the POTAs—he was campaigning to privatize the base, bring in civilian research-and-development staff from his brother-in-law's aerospace company, expose them to the POTAs, and exploit the hell out of the products of their Island Fever dreams. It would be, he'd told Dice several times during the flight, a Factory of Ideas where the Future Would Be Forged.

To judge by his grim little smile and stiff nods, Colonel Stock appeared to like Bliss's ideas about the commercial potential of the POTAs as much as Dice had.

At last, Bliss rose and at some length thanked the Good Lord for the bounty they were about to receive. Dice was afraid his daughter would get up and sing, but they were spared that. Rose-of-Mary's girl-rock gospel songs tended to revisit and revise Bible stories—she once told Oprah that if the woman caught in adultery had instead been caught coming out of an abortion clinic, Jesus would have cast the first stone Himself. What made it worse was that she had a bell-clear, water-stirring voice and set editorial messages fresh from Klan bed-sheets to tunes that infected the mind for weeks, like a bad case of brain flu.

Privates with starched white aprons over their pressed fatigues spooned chowder into the bowls of the diners. Dice had just taken his first mouthful when someone slipped into the empty seat to his right. It was the Brit, complete with watch cap, tattered uniform, wild beard, and funky jungle-survivor odor.

"WC Peter Redcliffe Brown, at your service, sah!" he stage-whispered. "WC, that's Wing Commander, not Water Closet. Wing Co Brown, RAF. RAF as in Royal Air Force, not raff as associated with riff. Some advice, man-to-man. I wouldn't touch the soup."

Dice thought of the radioactive coconuts. "Is it made from local fish?"

"Spiced with urine, sah! The good colonel's men tend to express their disapproval at their posting in, hem hem, basic fashion."

Dice set down his spoon. "Stock is that popular, huh?"

"These, on the other hand, are absolutely delicious." Wing Co Brown plucked an orchid from an arrangement, bit it in half, and said around the mouthful, "You're not wearing your hat."

"I'm not a hat kind of guy."

"Think of your brainbox, old chum. Defenseless against the pollut-ing onslaught of the evil blue peril . . . I hear on the old grapevine that you've met our Madonna of the pits, Queen of the POTAs. What do you think of her? Did she tell you anything interesting?"

"That's classified, Wing Commander."

Brown popped the rest of the orchid into his mouth and chewed with noisy relish. "And what about Susal and Wing? Who do you think is nuttier? Susal puts on quite a minstrel show, but when it comes to craziness I think Wing may have the edge."

He smiled when Dice looked at him, showing snaggled teeth stained with purple plant juice.

Dice said, "I'm trying to work out if either of them is screwier than you. What do you think?"

"I think you should wear your hat."

"I think you and me should have a discreet talk."

Brown shot to his feet and said loudly, "You should remember that I'm an officer and a gentleman, sah! I serve Queen and Country, sah, and will never never *never* kowtow to some colonial upstart!" He thrust his face toward Dice and added in a whisper, "I wouldn't touch the rest of the nosh, either. You don't have to be mad to work here, but if you don't start wearing that hat, you will be!"

Sergeant Haines came into the mess just as Wing Commander Brown was leaving, the two men tangling in a brief and awkward waltz. After Haines managed to disentangle himself, he crossed the room, face a study of mortification, and requested a private word.

It was a good point to leave. At the other end of the table, Rose-of-Mary was asking an officer—Dice realized he was the base padre—if she could lead a special service to give thanks for the incarceration of the POTAs and to ask God to lay bare their mysteries.

"With His help, we will discover their evil empire and mount a crusade against it. Isn't that right, Daddy?"

"Absolutely, my dear. And from that victory we'll forge miraculous new technologies that will help America bring an age of peace and prosperity to the whole world."

"*Christian* age of peace and *harmony*," his daughter said.

Dice wondered whether Rose-of-Mary had been allowed to try out her own brand of voodoo on the POTA in Pit Three. She was a much scarier proposition than her dear daddy.

Bliss's motivation for exploiting the POTAs was no more than the usual greed for power and riches that infected most people on Capitol Hill, but Rose-of-Mary had a Joan-of-Arc fixation, and was clearly ready to destroy the whole world if it failed to live up to her own ideals.

Once they were outside, Haines told Dice, "We're a prisoner down."

Dice thought of Chris Montori's knitting needles and said, "Suicide?"

"Much worse than that, sir. Jailbreak."

As they drove toward the brig, Haines explained that Walter Garrett had requested an interview with his lawyer. When Private Garrett and Lieutenant Shane had been left alone, the private had overpowered her, gagged her with her panties, and tied her wrists with her bra.

Dice said, "Why wasn't he cuffed?"

"He was, sir. To the table of the interview room."

"He overpowered her with just one hand?"

"Yes, sir. Then he used wire from her bra to unpick the cuff, knocked on the door, squirted her perfume in the eye of the MP who opened it, and made his escape."

"Did he take the MP's sidearm?"

"No, sir. Sir, I am willing to tender my resignation . . ."

"You'll have to talk to Colonel Stock about that, Sergeant, but I doubt that he'll allow you to get out of your new job so easily. What about Montori?"

"Still in her cell. Knitting what might be a hat. Four hundred and fifty-eight stitches when I saw her."

Dice tried to work out the angles of this latest development, but his jet lag seemed to be getting worse. His thoughts kept sliding away from one another. Beyond a range of flat-topped bunkers, across a blazing expanse of ocean, beneath thin bands of pink and orange cloud, the last sliver of the sun slipped below the horizon. A brief flash of green light embraced half the world, and off around the long curve of the conjoined islets a giant cross appeared, a phantom of golden light that had to be more than three hundred feet high, slowly rotating, the crucified figure blinking on and off.

It wasn't Jesus Christ up there. It was the three blue spheres of a POTA.

Dice laughed, remembering an urban myth about a Japanese store display that celebrated Christmas with a crucified Santa.

Haines said, "Lieutenant Glass's work, sir. He lashed it up from a flash memory card, some broken glass, the laser from a CD player, and a couple of Duracell batteries."

"The sunset was prettier. How's the book, by the way? Where are you at?"

"Page one forty-one line eight, sir."

"James Lee Burke is good on sunsets, isn't he?"

"All kinds of weather, sir."

There was a cautious note in Haines's voice.

"A New Orleans writer, I believe."

"Are you a fan, sir?"

"I'm not much of a reader of mysteries. They're too much like my work, and they unhelpfully raise your expectations. At the end, they all make sense."

Lieutenant Shane was waiting for them in the brig's office. She jumped up and flung herself at Dice, wrapping her arms around his neck and curling one leg up around his thigh. He registered that she definitely wasn't wearing a bra, and told Haines to give him and the lieutenant a few minutes. Haines discreetly withdrew and Shane burbled into Dice's neck about the horror of her experience, how frightened she'd been, how glad she was to see him . . . When she had run down, was simply breathing hot and heavy in his ear, he gently disengaged her and pushed her back at arm's length, met her swoony gaze.

"Just one question," he said.

"Anything."

"I think you'd better give me the handcuff key."

Shane went for Dice with nails and teeth, trying to knee him in the groin and snatch his Beretta. But he was braced for her attack, and caught one of her wrists, flipped her around, dumped her in a typist's chair, and cuffed her right wrist to the backrest.

She glared at him, puffed a strand of hair from her eyes.

He gave her his best smile. "Ever been to New Orleans, Lieutenant?"

"I want a lawyer," she said, suddenly serious.

"I'm sure you can see the problem there. One of those who-watches-the-watchmen, who-shaves-the-barber things. You *are* the lawyer, so when you *need* a lawyer, we have to send out."

"You'll get nothin' from me, coppa!" she said, snarling like Cagney, and ripped off her silver armband and snapped it at him like a whip.

Haines came into the room, a couple of MPs at his back and—uh-oh—Colonel Stock behind the MPs, leaning in the doorway and staring at Dice with a cold smile.

"He raped me," said Lieutenant Shane, holding up her ruined armband. "The bastard."

"Sergeant Haines," said Dice. "Fetch the base doctor immediately to administer the proper tests and evidentiary swabs."

"He *tried* to rape me," revised Shane and sat back, artfully arranging her torn uniform, showing off her recent bruises. Haines looked at Stock and Stock smiled at Dice, who only now noticed the nail marks on his hands.

"Oh, for fuck's sake," he said, exasperated.

Stock moved in for the kill, his voice calm and controlled and as cold as his smile. "Colonel Dice, you're under arrest. Surrender your sidearm to Sergeant Haines."

This was a good deal older than the Flavors Lock, and probably as difficult to escape from. Dice pulled his gun and put it on the table.

"Please yourself."

Haines took it. One MP uncuffed Lieutenant Shane; the other moved toward Dice, bracelets at the ready.

Dice ignored him and told Stock, "I'll come quietly."

The MP paused. Colonel Stock nodded and said, "Take the rapist son of a bitch to the cells."

"Thank you for a lovely evening, Colonel darlin'," Lieutenant Shane twinkled. "I'd offer my services as a lawyer but, la-di-da, conflict of interest."

Dice tried to think of a devastating retort but came up empty. He was suddenly so goddamn tired—shock, jet lag—that a spell in a nice quiet, cozy cell seemed welcoming. He let Haines and the MPs walk him down the corridor, through the barred door to the cell block. Two new guards were on duty outside Montori's cell. The chalk design had spread to the ceiling.

As one of the MPs unlocked the door of the cell opposite Montori's, Dice said, "Was this Stock's idea or the senator's? Or maybe doctors Wing and Susal set this up."

"A serious charge has been brought," Haines said stiffly. "It is my duty to see things done by the book. After what recently happened, we can't be seen to get sloppy about this sort of business. I'm sure you understand."

One of the MPs asked him for his belt, tie, and bootlaces, and Dice held out his arms as the man stripped him of possible aids to suicide, looking at Haines, saying, "Couldn't I have knitting needles? I'll let you count the stitches."

Haines's lips twitched, and a tiny giggle escaped.

"Good night, sir."

The cell was only a little smaller than his room back in the officers' quarters, and every bit as cold. The door slammed shut. The lock thumped.

The cot seemed child-size. When Dice put his head on the pillow, his knees dangled over the end, and he realized he hadn't taken off his boots. He sat up, trying to reach his feet, then fell back, dazed. He was starved, too, and his last thought before unconsciousness was that he should have had more than a spoonful of soup for dinner—an orchid would have made a nice *amuse-bouche*.

He had blue dreams.

It was an old one—he was back in basic, drill instructor's endless shout invading his skull, every bone and muscle aching, drawing punishment details from latrine digging through potato peeling to corpse retrieval. Senator Bliss was in his squad, sounding off about economic benefits as crystal armor-plate grew under his skin, distorting his face, swelling his uniform. Rose-of-Mary Bliss was singing "You're in the Army Now," accompanied by the Great James Island band with their mutant bugles and steel voodoo drums.

Then it was the Action, and he was in DC, frozen in a crowd as a whizzing shape, whirling like a child's top, swooped, scattering shards. Dice ignored flak as it passed through stone buildings and soft people like a buzzsaw through balsa wood. Everyone around him was dead or had run off, but he had to stand still.

The flying shell hovered in front of him.

It was weathered, deeply striated, with coral edges as sharp as razors. It had apertures like facial features, opening and closing with faint wet sounds. Spiny, multijointed limbs emerged, probes or Waldos reaching for him, drill-bit appendages homing in on his forehead, where he knew blue dots wavered as guide marks for incisions.

"You should wear your hat," said the alien, with Wing Co Brown's voice. "A fella's not dressed without the old titfer."

Dice was awake, staring up at a fluorescent circle buzzing behind steel bars high in a wall gouged and scratched with soldiers' graffiti.

The bit about the long insect legs with drills was his imagination. As far as he knew, no such appendages had been observed during the Action.

His heart still hammered. He was covered in cooling sweat.

Something was making a faint clack-clack-clack, as regular as a clock.

Chris Montori's knitting needles, in the cell across the corridor.

Dice sat up. His head felt as swollen and light as a balloon, bobbing on the end of his neck when he stood and slid back the iron cover in the cell door's little barred judas. The two MPs had their backs to him, engrossed in adding detail to the edges of the design spread from floor to ceiling on either side of the door of the cell across the corridor. When Dice called out to Montori, one of the MPs glanced at him over her shoulder. She had several different-colored chalks stuck between her teeth. After a moment she shrugged, and went back to her work.

Clack clack clack—the needles.

Dice said, "Private Montori. A word, please."

"Is that you, Colonel Dice, sir? I'm pretty busy."

"So I see. That's some design."

"I always liked to knit when I was little, sir. Momma said I had a gift for it."

"You have a gift for drawing, too."

Dice was certain that the MPs had caught Montori's particular strain of Island Fever.

Montori's voice said, "I guess. But girls like me, we don't get to go to college and study on art. We flip burgers, waitress at the Dairy Queen, make babies, or join the army."

"You won't ever have to flip burgers or wait tables, Chris. You're too famous for that now. There's already a Movie of the Week in the works."

"You old sweet-talker you."

"Talking is what I do, all right. What I want to talk about right now is the situation we're both in. How about helping me out, Private? How about asking one of your apprentices to unlock my door. It'll only take a few seconds, and I promise I'll leave you all be. You can knit and draw, whatever else you want, to your heart's content."

"Can't do that, Colonel, sir."

The needles' pace picked up. Clackclackclack.

"You don't have to be afraid of anyone, Christine. I'll make sure of that."

Dice meant it. He was certain that Chris Montori was no more than a stooge. A magician's box-jumper. The girl who held the man's cape, smiled big-time, and made graceful poses while he pulled live doves from a handkerchief.

Clackclackclack. After a long moment, Montori said, "What about the Blues?"

"The Blues?"

"The poor puppies in the pits."

"Whatever's planned for the Prisoners, I want to stop it."

Clack-clack-clack, the pace slowing now. Dice hoped it meant that he had her attention.

"The Prisoners are just like you, Chris. Recruits. Grunts. Victims of their circumstances. They were left behind while the ones who gave them their orders got away."

Clack-clack-clack. Montori said, her voice querulous, "How do I know you're not funnin' me?"

"I had a dream just now. About the Action, and about me."

"Yeah. I have dreams about the Blues, too. Everyone does, on the island, all the time. But ever since . . . well, you know what, mine have been different."

"You want to help them now."

"I want to, but I *can't*. I can't face them again." Clack-clack-clack. "If I get you out, will you do right by them?"

"By you and by them, Chris."

"All right," she said, and one of the MPs turned away from the intricate design and lifted a ring of keys from her belt, unlocked Dice's door.

He walked out of the door in his loose, unlaced boots. He was about to thank Christine Montori when the end of the corridor collapsed in a soundless blast of dust and grit.

Someone stepped through.

Wing Commander Brown.

The Wing Co slapped dust from his tattered blue uniform. He was wearing his black watch cap, and carried in the crook of one arm what looked at first sight like a baby tuba. No, it was a conch shell, ornamented with crystal. He seemed painted with woad, blue lines in a grid fashion, outlining his skull. The lines were pulsing. It must be some sort of optical illusion.

Dice wondered why he felt so calm. The first symptom of GJS was refusal to admit the infection. So surely it couldn't be anything to do with Island Fever.

The two MPs were working at their design—Chris Montori's design—as if nothing had happened.

"This is just your size," Brown said, and slid a watch cap over Dice's head. The foil lining scraped his scalp. Brown stepped back, studied Dice's face.

"Starting to see things more clearly, aren't we? It's not just the Prisoners that were getting to your brain waves, old mate. There've been many other emissions and transmissions and whatever. You're free of them now, and a spot of the old potential is sparking in the noggin. You'll be doing sums backward in your sleep, I'll be bound."

The blue grid on Brown's face was fading now.

"Time for a stroll? It's nearly dawn. You know how the song goes, 'Beyond the Blue Horizon . . . ' "

" 'There's a rising sun'?"

"That's the ticket. Sun-a-rise, she bring in de morning. Oh, by the way, here's a pair of bootlaces, and a belt. Thought you might need them. The only ties I've got are my regimental colors. As a heathen Yankee you're not entitled to wear them, so you'll hae to dae withaet, as the Scotchman sayeth. Hope that's not too big a disappointment."

Dice laced his boots and belted his pants.

Brown led him through the neat hole punched in the wall of the cell block.

The song had it right. There it was: a rich, electric-blue horizon, shading to purple-black, with a star canopy brighter than a city dweller could dream. Dice looked up, seeing the sky in a literal new light, transfixed like the first hominids by the join-the-dots pictures of the constellations.

"Our friends aren't from 'up there,' old thing. It would make things easier if they were."

Dice adjusted his scratchy cap, and Brown clamped a hand over his head.

"Naughty-naughty. Caps must be worn at all times on the quad.

Tassels denote prefects, who must be obeyed unto death. Appearance in public without a cap constitutes a Minor Offense and three Minor Offenses are a mandatory DT. Detention, that is, not delirium tremens. Appearance in public with delirium tremens is straight to the Head for six of the best and no argument."

Dice tried to focus and saw through the brig wall: Chris Montori sat up in bed, still knitting.

He had a brief spasm of panic—he had developed X-ray vision!

He remembered the joke about superheroes he'd made to Haines, and wondered if he could fly.

Then he saw the rubble and smelled the sharp tang of concrete dust.

"A little bit FUBAR," Brown said. "I blew out rather too much wall. Silly me. Your friend promised guides' honor she'd stay put, so no harm done."

The two MPs outside Chris Montori's cell door were under her spell, but where were the others? There should be sirens, roll calls, deployments, a clampdown, bodyguards piled on Senator Bliss to protect him from assassins.

"Ah, there's the clever part, you see," said Brown, answering a query Dice had not voiced aloud. "*Silent* explosion. Well, not really silent. It's just something a friend of mine rigged up out of this bit of old shell."

Brown held up the ragged trumpet. Its ridges and flecks of crystal were pulsing with blue light.

"It takes the bang, and makes it go somewhere else. I daresay some fellers in China got a fright, but they'll be used to it by now."

Montori smiled at them, and snapped off a salute. "Good luck with the Blues, Colonel. I know you'll do right by them."

Brown clucked like a hen. "Come on now, Dice. Don't dillydally."

Dice had been in the Pentagon during the Action, as baffled and panic-stricken as everyone else in the chain of command, from the commander-in-chief to the Newark, New Jersey, dogcatcher. As the swath of invaders cut south toward the border between Canada and the United States, all the alerts reached triple-redball and the president was evacuated from his second-best ranch in Montana to some Cold War–era mine shaft a mile under Kentucky by the Secret Service, where he declared war against the unknown enemy, vowing that they would be smitten utterly. On his live televised address, the president kept referring to the enemy as "analiens," but ADR retakes fixed up the slip for the taped versions that would go on the public record; the "Analien Invader" speech would go down as one of those "it would have been nice but didn't really happen" media legends.

Dice remembered the unholy, guilty, puzzled relief that broke out when the attack on Washington bypassed strategic centers of government and military command. Instead, the UFOs cut up a few tourist sites and directed their greatest force at an area of low-income, predominantly African American housing that senators a lot less reactionary than Jubilee Bliss tended to label a crime-ridden ghetto. Earth's first victory over the hostiles was actually scored by a posse of incredibly tooled-up drug-slingers who had somehow kept a stash of RPGs in reserve against anyone trying to claim their territory. They weren't on the official history, either—two of their three hits had been on flying terrors; the other had taken out a school bus.

After gearing up for a response against a purposeful, planned attack, it was almost a disappointment when it turned out that the "invaders" acted more like the weather than an army, devastating, impersonal, and not wholly predictable. Deadly shrapnel rained upon underinhabited, unimportant hinterlands as solidly as upon sites of strategic importance and areas with high-density populations. The attack did not even proceed in straight lines or with the prevailing winds, but shifted in a zigzag pattern that metastasized into some sort of fractal before analysts could get their heads around it. Once, half a dozen of the "enemy" deviated several hundred miles just to obliterate an abandoned farmhouse and the surrounding property, leaving unscathed an adjoining military research base, and then heading out to sea to dive-bomb a shoal of squab.

Like everyone else, Dice watched the Action on television. He was a soldier, but he was also a lawyer. So with a dozen fellow uniformed lawyers, he sat in front of a TV set in a lounge deep in the Pentagon's hive, watching everything Fox could show, speculating about how the Big Green Machine was going to pull the nation's ass out of the fire and how many lawsuits for reckless endangerment and property damage they were going to have to deal with when the dust settled.

As it turned out, except for clearing away the dead and tidying up the wreckage, it was all over by dinnertime. The UFOs were re-classified RFOs—Recognized Flying Objects, although being recognized wasn't the same as really knowing what they were. By the time the first instant book about the Action was number two in the Amazon.com listings, Dice was in Guam, investigating a drug cartel run by a corrupt chicken-hawk colonel and an enterprising corporal in the motor pool; when the first TV movie about the Action aired on NBC, he'd discovered that the chicken-hawk colonel had power-ful friends in places that counted; as Bruckheimer's movie of the Action entered pre-production, he was given a solo mission to the worst place in the world, to put a Band-Aid on a scandal the army was doing its best to bury.

And now he was on the front line of a fight for the hearts and minds of creatures that definitely didn't have hearts, and probably didn't have minds—certainly not minds as human beings understood them. Here he was, on the back of Wing Commander Brown's antique bicycle, heading for the island's recreation area at approximately sixty miles per hour.

The Wing Co had his feet off the pedals, which whizzed around in a noisy blur, powered by a contraption made from a wire coat hanger and a Duracell battery, another invention of Lieutenant Glass, he of the giant holographic cross.

Dice sat on the mudguard, hanging on to the Wing Co's waist. Yelling into his ear, "You got hold of the camera and sent it to the jour-nalist, didn't you?"

"Guilty as charged, sah!"

"This better not be some kind of British plot to take back St. James."

"Not in the slightest, old bean. It's a humanitarian plot to let the world know what's going on here. God bless the Queen, sah, but Her Government is mostly a frightful shower with their heads so far up your Yankee arses that they can look out through their big fat belly buttons. Call me mad if you must, but I was hoping that your great nation would be shamed into doing the right thing."

Dice noted that the Wing Co was dropping his krazy-kat lingo. "You were hoping for a big investigation. Trouble is, the Pentagon doesn't much care what happens to the POTAs as long as it doesn't embarrass them. So all you got was me."

"I'm sure that if you had enough time, you'd have worked everything out. The conspirators are as cunning as tax inspectors, but also as crazy as coots. Unfortunately, time isn't on our side."

"Why me? Why do you need my help?"

"If I did this on my own, a British officer taking on the US Army, it would cause an almighty diplomatic stink. Some folk remember who burned down the White House in 1812, and worry that we'd like to do it again. But you're a lawyer from the Pentagon. It's your job to conduct internal purges and the like."

"Do we have any other allies?"

"I've been handing out my hats, but I only had one roll of special tinfoil. Anyway, not many want to wear them."

"The hats really work?"

"Another of Glass's doodads. The tinfoil is *chemically* tinfoil, but Glass worked out a treatment that changed its quantum-mechanical properties. At least, that's what he said, but he also claims to have glimpsed God's hinderparts, poor fellow."

Brown halted the bicycle, as if at a railroad crossing with a train due. Dice got off, insides still rattled, mind racing.

"Let's get to the barracks," he said. "I can round up some men . . ."

"They'll be asleep," said Brown. "Or worse. That soup had something worse than piddle in it. The super-souped-up soup. Anyone who partook of it will be knocked out for the duration, and it wasn't only served at the VIP table."

Dice had taken only a spoonful, which had been enough to put him under for a couple of hours. A bad feeling rising through the blissful hum in his head, he said, "So it's just you and me?"

"More or less, old chap."

Dice wondered who was in the cult. Haines and Shane, of course. Chris Montori had been a priestess, but the Blues had got to her. At least one of the scientists was involved.

"It's Wing or Susal," he said. "Or Wing *and* Susal. How am I doing?"

"I believe Wing is the inside person," Brown said. "Susal's just a lone drummer marching to the beat in his head. Why don't you ask me who's really in charge."

"Ah, Senator Bliss?"

Brown giggled. "Wrong end of the stick, dear boy. Bliss is blissed out on soup, snoozing with his sidekicks. Didn't you notice who was only *pretending* to spoon soup into his gob? The guilty party is . . . *aargh, they got me!*"

Dice stopped breathing as Brown's eyes bugged out as if a dagger had just thunked between his shoulder blades. Then the Britisher rattled on again.

"Sorry: ill-judged attempt at comic relief. Won't happen again. I'll just come plain out and say that it's Colonel Stock. He's Head Man in the Cult of Conspiracy. He's the Butler What Did It."

Dice couldn't quite see it.

"Stock wants to turn the POTAs into zombies?" he asked.

"Oh no," said Brown, giggling again. "He doesn't want to *turn* them into zombies. He believes they *are* zombies, controlled by some insidious higher power. Gods of the Outer Darkness or some such. Stock spent a year in Haiti at the end of the last century, part of the peacekeeping force. Picked up some damn funny ideas if you ask me. What he wants to do with his silly ceremony and the salt is kill one of the Prisoners and draw down that higher power, so he can get something from it. Don't ask me what. He's bonkers."

That rang some dissonant bells.

"In voodoo, priests invite possession by spirits called *loas*," Dice said. "It's not Western demonic possession, it's as much caging the force inside you as it is being controlled by it. The priest takes on aspects of the *loa*'s power, beefs up with its juice. That'll be what Stock wants. Powerful Juice. Not surprising, really. He's got as far as he can in the army, and they aren't going to bump him up farther than Great James. His job here is just to make sure there's enough toilet paper and shoo away journos. The Frank-Einsteins get to issue all the orders that count. If you can't get a promotion or a medal or anything approaching respect, you swallow an almighty *loa* and become Lord of the Earth. In theory. Of course, there's no danger of it actually working."

As he said it, he wondered if he believed it. Admittedly, it was unlikely that Stock would come out of this as Brother Voodoo on Steroids. But with the Blues in the equation, who knew what might happen?

"How do you know all this voodoo gubbins?" asked Brown.

"The Internet. And the Library of Congress. Us army lawyers don't have much else to do but research. I boned up on it before I came here."

Brown was distracted for a moment, as if he heard something. Dawn light was gathering, and new day's hammer of heat banging down. Then the Brit was in focus again, in pre-mission briefing mode.

"You've no objection to going after a commanding officer?" he asked.

"Stock isn't *my* CO," Dice said. "He doesn't even outrank me. But I underestimated him. I thought he was a brokeback scared of losing face, and it turns out he's a fighting soldier. Trouble is, he's chosen his own war. And he's got Island Fever. One of the worst cases, I imagine. He has to be stopped, before he does any more damage."

"Aye-aye, sir," said Brown, saluting.

"I have to warn you, this isn't a *Free Willy* scenario. The Prisoners stay in their pits."

Brown shrugged, accepting the ruling. Dice had a stab of thought—

what was Wing Co Brown's real agenda with regard to the POTAs? Inside a day, Dice had gone from writing off the Brit as an arrant loon to accepting him as a reliable witness and a sound adviser. Was that GJS setting in? Had he just joined the Tea Party?

"One thing I should add," he said. "I've fired off plenty of cutting questions at an enemy, but never a gun."

"Me neither, old chum," Brown said cheerfully. "Bloody, isn't it?"

The invisible train had passed. Brown invited Dice to hop back onto the mudguard. He pedaled off again, picking up speed. The missile silos were in the other direction. Was Brown planning to circumnavigate the island and sneak up on them?

"Hold on to your hat, my boy," shouted Brown. "We're going down the rabbit hole."

They swooped through a grove of palm trees, braked in a shower of sparks, and climbed off, leaving the bike in the dirt.

A sign painted around a plywood archway announced the Great James Krazy Golf Course. The archway glowed white; the letters gold. Another sign floated in the air beyond, as pink as a blushing flamingo. DANGER: ORDINARY LAWS OF PHYSICS MAY NOT APPLY. Everything was glowing in vivid colors: the electric-green Astroturf; a clown's head with gaping mouth and red-carpet tongue; a giant custard-yellow top hat that spun on its brim; a windmill as white as snow. Several soldiers stepping around the revolving cross of the windmill-sails, dark shadows amid the candy-colored dawn-glow, aiming M16s and stainless-steel service automatics, opening fire in a blaze of muzzle-flash.

Dice didn't have time to flinch. A clattering rain of bullets dropped out of the air in front of them. The next moment, Brown flourished his shell, and the soldiers flew away into the glowing darkness, smashing into the crude plywood and polystyrene mock-ups of giant boots, armored vehicles, an atom-bomb mushroom cloud, an eight ball hovering with no visible support. One man landed on a red circle painted on one of the Astroturf greens and promptly shot up into the dark air as if launched by a giant spring, landing somewhere behind Dice and Brown with a wet thud.

"If you don't watch your step it could happen to you," Brown said, and grabbed hold of Dice's arm, hustling him toward the windmill.

"Someone invented antigravity?"

"It cancels gravity—more of poor Glass's tinfoil magic."

"And a force field. Those bullets . . ."

"Their momentum went the same place as the noise of my little explosions. In here," Brown said, and yanked open a yard-high door in the side of the windmill.

Dice ducked after him.

And fell for a long, floating minute through absolute black, Brown's long scream of delight the only anchor for Dice's unraveling sanity. Light loomed up, an electric glare suddenly all around him, and he landed on a collapsing pile of cardboard boxes, rolled off them in a cloud of dust, sprawling in dim red light on a concrete floor next to Brown, wind knocked out of him.

Private Walter Garrett, an unlit cigarillo clamped in the center of his grin, lumpy watch cap pulled over his shaven skull so that its brim was level with his eyebrows, reached down and helped Dice up, saying, "It's about time."

They had somehow landed in a low-ceilinged room full of metal racks crammed with tens of thousands of file folders, cardboard boxes, and plastic-cased CD-ROMs. No sooner was he over the queasiness of a fall through the void than Dice felt a pulsing like hot needles jammed against the fillings in his teeth. It was a sound that hurt, an arrhythmic thrum like the world wobbling on its axis.

Dice said, "Your Lieutenant Glass did what this time? Tamed a wormhole through other dimensions? Invented teleportation?"

Brown picked himself up and dusted himself down. "Dug a rabbit hole, so far as I know. It didn't have an explanation on the packet. Sorry. This is, ah, one of the surveillance center's document stores. And this, Colonel Dice, is . . ."

"Private Garrett, I know."

"We've already met," Garrett told Brown. "In the brig."

The big man was loaded for bear. An M16 slung over his shoulder. Grenades were clipped to bandoliers that crossed his broad chest.

"No hard feelings for the arrest, I hope," Dice said.

"Nope. I owe you for not having me hunted down and shot, which I believe was the general plan after my so-called escape. See, they just opened up the door of my cell and kicked me out. Might as well have painted a target on my back."

"What's your role in this unholy mess?"

"I'm an accomplished thief," said Garrett, with pride. "And a jealous ex-boyfriend. I didn't like it when Chris got picked up by the Voodoo Krewe, so I liberated their camera. When my bunky ditched me to become a *Mama-Loa*, I'm afraid I got good and pissed and thought the folks back home should see how she looked in her new church. A touch ignoble of me, I admit. Stock's got himself a new priestess now. Anyway, I gave the camera to my pal here and he got the pictures out. I told him to get them posted on the Internet but he went to the papers."

"Fat lot of good that did," Brown said cheerfully, inspecting his crystal-studded shell. "After all the fuss and bother, what does the army do? It sends a lawyer. No offense, old chap."

"None taken. But I thought Garrett shot the pictures."

"No way," Garrett said. "Man who took the pictures, that was Colonel Stock. All blacked up like an old-time minstrel for his voodoo show. Nothing more ridiculous than a white man painted black."

The pulse in the air was stronger. A drumming, nearby. There was wailing and chanting mixed in.

"They've started the ritual," said Dice.

"You bet," Garrett said. "I was beginning to think of testing their defenses by dropping a few explosive eggs on their heads. You know, just to see what would happen."

"It wouldn't do any good," Brown said. "They're mad, but they aren't stupid. They've made sure that the pit is secure from that kind of attack."

"They have a conch shell, too?" asked Dice.

"Not a shell, but something similar," Brown said. "It's a perfect defensive shield against projectile weapons—we'd all be retired from the war business if it got out. So if we do have to go up against them in the pit, I'm rather afraid you Yanks are going to have to forgo the pleasure of your shootie bang-bangs and rely on cunning and good old-fashioned fisticuffs instead."

"The hell with *cunning*." Garrett pulled a big hunting knife from a scabbard on his belt. "If their strings of garlic won't protect them against my fists, I reckon I can make good use of this."

They snuck out of the document store's steel hatchway, down a concrete-lined tunnel painted with yellow-and-black chevrons, to a T-junction with the wide passageway that led to the surveillance room Dice had visited earlier.

As they drew near, the sound of drumming grew louder and louder. Dice briefly wondered if Dr. Susal was the voodoo DJ, mixing hardcore hip-hop into the Haitian rites. When they entered the room, he realized he had done the Frank-Einstein an injustice. Susal was fixed to a swivel chair by duct tape wound around him mummy-wise, face red and bulging around tape that had sealed shut his nose and mouth and suffocated him. Dr. Wing's baffles were set on his head like huge, furry earphones. The corpse sat in the center of the control room, lit by the dead blue light of monitors and torchlight that danced behind the armored glass window that gave a view down into the pit.

The torches were fastened to scaffold poles planted in a ring around the big blue blob of the POTA. Half a dozen men stripped to the waist sat cross-legged, pounding tom-tom drums caught between their thighs, the sound transmitted by every speaker in the room. Two of the congregation were white, but blacked up with greasepaint. Colonel Stock and Sergeant Haines were also blacked up and swathed in white bedsheet robes. The colonel wore a top hat with toothlike shards of coral stuck through the brim and held up a long thin knife. Haines held a beheaded chicken by its clawed feet and shook it like a censer, blood from its neck-stump sprinkling everywhere. Anne-Louise

Shane, bare to the waist, pale skin painted with symbols from an alien alphabet, shimmied and writhed, slapping a tambourine, making circles around and around the tethered POTA.

Aside from Lieutenant Shane's breasts, the whole thing looked as cheesy as a frat-house initiation ceremony in some Midwest agricultural college. Then Colonel Stock, his knife and the right side of his white robe spattered with chicken blood, stalked across the pit and slit open a bulging Hefty bag, revealing a pile of fat crystals that pulsed with poisonous green corpse-light.

"He's not using sea salt anymore," said Brown.

"What is that? Crystals from a POTA?"

Brown nodded. "They've been irradiated. It's Haines. He's become quite the whiz at sums, and developed something akin to Lieutenant Glass's quantum-mechanical alchemy. It's amazing what people will tell you if they think you're barking. He gave me the full lecture. The shell research team has been bombarding crystals with anything that comes to hand, including hazardous waste left over from Anthony Eden's independent deterrent. Stock traded with the field boys, swapped medical data on the silo team's softball players' weaknesses for barrel loads of . . . what does it look like?"

"Kryptonite?" said Dice. "Red, green, and gold, mixed together."

"Kryptonite on crack," said Garrett.

"Sewing the stuff inside the prisoner's apertures," said Brown, "might well be like priming a warhead with what's that stuff called? Plasticine? No. Plutonium."

The drummers were going crazy. Sergeant Haines bit off the head of a chicken, squirted blood over Lieutenant Shane's writhing body.

"Better than the Playboy channel," said Garrett, grinning around his cigarillo. He pulled a Glock semiautomatic and handed it to Dice. "The colonel posted guards outside the silos, in case anyone missed their supper last night, but didn't know about the magic-carpet ride. As soon as the shit starts flying, the guards are going to come running. There's no anti-bullet flypaper in this room. They'll start shooting, an' you better shoot back."

Dice clicked off the safety, racked the slide to put a round in the chamber. "You mean, 'You better shoot back, sir.' "

Brown strode across the room, flipped dust covers from a set of panels, closed a set of knife levers. Constellations of multicolored pinlights lit up.

"The cooling system still works," he said. "Pit Three used to be one of the vertical-firing test beds, equipped with sprayheads pumping four thousand gallons of water a minute. Unfortunately for your countryman in the top hat, the drains were sealed when the engineers laid down reinforced concrete floors to turn the silos into cells. Fortunately for us, no one bothered to disconnect all the wires and pipes when the nukes were decommissioned. Never know when you'll have to batter your ploughshares back into swords. With your permission, Colonel?"

Beyond the window, down there in the pit, Stock shook blood from another decapitated chicken over the poison-green crystals. Blood boiled as soon as it touched crystal, spitting up thick curls of white smoke. Veins stood out in Stock's neck; this was a man who expected to become a god within the next ten minutes.

Dice said, "If you're going to do it, fly-boy, do it now."

Brown pulled his watch cap down over his ears, counted backward from five to zero, and daintily pressed a button.

In the silo, a hard rain came down.

Haines took the full force of a jet. It smashed him face-first into the spill of crystals, which immediately transfixed him, burrowing under his skin like angry inchworms. The rest of the cultists were washed this way and that by gushing torrents. The water dump had instantly turned the bottom of the silo into a pool, thigh-deep around the flailing voodooists, then waist-deep, neck-deep. Brown poked at another button: a second rainstorm smashed down. The frothing tide gently lifted the buoyant POTA against the constraint of the Flavor Lock, closing over its head-bump, lapping at the edge of the observation window and climbing higher.

Currents forced Shane against the window, breasts flattened against the glass, and then unglued her and whirled her away. Stock was dog-paddling, trying to keep his hoodoo hat on his head—without it, he would no longer be an avatar of Baron Samedi, just another fruitcake in a bedsheet. His chances of ascension were waterlogged at the moment, but he still clung to the hope of his reward on Earth.

Dice kept shifting his eyes between the observation window and the door through which he expected the guards to come. Garrett had positioned Susal's corpse as a natural target just in front of the door to draw fire, and had flattened himself to one side, the butt of his M16 resting against his hip, knife gripped between his teeth, ready to shoot or stab any intruders.

The expected charge didn't come.

Instead, the guards did the stupidest thing possible—they opened the hatch in the wall of the silo to see what all the shouting and splashing was about, and were washed off their feet by a muscular gush of escaping floodwater.

Stock, hatless, caught hold of the railing of the observation platform and was glaring at the window, face washed by clashing waves, legs scissor-kicking in foaming water. His mouth opened and closed—he seemed to be shouting. When Dice gave him a cheery wave, Stock pulled a gun from under his robes and fired a couple of rounds at the glass.

The cultists' anti-projectile-weapon hoodoo must not have been waterproof. Lead smeared glass tough enough to keep in an unrestrained POTA.

Brown leaned into a microphone and said gleefully, "Colonel Stock, I'm rather afraid I shall have to ask you to write out 'It is a severe breach of discipline to discharge a weapon at a fellow officer' five thousand times and present the lines to your house prefect before lights-out. Failure to comply will be punished disproportionately."

Stock raised his pistol to fire again, lost his grip on the railing, and was washed away, floundering around with the rest of his hounfort like mice in a washing machine. They were a spent force.

"Excuse me," Garrett said, "but do either of you two officers know the best way to escape from a Flavors Lock?"

"Don't worry," Dice said, "those things can't drown."

Garrett pointed at the window—at the drowned base of the silo. "Not what I meant. Best way to escape, it looks like, is to become something else."

The shackled POTA was completely underwater now, half hidden by whirling bubbles and debris but clearly changing shape. Stretching. Growing taller and thinner. With a sudden rush it escaped the eye-bending topology of the Flavors Lock and shot to the surface, sending violent waves splashing back and forth. It was shaped like a coin now, fattened in the center, knife-thin at the edges. Balanced on one edge on top of the water, bobbing up and down, gaining speed, bouncing higher and higher.

"Oh dear," said Brown. "Didn't expect that to happen."

Stock looked up at the thing in terror, and then it plunged down and drove him under the water. Dice couldn't tell whether it was a deliberate aggressive or defensive move or just a random motion.

On all the banked TV monitors displaying feeds from the other silos, all the POTAs were blurs bouncing off walls in chilling synchrony. The images could have been different angles on one individual.

"Simon Says," Dice remembered, aloud.

The water tanks had been drained; only light showers were dribbling from the sprayheads now. Most of Stock's followers were alive, clinging to the railing of the observation platform, clambering over it, crawling through the half-flooded hatchway. One of the guards floated facedown. Shane clung around the neck of another as he kicked toward the platform. Stock's hat sailed around like a busy little boat, bumping into a wash of chicken parts and tom-toms. At the bottom of the half-flooded chamber, what was left of Haines was pegged out like a ragged skin by spikes of crystal that glowed radioactive green through twenty feet of water.

The POTA was bouncing higher and higher, rebounding from side to side now, hardly ever touching the water, smashing into the cap of their silo. Someone beyond the window fired an assault rifle at the big blue disk, as if that had never been tried before. Bullets spanged off it and smashed chunks from the concrete wall. At least the anti-bullet shield had been washed away.

Someone was standing in the doorway of the monitoring room; Dice turned and nearly shot Moira Wing.

She wore a cheongsam and had an orchid behind one ear, still dressed for Colonel Stock's dinner. She held out her hands to show that they were empty.

"Aha, the Dragon Lady," said Brown. "Insidious Eastern temptress."

"Actually, I was born in Romford, Essex," Wing said.

She stepped around the taped body of her colleague, not giving him a second glance, walked across to her workstation, and studied the spiky traces on screens.

"You're not part of the Happy Hounfort, Dr. Wing?" asked Dice.

"Hounfort?"

"Voodoo cult."

"Oh that. No, not my scene at all."

"But the soup didn't send you to sleep, either."

Wing shrugged, more important things on her mind than being implicated or ruled innocent. Dice made a mental note that *someone* had mockingly put the baffles on Susal after he was mummified, and he remembered who owned the things.

"This is the behavior I mentioned earlier," she said, turning to the bank of monitors. "Highly synchronous movement. It's almost like a dance, isn't it?"

"They're jumping beans," he said.

Every time the POTA in the flooded silo hit the water, a mini tsunami broke against the observation window. The thumping pulse of its dance was a continuation of the drumbeat—had it learned the offbeat rhythm, or had Stock had his drummers sync with a pulse set by his big blue zombie? The floor trembled beneath Dice's feet; hanging light fittings swung to and fro overhead; a standing pattern of waves, target rings, appeared on the surface of the water in the chamber. Dice wondered how much longer the observation window would take the stress, saw with a start that something was growing across the lower edge, brachiate crystals like magnified snowflakes, growing right in front of his eyes.

Something was growing through the water, too. Jagged kelp extending through twenty feet of water, virulent green light pulsing in time to the pulse of the Prisoners' dance. Haines's body was gone, devoured by a holdfast of spines.

Wing noticed it, too, and stepped up to the window. "This is a new form," she said, rapt with fascination.

"Stock was going to load it into the Prisoner," Brown said.

Wing considered this, head cocked to one side. She might have been assigning the experiment a catalog number.

"Whatever it is," she said, "it could spread through all the silos now you've flooded them. The POTA may have added its own secretions to the mix. The growth is guided—see?"

"It'll be all through the silos," Brown said.

The crystal stalk had pierced the surface of the water, its top flattened out into a kind of cup. The POTA dropped down onto it, like a coin in a slot.

There was a long moment of quiet. The water calmed. Stock's body, facedown, eyes open, bumped against the window.

The POTA—like all the POTAs—balanced on its edge on a crystal cup that suddenly grew up around it. Then, newly enshelled, it began to spin like a top.

Dr. Wing clapped her hands like a delighted child.

"What are they doing?" asked Dice.

"I'd say they were getting ready to leave."

Dice knew she was right. He could feel a tremendous yearning that wasn't his, and knew Chris Montori had sensitized him somehow. The dream had been hers. Needles dug into his ears. He yawned and something popped inside his head.

Dr. Wing studied her computer screens, said, "Subsonics. It's causing overpressure. Interesting."

One of the screens cracked across, like a soprano's wineglass.

Dice said, "Will the silos hold?"

"We'll soon find out."

Brown had his hands over his ears, fingers under the rim of his cap. Garrett shook his head. He had a nosebleed.

Dice felt something shirr his internal organs. Vibration transmitted through the floor turned his muscles to water and he sat down hard, dropped the Glock. His vision was blurring. Something burst wetly inside his sinuses and he snorted blood. The air was singing. Beyond the glass, the POTA was a ghostly blue sphere spinning inside wreaths of steam. The top layer of the water was bubbling, boiling; the tall observation window shimmered and sang.

"Wing Commander," Dice said. "If we can pop the covers of the silos, I suggest we do it right now. Free Willy after all."

"I don't think so," said Dr. Wing. She had fallen into a swivel chair, was resting her right hand on the computer console, aiming a snub-nosed .38 at Brown, deathly pale but grim and determined.

Brown grabbed his shell, started to raise it, and she fired. The round blew the shell to shards, caught Brown in his shoulder, and threw him against the control panel.

"These are important experimental specimens," said Wing, "and I won't let you interfere with the work."

"Bitch," Garrett said, and lurched forward. He was bleeding from ears and eyes and nose, his face a mask of blood.

Wing kicked her chair around and Garrett stumbled into her and they went down in a clumsy tangle.

"If you could give us a hand, old thing," Brown said to Dice. "I seem to have come unstrung."

Dice went to the control panel. It was a bewildering array of switches and buttons. He had no idea which would flip the silo caps.

"Look for services humor, pal," gasped Brown, eyes rolling into a swoon.

Wing and Garrett were fighting like children. Pain drilled through Dice's skull, the super-audible whine vibrating his brittle bones. His vision swam.

Whatever happened next was down to him. He had no standing orders to cover the situation.

He found a panel of controls for the monitors, and switched to EXTERNAL VIEW. A new set of images came on the bank of TVs—lumps of concrete surrounded by scrubby, sun-blasted vegetation. Some of the slabs that sealed the silos were decorated with elaborate graffiti. One had the skeleton of a beach umbrella fixed into it. All were starting to crack, but the plugs installed at the end of the Cold War still held. Dice knew his head would explode before the caps shattered. Unless they could be shifted, everyone in this room would be dead of burst blood vessels—or brains—before the POTAs were free and about their incomprehensible business.

Services humor? What had Brown meant? Why couldn't he have just stated his case clearly?

Dice had to wipe blood-tears from his eyes and concentrate.

A section of the master board consisted of twenty handles, dirty and long unused. A faded sticker above them read DO NOT ATTEMPT WORLD WAR THREE UNLESS THE SILO LIDS ARE IN THE UPRIGHT POSITION. There must be hydraulics or explosive bolts, or some other manual means of opening the bottles to let the rockets fly. Dice turned Handle Three, and there was a *rush* as the pressure inside popped away.

Sunlight fell into the silo, onto the floodwater and the spinning coin of the Blue.

Dice turned the other handles, as many as he could manage, as quickly as possible.

On the monitors, one by one, silo caps popped like champagne corks. Groves of crystal trees sprouted from them.

The pressure was gone. The vibration was still there, but shifting to a different, nonlethal register.

"The silos are open," Dice told Brown, who was stirring. "Launch imminent."

Was this Stock's fault? Or would it have happened anyway? Being dead and all, the CO would certainly be taking the blame when Senator Bliss insisted on a full inquiry. Four or five other scandals could probably be laid at his door in a tidying-up exercise.

Dice hauled Brown off the floor and sat him in a swivel chair.

The Prisoners departed in precise formation, hanging above the mouths of the silos for a moment, then shooting skyward.

Brown whistled.

Dice prayed to God and Papa Legba and the Founding Fathers that Willy and his brothers were heading for the open oceans, and not about to institute a program of laying waste to the world's coastal cities. Perhaps the Blues didn't realize they had been tortured. Or perhaps they didn't have the human need for vengeance.

Wing cursed them roundly in working-class British with the odd Chinese word spat into the invective. Garrett was on his hands and knees at her feet, bleeding from nose and ears, but he'd managed to pin the sleeve of the scientist's cheongsam to the console, burying his big knife to the hilt. She couldn't get free.

By the time Dice and Wing Co Brown got out into the open and stood on the surface of Great James Island, the blue sky was empty apart from twenty white contrails that wind was already shaping into a row of upside-down question marks. All aimed north, and abruptly truncated.

Gone, through their own rabbit hole. Gone back to wherever they came from or on to wherever they were going next.

Out of the glare and heat-haze, Chris Montori wandered toward the silo, smiling like a six-year-old at her birthday party, trailing her knitted squid. Rose-of-Mary Bliss, saved from soporific soup by anorexia, was browbeating an MP, demanding immediate access to the base commander and medical attention for her sainted father. A couple of soldiers were picking their way through lumps of shattered concrete, peering into what was left of the mouth of Silo Three.

"That's the end of that," said Wing Co Brown, a hand pressed to the superficial wound in his shoulder, eyes bright and excited under the rim of his watch cap.

Dice wondered what he had just done and how he would answer for it.

Rose-of-Mary ditched the MP and charged up and demanded to know who was in charge.

Dice pointed at the wing commander. Rose-of-Mary did a double take, then fastened on Brown, bombarding him with questions.

Dice tuned out the shrill, vengeful angel and looked up at the empty sky. His scalp felt hot and itchy—he was still wearing the ridiculous and now superfluous cap. He took it off and folded it against his heart.

PHOTO: LORI DATLOW

ELLEN DATLOW was editor of SCI FICTION, the multi-award-winning fiction area of SCIFI.com, for almost six years, and fiction editor of *OMNI* for more than seventeen. Over her career she has worked with Susanna Clarke, Neil Gaiman, Kelly Link, Jeffrey Ford, Octavia E. Butler, Garth Nix, Gregory Maguire, Ursula K. Le Guin, Bruce Sterling, Peter Straub, Stephen King, Dan Simmons, George R. R. Martin, William Gibson, Cory Doctorow, Joyce Carol Oates, Jonathan Carroll, and others.

She has co-edited (with Terri Windling) the six *Snow White, Blood Red* adult fairy-tale anthologies; *A Wolf at the Door* and *Swan Sister*, both children's fairy-tale anthologies; and three young adult anthologies: *The Green Man, The Faery Reel*, and *The Coyote Road*. She has been editing the horror half (with Terri Windling, and now Kelly Link and Gavin J. Grant) of *The Year's Best Fantasy and Horror* for over twenty years. She and Windling also coedited *Sirens and other Daemon Lovers*, an erotic fantasy anthology, and *Salon Fantastique*, a nontheme fantasy anthology.

Solo, she is the editor of two anthologies on vampirism, *Blood Is Not Enough* and *A Whisper of Blood*; two anthologies on SF and gender, *Alien Sex* and *Off Limits*; *Little Deaths* (sexual horror), *Lethal Kisses* (revenge and vengeance), and *Twists of the Tale* (cat horror); *Vanishing Acts*, an anthology on the theme of endangered species; *The Dark: New Ghost Stories* and *Inferno*, a nontheme, all-original-horror anthology. She guest-edited issue 7 of *Subterranean* magazine, spring 2007.

Datlow has won the World Fantasy Award eight times, two Bram

Stoker Awards, the International Horror Guild Award, the 2002 and 2005 Hugo Awards, and the 2005 and 2006 Locus Awards, for her work as an editor. SCI FICTION won the 2005 Hugo Award for Best Website.

Datlow was named recipient of the 2007 Karl Edward Wagner Award, given at the British Fantasy Convention, for "outstanding contribution to the genre."

She lives in New York City. Her website is www.datlow.com.